The Good Servant

Fern Britton is the highly acclaimed author of nine *Sunday Times* bestselling novels. Her books are cherished for their warmth, wit and wisdom, and have won Fern legions of loyal readers. Fern has been a judge for the Costa Book of the Year Award and is a supporter of the Reading Agency, promoting literacy and reading.

A hugely popular household name through iconic shows such as *This Morning* and *Fern Britton Meets . . .* Fern is a much sought-after presenter and radio host. She has also turned her hand to theatre and toured with Gary Barlow and Tim Firth's *Calendar Girls*.

Fern has twin sons and two daughters and lives in Cornwall in a house full of good food, wine, family, friends and gardening books.

/officialfernbritton
@Fern_Britton
www.fern-britton.com

By the same author:

Fern: My Story

New Beginnings
Hidden Treasures
The Holiday Home
A Seaside Affair
A Good Catch
The Postcard
Coming Home
The Newcomer
Daughters of Cornwall

Short stories
The Stolen Weekend
A Cornish Carol
The Beach Cabin

Published in one collection as
A Cornish Gift

Fern Britton

The Good Servant

HarperCollins*Publishers*

HarperCollins*Publishers* Ltd
1 London Bridge Street
London SE1 9GF

www.harpercollins.co.uk

HarperCollins*Publishers*
Macken House,
39/40 Mayor Street Upper,
Dublin 1
D01 C9W8
Ireland

First published by HarperCollins*Publishers* 2022
This paperback edition published 2023
1

A catalogue record for this book is available from the British Library

ISBN: 978-0-00-822532-2

Typeset in Birka by Palimpsest Book Production Ltd, Falkirk, Stirlingshire

Printed and bound in the UK using 100% renewable electricity by CPI Group (UK) Ltd

FOREWORD

8th September 2022

I was out filming in the wilds of West Cornwall, standing in a field overlooking the Atlantic, hugging a warm coat around me. It was coming up to lunchtime. I was looking forward to a hot cuppa and a supermarket sandwich, standard location grub, when one of our crew looked up from her phone and said, 'The Queen isn't well. Her family are making their way to Balmoral to see her.'

I thought I hadn't heard her properly and asked her to repeat what she had said. 'It's the Queen. Prince Charles, Princess Anne, Prince Andrew and Prince Edward are on the way to her. Sounds serious.'

To say that this news gave us all pause for thought is too small a phrase. The Queen could not die. Not today. We weren't ready. I wasn't ready.

An hour later and we were back in the crew cars and driving in convoy to the next location.

While my make-up lady Katie drove, I tuned into BBC Radio 4 wanting to find any updates and hoping to hear that the Queen was fine, tucked up in her Balmoral bed, a kindly doctor at her side and the kettle on.

Katie and I went through possible scenarios.

'What's happened do you think? Has she had a stroke?'

'A fall maybe?'

'She has had a bad back and she said her leg was difficult to walk on without a stick.'

'I hope she's resting. The Platinum Jubilee must have exhausted her.'

I refused to believe that anything serious had happened. She was mentally so strong. So present. So invincible.

'She'll make a hundred,' I said. 'Her mum was 101 for goodness' sake.'

As a nation we had seen her just two days before in her drawing room at Balmoral. A welcoming room with two large green sofas either side of a blazing fire, walls decorated with favourite paintings, and furnished with vases and lamps. The Queen had looked relaxed and unusually smiley. She was wearing a tartan skirt, pale blue blouse and cardigan. Her handbag was firmly in place on her left wrist. She was holding a walking stick but what 96-year-old wouldn't?

She had called her outgoing Prime Minister, Boris Johnson, to Scotland to accept his resignation and shortly afterwards, on his departure, she welcomed Liz Truss, her new Prime Minister, granting her the request to form a new administration. Beaming, the Queen shook hands with her third female PM, and it was then we saw the large dark blue bruise on the back of her right hand. Well, older people bruise more easily, don't they? Especially after a possible blood test.

I got back home that evening in time for the BBC Radio 4 *Six O'clock News* and stood in the kitchen listening to a precis of the day's reports on the Queen's health.

She was under the medical care of her doctors and in the thoughts and prayers of many – including world religious leaders.

The mood at Radio 4 was changing. Jonny Dymond, Royal Correspondent for BBC News had the latest.

He told us it had been a curious and intense day but without much information, just 'signs and signals' of the seriousness of the situation.

He painted the picture of a few hours ago when the House of Commons was in full debate with Prime Minister Liz Truss and the Leader of the Opposition Sir Keir Starmer, facing each other over the despatch box. He described how a note had been passed to Nadhim Zahawi, the new Chancellor of the Exchequer, who then passed it to the PM, Liz Truss. Reading it, she quickly left the chamber. The air in the Commons had changed as MPs began to hear the rumour that was spreading and soon the Speaker read a statement extending best wishes to the Queen and the royal family.

Another sign?

And then another.

Sources in the Palace began reporting that senior members of the royal family were changing their plans so that they could move quickly towards Balmoral. Prince Charles and Princess Anne were already there while Princes Edward, Andrew and William were flying in an RAF plane from RAF Northolt.

Prince Harry, Duke of Sussex, was on his way.

Jonny Dymond stopped. I thought I heard a small intake of breath from someone in that studio – then presenter Mishal Husain told us, in a measured voice, 'We have just heard the news in the last few seconds from Buckingham Palace, announcing the death of Her Majesty Queen Elizabeth II.'

A tweet from the royal family confirmed it. 'The Queen died peacefully at Balmoral this afternoon. The King and The Queen Consort will remain at Balmoral this evening and will return to London tomorrow.'

This was news of great significance. The many listeners, including me, had only known one monarch. Queen Elizabeth II. On the throne for seventy years and as invincible as an oak, she had fallen.

The national anthem played, and I remained standing in shock and respect. I remembered her saying not long ago that she loved going to Balmoral – not least because it gave her the chance to sleep in the same bed for an entire twelve weeks. It felt right that she had had her final sleep there too.

This was hard to absorb.

We were in uncharted territory.

The transition of power was instantaneous.

The Prince of Wales was now King Charles III. On the Queen's death someone would have proclaimed the ancient phrase, 'The Queen is dead. Long live the King,' and kissed the new King's hand.

His wife The Duchess of Cornwall was now The Queen Consort Camilla.

London Bridge, the long-held code name for the Queen's death, had fallen.

On 6th May 2023 we crowned King Charles III with Queen Camilla at his side. The Crown had passed seamlessly.

But the old Queen, Elizabeth, will stalk the halls of history to the end of time.

She was loved and respected by many millions.

Stalwart, diplomatic, nobody's fool, a woman who understood the job of service and impartiality.

During her long life she never gave an interview. We saw her talking about bits of her life and recollections, but never as the answer to a direct question.

I have since wondered and hoped that before she died, she may have been persuaded to break that rule. As we get older there are certain things that we feel we would like to put straight or leave as a reminder for the coming generation. If such an interview exists, which is doubtful, it would not be aired for many, many years. Likewise, her diaries. We know she wrote in one each day and that they will eventually be released into the public domain but again, not while I am alive.

The Good Servant

The most famous woman on the planet remains an enigma. Did any of us really know her? Who helped to shape her character? Her thinking? Who gave her the chance to be more than just a royal child? One who had never been destined to become monarch?

We have caught vignettes, small glimpses, of a life well lived, and it's now, while reflecting on how challenging it must have been to have any semblance of an ordinary life in an extraordinary world, that I come to think of the characters within this novel. You may have heard of Miss Marion Crawford, the young, bright Scots girl who, at the age of 22, took the role as Governess to Princess Elizabeth (6) and her sister Princess Margaret (2).

You may also have heard that she betrayed the royal family by writing a tittle tattle book called *The Little Princesses*, which made her a lot of money while also ruining her character. Was she a cold-blooded money grabber who sold her soul for cash? Or was she the innocent victim of two unscrupulous American journalists who tricked her?

This is the story of Crawfie, The Good Servant.

Fern Britton

THE GOOD SERVANT

PROLOGUE

Buckingham Palace, 1949

George VI is on the throne. The King, his wife, and his two daughters enjoy great popularity. Princess Elizabeth has recently been married to Prince Philip. The abdication of Edward VIII – some twelve years before – has largely been forgotten, and the banished ex-king and his controversial wife are known as the Duke and Duchess of Windsor and are living in Paris.

Sir Alan Lascelles has known them all.

He is every inch a courtier. Six foot one, elegantly thin, with a centre parting in the exact middle of his scalp. He usually goes by the nickname 'Tommy'.

There have been many royal scandals behind the scenes which could have destroyed the Crown forever, but for Tommy's careful handling and iron fist.

You could say, he really has seen everything, *and* done it. A decent man and a stickler for protocol whose actions are not always popular amongst the royal household. But, by God, they know they are lucky to have him.

Today, he is sixty-two, a happily married man with three children, enjoying his job as private secretary to King George VI.

From behind his well-ordered desk in Buckingham Palace, he is reading over two court papers that the King will want to see.

It is a pleasant enough morning – until his secretary, Miss Jane Pepper-Thynne, knocks and pops her head around the door.

Tommy looks at his desk clock and smiles. 'Elevenses already, P-T?'

'No, sir. I mean yes, sir, but that's not why I am here.'

His eyebrows shoot up in their quizzical way. 'Well, then – out with it.'

'Her Majesty the Queen wants to see you straight away. She says it's urgent.'

'Oh, yes?'

'I believe it's something to do with Miss Crawford and' – she hesitates – 'a book, sir.'

This is news Tommy never wanted to hear and has tried to prevent in every possible way. His neatly trimmed moustache tenses in fury. 'Is it by chance the book I think it is?'

The Honourable Miss Pepper-Thynne squares her shoulders. 'Yes, sir.'

Tommy drops his fountain pen on his large desk blotter and stands up. 'I told the damned woman. I damn well *told* her.' His brimming rage is so quiet and contained it makes it all the more terrifying. 'And where exactly is Her Majesty now?'

'In her sitting room, sir.'

He buttons his jacket and straightens his tie. 'Heads will roll – but it damned well won't be mine.'

What happens next is the complete destruction of one loyal woman's character.

PART ONE

Chapter One

Dunfermline Station, March 1932

Twenty-two-year-old Miss Marion Crawford was waiting on the platform of Dunfermline station for the London King's Cross train. Her stepfather was waiting in the car park. Her mother was standing beside her, glancing up at the station clock. 'We are in good time at least.'

Marion had heard her mother say the same thing at least twice since they had arrived. 'Yes, Mother.'

'There's nothing worse than rushing for a train.'

'No. Look, Mother.' Marion sighed. 'There's no need for you to wait with me. Go home with Dad. It's been a long morning already, saying goodbye to all the neighbours – which, by the way, was really embarrassing.'

'I thought you'd like a proper send-off. It was a good turnout. Even old Mr Turner waved from his window, too cold for him to come out.'

'Too cold for everyone.' Marion lifted one foot then the other in an effort to warm them. 'Please, Mother, go back to the warm car. Dad will have the engine running.'

'I've been colder than this and survived.' Her mother sniffed. 'I don't know why your father wouldn't come out to see you off.'

'Because he hates goodbyes and so do I.'

Marion desperately wanted her mother to go. She needed to be alone to think. This was a big day. The biggest. She wanted to set herself straight, to think through, again, the enormous change that was about to happen in her life.

She just wanted to get to Windsor and start the job.

To find her feet.

'You will write when you arrive, won't you, Marion?'

'No, I thought I'd let you worry until I come back.' She flicked a glance at her mother, before muttering, 'I'll only be away for a couple of months. I have told them I have to be back for my university place.'

Her mother's breasts gathered up under her folded arms. 'And what happens if you're not back in time to start university? The worry your stepfather and I have had getting you through your exams.'

Marion almost stamped her foot in desperation. 'Of course I will be back for university. Mum, please don't make this so hard.'

Her mother sniffed and turned her back. Both of them kept their furious thoughts to themselves.

As mothers went, Maggie was challenging. She had told her daughter only this morning that the neighbours thought Marion was distant. 'I don't want people thinking you are getting too grand for us here,' she'd said.

Tall, thin and in possession of a rather plain face, Marion knew that she often came across as aloof. In her two years at Moray House, part of Edinburgh Provincial Training Centre, she had found it hard to make friends with her fellow students and most of her tutors. The principal had seen through her façade, though, and the end of the final term she had sought Marion out. 'Miss Crawford, would you come to my office after lunch? I would like a word.'

When Marion was shown into Miss Brown's sanctum, she seemed the picture of calm, though she was shaking within.

'Do sit down, Miss Crawford.'

She took the seat in front of the desk as the older woman sat opposite.

'I hope you have been happy here?'

'I have, Miss Brown.'

'You have worked hard for your place at Glasgow University. Their child psychology course is said to be the most enlightened and forward thinking of its kind. I am certain you will make a success of it.'

Marion flushed and looked down at her lap. 'Thank you.'

'I have had a note from the university saying it was suggested that it might be worthwhile for you to take a summer job to get some first-hand experience with children. Have you had any thoughts about that?'

'I haven't found anything yet.' Marion sat forward. 'You see, I want to help the children who need it most. If I could find something with children who have no chance in life, children who have no opportunity for a good education, children who live in such poverty that the little food they have is not helping to develop their bodies and their brains. I want to give every child a chance to learn how to read, write and know their numbers, to have at least one good meal a day at school, if not at home, to have manners so that they will never feel inferior to anyone.' She stopped. 'Sorry. But it does feel so important.'

Miss Brown slowly nodded. 'Never apologize for passion.' Her shrewd eyes scanned Marion's face. 'Would you be willing to work with any child, no matter their background? Just for the summer? To help a family at the other end of the social scale?'

Marion gave a small smile. 'One whose parents want to keep their privileged offspring busy and out of their hair during the holidays?'

Miss Brown acquiesced. 'It would be a temporary job. It would give you experience – and a nice financial benefit.'

'Who are they?'

She was passed a sheet of paper with an embossed letterhead and an elegantly written letter beneath.

*

The few travellers on the London-bound platform stamped their feet against the chill and began turning up their coat collars. One or two lifted their eyes to the end of the platform, where a colony of shiny jackdaws were chattering in the bare trees.

The sound of a woman's shoes clipped onto the platform opposite.

Marion recognized her, Lorna – an acquaintance of her mother's, and a gossip. Marion pulled her muffler over her chin to disguise herself, but she was too slow.

'Maggie, Marion!' the woman called, her voice ringing over the wide divide of rails and stone chipping. 'Marion, is it today you're leaving us for London?'

Marion pulled her face from her scarf. 'Good morning. Yes, indeed.'

'You'll have had to pack a whole new wardrobe, I suppose. Your poor mother.'

With nothing else to distract them, the bystanders trained their eyes and ears on the conversation.

Marion's mother called back, unnecessarily loudly, 'Off to London, aye!' She seemed delighted to have captured an audience. 'Everything in her case is new. I made two skirts and three blouses just this last week. Kept me busy, Lorna.'

'You must be so proud of her, Maggie.'

Marion wanted to clamp her gloved hand over her mother's mouth, but she was too late.

'I've always been proud of her, Lorna – even when she was all moonfaced over the Prince of Wales. She's still got those scrapbooks she made of him – hundreds of pictures cut from the papers and magazines.'

'Mum!' Marion felt tortured, but her mother carried on.

'And even though I am not a Royalist, the Duke and Duchess seem decent enough people.'

The waiting travellers were hooked.

Lorna shouted back, 'And those two bonny wee Princesses! To think that your Marion will be looking after them! She might even bump into the Prince of Wales himself. Who would have imagined that? I wouldn't come back if I were her.'

Maggie shook her head vehemently. 'No, no, no. She has her place at Glasgow. Nothing will stop her coming back.'

The rails began to hum and twang, bringing a warning that the London train was approaching.

Marion bent down to pick up her case and whispered, 'Mother, everyone is listening. Please stop.'

Lorna shouted back, 'Marion, make sure you write to your mother every week and let us all know how it is going.'

Marion shot her mother a pleading look, which Maggie ignored. 'I will let you know, Lorna, as soon as Marion can write.'

Marion turned to her mother and whispered wretchedly, 'Mother, for God's sake, shut up.'

Her last words were drowned by the incoming whoosh, hiss and squealing brakes of the train.

'Now, Marion Crawford, there's no need for attitude from you. Here, let me get the porter to help you.'

'Mother, please. I can do it myself.'

'You stop your snappiness, madam. I am trying to help you.'

'I know, Mother.' Marion sounded whiny and hated herself for it. 'I am grateful, really, but *please*.' She took the handle of her case and heaved it onto the train.

'This is the way it's going to be, is it?' Maggie whispered furiously. 'Just because you've got a job with royalty, doesn't mean you're better than the rest of us.'

Marion kept her head down, focusing on her case, in fear of letting slip the tears brimming in her eyes. 'Mum, it's just a temporary job.'

Her mother reached for her hanky, her anger subsiding. 'I will miss you so much.'

'I'll miss you too.'

The guard's whistle blew shrill, making both women jump.

'All aboard please, ladies.'

Marion lifted her bag and stepped up into the carriage. Her mother reached up for a last hug. 'I love you and I am very proud of you. You know that.'

'I love you too, Mum.'

The stationmaster blew his whistle again and slammed Marion's door.

Then the train began to move.

'Now don't be shy with them!' Maggie called up through the open window. 'Let me know you arrived safely – and please, grow your hair back again!'

Marion blew a kiss. Walking along the narrow corridor, she peered inside each compartment until she found an empty one. Her mother had walked along the platform to follow her and was now standing below the window, wiping her tears, waving. Marion knew it was cruel, but she forbade herself to look at her. Right now she needed to calm herself. She arranged her case on the rack and folded her coat neatly on its top. The train jolted and began to move forward. Outside, Maggie moved too, knocking on the window. Marion now acknowledged her and waved back guiltily.

'Bye, Mother,' she mouthed. The train was picking up speed and Maggie was running out of platform. The last sight Marion had was of Maggie fluttering her hanky and crying.

She sat down with a sigh of relief. At last, she was free to concentrate on all that had happened since Miss Brown had slid the letter across her desk to her.

The older woman had watched as Marion read the letter quickly, then a second time, more slowly, taking in all it offered. It was from Lady Elgin of Broomhall. She wanted a history teacher for her seven-year-old son, Andrew, Lord Bruce. There were three younger children – Lady Martha, Lady Jean and the Honourable Jamie – who would wish to join in more suitable lessons, as and when.

She put the letter down. 'The Elgins?'

'Yes.'

'I am sorry, Miss Brown, but no. I don't approve of inherited wealth. These children do not need me. They will do fine without me.'

Miss Brown leant her elbows on her desk and steepled her fingers. 'Lord Elgin is a decent man. He cannot help his birth into good fortune, but you can learn a lot from him and his family.'

Marion was not inclined to think so. 'In what way?'

'It is important to see all the colours in the rainbow, Marion, even if there are colours you really don't like. Without blue, there would be no green; without red, no purple. Poverty and wealth can be brought closer together if one understands the other. Do you see what I am getting at? The wealthy can help the poor financially, while the poor can educate the wealthy in finding the small joys of life and humility. Isn't that what you would like to achieve?'

Marion was thinking. 'Well, yes . . . I suppose so.'

'Good. Then I shall write back to the Elgins and request an interview.'

As prejudiced as she was, Marion had found Lady Elgin warm and welcoming at their interview. She clearly loved her children and wanted them to be well-educated. So, when Marion was offered the job, she spent two nights thinking hard, then finally accepted, despite her misgivings. She wanted to help her parents by paying back some of what they had invested in her own education. Her stepfather refused to take her money, but her mother accepted it gladly. She'd said with a grin, 'Rob the rich to pay for the poor. I am all for it.'

Marion had soon learnt first-hand the interior workings of an aristocratic family and its household. Breakfast was at eight, with prayers and hymns, then the schoolroom for a couple of hours, followed by elevenses. The family had their drinks and small cakes in the sitting room, while the domestic and garden staff had their own bread and cheese in the stables or the still-room. Marion was fascinated by it all.

Visitors came and went, dropping in at all times. One day the Duchess of York, who was married to the King's second son, came to visit. She brought with her her two beautiful daughters: Princess Elizabeth, six years old, and Princess Margaret Rose, who was coming up for two.

Marion was not able to sleep on the train, or to eat the carefully packed sandwiches her mother had insisted on giving her. Anxiety, and a sudden bout of homesickness, prohibited both.

What on earth was she doing? Leaving Scotland, leaving everything she knew? And all on the whim of the Duchess of York, who had decided that her two girls needed a governess exactly like Miss Crawford.

Marion couldn't quite remember how or when she had agreed to the sudden change. Before she knew it, it was all arranged. The Duchess of York was hardly a woman you said no to. Her manner was sweet and charming, beguiling even. Marion had fallen prey to the smile that lit the Duchess's cornflower eyes, the merry laugh and obvious love and concern she had for her daughters.

'The Duke and I would very much like you to come to London and start the girls' education. They need someone young and fun,' she had said.

'I am very flattered.' Marion really was. 'But I have a place at Glasgow University to study child psychology, so I am sorry, but I shall have to say no. Thank you.'

The Duchess put her hands together as if in prayer, 'That will work perfectly. We can have you back in Glasgow ready for the start of term.'

Once her mother came round to the idea, she was in a state of high excitement and condemnation. 'Why would they want *you*?' she had asked. 'A girl from a good, working-class family? What do you know about how these people live?' She had stared at Marion, almost in reverence. 'Working for the royal family . . . They must have seen something in you. *My* daughter.'

On arrival at King's Cross Marion took the underground to Paddington. She found the right platform for the Windsor train and, as she had a little time to wait, ordered a cup of tea, a scone and a magazine from the station café.

She tried to imagine what her mother and stepfather were doing right now. They'd have eaten their tea and have the wireless on, tuned to the news, most likely. Her mother would have her mending basket by her side, telling her husband all about Marion's send-off and how rude she had been to Lorna. She imagined her mother rambling on as the fire in the grate hissed and burned.

The train was quite full, but Marion found a seat and settled down to flick through her magazine. However, her mind couldn't focus. Through the dusk she watched the alien landscape and houses spool out beside her. Rows of neat red brick houses, blackened with soot, giving way to fields and small villages – not a granite tenement to be seen.

Dear God, what was she doing here, so far away from family and home? What was she walking into?

When the conductor walked through the carriage announcing that Windsor would be the next stop, she began to breathe deeply and calmly, as she had been taught to do before her exams. She took from her bag, for the umpteenth time, the letter from her new employers. The instructions were clear: she was to leave the station and look for a uniformed driver with a dark car.

She gazed out of the window as the train began to slow. She took a deep breath, stood up and collected her case and coat. *Come on, Marion. It's only for a few months. You can do this.*

Chapter Two

Windsor, March 1932

'Good evening, Miss Crawford.'

A smart young man in uniform was waiting on the platform when she stepped off the train.

She was startled. 'Aye. That's me. How did you know?'

'Easy.' He smiled. 'There aren't that many young ladies travelling alone on the train from King's Cross and wearing a tartan scarf.'

She followed him through the station, where a car was waiting. He opened the front passenger door for her, before putting her bags in the back and hopping into the driving seat.

'Thank you so much.'

'All part of the service.' He turned the ignition over and let the handbrake off. 'Have you been to Windsor before, Miss Crawford?'

She shook her head. 'I've never been out of Scotland until now.'

'Welcome, then, Miss Crawford.'

'Please . . . call me Marion.'

'And you can call me Peter, but to the rest of the household I'm known as Jackson the Chauffeur, just as you'll be known as Miss Crawford the Governess – or something else. If I know anything about the family, you'll get a nickname sooner rather than later. They love that sort of thing.'

'Just Marion will do me fine,' Marion replied. She was looking at all the shops lining both sides of the road, their lights shining onto a drizzled pavement. 'This is a lovely street. I have never seen anything like it. Where are we?'

'Peascod Street. Beautiful, isn't it? Look up ahead.' He pointed to the windscreen. 'See the walls of the castle?'

Straight ahead of them, the fortress walls of the castle began to emerge, rounded and as solid as the day they were built, over eight hundred years before.

Marion's mouth gaped for a second. 'Is this where I am to live?'

Jackson laughed. 'Not unless you've been bad; then you might be thrown into the dungeons.'

Marion laughed too. 'Don't say that!'

'You won't be working here. This is where the King and Queen spend their weekends. Not bad, is it?'

'It's unbelievable. Where shall I be, then?'

'You'll spend most weekends at Royal Lodge.'

'That sounds a lot more cosy. Is it a sort of gate house to Windsor Castle?'

'It's bigger than that – very grand. You'll see. It's where I am taking you now, but during the week you'll be holed up in 145 Piccadilly, the Duke and Duchess's London home.'

After about ten minutes, Jackson slowed the car and turned left down a short drive, leading them between two gates. 'Almost there.'

The drive snaked gently through the dark trees until Royal Lodge loomed ahead of them. It was white, pretty and huge. 'It's a palace,' Marion said.

Jackson jogged round the car to open her door. 'Royal Lodge has only thirty rooms. The Palace has at least twenty times that. Mind you, the inside is all gold leaf, priceless rugs and crystal chandeliers, so it does feel like a palace.'

He took her cases from the boot and carried them to the porticoed front door. 'Welcome to your new home,' he said, with a mock bow. 'And if you like a walk there's ninety-eight acres for you to plod round.'

In moments the front door was opened, flooding the front steps with the glow from within.

'Good evening, Miss Crawford. We have been expecting you.' A man stood before her, in the black tailcoat and striped trousers of a butler. 'Do come in. You must be tired after your journey. I am Ainslie, their Royal Highnesses' butler.'

'Thank you.' She was in awe. 'I am pleased to be here. Do call me Marion.'

Peter returned with her case. 'Delivered safe and sound, Mr Ainslie.'

'Thank you, Jackson. You may take the car round to the stables. It won't be needed again tonight.'

'Right ho, Mr Ainslie.'

From nowhere a young man, dressed in what Marion assumed was footman attire, arrived to lift her bags.

Ainslie closed the door against the dark. 'The Duke and Duchess send their apologies,' he said. 'They are detained in Town but will be back later. I have been instructed to take you straight to the nursery, where the Princesses have delayed their bedtime until your arrival.'

'Oh, dear. I hope I won't have upset their routine.'

'Alah, the Princesses' nurse, will have made sure all is well. Follow me, please.'

She followed him across the elegant hall with its black and white chequered tiles. The walls were covered in eau-de-nil watered silk, and the polished side tables were awash with extravagantly scented flower arrangements in each corner.

'Top floor,' Ainslie told her. 'You are young – you will not feel it.'

Marion followed him upstairs. She stopped counting the steps when she got to forty-five. Each floor absorbed her, as she spotted corridor after corridor of beautiful paintings and objets d'art.

At last, the stairs finished, and she found herself standing on an airy landing with large windows, giving a double aspect to each side of the house. Leading off the landing were two corridors, one to the left, the other to the right. A table with four chairs sat in the middle and there was a bookcase filled with children's books, an abacus, two teddy bears and a jam jar stuffed with paintbrushes.

'The Princesses play up here in inclement weather.' Ainslie smiled. 'The nursery suite is to the left, Miss Crawford.' He stopped and knocked on the nearest door.

'Come in,' a woman's voice answered.

Ainslie stood back to allow Marion to pass.

The room was dimly lit and decorated in soft pink and beige, furnished as a child's bedroom. A woman stood close to a small fire with a guard around it, little vests and pants hanging from it to air. Tall and noble, she was the epitome of infallible calm and kindness. She took a step towards Marion, her hand outstretched. 'Good evening, Miss Crawford. I am Clara Knight, the Princesses' nurse. But everyone calls me Alah.'

'Hello, Miss Crawford,' piped a little voice from one of the two small beds. 'We've been waiting for you. My name is Lilibet and that' – she pointed at the second bed where a small shape was sleeping soundly – 'is my sister Margaret Rose. She's very tired. You are just in time for a trot round the park. Come on, Alah. Pass me the reins.'

Alah took a dressing gown cord and began to wind it around the bottom bedposts, handing the ends to the little Princess. 'Just a quick one, please, Lilibet. Miss Crawford will be tired from her journey.'

Lilibet frowned. 'No one could ever be too tired for a quick carriage ride.' She shook the dressing gown cord and encouraged her invisible horses. 'Walk on, giddy up – we haven't all night.' She proceeded to tilt her body round unseen corners until Alah tapped her watch. 'That's enough now.'

'Whoa, boys. Good boys.' The Princess reined them in to a halt. 'Alah will take you back to your stables, and maybe there will be a carrot for each of you.'

Alah unrolled the dressing gown cords from the bed posts, and settled her charge to lie down.

Marion smiled. 'Do you often drive your horses in bed?'

'Oh yes. I have to exercise them, you see. Are you going to stay with us for long?'

'For a little while, yes.'

'Good. Grandpa says I need someone to teach me neat handwriting. By the way, what has happened to your hair?'

Marion smiled conspiratorially. 'Well, I used to have very long hair but it took a lot of looking after, like a horse's mane or tail, so . . .' She lifted her hat. 'I had it cut short.'

'Goodness!' Lilibet looked shocked. 'I have never seen a girl with short hair before.'

Marion feigned surprise. 'But I heard that it's all the fashion at the moment.'

The little Princess frowned. 'Is it?'

'Yes. It's called the Eton Crop.'

'Like the Eton schoolboys? How funny. Alah, may I have an Eton crop, please?'

Alah frowned. 'Now, young lady, you just lie down and go to sleep. Miss Crawford has come all the way from Scotland and she'll be tired and hungry. Settle down now. You'll see her in the morning.'

'Very well.' Lilibet rested her head on the pillow. 'Goodnight, Miss Crawford.'

'May I call you Lilibet?' Marion asked, not wanting to make an unpardonable mistake.

'Yes, please.'

'In that case, goodnight, Lilibet.'

Alah signalled for her to leave as she tucked the little Princess in.

Waiting on the landing, Marion heard Lilibet whispering to Alah, 'She's nice, isn't she? I like her. I hope Margaret does too.'

'I'm sure she will. Now close your eyes and sleep well.'

Marion moved away from the door and went to one of the windows, not wanting Alah to think she had been eavesdropping.

Alah gently closed the door behind her. 'Miss Crawford, you must be tired after your long journey.'

'I'm fine, thank you.'

'I have asked the kitchen to send a supper tray to your room.'

'Thank you. That's very kind.'

'Not at all. You're across the landing here.'

Alah opened the door onto a comfortable room, decorated in the same pink and fawn hues as the Princesses' bedroom. A fire was burning gaily in the grate and in front of it was a small card table with a supper tray set upon it.

'It's a pretty room, isn't it? The Duchess's favourite colours.' Alah reached for the coal tongs and took two lumps from the scuttle to place on the flames. 'If you find yourself needing more coal, just ring for the housemaid. The bell pull is by the mantelpiece.'

'Thank you. It seems so much warmer down here than I am used to in Dunfermline.'

Alah was lifting two silver domes on the supper tray. 'Cold pork. Trifle to follow. There is hot cocoa in the flask. Will that do you?'

'Perfectly.'

'This is your corridor, Miss Crawford. There is a bathroom opposite for your use and a couple of boxrooms further down. We keep luggage, etc, stored there.'

'I see.'

'Then there is the Princesses' bedroom, a sitting room, and a small kitchen. Bobo, the young nurserymaid, and I sleep on that side to be close to the girls, but you are welcome to use the kitchen and sitting room.'

Marion tried to stifle a yawn. Alah noticed and patted her arm.

'You are tired, of course. I will say goodnight and let you get some rest. The Princesses are busy little bees, always up early, so make sure you get enough sleep. I will bring them to you at 9.00 a.m. They will wear you out if you let them.' She smiled. 'Fortunately, you have the benefit of youth.'

'I shall certainly sleep well. Goodnight, Alah, and thank you.'

Alone at last, Marion took in her room. It was much larger than her bedroom at home and decorated so prettily – not so grand that she was scared to touch anything, but grander than anything she had ever known before. The bed was most inviting, piled high with pillows, blankets and a plush eiderdown.

She turned to look for her luggage. She couldn't see it, though she was certain the footman had carried it up here. She checked around the corners and underneath the bed and finally found it, empty, in the wardrobe where her clothes were hanging with precision on their wooden hangers, her nightdresses and under-wear folded neatly in a generous George III mahogany chest of drawers. Marion was horrified. Who had unpacked her clothes? Her outer and underclothes were very plain and simple but none the less intimate for that. She was so terribly embarrassed. Perhaps the nurserymaid had done it? That would be less bad. Maybe in grand houses like this it was normal for men or women to unpack someone's personal wear. She would have to ask Alah in the morning.

A rush of exhaustion and hunger overtook her. She kicked off her shoes and relaxed into the comfortable armchair. She would write to her mother tomorrow and tell her all about it.

The cold pork was served with pickle and slender slices of bread and butter, all the more delicious because she'd expected nothing, and the trifle was like no trifle she had ever tasted before.

Full and contented, Marion sat back in the chair and closed her eyes. Immediately there was a gentle knock at the door. Expecting Alah, she said, 'Come in.'

A small and pretty woman wearing a hyacinth-blue evening gown popped her head around the door. 'Am I disturbing you?'

It wasn't Alah; it was the Duchess of York. Her sweet smile and the sparkle of her blue eyes and the twinkling of her diamond tiara made Marion jump in shock.

Scrambling to her feet, she bobbed what she hoped was a good enough curtsey. 'Your Royal Highness.'

'I just wanted to welcome you, and apologize for not being here when you arrived. I hope you are settling in well?'

'Yes, thank you, ma'am.'

'I shall leave you to your rest. See you tomorrow. I am sure you shall be happy here. I do hope you shall like us.'

'I am sure I shall, ma'am.' She bobbed again. 'Goodnight.'

Left to herself again, Marion's mind began racing. Pulling her journal and a pencil from her handbag, she began to make a list. If she was to see the Duchess, and possibly the Duke, tomorrow she had better have some clear thoughts and questions about the Princesses and her role. She wrote fast, thinking hurriedly:

1. *What are their favourite activities?*
2. *How much can Princess Elizabeth read yet and how much can she write? (she is six years old)*
3. *What stories do they like?*
4. *What subjects do you wish me to teach first?*
5. *How much outdoor activity do they like?*
6. *Princess Margaret Rose is still so young (two in August?). Where and how would you like me to start her lessons?*
7. *Do you have a schoolroom?*
8. *How much of the world outside their front door are they allowed to explore – how shielded are they?*
9. *Who are their best friends that we may meet for play and teas?*
10. *I am here for only a few months (as discussed, I return to Scotland in the autumn to start my child psychology diploma). What would you like me to have achieved by then?*

She tapped her pencil against her teeth and read it all through. She didn't want to come across as too prescriptive or bossy, but she wanted them to know that she was taking her responsibilities seriously.

Satisfied for the moment, she jotted down a few further notes of the day so far. Her mother would want to know all the details.

Finally, Marion got ready for bed. She wasn't used to sleeping in so warm a room, so she opened her window wide onto the dark outside. The cool air felt so much warmer than a Scottish night in March. She drank it in and gave a small laugh. 'Well, lassie, look at you now.'

She checked her watch. It was getting late: if she was to be up and ready for her first day, she'd better get some rest.

Chapter Three

Royal Lodge, Windsor, March 1932

Marion woke to the sound of her window being firmly shut. Blinking against the light, she saw the outline of a young housemaid securing the curtains with tiebacks.

'Good morning,' Marion said, rather alarmed to find this stranger in her room.

'Morning, Miss Crawford. You must be cold, with the window open all night. It's very chilly outside today. I've laid your breakfast on the table by the fire and put a couple of lumps of coal on the embers too, so you'll be warm in no time. How did you sleep?'

'Very well, thank you.' She sat up with a thought. 'Was it you who unpacked my cases last night?'

'Yes, Miss Crawford. Have I made a mistake?'

'No, no. It's just that I am not used to others, erm . . .'

'I quite understand, but don't worry. It's my job.'

Marion lay back in relief. 'I was worried in case it had been Mr Ainslie or the footman.'

The maid giggled. 'Wouldn't that be awful!'

The giggle was infectious, and soon Marion was joining in, until the pair of them had to wipe their eyes.

Marion's heart was lifted. 'I needed that. My nerves have been in knots for days.'

'I was just the same when I started.'

Marion sat up again, lifting her legs out of bed. 'I'm Marion. What's your name?'

'Maria. It'll be me who looks after you, so anything you need to know, just ask. I've brought you a boiled egg and toast, orange juice and a pot of tea. I hope that's all right.'

Marion tucked her short curls behind her ears. 'Sounds delicious. Thank you.'

'I do like your haircut. I'd like mine short too, but it has to be long enough to stay off my face and under my maid's cap.'

'Do you think mine is too short – for the job, I mean?' Marion asked anxiously.

'Bless your heart, no! It'll be perfect for you running after those two little girls.'

'Are they nice?'

'Princess Elizabeth is rather serious but very sweet, and Princess Margaret Rose is a little monkey. Runs old Alah ragged.'

Somewhere a clock chimed eight and Maria hastened to the door. 'I'd best be gone, but anything you want to know just ask me, Miss Crawford.'

'Marion, please.'

'Marion.'

With a quick smile, Maria left the room, closing the door softly behind her.

Marion opened her window again and sat by the fire to eat her breakfast. It was a bright spring day and the birds were busy singing, accompanied by the shrieks of children. Tea in hand, she stood up to look out on to the garden below. There was a large terrace and a bird table covered with crumbs and bluetits. A door opened beneath her window and two little girls ran out giggling, pursued by a man.

'Papa, Papa!'

'Come here, you little imps.' He lunged at Princess Margaret, who was still in her nightclothes. She swerved away from him and tripped, landing on her knees. For a moment there was silence and then the shocked wailing began.

'Mummy, Mummy!' the baby Princess cried.

Her big sister leapt to comfort her. 'It's all right. You just tripped. Let me see your knee.'

Marion watched from above as the Duke looked anxiously back towards the house. 'Darling? Margaret has fallen. I think you may be needed.'

'I did say,' the Duchess's voice came. 'I knew it would end in tears.'

Marion withdrew from her window and latched it as quietly as she could. It wouldn't do to be thought of as an eavesdropper.

By nine Marion was dressed and waiting in her room. She had practised a curtsey, several times, and now the wait for the Princesses' arrival was making her nervous.

Finally there was a knock at the door.

'Come in.'

Alah led the Princesses in.

Marion gave her most reassuring smile and, forgetting to curtsey, said, 'Good morning.'

'Hello,' Princess Elizabeth said shyly. 'Are you ready for us?'

'I certainly am.'

Alah nudged a reluctant Margaret towards Marion, and checked the nurse's fob watch on her bodice. 'This is a new routine for us all. We have always had sole charge up until now.'

'We?' asked Marion.

'The nurserymaid, Bobo, and I.'

'Oh, I see.' Marion smiled nervously. 'Nine o'clock it shall be from now on then.' She tried to sound reassuring.

'You are our first governess. I would be grateful to know your schedule, so that we can fit your activities with the Princesses round their normal daily routine.' Alah's shoulders went back, her hands tightly folded over her skirts. The tiny gesture reminded Marion of her mother. Last night Alah had been much more approachable, but last night she hadn't been handing over her little Princesses to another woman.

Marion acknowledged the metaphorical gauntlet thrown before her. She had been expecting it. She knew she'd be thought of as too young and too inexperienced to have such a position. There would be raised eyebrows and whispered conversations about her.

She was more than ready for it.

'As today is our first day,' she said, wanting to sound confident, 'I thought the Princesses might show me around the garden and they can tell me about the games they like to play.'

Alah built her first defence. 'The Duchess likes them to have refreshment with her at eleven o'clock.'

Marion smiled again. 'Perfect.'

Another parry. 'And at midday the girls take their rest.'

'Very sensible.' Marion was beginning to wonder how the children would have any time for lessons.

'Luncheon is at one fifteen, with the Duke and Duchess.'

'How lovely. And what happens after lunch?'

'If the Duke and Duchess are at home, they like to play outside, as a family. The Duke is very good at hopscotch.'

Little Lilibet, who was bored and getting fidgety, looked up at this. 'Papa is better than any of us at hopscotch. He is a very fast runner too.'

Marion looked at the three expectant faces, waiting for her to say something. 'I am a very good runner myself and when I was at school, I was on the hopscotch team.'

'Were you?' Lilibet took her hand. 'I will tell Papa and you can have a competition.'

'All right. Why don't you show me the best bit of your garden to practise in?'

'They will need to put something warm on first,' Alah interrupted. Turning back to the door, she called, 'Bobo?'

A voice from the small kitchen called back, 'Yes?'

'Bring warm cardigans for the girls, please.'

A fresh-faced woman of twenty-eight, wearing the uniform of a nurserymaid, came in with two matching scarlet cardigans. 'Here we are.'

Alah introduced her. 'Miss Crawford, this is Bobo. Say hello to our governess, Bobo.'

Marion wondered what her real name was.

Bobo smiled broadly. 'Hello, Miss Crawford, and welcome to our little kingdom on the top floor. We have been ever so excited to meet you, haven't we, girls?'

Margaret hopped on one foot and wriggled into her cardigan. 'Yeeees.'

'Margaret, keep still,' Lilibet told her. 'Bobo can't put your cardigan on if you are hopping.'

Margaret stuck her tongue out and blew a raspberry in reply.

Togged up and clinging on to Marion's hands, the three of them finally made it out into the garden. The sun was watery but the air held a promise of warmth. The sound of a mower came from somewhere and the smell of freshly cut grass hung over the garden.

Margaret began to sing: 'Neigh neighs, la la la, neigh neighs.'

'No, Margaret.' Elizabeth took her sister's other hand. 'No horses today. Remember you have a sore knee.'

Margaret stopped singing and pulled her hand from Marion's. Bending down, she unfolded her sock and pointed at a fresh graze on her shin. 'Ouchy,' she said. Marion could tell from the freshness of the wound that this was the result of the game she had witnessed earlier.

Lilibet became very matter of fact. 'Don't be silly, it's just a scratch. Mummy says you might get a bruise but that's all. You can still skip, can't you?'

Margaret grinned and immediately began to skip across the grass, Lilibet and Marion following behind.

The lawn led down to a gravel path lined with forsythia and sweet-smelling Daphnes. The last daffodils shook their golden heads as the girls skipped by.

'Where are you taking me?' Marion laughed. 'Fairyland?'

'Wait and see,' Lilibet replied breathlessly. 'We are nearly there.'

The three of them skipped round the last corner of the path and Marion saw a miniature cottage sitting in a clearing, with its own little garden surrounded with white picket fencing.

'What's this?' Marion asked.

'It's our Little House,' shrieked Lilibet. 'Come and see.'

Built of brick and whitewashed, with a thatched roof, the two-storey cottage was about a third of the size of a real house.

'Goodness!' Marion stood open-mouthed. 'Is this your play-house?'

'Yes.' Lilibet reached the front door and turned the handle. 'Come in and see.'

'Will I fit?'

'You'll have to bend down a bit.'

Marion crouched, squeezing herself into a tiny hallway. She saw one room to the left and one to the right with a staircase in front of her.

'Come into the kitchen,' Lilibet said. 'Look, the taps work, and the lights. And we've got the wireless, too. I would make you a cup of tea but we didn't bring the milk.'

Marion marvelled. 'It's wonderful. Better than fairyland.'

Margaret pulled her skirt and ran to the room next door.

'Margaret wants to show you our sitting room,' said Lilibet.

Marion shuffled backwards then forwards, finally managing to fit in the sitting room. It was furnished beautifully, with two little sofas, a miniature armchair in the bay window and a portrait of the Duchess hanging over the real fireplace. 'It's so beautiful.'

Margaret had crawled onto a sofa and began jumping on it.

Lilibet was like a proud housewife. 'Don't jump on the sofas, Margaret. You know what Mummy has told us.'

Margaret immediately dropped to her knees and began to cry.

Marion comforted her by swinging her onto her hip. When she looked round, Lilibet had vanished.

'Where's your sister gone?'

Margaret wiped her nose and pointed back to the hall. 'Up,' she told Marion.

'There's an upstairs too?' Marion pretended not to believe her, even though she had just heard little footsteps going up the stairs.

'Yeeees.' Margaret laughed. 'Silly-billy.'

Elizabeth called from upstairs, 'Come on, you two.'

Marion put Margaret on to the stairs and they both crawled up together. On the bright landing, Marion could finally stand up. 'I am a giant!' She laughed. 'Like Gulliver in Lilliput.'

'That sounds like my name.' The elder sister was busily tucking Margaret Rose into a tiny bed. 'Margaret calls me Lilibet because she can't say Elizabeth properly.'

Little Margaret, comfortable under her blankets, began giggling. 'Lilibet, Lilibet, Lilibet.'

'See? And now everybody calls me that. Come on, Margaret, you've got to get up now.' Lilibet gently extricated her sister. 'Now I must make the bed properly again or Mummy will tell me off.'

'Do you do all the housework yourself?' Marion asked jokingly.

'Oh yes.' Lilibet was serious. 'Mummy says we must not let people do everything for us. We must learn to do it ourselves.'

Marion was impressed. 'Good for you.'

Outside, the three of them began a gentle game of tag, which came to an abrupt end when Margaret tripped on her bad leg.

'Brave girl,' Marion told her, giving her a hug. 'Show me where it hurts.'

Again the tiny Princess rolled down her sock to reveal her graze. Marion dropped a kiss onto it. 'No harm done.'

Lilibet stood with her hands on her hips, watching as Margaret bravely pulled herself up. 'Oh, what are we going to do with her, Miss Crawfie?'

'She's all right,' Marion said, brushing the little girl down and lifting her into her arms.

Lilibet started to laugh. 'I said Miss Crawfie, not Miss Crawford. Crawfie. I like that.' Her laughter was so infectious that Margaret started to laugh too. 'That's a good name for you, isn't it? Can we call you that?'

Marion thought about it for a moment. It seemed that everyone else had nicknames. Bobo, Alah, Lilibet. She grinned at Lilibet. 'Why not?'

Returning to the house, Marion found that they were a little late for elevenses. The Duke and Duchess were sitting together on the terrace, the table before them set with refreshments, including tea, a jug of lemonade and a plate of biscuits.

'There you are.' The warmth in the Duchess's voice welcomed them. 'Have you had a good morning?'

Marion delivered the Princesses and curtsied, while the girls ran straight to their father.

'We had a lovely time,' said Lilibet. 'We showed Crawfie our little house.'

'Crawfie?' The Duchess raised her eyebrows. 'And who thought of that?'

'Me,' Lilibet said proudly, 'and it's all right, I asked her if we could call her Crawfie and she says we can.'

'I like it,' the Duke said approvingly, 'As long as that is all right with you, Miss Crawford?'

'Perfectly all right with me.'

'Isn't that marvellous? I knew as soon as I saw you at the Elgins' that you would be fun.' The Duchess motioned to a chair. 'Come and join us for tea. Or perhaps you prefer squash?'

Marion hesitated. She had expected to be dismissed. 'I'm sure you might like some family time?'

But the Duchess insisted. 'Take a pew. My husband and I have a lot to ask you.'

Sitting with her tea and trying not to show her nerves, Marion watched the family. She admired the obvious fondness and ease between parents and children.

The Duke was a handsome man but very slender and clearly shy. Putting down his teacup, he lit a cigarette and asked, through a bad stammer, how Marion had found the girls so far.

'They are delightful, sir.'

The Duchess, pretty in a lilac-blue tea dress and warm fur tippet around her shoulders, sat back in relief. 'My husband worries so.' She reached for his hand and patted it. 'You see, Miss Crawford, neither of us had much of a formal education, but we want our daughters to have a broader view of the world than we were given, or indeed we can give. It's impossible to send the girls to an ordinary school, obviously, but this is 1932. We want them to grow up as modern young women. Do you see?'

This was music to Marion's ears. 'I do, ma'am. The last war has shown us that women can do more than was expected of them before, and do it willingly.'

'Quite so.' The Duchess glanced quickly at the Duke, who took another lungful of tobacco smoke. 'They won't be expected to find paid work as such, but as the King's granddaughters they will work within the royal family, representing all that the monarchy does around the world.'

'B-b-bally hard work too,' the Duke said.

Marion put her cup on the table and leant forwards. Her confidence was growing in the company of these forward-thinking parents. She was going to tell them how much she cared about education. 'You would like them to gain qualifications, perhaps? Having my teacher training under my belt has given me the opportunity to study child psychology from this September.'

'Where did you study?' the Duke asked, his speech more relaxed now.

'Moray House, part of Edinburgh Provincial Training Centre.'

The Duchess put her hands together in joy. 'Edinburgh. Isn't it a marvellous place? So good for shopping. The linens are exquisite.'

'So I have been told, ma'am, but rather beyond my purse as a student. I trained with some of the poorest children in the city.'

'Oh dear,' the Duchess said. She looked a little less comfortable.

'The children have very little and their nutrition is so poor that it hinders their ability to develop through education.'

'Goodness.' The Duchess touched her pearls. 'But there are so many lovely open spaces for the children to run in. That must help them?'

'Oh yes, you're right – but still, so many children suffer trauma and sadness in their young lives. With modern practices we ought to be able to save them from a life of low wages and ill health.'

'I see.' The Duchess seemed to want the conversation back on safer ground. 'Well, yes, that sounds very important for unfortunate children and their families – but you must see it is quite different for our girls. What would they need qualifications in?'

'I would start with the basics. English, history, arithmetic, geography.'

'And they would have to take examinations in these subjects?' the Duchess asked.

'It is proven that being qualified in certain subjects can really boost a child's self-esteem, yes.' Marion smiled, thrilled to be able to have this conversation so openly.

The Duke put out his cigarette, and through his difficulty in speech, asked, 'And how often would the girls be taught all this?'

'About two hours in the morning and the same in the afternoon, to start with, but as they get older, the hours would naturally get longer.'

'Every day?' asked the Duke.

'Yes.'

'When would we see them?' The Duchess sounded anxious. 'The Duke and I like to spend as much time with our daughters as possible.'

Marion began to realize she might have unsettled their Royal Highnesses. 'Of course, I am only here until the end of August, as you know,' she said. 'I have to get back for my first term of psychology. I worked so hard to get my place. But I would think that any governess you employ would suggest the girls get some proper qualifications.'

Inside, a telephone rang and the Duke checked his watch. 'That'll be the PM for me.' He bent to kiss the girls, who were sprawled over his knees. 'See you two at luncheon.'

And then he returned inside.

The Duchess stood, and Marion did the same.

'Girls, say goodbye to Miss Crawford. It's time for your nap and a story. Miss Crawford will see you again after lunch.'

Marion curtsied. She watched as the mother and daughters, chattering away, left her alone in the garden.

Chapter Four

Not knowing where else to go, Marion returned to the nursery.

'How was your first morning?' Alah asked over the tops of her glasses, as she folded socks from the clothes horse. 'You'll have lunch with me and Bobo, won't you?'

'I don't quite know. *May* I have it with you?'

'We have some soup and sandwiches coming that you are welcome to share.' Alah gave Marion a careful glance. 'We've never had a governess to cater for before.'

'I must be a bit of a guinea pig for you all,' Marion said lightly.

Bobo, who'd been quietly ironing Margaret's napkins in the corner of the nursery, said, 'We didn't know if you'd want to be up here with us. Alah thought you might want to eat with the household staff, you being a teacher.'

'Am I not eating with the household staff right here with you?'

Alah sniffed. 'We are *nursery*, Miss Crawford. The household staff are Mr Ainslie and the others.'

'Oh.' Marion hadn't realized that there was such a hierarchy.

Bobo continued, 'And then there's kitchen staff and house staff—'

Marion stopped her. 'And where does the governess belong?'

Alah took up another pair of socks. 'Well, that's the puzzle. We've never had a—'

'You've never had a governess before, I know.' Marion slumped into the nearest armchair in agitated frustration. 'I suppose it's up to me to make my own position. That way, when the new governess arrives after I have left, you will be able to tell her where she eats, what she teaches and the hours in which she is permitted so to do.'

Bobo stood open-mouthed, while Alah tucked another ball of freshly paired socks into the laundry basket. 'I think we need to have a little talk over lunch,' she said. 'Bobo, prepare the table.'

Settled with plates of sandwiches and bowls of soup before them, Alah began.

'Miss Crawford – Marion – having been in service for too many years, I forget how lost a newcomer can feel. I was younger than both you and Bobo when I began working for the Duchess's mother as the Duchess's nursery nurse. I had been sent to work for them by *my* mother. I had experience of looking after my own younger siblings and was thought mature enough to look after a new born. I was fifteen.'

'I was sixteen,' Bobo told Marion.

'Gosh.'

'I am speaking, if you care to listen,' Alah said, quietening the younger women. 'Now, the Duchess's father, the Earl of Strathmore and her mother, the Countess, live in Glamis Castle. You might know it?'

'Aye. I do. A beautiful place.' Marion had been to see the gardens with her parents.

'Indeed. But for a young girl who had never left home, it was frightening. Castles are draughty and the stories of hauntings meant I didn't get a wink of sleep in my first two weeks.'

'I wouldn't have,' said Bobo, shivering. 'Not with the ghosts and the baby up all night.'

Alah silenced her with a sharp look. 'May I continue?'

Bobo nodded, eyes cast down.

'So, as you can imagine, I was tired, cold, anxious over my new responsibilities – and very, very hungry.'

'Hungry?' asked Marion.

'Oh yes. No one had bothered to tell me that my breakfast, lunch and dinner were waiting for me in the kitchen. When I didn't come for it, they thought I must have my own rations in the nursery and didn't bother me.'

Marion was incredulous. 'But how could they not think to ask?'

'They'd never had a nursery nurse before. Nothing had been planned for me.'

'Ah.' It began to come clear to Marion. 'And because you've never had a governess . . . ?'

'Quite so.'

Marion thought for a moment. 'If it is quite all right with you, I should like to share my meals with you both in the nursery.'

'You are welcome to, Miss Crawford.'

'As long as you call me Crawfie,' she added. 'Lilibet today decided that is my nickname. Alah, Bobo and Crawfie – we sound like quite a team.'

Alah pursed her lips. 'Well, let's not jump our fences before we are in the saddle,' she said. 'It's not as if you will be with us past the summer, is it?'

The Princesses were returned to Marion's care after lunch and were ready for an afternoon of fun.

'Have you seen the little pond yet?' Lilibet asked.

'Are there frogs?' Marion asked.

Lilibet wrinkled her nose. 'I think so.'

'Good. Then we might find some frogspawn?'

'Papa calls it tapioca,' laughed Lilibet. 'Margaret doesn't like tapioca, do you, Margaret?'

'Ducks,' said Margaret, grabbing Marion's hand.

'Oh, are there ducks too?'

Lilibet skipped ahead. 'Ducks and slimy frogspawn.'

Across the lawn and down some wooden steps was a large pond surrounded by budding maple trees and tulips. Across the middle were stepping stones and a little bridge.

'This isn't a *little* pond.' Marion smiled. 'It's big enough to swim in.'

'You haven't seen Grandpa's pond. That's huuuuge.' Lilibet spread her arms wide. 'You can take a boat on it.'

'And where's Grandpa's pond?'

'At his house called Buckingham Palace.'

Marion shook her head, smiling. 'Of course it is.'

They reached the water's edge and began peering into the depths.

Lilibet pointed to the stepping stones. 'Margaret is not allowed to go on those or she'll fall in, but if we all hold hands we *are* allowed to walk the bridge to the little shelter.'

They did as Lilibet suggested, and in the middle of the bridge they stopped and looked down. With her free hand, Lilibet pointed out her father's collection of koi carp. Some lingered under lily pads, and some came up to greet them.

'They are very friendly.' Marion was enthralled. 'Next time we could bring them some food perhaps.'

'Oh no.' Lilibet shook her head seriously. 'Papa or the gardener are the only two people allowed to feed them.'

'Oh, look!' Marion pointed to the furthest edge of the pond. 'There is some frogspawn.'

Margaret wriggled and hopped singing, 'Fogspa. Fogspa.' Marion kept a tight hold of her hand.

A large frog they hadn't seen sitting on the muddy water's edge leapt in fright, dropping into the water with a large plop.

'Eeeee.' Margaret held her little arms up to Marion. 'Cab me.'

'She's asking you to carry her,' Lilibet interpreted. 'I wish I could be carried but Mummy says I'm getting too big.'

Marion collected up the trembling Margaret. 'Now, who wants a story?'

Lilibet hopped up and down. 'Meeee!'

The little shelter had three walls to keep off any breeze and a sunny, open side from which to watch the pond and the birds dipping and flitting above it. There was a white bench on one side, and Marion sat the girls down either side of her. They snuggled under her enfolding arms. 'Let's get comfortable,' she said. 'What is your favourite story?'

'Do you know a story about horses?' Lilibet asked.

'I can tell you the story of a horse I met on holiday when I was little.'

'Yes please.' Lilibet politely folded her arms and began to listen.

Marion told them about a pony she had ridden on a beach in Skye when she had been around six years old. Looking back, it must have been the time her mother had remarried. Marion had never known her father who had died when she was just a year old. When her stepfather came along five years later, Marion was uprooted from the house in Kilmarnock, where her grandfather, her mother and she had been born. Her stepfather took them to his house in Dunfermline, where she was enrolled in a new school. Her stepfather was kind, easy-going and made her mother happy. Life had felt more secure from then on. Marion had always thought of him as her father and called him 'Dad'.

The trip to Skye might have been her mother and stepfather's honeymoon. She hadn't thought of that. It had been a good holiday. The pony ride on the sand had been an extravagance that her mother had tried to stop but her stepfather insisted. Marion was sorry she hadn't enjoyed the ride – but she hadn't. The rolling gait, the stirrups slipping from her feet, the ground so far beneath her. She had gripped the pony's mane so tightly that the horse man who walked beside her had told her off and she'd wanted to cry. She had not been near a horse since.

'. . . And the big brown horse took me all the way into the forest, and there we met his friends.'

'What friends did he have?'

'Well now, let me see. There was Mr Fox. He let me stroke his whiskers.'

'Did he?'

'Very gently. Then I met Mrs Rabbit with her children walking back from school.'

'How many children?'

'Three. Two boys and a baby girl.'

'What was the little girl's name?' Lilibet wanted to know the details.

'Primrose.'

'That's nice. Carry on.'

'And then I met the big old owl.'

'Woo woo,' said Margaret.

'It's not woo woo, Margaret.' Lilibet wagged a finger. 'It's twit-too-woo, the way Papa tells us.' She looked up at Marion. 'Go on. What happened next?'

Marion wrapped the story up on a happy note, with the horse going back to its stable for a brush, a carrot and an apple. Lilibet seemed satisfied.

'Now then, girls.' Marion gathered them up. 'I expect you are ready for your tea?'

Lilibet led her to the drawing room. 'Mummy, Papa, we've had a lovely day, but Margaret still can't say twit-too-woo.'

Margaret frowned and began shouting, 'Woo woo,' all around the room.

'Poor Miss Crawford.' The Duchess put her arm out to catch the noisy Margaret as she sped past.

'She's called Crawfie now, Mummy,' Lilibet managed, as she followed her sister.

'So I understand.' The Duchess smiled graciously. 'My husband and I wondered if you would like to join us for a little cocktail when the children are in bed? We would like to talk more about your work here.'

Marion had never had a cocktail in her life. She didn't really have any idea what they were. 'Oh, I . . . That's very kind, thank you.'

'Very good. We'll see you here at, say, half past six?'

Marion stood where she was for a moment too long, before realizing that she had been dismissed. She gave a smart curtsey and left.

She ran up the stairs to the nursery in an absolute panic. 'How do I dress for cocktails?' she gasped at Alah and Bobo. 'I don't have any evening wear.'

Alah, the font of all knowledge, was only too happy to tell her. 'I assume this is with their Royal Highnesses?'

'Yes.' Marion was wringing her hands. 'I don't even know what a cocktail is.'

Alah took on the stance of the superior servant. 'A clean skirt and blouse will do. Wash your face and brush your hair. You'll only be with them for twenty minutes at most. And be careful of the Duke's measures.'

'G-g-gin and tonic?' The Duke was at the drinks table. 'Ice and lemon?'

'Thank you.' Marion was nervously perched on a chair opposite the Duchess. She had no idea what a gin and tonic tasted like. 'Just a small measure, please.'

The Duchess laughed. 'My husband doesn't know the meaning of the word. You have been warned.'

Crawfie took the glass that was offered.

'Chin-chin.' The Duke raised his glass to both women. Marion took a tiny sip. It was perfumed and rather bitter.

'Now, Miss Crawford,' began the Duchess, 'my husband and I have talked over the conversation we had with you earlier, and would like to make some suggestions as to our daughters' lessons.'

Marion smiled. 'Yes?'

'And we would like to make some suggestions of subjects.'

Marion took another sip of her drink and tried not to cough.

'We think that lessons in dancing, painting, piano and lots of outdoor play are very important.'

'Well, I remember some Scottish Country dancing from my own schooldays,' Marion said. 'But it's hard to do on your own. Might I invite the Princesses' friends over to make up the numbers?'

The Duke and Duchess looked at each other. 'Our daughters don't have many friends,' said the Duchess 'They have us.'

'Oh.' Marion was a little surprised. 'I am sure we can manage to find some friends.'

'The thing is' – the Duchess looked over at her husband again – 'we think that too much time in the classroom means less time out in the fresh air and having fun.'

Marion was bemused. 'Yes?'

The Duchess began again. 'Margaret is still so young. She needs her morning nap and she likes stories.'

'And I am happy to teach her to read. Lilibet tells me she knows her letters already and can write her name.'

'The Duchess has taught her,' the Duke said with pride. 'But what will Lilibet do when you are reading to Margaret?'

Marion thought on her feet. 'I suggest that the mornings are taken up with some drawing and colouring, which I am sure Margaret would enjoy, and while she is having her nap I can start Lilibet with some proper learning. Each day we would do a different subject. Writing, arithmetic, geography . . .' She waited for her employers' reaction.

'Can you do those things outside?' asked the Duke.

The Duchess nodded. 'Oh yes. Fresh air is so good for them.'

'I don't see why not.' Marion improvised again. 'We can do some nature study at the pond, watching the frogspawn grow into frogs. We can take the paints outside, look at maps of the world. Just to get them both ready for when they go to school.'

The Duchess stopped her. 'But as I said earlier, they won't be going to school.'

Marion had not fully realized that they would *never* go to school. 'I thought that perhaps by the time they were about eleven or twelve you might want them to experience school life, make friends. It really would be a wonderful opportunity for them.'

The Duchess smiled stiffly. 'No.'

Marion took a larger sip of her gin and tonic; it seemed to be warming her veins. 'So they will always be taught at home?'

'Yes.' The Duke smiled. 'It is royal tradition.'

The Duchess visibly relaxed and put her hand on her husband's knee. 'We just want them to be happy.'

Chapter Five

Royal Lodge, Windsor, July 1932

Dear Mother,

I am so sorry that I haven't made it back home yet. I find myself in rather a difficult situation. The Duke and Duchess have said nothing about finding my replacement, although they know I have to be back in time for the start of term. They brush the question away when I try to ask.

If only I already had my degree, I would be happy to stay here. The girls are lovely wee lassies and I am growing so fond of them. We have such fun together and our routine is establishing nicely.

I must say that, as much as I enjoy living in London during the week, I am always very glad when we decamp to Windsor and Royal Lodge on a Friday night for the weekend. The Duke and Duchess are so relaxed when we are there. Just like any other young couple, they sit by the fire after dinner and listen to the wireless. We get very few interruptions of visitors. Unlike 145 Piccadilly, where the front door bell seems to ring constantly.

Last weekend, who do you think just 'dropped in' from Windsor Castle? The King and Queen!

Mr Ainslie gave us all fair warning and dear Maria (you remember, the housemaid?) ran to my room with an especially pressed shirt for me (the pink cotton). We, the entire household, lined up on the drive, either side of the front door, checking our nails and hair. When the royal car swooped onto the gravel we were all flapping a little – apart from Mr Ainslie, of course, who remained utterly unflapped.

As Their Majesties were helped from the car, I swear that the very air felt changed, as if there was gold on the breeze. They shone so brightly.

Even the Duke and Duchess seemed in awe. If it wasn't for those two wee Princesses curtseying nicely then bounding about their grandparents, tugging on the King's sleeves like puppies, I think we would all have stood there, just staring, for hours.

Once the King and Queen were safely in the house, I made myself scarce. I didn't want to get in the way of a family get-together, so I went to my favourite bench under the wisteria walk in the back garden. Can you imagine how terrified I was when I saw Their Majesties stepping out of the drawing room, onto the lawn and heading towards me? I looked for somewhere to hide but, alas, there was nowhere I could go. I just stood there, head down, like a lamppost.

I thought that maybe, if I stayed still, they would pass me and carry on to inspect the gardens.

But, no, they came straight up to me. I could hardly breathe and certainly couldn't speak, but I managed a curtsey and fully expected them to move on.

They didn't.

Queen Mary is very tall (taller than me!) and imposing, with the most immaculate posture. She had her hair piled high, with a large hat on top, giving her an extra six inches at least. She was wearing her choker of pearls. Six rows! The sunlight on them made them gleam like little rainbows.

And her dress! So elegant, if a little old-fashioned. Blue silk with cream lace, a small bustle and a corseted waist. No wonder she has good posture. I wouldn't be able to breathe in anything so tight!

Her parasol matched her outfit and she used it as a walking stick. As she looked, I could see she was forming an opinion of me. Goodness knows what! She didn't speak, but King George, looking rather fearsome with his full set of whiskers, prodded the ground with his stick and grunted a sort of acknowledgement. Then in his booming voice (which I suppose he must have found useful at sea) said, 'For goodness' sake, teach those girls to write a decent hand, that's all I ask! Not one of my children can write properly. They all do it in the same illegible way.' I thought he had finished, but he looked me straight in the eye and said, 'I like a hand with character in it.'

'Yes, Your Majesty,' I managed and curtsied again.

The Queen gave me a final once-over, nodded and then both of them walked away, leaving me in a puddle of emotions.

Imagine! Me meeting King George V and Queen Mary! I only wish you could have been there.

Later that evening the Duchess told me that Their Majesties had wanted to meet me, because they thought I might be too young for the job. But they seem to think I am suitable after all. I must confess I am pleased to have their good opinion.

There was another day I wanted to tell you about. The other morning, we got a call in the schoolroom for Lilibet to find her field glasses and look out of the window towards Buckingham Palace.

Suddenly she was all action. 'Crawfie, we can wave to the King!'

It seems that when the King is able, he stands at the window of his office at BP (as they call Buckingham Palace here!) and trains his own field glasses onto our schoolroom window, then waves to the girls. Isn't that wonderful! He even waved at me when I had a go. God bless him. What a wonderful grandfather he is.

As good fortune has it, Lilibet is very conscientious with her work, and her handwriting is coming along clear and strong. I am very glad.

I have, at last, made a timetable of lessons which, mostly, the Duchess allows me to follow.

Depending on the day of the week we start with:

9.30 Arithmetic, Bible studies or history for Lilibet, and a story or colouring (scribbling!) for Margaret

11.00 Elevenses, outdoor games, reading or resting

1.15 Lunch

2.30 Walks, singing, dancing, painting or (the girls' favourite) hopscotch or chase with their father. He is excellent at both, being slim, athletic and agile. I have never been able to outrun him, but I do occasionally beat him at hopscotch.

The Duke and Duchess almost always join in the girls' bath-time fun. Fortunately that is where Alah comes in to her own, and I go 'off duty'. But I can still hear them, shrieking and splashing! You would never have allowed it.

I do miss you, Mother. Tell Dad I'm asking for him. I will be home as soon as I possibly can. I will let you know as soon as the Duchess releases me.

My dearest love,

Marion

AKA *Crawfie xxx*

Chapter Six

145 Piccadilly, London, August 1932

'Crawfie, Crawfie!' Margaret and Lilibet had burst into her room. 'We've got a surprise for you!'

Marion was jolted out of her post-lunch forty winks. It had been a hot morning in the schoolroom, even with the windows open, and the heat didn't agree with her Celtic blood. 'I think you've just given me one, young ladies.'

'Come on!' The little girls giggled as they pulled her out of her chair. 'Mummy wants to show you.'

They waited impatiently, hopping from foot to foot as Marion relaced her shoes.

'Ready,' she said finally. The moment she stood up, she was tugged down the stairs to the hall.

'Close your eyes,' Lilibet told her. 'The surprise is in the garden.'

Marion gave herself up to Lilibet's steering, as she was guided through the doorway and out on to the terrace.

'Now you can open your eyes.'

Blinking in the sudden sunlight, Marion saw the Duchess sitting at the garden lunch table beneath the shade of a spreading magnolia tree. Sitting on her lap was a small golden puppy with long pricked ears.

Marion grinned. 'A puppy!'

Lilibet jumped up and down with glee. 'He's called Dookie and he is ours!'

'Dookie,' repeated Margaret, beaming.

'What sort is he?' asked Marion, looking at him closely.

Lilibet recited, 'He's a corgi from Wales and his proper name is . . . What is it, Mummy?'

'Rozavel Golden Eagle,' said the Duchess. 'Isn't he adorable?'

'We've never had a dog before.' Lilibet and Margaret were now kneeling by their mother and rubbing their fingers and faces against the little dog.

The Duchess laughed. 'Darlings, be careful with him. He's only just getting used to us.' She looked at Marion. 'My husband has his Labrador gun dogs but they are not pets, and I think it's terribly important for children to have pets to care for. Don't you?'

'I do,' Marion agreed. 'We had one when I was little. A Scottie called Rory.'

'You've never told us that,' Lilibet said indignantly. 'What colour was he?'

'Black. He was very naughty – always in trouble.'

Lilibet turned back to Dookie. 'Are you going to be a naughty boy, too? Like Rory?'

Dookie growled and snapped at Lilibet's little fingers, but she wasn't afraid. 'Stop that,' she commanded, and the puppy hid his face in the Duchess's lap.

'That's right, darling, you tell him who is boss.' The Duchess laughed. 'Now, girls, go and play with him on the lawn, but be careful not to wear him out. Remember he's only a baby. Crawfie will keep an eye on you.'

Marion hid a sigh of frustration, knowing her afternoon timetable with the Princesses would now be abandoned. This was not the first time it had happened.

'It's lovely to see them happy, ma'am.'

The Duchess smiled. 'Happiness is all I ever want for them.'

Marion watched the girls for a moment, as they ran out onto the lawns, the little puppy following them. Then she turned to the Duchess. 'Ma'am, while they are playing for a minute, do you have time for me to ask you something?'

'Yes, of course. Fire away.'

'Well, I have been here now for almost five months and . . .'

'Is it as long as that? Goodness. And are you happy here?'

'Oh yes, very happy, but if—'

The Duchess spoke over her. 'My husband and I have noticed how well the girls are doing. Lilibet is reading so well, spelling out her letters to hear the words. A child's brain is quite a marvellous thing, is it not?'

'That is true, and—'

'And our dear little Margaret Rose – I know how headstrong she can be, but you have a very good understanding of her. They are both so fond of you.' The Duchess turned her eyes to the garden. 'Look at them playing with that puppy.'

Marion took a deep breath, determined to ask her question. 'Yes, ma'am. And I am loath to leave them, but as you may recall, I have a place waiting for me to study child psychology in Glasgow, starting next month.'

The Duchess's smile shrank and her face fell. 'You can't leave us now. That would not be good for the girls.'

'Ma'am, I love working with the girls, and you and the Duke, but they have everything a child could need, and I wish to help the children from poor families, those who are hungry and have no access to an education, no hope of bettering themselves. But I could give them that chance, if I can go to university and study.'

The Duchess fussed with the lace at her cuff. 'I don't know what to tell you. I had no idea you would want to leave. I assumed things would continue as they are.'

Marion blinked. She had told them about her university place from the first, but it didn't seem to have sunk in. 'For how long?' she asked.

'Until the girls are educated.'

Marion looked blank.

The Duchess gave her one of her quick smiles. 'You see, in this family, we like continuity, and we like to have people we trust around us. We trust you. The Duke and I think you have settled in very well and my daughters are very fond of you. We don't want to let you go . . . if you are happy to stay.'

Marion's brain was recalibrating. If she didn't go to university now, she might never get the chance again. What was she to say?

'I am very happy here,' she began. She was about to add that she was only twenty-two, that she would like to stay but she really needed her qualification in order to get the career she wanted.

But for the Duchess, the matter was decided. 'Good. That's settled then.'

Lilibet ran over from the lawns, shrieking with laughter. 'Margaret has put Dookie in a flower pot and we can't get him out!'

The Duchess wafted a hand towards Marion. 'Crawfie, dear, you have your afternoon's work cut out for you.' She smiled. 'I am so pleased we have come to this arrangement.'

With a curtsey, Marion left to rescue Dookie and spend the hot afternoon looking after the girls. She felt deflated and anxious. It was flattering to be wanted, of course, but she was not ready to give up the future she longed for. What was she to do?

Dookie was exhausted by the time Marion and the girls were called in for the day. The August afternoon air had turned sticky, and black clouds were starting to billow over the tall plane trees of Hyde Park, which stood just across the road.

Marion felt the atmospheric pressure in her head. She had always been susceptible to migraines and found that the oppressive London air made them worse.

With Lilibet carrying the puppy under one arm and Marion carrying a droopy Margaret, she steered them up to the nursery.

Alah was ready and waiting for them. 'So, this is the new baby in the nursery, is it?' She took the weary Dookie from Marion and gave him to Bobo. 'Take him to the kitchen and find him some supper while I bathe the girls.'

The Princesses begged that Dookie be allowed to stay in the nursery while they slept, but Alah was not to be moved. 'I will not have a dog in the nursery – it's enough that we have invisible ponies all over the place. Now, into the bathroom, clothes off. Your bath is ready.'

'Are their Royal Highnesses not coming up for bath time, Alah?' Marion asked, rubbing her temples. She could already hear water being splashed about in the bathroom.

'Not tonight,' Alah replied. 'The Prince of Wales is coming for dinner and they need a rest before any visit from him.'

Marion's ears pricked up. 'The Prince of Wales? Coming here?'

Lilibet shouted from her bath. 'I want to see Uncle David!'

'Me too,' said Margaret. 'Want to see Uncle Bavib.'

Lilibet laughed. 'It's David.'

'Bavib bavib,' giggled Margaret.

Alah tutted as she went into the bathroom. 'Little girls should not have big ears to hear things they shouldn't. Lilibet, get in the bath. Uncle David will not want to see you all dusty and hot, will he?'

Before closing the door on the bath steam, Alah had one last word for Marion. 'Now, don't *you* go getting moony over the Prince. I have enough trouble with Bobo half fainting whenever she gets a glimpse.'

Back in her bedroom, Marion sat on the bed and held her head in her hands. She couldn't tell if it was the latent migraine, or the idea that her schoolgirl crush, the Prince of Wales, was going to be here, under the same roof as her, that was making her head so painful. She made herself stand up, took off her skirt and blouse, splashed her face in the little sink and lay down on her soft bed, in her underwear. The Prince of Wales would be just downstairs and here she was, feeling dreadful.

Sleep came to her quickly – and just as quickly left.

Bobo was at her door. 'The Princesses want to say goodnight to Dookie. But he's in the kitchen, and I can't go down because Alah needs me up here. Can you bring him up?'

Wearily, Marion got up and pulled on the clothes she'd so recently discarded. She noticed grass stains on the back of her skirt and a streak of dust on her white shirt from playing with Dookie, but she didn't feel like finding clean clothes. No one would see her. Her errand would take only a couple of minutes.

Creeping downstairs to the softly lit hall, she made her way to the scullery. There she found Dookie, curled on top of a tartan blanket. His eyes opened a little and he managed a small thump of his tail in greeting. 'Come along, young man. A quick goodnight upstairs and then you can go back to bed. I'm as tired as you are.'

Picking him up, Marion caught sight of herself in the reflection of a cabinet. She seemed pale and her lengthening hair looked untidy. She groaned and made a half promise to go to the hairdressers.

As she returned to the hall, still wincing at the pain in her head, the storm that had been threatening all afternoon broke. The first bolt of lightning blinded her and the immediate bang of thunder that followed shook the floor beneath her feet. Dookie leapt from her arms in fright.

'Dookie!' she shouted.

The hall chandelier was suddenly switched on.

The brightness exacerbated the pain of her migraine. Feeling both faint and nauseous, Marion felt for one of the hall chairs to sit down and cover her eyes.

'What the hell is the dog doing in the hall?' She recognized the Duke's voice but a fresh wave of pain hit her and she couldn't reply.

'Crawfie! Whatever is the matter? David, get some water. Our governess is unwell.'

'I am fine,' she whispered, still keeping her eyes tight shut. 'Just a headache. So silly.'

Another flash of lightning came, but the thunder was not as close this time.

'I'm not surprised with all this racket going on,' said the Duke. She felt a glass being pressed into her hand.

A man's voice, similar to the Duke's, spoke next. 'Sip this. Slowly now.' A cool, soft hand took hers and wrapped her fingers carefully around it.

'Thank you.' She took a sip but kept her eyes closed and her head down. 'I will be all right in a minute.'

Now the Duchess's voice, flustered. 'Bertie, shouldn't we call the doctor?'

Marion shook her head. 'I am fine. Thank you. Really, I am. I don't mean to be a bother.' She half opened her eyes and saw three familiar faces. Two she knew in person – the other only from her scrapbook of cut-out photographs. The Prince of Wales, whose blue eyes were watching her anxiously. A lopsided smile dazzled her as she looked at him. He was more handsome than any photo she had ever seen, and she had seen hundreds.

She made herself stand and gave a wobbly curtsey. In the flesh, the Prince was so close that she had to shut her eyes again.

'I came to take Dookie to the Princesses,' she said. 'They wanted to say goodnight to him. And then . . .'

Almost from nowhere, Ainslie the butler appeared, with Dookie in his arms. 'I shall help Miss Crawford to her room.' Ainslie offered her his arm. 'Come along.'

'I hope you feel better soon,' said the Duke.

The Prince, his brother and sister-in-law returned to the drawing room, and Marion heard the door click shut behind them.

'I am so sorry, Mr Ainslie. I have made a fool of myself. I get these awful headaches sometimes.'

'No harm done. You need to rest. I will let their Royal Highnesses know that all is well.'

Another flash of lightning, softer this time, lit the stairs as Marion gratefully leant on Ainslie's arm. 'That was the Prince of Wales?'

'Indeed.'

'And I have grass stains on my skirt.'

Ainslie grunted and murmured something which Marion thought afterwards sounded like: 'It wouldn't be the first time he's seen a lady with grass stains on her clothing.'

Chapter Seven

145 Piccadilly, London, August 1932

Marion had spent the last two days worrying about her university place. She wanted it – and the future it would bring her – more than anything in the world but . . . her work here with the Princesses was of importance too. Without her, Lilibet and Margaret would never get to experience the normalities of life. She could teach them so much about the world beyond their front door. If she left, who knew what kind of governess would replace her? Perhaps someone from the upper classes, who knew as little of real life as them. But Marion could show them how real working people lived, in ordinary average homes where children did not have cupboards of lovely clothes and mothers who wore tiaras. She could mould them into women with social conscience, able to use their privileged platform for humanity.

The decision was splitting her in two.

She loved the Princesses, but her heart was full of all the poor children in Glasgow and beyond who had nothing: no food in their stomachs, no shoes on their feet, and a future as bleak and cold as a winter's night. How could she think that looking after two of the planet's most cosseted girls compared with those desperate children?

'What should I do?' she asked herself over and over again, pacing her bedroom in the small hours, unable to sleep. She crept into the nursery kitchen and put some milk on the gas to heat. Warm milk always soothed her. Waiting for it to come to the simmer, she sat at the small table and put her head in her hands.

'God, if you are listening, what am I to do?'

No answer came.

Taking her milk to bed, Marion pulled the blankets up around her and lay back against her pillows. 'What am I to do?'

Three thoughts suddenly came to her:

1. She would have to talk to the Duchess again, to try and make her see that training to be a child psychologist was what she was going to do. But how could she explain that to someone who wouldn't listen?
2. She would write to Glasgow University and ask if they could hold her place for another year, perhaps two, so that she need not let the Duchess down immediately.
3. Her mother must not hear any of this until she had found the solution.

And so, before breakfast, she wrote to the university – a simple, truthful letter, explaining that she was working for a decent family with two interesting daughters and that she was being given an invaluable apprenticeship which would only help her when she came to study. In view of this, she would like to post-pone her course for two years.

She felt a lot better having written that. Now she had to find the perfect moment to speak to the Duchess.

Two days later, an envelope arrived with Glasgow University stamped across its front. As soon as she was able, Marion hurried back to her room and closed the door. Her hands shook as she read the single page:

Dear Miss Crawford,

We confirm receipt of your letter regarding your place on our child psychology course.

Unfortunately, while we can accept your withdrawal, we cannot carry your name forward to any future student intakes.

Our applicants are selected on merit, and it may be that there are more suitable candidates ahead of you in two years' time.

Please confirm by return post your acceptance or withdrawal for this year.

Yours sincerely,
Miss B.A. Young
Secretary to the Dean

Well, there it was. No help at all.

It was Alah who heard the sniffles coming from Marion's room and knocked on the door.

She quickly wiped her eyes. 'Who is it?'

'Alah. Are you quite all right?'

'I'm fine, thank you.'

'Had I better come in and see for myself?' Alah opened the door without waiting for an answer. Marion was sitting with her back turned, looking out at the garden.

Alah was no fool; she had tended to little girls all her life, long enough to recognize wretchedness when she saw it.

She sat on the bed and put her arm over Marion's shoulders. 'Why don't you tell Alah all about it?'

Alah listened without interruption, rubbing the heartbroken girl's back, lending her handkerchief when necessary.

When Marion had nothing left to say, Alah stroked the young governess's forehead, pushed the tear-damp hair from her eyes and said, 'You don't need to go to school to learn your job, lassie. Right now, you are learning at the very best school of all – life! I know how you feel about those poor children – but maybe God does not need you to do the hard work. He has put you here, on an off-chance, a special mission. And do our two little girls not deserve love and nurturing too? They who will grow up in a gilded cage – beautiful canaries who will never know the freedom of independence? Think of the friends they will never make, the small things that other children take for granted. They can't go to a funfair and eat toffee apples, or take a trip to the seaside and watch a Punch and Judy show with children of their own age. I believe that the Lord has taken a hand in your destiny, Crawfie. You are just the right normal sort of girl who can give the Princesses a glimpse of reality. I thank God every night that the Duke is the second son. He will never have to face the burden his older brother will shoulder. Imagine the future the Prince of Wales sees laid out before him and then before his unborn children – chained to the throne by an accident of birth, born with a silver spoon in his mouth but iron shackles around his freedom.'

Marion wiped her nose, astonished by Alah's speech. 'My mother wouldn't agree with any of that. She's all for the revolution.' She managed a sniffly smile.

'Well, that is where we differ. The work you and I do is not just vital to the wellbeing of this family – it is vital to the welfare of this country. The royal family brings security and admiration from around the world. And they can't do it without us. We dress them, drive them, feed them, care for their children, make their lives as smooth as clockwork, wash their linen, wipe their arses.'

'Alah!'

'It's true! And why do we do it?'

Marion sighed. 'I don't know.'

'Because we keep the good ship HMS *Britain* sailing. That's why. A solid monarchy means a solid country.'

Marion stared at her. 'Goodness, Alah! I never realized what a firebrand you are! My stepfather would have you shot.'

'No, he wouldn't.'

'He would.'

'Not while I'm looking after his daughter, he wouldn't.'

'Oh, Alah.' Marion managed a smile. 'Thank you. Do you think I should talk it over with the Duchess, though? I want her to understand that I love the girls but . . .'

Alah gave a short laugh. 'Ha! Do you want her to make the decision for you? We know what the answer will be, don't we? No, you must be brave. Accept what you have been given and be the best for the best. Yes?'

'I suppose so.'

'That's the spirit. You are lucky. God gave you two choices and that's two more than the average young girl gets. Courage, child. Courage.'

'I am very lucky to have you, Alah.'

'I agree with you.' Alah smiled. 'And I am proud of you. Decision made.'

'Yes. Decision made.' Marion took a deep breath. 'Now, all I have to do is tell my mother.'

Chapter Eight

Dunfermline, late August 1932

Marion paid the taxi driver and walked up the familiar path towards her parents' front door.

Before she had time to knock, the door flew open and Marion's mother took her in a warm embrace. 'We would have picked you up from the station! How much did the taxi cost you?'

'Less than it would in London.'

'Let me take your coat. Robert,' she called, 'take Marion's case up to her room, please.'

Marion heard the rustle of a newspaper being folded and could imagine her stepfather's sigh as he pulled himself out of his comfortable armchair. 'Ah. There you are.' His gentle face appeared from the front room. 'I've missed you.'

'Hello, Dad.' She hugged him. 'I've missed you too.'

'Take Marion's bag up and I'll make the tea,' bustled her mother, 'I see you've let your hair grow. Much better.'

Robert gave Marion a wink and lugged her bag to the stairs.

'It's good to be home.' Marion looked around at the kitchen. It was warm, secure and comforting.

'Not what you're used to, I suppose.'

Marion buried her irritation. 'Don't say that, Mother.'

Maggie handed her daughter a new tin of Scottish shortbread biscuits. 'Put some of those on a plate, would you? I hope you still like them.'

Marion smiled. 'The Duchess's favourite.'

'Are they? Well, she's a good Scots lassie, that one.'

Robert came back into the kitchen, smiling. 'You've brought the sun with you, Marion,' he said.

She looked out of the kitchen window to the garden beyond. Standing in their serried ranks were the usual golden marigolds, white alyssum and blue lobelia, waiting for inspection. 'The garden looks lovely, Dad,' she said.

Her mother tutted. 'Always the same. I don't know why he does it – it's too much work now he's getting older.'

'I am perfectly fit, thank you,' Robert said. 'Anyway, it keeps me from getting under your feet.'

'Aye, and that's a blessing. Get the milk from the cool shelf, would you?'

'Well, I think it looks lovely.' Marion patted her stepfather's shoulder. 'Shall we have our tea in the garden?'

Sitting out on the old deckchairs, her mother fussing and guarding the biscuits from any wasps, Marion was building up to telling her parents her news. Should she tell them now? Or wait a couple of days? The sun was shining. Her parents were bickering happily. Everything was calm and peaceful. Why spoil the cheerful mood?

'More tea, Marion? I think I can squeeze a cup out.' She tipped the teapot but there was only a trickle. 'Robert, go into the kitchen and make a fresh pot?'

Marion started to stand. 'I can go.'

'No, no, you stay where you are.' Her mother stopped her. 'It's good to have you home at last and you have had a long journey. Rest while you can. You'll be leaving us for Glasgow soon enough.'

'Um, we need to talk about that.'

'We do,' her mother agreed. 'Your father and I will drive you there and get you settled in your rooms. I haven't been to Glasgow for a long time and I thought I might take a look around the shops.'

'Here we are. Fresh pot.' Her dad was back. 'Just let it mash for a few minutes.' He sat down. 'As your mother was saying, we were thinking we would take you to Glasgow and get you settled.'

'Thank you. That's very kind of you, but . . .'

'We can stop and get some lunch on the way. What time are they expecting you?'

'I don't . . .'

'You haven't got hold of them yet?'

'I have, Mum, but, well . . .' Marion took a steadying breath. 'I have decided not to go, after all. The Duke and Duchess want me to stay and look after the girls until they have finished their education.'

The silence was deafening.

Her stepfather scratched his head and avoided looking at Maggie by picking up a teaspoon and stirring the pot.

Marion waited for her mother's reaction. It came quietly at first.

'I hope this is a joke?'

'No, Mum.'

'But what about those poor wee children you were going to fight for? Give a future to? You were going to do wonderful things for them, help them escape their dreadful poverty.'

Marion watched as Maggie's colour rose, first blotchily across her chest, then her throat and now her cheeks.

'Mum, I understand how you must be fee—'

'You don't understand anything about how I am feeling.' Maggie spoke very slowly, with an anger that was making her tremble. 'You are damn well going to Glasgow if we have to drag you there. I brought you up as a good Scottish working-class socialist, and what has become of you, eh?'

Robert held a hand up to his wife. 'Maggie, just listen to the girl. She will have her reasons.'

'Reasons?' Maggie was shouting now. 'Oh aye, there'll be reasons all right. She's too good for us now, isn't she? Her lah-di-dah life in London has gone to her head. We are beneath her now! I am surprised she hasn't asked us to curtsey before her.'

Marion sighed. This was exactly what she had hoped to avoid. Her mother was highly strung, and she didn't take change well. It frightened and unsettled her – a symptom of the grief and shock that drowned her when Marion's father had died. Marion had been only three but she remembered going to live with the grandmother she had been named after. She was told that her mother had 'gone on holiday for a rest' but she was away for a very long time.

It was only when Robert met her mother that life began to settle. He was a loving man who gladly took Maggie and Marion on. But trauma leaves scars, and Maggie's scars hurt when things did not go the way she had planned. The pain made her judgmental, difficult. Marion knew it was fear that drove the behaviour, that her mother loved her underneath all the criticism and hateful words. When she was growing up she had resented her mother's behaviour, but Robert had always been there to smooth the waters. She had watched and learned.

She said now, 'Mum, please. Let me explain.'

'I don't want to hear.' Maggie was sulking now. 'What will I tell our friends? You have thrown everything I have ever done for you back in my face, and for what? For two overprivileged little royal Princesses! *They* will never have to be ashamed of their one pair of boots with holes in. They will never have to deal with their fathers hitting their mothers, or the pain of hunger, day after day, will they?'

'*Maggie!*' Robert, who never raised his voice, shocked his wife into silence. 'Stop.'

Maggie stared at him as if he were a stranger. Slowly she stood up with all the dignity and tragedy of a burning martyr. 'I am going to lie down,' she said, 'and the bedroom door will be locked.'

Left alone, Marion and Robert said nothing for some time. Then Marion said, 'I'm so sorry.'

'Would you like some whisky in your tea?' Robert asked. 'I think it's what the doctor would order. Then you can tell me the full story.'

Her dad listened attentively and when he had heard it all, he said, 'You were put in a very awkward position.'

'I was. Have I made the right decision, though?'

'You are the only person who can answer that, Marion.'

'I know.'

They were still sitting in the garden, but the air was chill now. Bats chased through the silver shadows cast by the moon. Marion wrapped her arms around her body and rubbed her upper arms for warmth.

'Before we go in,' Robert asked, 'did the Duchess bully you into staying? Was your arm twisted so hard you couldn't say no?'

'Gosh, no. Nothing like it. It was my choice.'

He nodded. 'Good. So, no regrets about Glasgow?'

Marion shivered slightly then said, 'I might always wonder what I could have done in Glasgow, but I honestly feel the Princesses and I are meant to be together. I have the unique opportunity of preparing them for their life as rounded women who will hold their own in any situation they find themselves. They will be well-placed to help to recognize causes that they can champion on my behalf. I can make a real difference.'

'Well said.' Robert stood up. 'Now, come in. I'll make cocoa for you and your mother. You can take it up to her and tell her everything as you just told me. She'll understand.'

Balancing the small tin tray on one hand, Marion knocked on her mother's bedroom door. 'Mum? It's me. Marion. Can I come in?'

'What do you want?' Her mother's voice was dull.

'I have cocoa for you. Dad made it. Would you please let me in?'

There was a brief silence, then a rustling and the sound of the key turning. Maggie's face was drawn and pale, her eyes swollen. 'Where is your dad?'

'Downstairs.'

'Good, because he's not coming in here.'

Marion slid through the barely open door and closed it behind her. 'Are you all right, Mum?'

Maggie slumped on to the bed. 'What do you think? My daughter has broken my heart. My friends will laugh behind my back.' She raised her weary eyes to Marion. 'What were you thinking?'

Marion sighed. 'To be honest, Mother, I don't have an answer, other than I feel the Princesses need as much help in navigating the real world as poorer children do. I feel so responsible for their learning and their ability to see the world through a better lens than they would get otherwise. I can make them understand real life much more than someone from their own class could. You would understand if you met them.'

Her mother scoffed. 'As if I should ever meet them.'

'Well, you might.' Marion shrugged her shoulders. 'They are up at Balmoral with the King and Queen right now.'

'And that's the only reason you are here to visit, isn't it?' Maggie's lips curled. 'You wouldn't have come to see *us* if *they* had wanted you to be on holiday with them.'

'I chose to come here because I wanted to. I haven't seen you for months and I miss you and Dad.'

Maggie's face crumpled. 'And we have missed you. Every day.' She opened her arms. 'Have you got a wee hug for your mother?'

'Of course.' The two women held their embrace until Maggie asked, 'Did Robert really make the cocoa?'

'Yes. He knows it helps when things upset you.' Marion passed one of the warm cups to her. 'I am so sorry to have done that.'

'It was the shock.' Maggie took a sip of her drink. 'I will get over it.'

'And you will see that it is for the best after all.'

Maggie managed a short laugh. 'I won't hold my breath.'

There was a light knock at the door and Robert stuck his head round. 'How are you feeling now, my love?'

Maggie raised her cup. 'All the better for this.'

'Good. Am I allowed back in here tonight?'

'Are you thinking of going anywhere else, you big lummock?'

He smiled, and sat down on the bed next to her. 'So I don't have to cancel all the visitors coming tomorrow, then? Only it would be a terrible waste of all the cleaning you've done this week.'

Marion raised her eyebrows in alarm. 'What visitors?'

Maggie waved a hand dismissively. 'Och, it's nothing. Your father is pulling your leg.'

Robert feigned innocence. 'Am I? Then why have you asked the whole road to come and "drop in" tomorrow?'

Marion banged her cup down on the tray. 'Oh, Mother, you haven't!'

'Of course, I haven't. Just Auntie Linda, Bessie and her boy, Sheelagh and Ross and—'

'Mother!'

Maggie stood her ground. 'Is it wrong for me to be proud of my daughter?'

'She wants to show you off,' said Robert. 'There's no harm in that.'

It was a full and exhausting three days for Marion. She was interrogated and marvelled at by all their friends and neighbours. Her mother showed her off like a doll in a box, cueing her responses to make her talk:

'The Princesses have given her a nickname too. Go on, Marion, tell them what it is.'

'The Duchess has wonderful clothes, even a mink coat. Marion, tell them all about it.'

'She's met the King and Queen too, and the Prince of Wales. He's very handsome, isn't he, Marion? Tell Sheelagh how you met him.'

Finally, there was not a person in the street left unsatisfied by Marion's stories. She kept her details to a minimum and her protective instinct towards the royal family made certain she never disclosed anything that the newspapers had not described already.

On the fourth day, a large white envelope with the royal crest raised in gold arrived on their doormat, addressed to Marion.

Maggie hovered as she opened it.

'What does it say? Are they calling you back to work?'

Marion scanned the page. 'You know I said there might be a chance for you to meet the Duke and Duchess and the Princesses?'

Maggie tutted. 'Ho! As if.'

'We have tickets for the Braemar games.'

'Who gave you those?'

'I did mention to the Duchess that I had never been and would love to go one day. I suppose she must have remembered.'

'Away with you. I can't go. Not without your dad.'

'We have three tickets. He can come too.'

Maggie pulled her cardigan over her chest in defence. 'How will we get there? It must be almost a hundred miles from here.'

'We'll go by train.'

'But I've nothing to wear.'

'Something warm with a bit of tartan would do you fine.'

Maggie stared at her daughter hard. 'Have they really invited us?'

'Yes.'

'Hm. Robert!' Maggie called out. 'Do you want to go to the Braemar games?'

Chapter Nine

Ballater, September 1932

The train journey involved two changes to get to Ballater station, where a healthy queue of taxis was taking advantage of the extra business the games brought in.

The driver was happy to be their guide and royal expert. 'You'll be wanting to see the King and Queen, I suppose?'

Marion shot a warning glare at her mother, before replying with a smile, 'Wouldn't that be the thing.'

They heard the noise of excited shrieks and the bang of drums and applause as soon as they got out of the car. The party mood was infectious.

Joining the line of people at the main gate, they could see the huge field busy with onlookers and above their heads the tented royal stand.

'I could do with some refreshment,' Maggie said, taking off her warm jacket. 'Robert, get Marion and me a cup of tea, please? My mouth feels like a desert.'

'Would you not rather have a nice cold shandy?' he asked, rubbing his hands hopefully. 'I can see the beer tent.'

'Oh, be off with you.' Marion laughed. 'And yes, get Mother and me a shandy each. We'll be over by those wee girls doing their Highland dances.'

Marion took her mother's coat from her and together they walked through the happy crowd, the men in kilts, the women in tartan dresses or summer frocks.

They managed to nab three deckchairs from a departing family and got themselves comfortable to enjoy the Highland dancing. The girls were no more than twelve years old, moving their nimble limbs with precision and speed, kilts flaring. Marion saw several proud families beaming their support.

Maggie gave her running critique. 'Now when I was dancing for the Kilmarnock team, we'd be disqualified for that sort of step . . .'

Marion wasn't listening; she was glancing around for any sight of the royal party.

When her father arrived with the drinks they moved on, at Marion's suggestion, to watch the muscled hammer throwers in action.

From there, Marion could see a little more of the royal stand. She saw the waving plumes of the feathers in Queen Mary's hat first. Regal and upright with a bouquet of heather in her lap, she was tapping her feet to a group of six pipers. Next to her, the King was watching and applauding the long jump competitors in front of him.

Marion scanned the rest of the royal party but there was no sign of the Duke and Duchess of York or the Princesses. She had her hopes of introducing Lilibet and Margaret to her parents, but beyond that, she was also desperate to see them again, to deliver hugs and ask how their holiday had been.

She sat back in her deckchair and gave herself up to the pleasure of the sunny day shared with her parents, and to the fun around her.

There was the tug-of-war, running races for children, cabers tossed by men who were bigger and brawnier than any man she'd ever seen – and finally, as the sun began to lose its heat, there was a massed band of pipes and drums, marching in intricate patterns to ancient battle hymns.

Robert, on the outside of three pints, stood and sang as loudly as the others around him. 'Get up, Maggie. Get up and sing!' he told her, and to Marion's astonishment, Maggie did just that, with tears in her eyes.

The cheering and applause when the performance was over was deafening. ''Tis a great day to be Scottish,' Robert yelled, hugging Maggie to him.

'Aye.' Maggie laughed. 'It's wonderful.'

The crowd grew quiet and the band became rigidly still as they began the National Anthem. Everyone on the field stood and sang lustily until the last note faded. Then the applause rang out as the royal party moved towards their waiting cars. The people parted like the sea to let them through, and Marion saw that they would pass by so that she would be within touching distance. Her heart swelled with affection as the King and Queen passed. She curtsied automatically and felt her mother do the same beside her. Even her stepfather bent his head.

The Prince of Wales followed, nodding and smiling at the young women whose curtsies were deepest.

And then Marion heard the chirrup of two little voices chattering happily, and a familiar voice saying gently, 'Come along, you two. All these kind people have come to see how well you can behave.'

A man wearing a tall hat pushed his way in front of Marion, obscuring her view. She gently nudged him aside. 'Excuse me. Please. I can't quite see.'

He looked down at her and took his cigarette from his moustachioed lips. 'I beg your pardon. Of course.'

'Thank you.'

As Marion shifted forwards to the front of the crowd, Lilibet spotted her and tugged at her mother's hand. 'Crawfie! Look, Mummy, it's Crawfie!'

Marion waved and smiled. The Duchess passed by and raised her eyebrows with a small smile of recognition, but continued walking towards the cars.

Maggie had not noticed the exchange as she had been studying the Prince of Wales. 'Not very tall, is he?' she was saying to the woman standing next to her. 'I thought he'd be at least six feet tall but I suppose it's come from the old Queen's side. Victoria wasn't even five feet, was she?'

Marion remained in a world of her own. Lilibet had seen her and she was sure that the Duchess had too. She watched until all the cars were loaded with their royal passengers and lifted her hand to wave. When the wave wasn't returned, Marion forgave them. How could they see her in a crowd like this?

She glanced around for her parents – they mustn't miss their trains. She soon found them. They had retreated to some empty deckchairs, both glowing from the sun and beer.

'Have you enjoyed yourselves?' Marion asked as she reached them.

'Oh, Marion dear, it was wonderful,' her mother said. 'And although I believe in an independent Scotland, I must say, seeing them like that . . . Well, they do a good job.'

Marion laughed. 'Praise indeed! Now, give me your hand and I'll pull you out of that chair, and then we'll find a taxi to the station.'

Before they could get out to the road, Marion heard someone call her name.

'Crawfie! Crawfie!' It was a man's voice, from somewhere behind her. 'Crawfie! Hold up. I can give you a lift home.'

She turned to see Peter Jackson, the young chauffeur who had collected her that first night in Windsor, and since then had often driven her and the Princesses.

'Peter! What a lovely offer. We are going to the station, if you could drop us there?'

'Duchess's orders. She told me to take you all the way home.'

'The Duchess? But we live in Dunfermline – it's a very long drive.'

'The Duchess insisted. I am not allowed to take no for an answer.'

Her parents were watching closely. Maggie seemed in awe, but Robert was immediately suspicious.

'Young man, I am Marion's stepfather.'

Peter stood taller. 'Sir, I am very pleased to meet you. My name is Jackson. If you'd care to follow me to the car, I can get you home toot sweet.'

Maggie was uncharacteristically agog with silence.

Peter gave Maggie a smart neck bow. 'And this lady must be your sister.'

'Get away with you,' she whispered.

Marion smiled. 'Mother, meet Peter Jackson. Peter, this is my mother, Maggie.'

'Your mum? Never.' He opened the back door. 'I am at your service,' he said, helping a bemused Maggie into the car and pulling a tartan blanket over her knees. 'Her Majesty has a rug for her knees, so why shouldn't you, ma'am?'

Maggie gasped. 'And you know my daughter?'

'Know her? She's like a sister to me. I drive her and the little 'uns forwards and backwards between London and Windsor, all the time.'

Maggie pursed her lips. 'She never tells me anything.'

Jackson tapped his nose. 'That's the way the family like it.' He turned to Robert. 'Now, sir, would you like to sit up front with me? While the ladies watch the world go by, you and me can have a chat.'

Robert agreed readily. 'An Austin, eh? How does she handle?'

'We have got eighty-odd miles to put her through her paces.' Jackson grinned. 'Ask me anything you like as we go.'

Watching from an open edge of the beer tent was the man Marion had asked to let her through the crowd.

He'd heard Princess Elizabeth call out her name – Crawfie, was it? What a strange name – and he'd seen the Duchess's subtle acknowledgement of her.

He had examined her closely after that.

She was not a great beauty, perhaps, but there was something about her face that caught his attention.

And whoever she was, she warranted a royal car. Interesting.

He finished his whisky, wiped his moustache and lit a cigarette. Who the hell was she? Maybe he'd ask around.

Picking up his hat, he turned to the bar man dismantling the makeshift pub. 'I'll be off now, David.'

'Take it easy, Major Buthlay,' came the reply.

Chapter Ten

145 Piccadilly, February 1934

'Come on, Crawfie. You must stamp and paw the ground while you are waiting for me to make a delivery.' Princess Elizabeth was playing her favourite game. 'Now, you be a good horse while I drop this parcel off for old Mr Buggins.'

Crawfie stamped a foot obligingly and whinnied. The air so cold that the streams of breath from her nostrils were exactly like a delivery horse's.

They were playing in Hamilton Gardens, a large communal space with trees and shrubs, in which the local children could play. As expensive and luxurious as Mayfair houses were, they had very little outdoor space of their own, but the Princesses were safe within the metal railings of Hamilton Gardens, and took no notice of the public, who would stand and gaze at them as if they were exotic animals in a zoo.

Lilibet returned from her imaginary delivery to the imaginary Mr Buggins and picked up the bell-pull rope she had tied around Crawfie's waist as reins. 'Walk on, lazybones.'

Crawfie obeyed. 'And how was Mr Buggins? Has he heard from his nephew in Ireland yet?' asked Crawfie, in the horsey voice Lilibet insisted on.

'No, I am afraid not. Mr Buggins thinks he must have got the flu and died.'

Crawfie stifled a smile. Lilibet's sense of drama was getting as good as Margaret's. 'What a shame. Poor Mr Buggins.'

'That's just what I told him. Stand here while I take the milk in for the Earl.' She dropped the reins again and skipped off to a gnarled old tree trunk – the home of the Earl of Hamilton.

Crawfie wished she had brought her gloves. Less than a year in the South and her blood was thinning. She must ask her mother to knit some mittens.

She thought of her parents every day, and felt a complicated kind of gratitude to be so far away from them. There was no doubt about it: her mother was easier to love from afar. She marvelled at her stepfather's patience. How did he cope with her day in, day out?

Marion hoped that, eventually, she would find a husband who showed the same kind of love.

But, right now, she was in London, and she could do anything she wanted without her parents' knowledge or judgement. She was free as a bird and loving it.

Bobo and Marion had grown closer lately. Together, on their days off, they would explore the shops. She and Bobo had gone to Selfridges and seen for themselves all the wonderful things the huge department store had. Neither of them could afford to buy anything, of course, but it kept them in conversation, and Alah's tutting, for weeks.

Marion had begun to dabble in make-up bought from the old chemist on Kensington High Street. A little rouge and a dark red lipstick. She hadn't had reason to wear them yet, but the fact they were sitting in her drawer was enough for now.

Her hair, which had grown a lot in the last eighteen months, had recently been trimmed by Alah and now curled softly at her shoulders. It was long enough to pin up for work.

Life in the nursery and the schoolroom was suiting her. It brought her more happiness than she had expected and the girls, the Duke and Duchess, Bobo and Alah were becoming her family.

The quiet evenings sitting with Alah by the nursery fire, chatting, mending or reading while the Princesses slept – these were precious moments of contentment, time that she would be able to look back on and never forget.

On one of these evenings, Alah told Crawfie something that shocked her.

'I don't know how the Duchess remains so calm,' she said.

Crawfie smiled. 'I know, she's always so serene.'

'I just wish the Duke was the same.'

'Yes, I know. He's so shy and his stutter must frustrate him.'

'That's one way of putting it.' Alah snipped the thread of the hem she was letting down for Lilibet. 'Cook told me there was another plate broken last night.'

'Who dropped it?' asked Marion casually, expecting that a footman or kitchen maid had been told off.

'The Duke broke it.'

'No harm done then.'

'Luckily.' Alah lowered her voice. 'The plate hit the wall – was thrown at the wall. And it's not the first time.'

Crawfie was incredulous. 'The Duke broke a plate deliberately?'

Alah nodded.

'Why?'

'Cook says it started when he got a phone call just before dinner. His tempers can come from nowhere. Apparently the Duchess went on as if nothing had happened and just asked him to calm down.'

Crawfie couldn't believe this was true. After thinking about it for a few moments, she said, 'I don't believe it. The Duke is such a kind man – look how he is with his daughters and the Duchess. It must have been an accident.'

Alah raised her eyebrows. 'It's happened before.'

Crawfie became very indignant. 'I admire them both too much to believe kitchen gossip. I would rather die than talk of them like that.' She closed the book on her knee and stood up. 'I will pretend you never said these terrible things, Alah. If you will excuse me, I shall say goodnight.'

As she left for her own room, Alah called after her, 'You'll see!'

It took a couple of days for the atmosphere between the two of them to warm up again. In the meantime, they each privately thought the other was in cloud cuckoo land.

The Duke and Duchess always came to the nursery to say good-night to their daughters if they'd been unable to be present for bath time.

One particular evening towards the beginning of spring, they arrived upstairs in full evening dress.

'Do you think we'll do?' the Duchess asked the Princesses, giving them a whirl of her ball gown.

'Mummy, you look very pretty indeed,' said Lilibet. 'Where are you going?'

'To the opera.'

'Real diamonds, Mummy?' asked Margaret, reaching up and trying to touch her mother's necklace.

'Yes, but don't tell anyone.'

Lilibet suddenly ran to the window. 'What time is it? Have we missed Mr Coachy and his horses?'

'Who is M-M-Mr Coachy?' the Duke enquired

Crawfie thought she had better explain. 'Sir, ma'am, each night at about this time Lilibet and Margaret look out for some friends of ours. Have you the time to meet them?'

The Duke was about to say no but the Duchess jumped in, 'Bertie, darling, they can't start the opera without us. We'll only be ten minutes late.'

The Duke clenched his jaw in irritation but said nothing.

Outside, Park Lane was dark and slick with rain. The street-lamps gilded the puddles and headlights glittered on the tarmac.

'Who are we w-w-waiting for?' asked the Duke.

Lilibet flapped her hands at him. 'Here they come.'

A Fuller's Brewery dray, pulled by a handsome pair of black horses, was trotting along Park Lane towards them.

Margaret pushed her way to the window and Lilibet held her up. 'There! See them.'

'And these are your friends?' the Duchess asked fondly.

'Wait, Mummy. If the lights go red he'll have to stop and the driver always waves up at us. But I worry about the horses if they have to stop because then they have to pull even harder to get going again and it is a horrid wet night and they might slip.'

The little family watched as the dray approached the traffic lights. 'They're still green!' the girls shouted. 'Come on! Keep going.'

But as the horses approached, the lights turned red, and they were pulled up by their driver.

'Oh dear!' The Duchess clutched her daughters' shoulders with genuine anxiety.

'Mummy, look, he's waving at us! The Coachy! Wave back everyone!'

The coachman squinted up at the familiar window and the two little girls – and the two highly recognizable adults with them today. With a grin, he immediately doffed his cap and gave them a thumbs-up.

The Duke and Duchess were delighted and waved graciously.

'The lights are green!' Still waving, Lilibet pointed at the traffic lights. 'The lights are green.'

'I don't think he can hear you, darling,' laughed the Duke. 'And they're off!'

'Bye-bye horsey,' Margaret squealed.

'Goodness.' The Duchess smiled. 'That was more exciting than Aintree!'

Crawfie hugged these special moments to herself, saving them up in order to share them in one of her weekly letters home.

The Good Servant

Dear Mother and Dad,

The Princesses and I have been on some new adventures. Hamilton Gardens has become our Wild West. I was a Red Indian chasing after those two cowboys. Honestly, if you could have seen them! There were some pretty hairy ambushes in the shrubbery, but of course they captured me and took me back to their ranch where I became a horse again and was groomed to death. They are so funny! We all got a ticking off from Alah though, when we arrived in the nursery with dirty clothes and faces. I don't think they have ever been allowed to get really dirty before now.

I think I've started something now though, because when I asked the girls over tea what they would like to do as a treat, you wouldn't guess the list I was given:

1. *Walk to the Round Pond in Kensington Gardens and watch the toy yachts being sailed. (Ordinary children fascinate them!)*
2. *Travel on an underground train.*
3. *Ride on the top deck of a bus.*
4. *Take a trip to Woolworths to buy Granny (Her Majesty to you and me) a wedding anniversary gift. The whole family love the Woolworths trinkets. The girls have their eye on a tiny horse ornament with a rider on its back, and have been counting up the pennies in their money boxes.*

I think they are old enough to do those things now. Lilibet is nine and Margaret almost five. I shall ask the permission of the Duke and Duchess of course, and I suspect we would have to have a detective or two with us, but I would be glad of them! Imagine if I lost the Princesses!

It will be a welcome change (for me) from the usual games of sardines and hide and seek.

We are all in awe of Her Majesty. She can be very imposing. She comes into the schoolroom now and again to watch a lesson or two. The girls adore her and although they are on best behaviour Margaret can always make her grandmother laugh with a little song she has made up or a silly dance. I cannot believe that I no longer squeak with nerves when she appears, but she is so good and kind that I am beginning to take her company in my stride. Something I never dreamed I would have the confidence to say!

I cannot believe that I have been here for more than three years.

I do wonder sometimes where I would be now if I had gone to Glasgow and got my degree. Probably working in the tenements. But it has all worked out for the best. No regrets.

I have good news, too. I shall be home for the summer. A whole six weeks for you to get thoroughly tired of me, and me of you! That is a joke, of course. I am so looking forward to seeing you.

My fondest love,
Your Marion xx

Chapter Eleven

Dunfermline, August 1935

'Welcome home, Marion.' Her mother opened the door, wearing a tartan apron. 'Come on in. I'm baking a Dundee cake for you.' She looked at her daughter with a critical eye. 'It looks as if you could do with some – you've lost weight.'

'It's running after the girls,' Marion answered sharply. Her mother could never resist a criticism.

'Aye, I was skin and bone when I had you. You ran me ragged for the first ten years.'

Marion held her breath and counted to ten. 'Where's Dad?'

'Where do you think? In the garden, of course.'

Marion went to find him. He was kneeling on the grass, grubbing up dandelions.

'Hello, Dad.'

'Hello, lassie.' He wiped his hands on his old trousers and held them up to her. 'If I get up now, I'll never get down again. Come and give me a kiss.'

She knelt and he gave her a hug. 'My, but you're a sight for sore eyes.' He held her hand in his big earthy ones. 'Your mother's been on at me all week. Get the garden done. Wash the car. Don't come in the house with your shoes on.'

Marion smiled. 'She'll never change.'

'Aye. She's got a good heart, but sometimes I pretend I can't hear her.'

'I'll tell her, shall I?'

'Don't you dare! She'll have me at the doctors getting my ears syringed.'

'Oh, Dad. I've missed you.' Marion put her arm around his shoulders.

'And me you, lassie, me you.'

Maggie came out of the back door holding a tray. 'Robert, take your trowel off the garden table! You know we are having tea out here.'

'Sorry, dear. Pull me up, will you, Marion.'

As she helped him up and he went to collect the offending trowel, Marion noticed a stiffness in his walk.

'Are you all right, Dad?'

'It's his hip,' Maggie told her. 'Arthritis. But will he go to the doctor?'

Robert ignored her and sank gratefully into his old deckchair. 'Maggie! Dundee cake.' He smiled. 'My favourite.'

'Don't change the subject.' Maggie shook her head. 'Anyway, I made it for Marion, not you.'

'In that case, I'm even happier to see Marion home.' He picked up the cake knife. 'Shall I be Mother?'

The tea was poured and the cake was eaten and Marion felt the comfort of being home again. 'So, tell me, Mother, what's the latest gossip?'

Maggie was a great talker and over the next hour she managed a constant stream of words. Marion heard but didn't listen. She had only asked her mother about local gossip because she knew it would please her.

'Oh, and your father has a friend coming over for his tea tomorrow. A very nice man.' She looked intently at Marion. 'He would suit you very nicely.'

'Oh no.' Marion laughed, 'I don't think so. No thank you, Mother.'

Maggie couldn't stop herself. 'Why not? Have you met someone?'

'I've *met* plenty of people.'

'But not this one.' Maggie nudged Robert. 'Tell her about him.'

'Please don't,' begged Marion, only half joking.

'Shush,' Maggie told her. 'Go on, Robert. Tell her.'

Robert did as he was told. 'He's a nice chap. Ex-army. Dabbles in motor car sales.'

Maggie interrupted. 'They met at a rally. You know how your dad loves cars?'

'Aye, and we got chatting and it turns out he's newly returned to the area, living on his own. I felt a bit sorry for him and I thought, with you coming home, it might be nice to invite him over. A new face for us all.'

'I smell matchmaking.' Marion raised an eyebrow at her mother. 'And I am not going to fall for it – or for a stranger Dad picked up at a car rally.'

Maggie tutted. 'You're twenty-six, Marion! You shouldn't be leaving it so late!'

Marion looked pained. 'I am enjoying my work. I like my life. There's plenty of time for a husband.'

'Aye, but—'

Robert threw Maggie a warning look. 'That's enough. Leave the girl be.'

Maggie twisted her lips and said huffily, 'Oh, so you don't want to be a grandfather then?'

With gentle diplomacy, Marion stepped in. 'One day, I promise, I shall get married and have a wee girl and a wee boy and you two can spoil them rotten. But not yet. Now, I will wash this up for you and, if you don't mind, I would love a bath. It was awful hot on the train.'

*

The next day, Maggie threw herself into a frenzy, preparing the house and the food for their visitor.

'Mother, you will work your way into one of your headaches.' Marion tied an apron around her waist. 'Sit down and give me orders.'

'Where's your father?'

'I'm here.' Robert came in through the back door with a handful of freshly dug carrots and some horseradish root.

'Does your friend like roast beef, Robert?'

'I am sure he does.'

'You didn't think to ask?'

Robert sighed. 'Maggie, what man doesn't like roast beef?'

'When I asked the butcher, he said the same. But you never know. Should I have bought salmon?'

Marion stopped her. 'Mother, your roast beef is the best.'

Slightly mollified, Maggie agreed. 'Your poor late father always loved it.'

'And so does your poor living husband!' Robert kissed her cheek. 'Shall I boil some tatties?'

'Why would I want boiled tatties, Robert?' Maggie asked him as if he were an idiot. 'Has anyone ever had boiled tatties with beef? You have roast tatties with beef!'

Robert picked up his newspaper. 'Ah yes. Your roast tatties are legendary. I will leave you girls to it then.' And he retreated to the garden, smiling to himself.

'What time is our guest coming?' Maggie called after him.

'Six o'clock.'

Maggie began to fret again. 'It's eleven o'clock now so . . .' She thought hard. 'He'll be here in seven hours! And I haven't even ironed the tablecloth.'

Marion turned the sink tap on and began washing the carrots. 'Come on – I'll help you and then you'll have time to get yourself ready.'

By five o'clock, all was nearly done. The beef was doing well, the potatoes waiting to go in the oven, and carrots, cabbage and peas waiting in their pans to be boiled.

Maggie was half up the stairs to get ready before dashing back down. 'Gravy!'

'Yes, Mother. I've got the browning ready and the horseradish sauce is made. Now go and get changed while I check the table.'

With minutes to the momentous arrival, Robert was stationed by the small drinks trolley, Maggie was applying lipstick in the cracked kitchen mirror and Marion was upstairs sitting on her bed, looking out onto the road. She had no desire to find herself a husband but she found herself curious to meet this man. His name was George Buthlay and he had come out of the army as a major. By staying upstairs she'd have the opportunity to get a glimpse of him before meeting in person.

'Marion, come downstairs,' Maggie called.

'I will in a minute. Almost ready.'

She saw a little car as it came round the corner – small and green with large chrome headlamps and narrow tyres. It slowed as it looked for the right address, then pulled into the drive in front of her father's garage.

'He's here, Marion,' Maggie called again. 'Quick, quick!'

'All right!' Marion stayed where she was, waiting for the driver to reveal himself. The engine was killed and he stepped out of his car.

He was older than she had expected, in his forties at least. Average height, dressed in a black suit and highly polished shoes. Closing the car door, he glanced up at the house. His face was round, his hairline receding, but his well-clipped moustache lent some style.

'Hello, George Buthlay,' Marion said to herself

She heard the doorbell ring and went downstairs to meet him.

Maggie was standing at the front door, introducing herself. 'How lovely to meet you, Major Buthlay. I'm Robert's wife.'

'Mrs Crawford, thank you so much for inviting me. I have been so looking forward to meeting you.'

'It's our pleasure. Please, call me Maggie. Come on in.'

Marion watched from the last step of the stairs. Her mother's effort to charm was mortifying.

She stepped down into the hall and introduced herself.

'Good evening, Major Buthlay. How nice to meet you. I'm Marion.'

'Yes,' fluttered Maggie. 'Marion's my daughter by my first husband.'

'Good evening, Marion.' He took her hand and held it briefly to his lips.

Maggie's eyes widened in delight.

Robert ambled in from the sitting room. 'George, how good to see you. Come in to the warm.'

'Oh yes, do come through.' Maggie stepped back to let Major Buthlay in and then winked at her daughter before closing the front door.

In the sitting room, the two men had taken up the armchairs, leaving the sofa free for Maggie and Marion. Marion was relieved; the last thing she wanted was to have to sit on the sofa with Major Buthlay when her mother was on a mission to throw her at him.

Robert poured two whiskies and two sherries, and Major Buthlay commented on Maggie's knickknacks and taste in décor. After that, Maggie and Marion withdrew to the kitchen to finish off the gravy and boil the veg.

'What a charming man,' Maggie whispered as she drained the carrots.

'He seems polite enough,' Marion replied, with no noticeable excitement – but her hand was tingling a little from his lips. No one had ever done anything so courtly before and it had rather disarmed her. She tried to distract herself. 'Did you put the horseradish sauce on the table?'

'Yes, and the mustard.' Maggie lowered her voice. 'Doesn't he have lovely manners? And so good-looking. A man like him, a major, would suit you very well.'

Marion glared at Maggie. 'Mother! Stop!' she hissed. 'I can find my own husband, thank you. I don't need Dad's friends to be paraded in front of me in the hope that one of them will take me off the shelf.'

'There *is* a man friend in London, isn't there? You know you can tell me anything.'

Marion gave her a glare.

'How did I get such an obstinate daughter?' Maggie shrugged her shoulders. 'Put those roast tatties in the warm dish, would you, and call your dad in to carry the beef.'

Marion, seated opposite Major Buthlay, observed him covertly. She listened carefully, spoke when she was required and weighed him up. His eyes were dark and amusing, lively. His lips well-shaped, neither too plump nor too thin. He held himself well and listened attentively to her mother's rambling stories. His hands were nice. She thought of the warmth and dryness of his fingers when he had taken hers. Of course, he was shorter than her, but as her mother had always told her, she was too tall for any decent man.

Major Buthlay – George, as he insisted they all call him – ate heartily and accepted seconds. 'This beef is the best I've ever tasted, Maggie.'

'Thank you, George. I suppose it's just practice. Would you like dessert? Marion made an apple crumble this afternoon. Our own apples. She's a very good cook, you know.'

George looked across at Marion in a way that produced an unfamiliar feeling of warmth within her. 'Tell me about yourself, Marion.'

'I am a governess. I work in London.'

'That sounds very interesting.'

'It can be.' She changed the subject, not wanting to be drawn to say more. 'And what about you? I hear you met my dad at a car rally?'

George took his napkin from his knee, rolled it carefully and placed it on the table. He smiled. 'Robert and I have a shared interest in motorcars and I was with a friend who owns a car salesroom in Stirling. I help him out with the business now and again, and we bumped into Robert while looking over a Rover Sports tourer. Superb motor – and way beyond the reach of an army pension.' He laughed. 'Robert and I drooled over it together.'

'We did that.' Robert smiled. 'Triple cylinders, elbow dip doors. I could see you and me, Maggie, driving down to Dover, catching the boat train and travelling down to Monte Carlo.'

'Get away with you!' Maggie was coquettish after an extra sherry. 'And where would we get that sort of money? Or a passport!'

'For you, my darling, anything.' He smiled at her fondly.

Marion stood up. 'I'll get the crumble. Custard or cream for you, George?'

'Now there's an offer.' His smile was so innocent and yet Marion found herself blushing.

In the kitchen, she opened the back door and fanned her cheeks to cool them. 'Pull yourself together,' she muttered.

Placing his spoon into his empty bowl, George wiped his lips on his napkin and told Marion, 'I have never tasted apple crumble as perfect as that. You have inherited your mother's talent for cooking, Marion.'

Maggie reached over and clutched at his arm. 'She would make a fine wife one day.'

Marion winced.

Robert came to the rescue. 'One day, I have no doubt – but at the moment Marion's career is in London, where she is doing very well.'

'You must be very proud of her.' George grinned and checked his pocket watch. 'I fear I would be outstaying my welcome if I didn't take my leave of you now.'

'Is there anything else I can offer you?' asked Maggie, verging on desperation. 'Another tea?'

'Another whisky?' Robert mimed pouring a glass.

'No, no. I am working tomorrow.'

At the front door they said their goodbyes, with Maggie inviting him to 'Come again any time. Don't be a stranger.'

George shook their hands, leaving Marion until last. 'My dear Miss Crawford, I hope we may meet again.'

'It's been very nice to meet you,' she said and, as she began to release her hand, his grip tightened.

'The pleasure has been all mine. Would you perhaps join me for a walk on Sunday? The forecast is for sun. I could pick you up around ten and we could find a nice spot for lunch?'

Marion felt her mother's eyes on her, willing her to accept.

'That's very kind of you but I can't this Sunday.'

He took the knock. 'Maybe another time.'

They watched him as he drove away, Maggie waving theatrically.

When the front door closed and they were all inside, Maggie spoke her mind. 'A lovely man like that and you turn his invitation down?'

Marion smiled tightly. 'Why don't you and Dad go up to bed? I'll clear up down here.'

Alone in the kitchen, she mulled over the evening. George did seem nice. He had manners and was a good conversationalist. Her parents clearly liked him and she felt he had liked her. And that was a new experience for her. No man had ever kissed her hand. And for that matter, no man had ever invited her out for a . . . for a date? Is that what he had done?

She pulled the plug from the sink and watched the greasy suds drain away.

She wished she could talk openly to her mother about this sort of thing, or that she had a best friend to discuss it with. Even Alah and Bobo would do – not that they'd be much help. Alah was a spinster, and Bobo had her head in cheap romance books. Neither of them had any real experience of men either.

Still, she wouldn't be seeing them for several weeks and she suddenly found she missed them dearly. The three of them formed an unusual friendship – colleagues who didn't go home at the end of the day, women who kept their work discreet. Loyalty was everything.

Marion hung the damp tea towel on the stove to dry, then turned the lights out. As she walked up her parents' stairs, she suddenly realized who she wanted to share her thoughts with. A true matriarch – unflappable, trustworthy and intelligent.

She sighed. If only her own mother could be more like Queen Mary.

Chapter Twelve

Royal Lodge, Windsor, early November 1935

'Help me, Crawfie, help me!' Margaret had slipped over on the ice again.

Lilibet was bent double laughing. 'Get up!'

'I can't,' wailed Margaret.

Crawfie, who had skated since she was a small child up in Scotland, glided over to the prone Princess. 'Up you get. Oh, your mitten is all wet. Hold my hand and I'll warm you up.'

'Look at meee,' shouted Lilibet, whizzing past. 'I'm better than you, Margaret.'

'No, you're not,' Margaret yelled, then looked up at Crawfie. 'She's not better than me, is she?'

'I think you are both doing fine. Look at your mummy, skating with a chair to hold onto. That's clever of her, isn't it?' Crawfie was intrigued by another figure on the ice. 'Who's that lady?' she asked.

'That's Uncle David's friend, Mrs Simpson,' said Margaret.

'Is it?' Crawfie was suffering from an attack of proprietorship. The Prince of Wales could not, surely, be involved with this brittle-looking woman? She was too thin, overly made-up and laughing girlishly as the Prince held her waist.

The moment Mrs Simpson had arrived at Royal Lodge, on the arm of the Prince of Wales, backstairs gossip had been rife, but Marion had not met her yet. Word had it she was an American who was on her second husband and who had the Prince wrapped around her finger.

'She's not as pretty as Mummy,' Margaret said. 'And she doesn't like me and Lilibet very much.'

'Of course she does,' Crawfie said.

'No, she doesn't. I can tell. I don't think she likes children. Mummy loves children.'

'Well, let's go and show Mummy how well you can skate.'

That evening, up in the nursery, Bobo was setting the table for the Princesses' dinner and Alah was warming two sets of pyjamas on the fireguard.

Crawfie was sitting in an armchair. 'I haven't skated for a long time. I'll be bruised and sore in the morning.' She stretched her long legs in front of her. 'I don't how the Duchess will have the energy to entertain the Prince of Wales and Mrs Simpson.'

'She's always had stamina. Even as a baby.' Alah sighed. 'Just like those girls of hers.'

As if on cue, they heard two sets of little feet pounding up the stairs.

Then the Prince of Wales's voice, deep and monsterish. 'I'm coming to get you!'

'*Nooo*. Uncle David! Arrgghh.'

'I'm going to eat you all up.'

'Stop it. Papa! Uncle David's going to eat us.'

The nursery door flew open and Margaret and Lilibet charged into the room, with the chasing Prince and their father behind them.

'Crawfie, save us!' Dramatically, they both threw themselves at her as she hastily stood up and curtsied.

The Prince was holding a book and panting hard. 'You two little monkeys are too quick for me.' Then, throwing the book down, he suddenly pounced on them, almost knocking Crawfie over.

Falling to the floor, he rolled onto his back, looked up at Alah, Bobo and Crawfie and said, 'I am most awfully sorry. It's all my nieces' fault. Dreadful little girls.'

The Princesses fell on top of him and another wrestling match began.

Alah stopped it all.

'Ladies! Would you kindly get up and wish His Royal Highness and your father goodnight?'

They did so immediately, though Margaret could not suppress a giggle.

The Duke helped the Prince up. 'My apologies for the disturbance,' he said. 'My brother is a rogue.'

The Prince grinned at Crawfie, Bobo and Alah.

'Goodnight, ladies.' He turned to follow his brother out but stopped. 'And er . . .'

Crawfie's heart skipped a beat. Had he recognized her as the woman who had nearly fainted in front of him all that time ago?

'I promised my nieces a story, but perhaps you would do the honour on my behalf?' He pointed at the book he had thrown on to the carpet.

Crawfie breathed with relief, but was somewhat miffed. So he hadn't recognized her after all.

'Of course, Your Royal Highness,' Alah said. 'And you are always welcome in the nursery.'

'I shall take my leave of you.' He went to the door but again turned back. 'My friend from America has received a shipment of gramophone records and after dinner we intend to play them and enjoy a little dance. I apologize for any extraneous noise in advance. Good night, Lilibet. Goodnight, Margaret. Goodnight, ladies.'

'Goodnight, sir.'

The Princesses were already collecting up the abandoned book. 'Come on, Crawfie.' They pushed it into her hands and pulled her towards their bedroom.

'And what is this book all about?'

'Murder and mystery.' Lilibet's eyes lit up. 'Uncle David said we would love it.'

Crawfie read the cover. '*The Mystery of the Blue Train* by Agatha Christie?' She doubted that the girls, aged nine and five, would stay awake long enough to be enthralled by it, but she would enjoy it enormously.

The Prince of Wales hadn't been wrong. Cold though the night was, the party downstairs had spilled out on to the terrace, and through the open doors of the drawing room the sound of Cole Porter's 'You're the Top' was travelling up on the night air and in through the curtains of the nursery sitting room.

'Here, this will help us sleep.' Crawfie was carrying a tray of hot milk. 'I don't know how the girls can sleep through this.'

Alah looked at the clock on the nursery mantelpiece. 'It's past midnight.'

'Lovely music though,' said Bobo.

Hush suddenly fell.

'Oh. It's stopped.'

'Thank goodness.' Alah pulled her shawl around her.

There came an explosion of helpless laughter and whoops, then the sound of something being smashed.

'What was that?' asked Bobo, wide-eyed.

'I shall go and see.' Alah tightened the belt of her long dressing gown and tucked her shawl securely around her chest. 'I hope to God no one is injured.'

Crawfie and Bobo followed her.

Out on the landing, the three of them leant over the bannisters and could see Ainslie, three floors down, with a dustpan and brush in his hands.

'What's going on?' Alah called quietly. 'Is anyone injured?'

His weary eyes looked up at her. 'The only injury is to the Japanese table lamp. Beyond saving, I'm afraid.'

'What are they playing at?'

'The Prince discovered that a gramophone record, when thrown like a flying saucer, is enormous fun until things get broken.'

A volley of raucous laughter came from the drawing room and the Prince of Wales shouted, 'Ainslie? We need more cocktails.'

Ainslie raised his eyes to the women above and sighed. 'Yes, sir. Of course, sir.'

145 Piccadilly, December 1935

Dear Mother,

I can never tire of Christmas in London. So different to Dunfermline. You should see the Christmas tree we have here – at least two feet bigger than last year's and I thought that was enormous! The Duke and Duchess both adore the season and together with the Princesses they have decorated it beautifully. They have baubles dating back to Queen Victoria that have been passed down through the family. It is standing in the hall as usual and I daren't breathe when I go past it for fear of knocking one on to the floor.

Dookie the dog is kept well away.

Dear Lilibet and Margaret are getting so excited, desperate to write their letters to Father Christmas.

You remember that the Duchess always takes them to Harrods to have a look at what they might like to add to their list? (Not that they are spoilt – not at all!) This year, the Duchess invited me to join them because Alah, who usually goes, had a dreadful cold. I have walked past it many times but always been a little intimidated by the sheer size and glamour of it. And now, to be driven up, sitting next to the Duchess, and have one of the green liveried doormen help us out and into the shop, was wonderful.

The shop was closed and we were the only customers. Can you imagine?

It smelt of leather and perfume and it was all lit up and so warm. Our small party was taken up in one of the many lifts to the fourth floor. The Princesses giggled all the way and, when the door opened, we were in the toy department – an Aladdin's cave filled with the smallest bag of marbles to a mini replica of King George's Rolls-Royce Phantom. The girls were each allowed to sit in it and pedal around the department. When they had done that, they took little notebooks and pencils out of their small bags and began making a list.

Lilibet fell for a small farm with stables and fences to make two fields. 'Look, Mummy. And it has two horses and little jumps to go over.' The Duchess told her to write it in her book, and that if Father Christmas thought she had been good, perhaps she might receive it for Christmas.

'When I'm grown up,' Lilibet told me, 'I am going to get married, live in the country and have lots of horses, dogs and children.'

Of course Margaret found the dressing-up clothes and immediately wanted the most sparkly fairy dress with a wand and a tiara. 'I have been good, Mummy. I have.'

The Duchess was so good with them, making sure everything was written down and no promises made.

After they had finished their lists, we were taken down to do a bit of shopping ourselves. The Duchess was interested in gloves as gifts for her friends and I bought you and Dad a Harrods souvenir. But that is the only hint I shall give you!

The next day, feeling like Cinderella after the ball, I took the Princesses to Woolworths to buy their presents for the family. This time we shared the shop with many customers but the little girls were very good at not drawing attention to themselves. I think, with the detective in tow, we looked like any other family.

It was so sweet to watch them choosing small trinkets for their grandparents: a scrapbook for the King to put his stamps in, and a small china posy of violets for the Queen. Then they picked out a brooch fashioned like a dog for the Duchess and a hand fork and trowel set for the Duke. (Although I think Dad has a better one!)

The Good Servant

It's very much all go here. Everything required by the family for their Christmas stay at Sandringham is being packed up and sent to Norfolk for their arrival. Alah and Bobo have been very busy as you can imagine. I, on the other hand, have been setting a little homework for the girls to take with them. I don't want them to lose the habit of reading and learning just because it's Christmas!

Queen Mary came to tea last week and asked me how their lessons were going. She is very encouraging and understands how the Duchess perhaps doesn't take the girls' education as seriously as she might, or that I would like. Her Majesty is keen for them to know their history and has offered to write to the royal librarian, Mr Morshead, to put on one of his historical tours of the Royal Palaces for them. I did say that I got a little discouraged at times because the Duchess does disrupt the teaching timetable with appointments for the dentist or hairdresser. The Queen passed over my indiscretion and told me that Mr Morshead has been concerned that the last eighteen books ordered by the Duchess had all been P.G. Wodehouse. 'It's all very well to enjoy some light reading and lots of fresh air, but at some point they must read some Dickens, Austen and Shakespeare,' she said.

I thanked her with relief and couldn't agree more. She's a wonderful woman, warm and intelligent.

I had heard that the King has been unwell and wanted to ask her how he was, but it's not my place. Sandringham is his favourite home and I hope he will feel a lot better for resting there.

It won't be long now until I see you. Don't put the tree up until I get home, will you?

Fondest love to you and Dad.

Marion

Chapter Thirteen

Sir Alan Lascelles, MC, known to all as Tommy, arrived at Buckingham Palace with no small amount of trepidation. The last time he had left the building was more than six years before, when he had resigned as assistant private secretary to Edward, known as David, Prince of Wales.

Now, here he was again, fresh from a four-year stint abroad as private secretary to the Governor-General of Canada, flattered into taking up the post of Assistant Private Secretary to King George V.

Tommy had left the services of the King's son in 1929, openly admitting that he didn't like the man and thought him unworthy of his position as Prince of Wales – so he was uncertain as to why the King had thought to give him the job.

However, here he was, with a salary of £1,500 per annum, a grace-and-favour home and the encouragement of his wife, Joan.

The Lord Chamberlain had written the confirmation letter with an instruction to pack a full-dress coat and knee breeches.

A costumed footman welcomed him. 'Good morning, Sir Alan. I am ordered to take you to your new office and get you settled in.'

Behind his new but antique desk, he ran a finger inside his tight wing collar and surveyed his new office: one large-paned window looking over Constitution Hill and Green Park beyond, two walls of bookcases, and a door leading to a corridor which led to his new and not-so-antique secretary, Miss Pepper-Thynne.

'Good morning, Sir Alan. May I get you a cup of tea?' she asked brightly.

'That would be splendid, thank you.'

'How do you like it?'

'Strong, splash of milk and two sugars, please.'

On her return, it seemed she had added two biscuits to his order.

'There you are, sir. If you need anything, just give me a buzz.' She pointed to a machine on the desk. 'One buzz for anything. Two buzzes for emergency.'

He smiled. 'Emergencies, eh? Are we expecting many?'

'You never know, sir.'

He liked a woman with a sense of humour. 'Very good. Thank you, Miss Pepper-Thynne.'

'Please call me P-T. Everybody does. It's so much easier.'

Tommy nodded.

'And one more thing, sir – the blue file on your desk is the latest briefing for today. Underneath that is the schedule for the rest of the week.'

'Very efficient of you, P-T.'

'You will see that His Majesty has asked you to meet him at 11.30 for thirty minutes.'

'Right.'

'And remember, one buzz for anything, two buzzes for emergency.'

She closed his office door quietly behind her.

For a moment or two, Tommy absorbed his situation and bit into one of his biscuits. The traffic outside was busy but thinning as the rush hour slowed. The quiet of his office and the corridor outside was soothing. He took a sip of his tea, which was perfectly made, and checked the time: 9.20. He had two hours in which to focus his thoughts on his meeting with the King and acquaint himself with P-T's well-typed schedule.

*

At 11.28, Tommy arrived outside the King's office. At 11.30 on the dot, a footman, acting on an unseen signal, opened the King's doors.

Tommy entered and performed a perfect neck bow, then waited for the King, who was signing a document, to acknowledge him.

'Ah, Tommy.' The King stood and came round his desk to shake hands.

'Your Majesty.'

'How are you? Good to see you again.'

'Glad to be back, sir.'

The King indicated two brocade sofas, one either side of a glowing fire. 'Take a seat. This place is always so damned cold. But I expect you remember that.'

'After four years of Canadian winters, London feels quite warm.'

'Quite so.' The King took a cigarette from the table beside him and lit it. 'So, Tommy.' King George V inhaled deeply, leaning against a cushion. 'Why have you agreed to come back to the Old Firm?'

Tommy uncrossed and crossed his legs, hitching his trousers at the knee lightly. He was prepared for this. 'It is a privilege to be asked to serve one's monarch, sir.'

The King smiled slowly. 'Hmm. Even though you resigned as APS to my son? The Prince of Wales? The *future* King?'

Tommy coughed. 'Sir, it was a privilege to serve the Prince of Wales.'

'Ha.' The King dismissed him. 'A privilege? I heard it was anything but. My son and heir is a popular and handsome young man, but the Queen and I are neither blind nor deaf to his antics. I know very well that you resigned because you were tired of defending him, covering for him, and clearing up after him.'

Tommy gazed stoically at the carpet.

'You have nothing to say?'

'How is the Prince of Wales, sir?'

'No change. One unsuitable woman after another. Usually married.'

'I am sorry to hear that, sir.'

'Yes, well, the Queen worries. If only David could be more like Bertie. Bertie's marriage to dear Elizabeth, and his two little girls, make him a much better future sovereign, on paper, although his nervousness and the stutter would never do. Accidents of birth, eh?' The King stroked his beard in thought, staring into the fire. 'If my elder brother hadn't died I would never have been king. You know that Queen Mary was engaged to my elder brother, don't you?'

'I do, sir, yes.' Tommy watched his King carefully, noting the pallor in his cheeks and his yellowing eyes.

'But he died and I got the Throne, Mary accepted my proposal, and here we are. Four sons, one daughter, and the firstborn a rogue and a lush.'

At a soft knock on the door and the arrival of the footman, Tommy knew his designated thirty minutes were up.

The King stayed seated while Tommy stood. 'Good to see you, Tommy.'

'And you, sir.' Tommy bowed at the neck and withdrew from the King's presence.

Back in his office he buzzed for P-T. 'Yes, sir?' her distorted voice asked.

'Where does one go for lunch around here?'

145 Piccadilly, December 1935

Dear Mother,

Only another week and I shall be back home. Yesterday the King and Queen held the annual household Christmas party. The Palace looks really wonderful, all decorated and lit like a

Dickens novel. Princess Margaret galloped around the tree, getting closer and closer to every priceless bauble. Her grandparents take great pleasure in her antics.

I was just about to step in to prevent any accidents when Lilibet managed to catch her. I heard her whisper to Margaret, 'You will break something, Margaret. Stop being silly,' in her no-nonsense little voice.

M immediately burst into tears and made a dash for her mother's skirts.

L is such a thoughtful girl. She knows how to have fun but also how to rise to any occasion. She will make a fine young woman. M on the other hand is so amusing and very good at taking centre stage, but quite a handful too. Imagine the beaus she will have!

The Queen was as gracious as always but the King didn't look very well.

They both work so hard. I am sure they need their Christmas at Sandringham.

Is there anything else I can bring home with me? I got the marmalade you like but what about Dad? How is he for socks? Vests? I only ask because Ainslie tells me the Army and Navy store is very good for men's underclothes. I don't know how we got onto that conversation! But if the A&N are good enough for a royal butler, I think they are good enough for Dad. What colour tie doesn't he have?

See you next Monday.

My love,

Marion xx

PS I miss you both very much. Where does the time fly?
PPS I found some of the stockings you like. I bought you two pairs.

Chapter Fourteen

Sandringham House, Norfolk, January 1936

12th January 1936

Darling Joan,

I hated leaving you and the children this morning. You know how badly I feel about being here instead of with you. You are so wonderful at understanding.

I am in my bedroom in 'The Bachelor's Wing'. So archaic. As if I presented any danger to a young parlourmaid! The room is small and I wouldn't give £15 for the furniture but it has a good fire which is sorely needed. The house is homely but cold and is a very rum place for a king to love. Everything is pitch pine and trophies. Quite hideous.

Open the front door and you immediately step into the large and draughty hall. A roaring fire in the grate makes no difference to the temperature, but there is a large table, half completed jigsaw on top, and two chairs to encourage visitors to pop a piece of the puzzle in place. Then endless stairs, corridors and ugly paintings on the walls. I constantly feel I shall bump into the ghost of Queen Victoria, lurking round every corner.

The train journey was interesting. I was placed in a first-class compartment with my name on the door. Most uncomfortable as people would stop to read it and stare at me. The guards all hailed me as My Lord. Fearful.

About halfway through the journey, a young man appeared in the doorway. I was about to tell him to go away, when I recognized him as the Duke of York. I hadn't seen him for eight years. He joined me and we had an amiable chat which he started with, 'What's all this I hear about the King not being well?' I could tell him nothing more than I had been told, to wit there seemed to be no obvious illness, it was just the old machine running down.

When we arrived there was an inch of snow, and in the last two hours it has begun snowing rather more heavily. The Duchess of York is not here; she has succumbed to a very heavy cold, and the Princesses are with her in London. The sombre atmosphere of the house would not be suitable.

The Prince of Wales is due later.

Sleep well, my dear Joan.

My fondest love,

Tommy

15ᵗʰ January 1936

My dearest Joan,

The Prince of Wales has arrived. He burst in, disrupting us all. He had been sent for and was not happy to have been called from his Windsor shooting party. I am afraid I made myself scarce. I couldn't face meeting with him before bed. The last words I had with him were six years ago and none too complimentary. He may not remember me, of course, but I should like to have a good sleep and a breakfast inside me, if and when he does.

The King – and keep this strictly to yourself – is clearly not at all well. He has been in bed for the last three days and seems unlikely to leave it. The King's surgeon apothecary, Sir Stanley Hewett, and the royal physician Lord Dawson of Penn are with him. They arrived under the cloak of secrecy so as not to excite the nation.

I walked in the grounds this afternoon, the mood of the house being so grim and oppressive. Nothing much to see. Rather *ordinary shrubs: berberis, myrtle, fancy hollies and variegated laurels.*

I have not seen the King myself. My main purpose, if and when the time comes, will be to oversee communiqués to the press.

How are the children? Take no nonsense from them.

Your Tommy

16th *January 1936*

Darling Tommy,

It's been very hectic here. One of the children's trunks burst its leather straps when I took them back to school. Then, when I returned home, a frightful clonking and clanking was coming from the boiler. The upshot is no hot water. I think I would rather be at Sandringham. Consider yourself lucky!

Poor you having to share time with the Prince of Wales. And of course he will remember you – you worked with him for years! But will he have forgiven you for telling him you couldn't stand his drinking and womanizing ways a moment longer, and leaving him? He didn't pay much attention to that piece of advice, did he?

Speaking of which, has Exhibit A – AKA *the ghastly Mrs Simpson – put in an appearance? She is definitely playing to be the next Queen of England. I suspect, my darling, you will be asked to get your thinking cap on as to how to nip that little scenario in the bud. Can you imagine? Divorced from her first husband, still married to the second and getting her well-manicured talons into a future king? To be honest, we could probably forgive most of that but the British public could never forgive her for being American.*

Now, darling, do let me know how the King is doing. I like him very much. Poor Queen Mary. If appropriate, send her my regards.

I'm off to get some logs with which to light the fire in our bedroom. Could barely sleep for the cold last night, even though

I put my mink on the blankets. Woke up to frost on the inside of the windows.

All my love,
Joan

17ᵗʰ *January 1936*

Dearest Joan,

The Prince of Wales left this morning for London. The King is fading and the subject of succession needs to be discussed with the PM, etc.

Before he left, the POW went to the King's sickroom, where he found his father sitting sleepily by the fire, wrapped in his favourite Tibetan dressing gown. He opened his eyes and briefly recognized his son, but it wasn't long before His Majesty relapsed back into his twilight world.

The Queen was pleased to have your message and asked after you which, in the circumstances, shows what an extraordinary woman she is.

I have been busy writing statements on the King's health for publication in the newspapers and radio bulletins. Maybe you have heard them? It is true that his heart appears to be growing weaker and his condition is being regarded with some disquiet. The blessing is that he is without pain.

Darling, I hope you are not too cold tonight. Why not actually wear your mink in bed?

My love to you and the children,
Tommy

18ᵗʰ *January 1936*

Darling Tommy,

The postman has just delivered your latest communiqué. He is new and very nosey. He sees Sandringham on the envelope and almost bows to me. I can see he is desperate to ask questions. I take the post from him, thank him and promptly close the door.

If he thinks me rude, then let him. We are about to be plunged into national mourning. We are losing a much loved monarch and replacing him with a weak and easily influenced successor. I'm sorry, darling, but it's true. I know you know it as well as I do.

Mr Williams, the plumber, is coming out today to give the boiler a wallop.

I really am longing for a hot bath.

Fondly,

Joan

19th *January 1936*

Darling Joan,

Dear girl, I do hope Williams's wallop did the trick? I have some army combinations in the attic. Dig them out and you'll be as warm as toast, I guarantee.

The days here at Sandringham are becoming more surreal. Life goes on, fires are lit, maids scurry. Meals are made and dinner served, with no hint that the King of England is upstairs, in his bed, dying.

The Queen's unwavering fortitude upholds us all.

This morning the Prince of Wales returned, looking very sombre. Clearly the thought of his succession is weighing heavy. I cannot say more.

This afternoon I spotted the Queen walking in the grounds with all her children. The Prince of Wales looked more downcast than I have ever seen him. The Duke of York, Duke of Gloucester, Duke of Kent and Mary the Princess Royal flanked their brother and the Queen as they perambulated the misty grounds. One can only imagine their conversation.

On my own walk, I spotted people gathered at the main gate like grey spectres. Their loyalty is touching but seeing them only underlines the whole terrible business.

They are like us and we like them. All of us waiting for the inevitable news, while behaving as if everything were quite normal.

Would you be kind enough to send me asap a pair of black mourning trousers – bottom drawer in the wardrobe of my dressing room – two white flannel shirts with a black stripe, and two pairs of my black woollen socks? All in the small drawer of the big wardrobe.

I have just been working with Lord Dawson, the royal physician, on the medical communiqués. He has a beautiful sensitivity. When the time comes, he has proposed these words: 'The King's life is moving peacefully to its close.'

When I read it, I am not ashamed to say I wept a little. So beautiful.

Sadly, you will surely hear those words for yourself, in the next few hours.

Your Tommy

Sandringham House, Norfolk, 20th January 1936

Tommy woke to a cold morning, and his first thought was for the King. Had he survived the night? He checked his watch. Six thirty. The sun was not yet up and yet he could see that it was snowing. The lower quadrants of his window panes had collected small piles of the stuff and more flakes were joining them.

In the muffled silence, Tommy carefully shaved, washed and dressed. If the sovereign died today, Tommy would be ready.

With the snow showing no signs of stopping, the house took on a muffled atmosphere. The staff flitted through the rooms, adding logs to the fires, producing meals and hot drinks, but never speaking of death.

A few hours later, the Prince of Wales and Duke of York sent for Tommy to join them in the library.

The royal brothers were both smoking. The Prince was slumped by the fire, his thin legs crossed, an empty coffee cup and the day's *Times* by his side. The Duke was at the window watching the snow.

Tommy bowed to them both. 'Good morning, sirs.'

The Prince smiled weakly. 'Sit down, Tommy.'

Tommy sat. 'What news of the King?' he asked.

From the window the Duke said, 'He is asleep. The doctor has told us he will not wake up. It's just a matter of time.'

'I am very sorry to hear that.'

The Prince lifted his red-ringed eyes to Tommy. 'I bet you are, knowing his successor is me.'

Tommy chose his words carefully. 'Sir, I have always believed in the words of St John: "Cometh the hour, cometh the man".'

'Ha.' The Prince reached for his cigarette case. He took a cigarette and lit it from the end of his previous one. 'But as you know, I am no saint.'

Tommy looked at the man who would be king. A weak, unreliable man, wedded to a life of parties and pleasure. But he was glamorous and loved by the public. He had a heart and wanted to improve the living conditions of the poorest people. He had the common touch – an asset rare in this vaulted bloodline.

The Duke of York returned from the window and rang the bell by the fireplace. 'I think we could do with our pre-luncheon whisky and soda.'

'May I ask why you sent for me?' Tommy asked the Prince.

The Prince picked a stray strand of tobacco from his lip. 'I need some help, Tommy.'

'I am here to help.'

The Prince coughed and looked slyly at his brother, who turned back to stare at the snow. 'I want my friend, Mrs Simpson, here.'

Tommy blinked. 'I see.'

'I need her by my side when the . . .' The Prince was close to tears. 'When the time comes.'

'I see,' Tommy said again. 'But I suggest that—'

The Prince's temper flared. 'I need her by my side.'

Tommy tried again. 'But the Queen—'

'Won't know.'

Tommy's smile was perplexed. 'So, we are to smuggle Mrs Simpson into the house and not tell the Queen?'

'Yes.'

'Ah.' Tommy hid his anger. And said with reason, 'That would put us all in a most awkward position at this delicate time.'

The Prince threw his cigarette into the fire and put his head in his hands. 'In a few hours I shall be King. You have to do as I say.'

Tommy wanted to say a lot of things – most of which was to tell the man in front of him to pull himself together. But he decided to keep his own counsel. 'The King is dying and that must be the focus of my work.' He stood up. 'I shall take my leave of you, sir.'

The Duke of York moved from the window to Tommy. 'My brother is grieving for the King. He is not in his right mind.'

'Understood, sir. I believe none of us are.'

As Tommy left for his office at the back of the house, he bumped into a footman. He was carrying a tray with a whisky decanter, a bowl of ice, two glasses and a soda syphon.

'Don't let them have too much,' Tommy said as he walked past.

His mind was in a fury at the selfishness of the Prince of Wales. How dared he ask for Mrs Simpson? The Queen would never accept her here and Tommy would never smuggle the woman in under the Queen's nose. 'God save us from the man.'

When he reached his temporary office, P-T was waiting for him. 'Sir, the latest update.' She passed him a folded note.

'From the King's physician?'

'Yes, sir.'

A wave of exhaustion suddenly swamped him. 'Would there be any tea on the go, P-T?'

'Of course. I will bring it in to you.'

'Thank you.'

He sat down at his desk and took a deep breath before unfolding the missive.

Midday bulletin

Dear Lascelles,

The King's condition is weakening. The pulse is slowing and his breathing more shallow. There is nothing to be done other than to wait.

The Queen is with him, as is the Princess Royal.

Lord Dawson

Tommy felt a rare constriction of his throat. He had not cried for longer than he could remember, but now he let his tears free.

The afternoon wore into night, the house grew more silent and the ticking of the many clocks seemed to Tommy to be growing louder by the hour. It all set the scene for the death of a king.

At nine thirty that evening, Lord Dawson sent another note.

Dear Lascelles,

I suggest now is the time to release the bulletin we agreed on.

Dawson

Tommy opened his desk drawer and removed a single sheet of paper on which the words: *The King's life is moving peacefully to its close* were typed. He called for P-T, whose temporary desk was just outside in the corridor.

'Telegraph this, please.'

He heard the catch in her breath as she recognized the note and saw a gleam of tears in her eyes. But her voice did not betray her. 'Yes, sir.'

'And we had better have ready the final bulletin.' He pulled another sheet of paper from his desk. It read: *Death came peacefully to the King at (insert time) (insert date).*

It was the sound of running footsteps coming down the corridor that signalled to Tommy the King's passing.

A tearful footmen handed over a note. 'From Lord Dawson, sir.'

Tommy ran his eyes over it and called in P-T. The final message, gaps filled, was released to Fleet Street.

Just after midnight, Lord Dawson came to Tommy's office, and said simply, 'It is over.'

Tommy stood up. 'My dear fellow. You must need a drink.'

'I think so. Yes, please.'

'Sit down. P-T,' he called, 'whisky please.'

She came in moments. She kept a bottle under her desk with glasses and soda, just in case. 'Here we are, sir.'

Lord Dawson took the glass with a shaky hand. 'Thank you.'

Tommy looked at his loyal secretary. 'P-T, would you care to join us?'

'Thank you, sir.' She looked anxiously at both men. 'How is the Queen?'

'Steadfast. Sitting with him,' Lord Dawson answered. 'With all her children around her.'

'Oh golly.' P-T paled and sat down on a wooden upright chair. 'Oh dear.'

'Indeed.' Tommy raised his glass. 'The King is dead. Long live the King.'

P-T gulped her whisky.

'Come along, P-T,' said Tommy when she had finished, 'you need to sleep. We shall be busy tomorrow.'

'Yes, sir,' she replied. 'I am so sorry. For all of us.'

When she had left, Tommy poured himself and Lord Dawson another glass.

'He did not suffer?'

'No,' said Dawson. 'At least I could help him with that.'

'Thank God.'

'Indeed, but' – Dawson faltered – 'I have done something, and I hope God may forgive me.'

Tommy looked at the man. He seemed to be suffering some inner turmoil. 'What have you done?'

'If I tell you, would you promise to keep it within these four walls? Please?'

Tommy sat forward. 'If this is a confession, I am no priest.'

'I need to tell someone I trust and that is you.'

'All right.'

'Earlier this evening, I injected 750mg of morphine and a gram of cocaine, into the King's veins. I hastened his death.'

Tommy's tired brain was in overdrive. 'What? Why?'

'I thought it suitable that his death should be announced before the presses of *The Times* newspaper rolled at midnight. This way the country will wake to the news at breakfast. If he had passed away any later, the solemnity of his death would be reported by the lesser evening papers.'

Tommy was stunned. 'Good God!'

'The Queen and the family can sleep tonight and be stronger tomorrow as they face the agony of grief and burial and succession.'

Tommy twisted the glass in his hand, taking all this in, then he said, 'You will not speak of this again. As for me, I shall wipe this conversation from my mind. You did what you felt was right. Let us leave it at that.'

21st January 1936

Darling,

He has gone. At five to midnight.

All the family were with him as he breathed his last.

I am told that the Queen, who has maintained a long vigil at his bedside, instantly turned to her eldest son and, bowing, took his hand in hers and kissed it. 'God Save the King,' she said unfalteringly before stepping back with a small curtsey.

The King is dead.

The house is now brimming with the quiet efficiency of state.

It is two o'clock in the morning now. I have just returned from visiting the old King in his room to pay my respects and thank him for his life of duty. Like all our generation, I have seen too many dead men, but none has ever had a more peaceful face.

The new King will return to London tomorrow to present himself to privy councillors who, no matter how they judge him, must swear allegiance to him.

He is taking his own aeroplane to do so, apparently creating a kingly precedent. His father never flew in his life.

I will write again tomorrow, but for now I am going to get some sleep.

Thank you for the clothes parcel. Tomorrow will be all hands to the pump.

With grateful love,

Tommy

Chapter Fifteen

Dunfermline, 21ˢᵗ January 1936

Maggie's eyes were swollen with tears. Whether they were for the dead King or Marion's insistence on returning to Windsor and Royal Lodge, she couldn't have told you.

'Surely they can do without you for another day?'

Marion had reached the end of her forbearance. She had been awake since Alah had telephoned in the early hours. The poor woman had sobbed down the telephone, hardly able to get her words out. And now, dealing with her mother's bleating was the last straw.

'Mother!' she snapped. 'This is not about me staying here to comfort you! It's my job to go to London and comfort two little girls who have lost their grandfather! Read the telegram if you don't believe me.' She handed the flimsy piece of paper to her mother. 'The Duchess isn't well. She has flu. The Duke is in mourning. The girls need me and that's that.'

'What about me? *I* need you.'

'Stop it!'

'You've changed, Marion. You used to be a loving daughter but now . . .'

'Pass me my cardigan, would you?'

Pathetically, Maggie looked around her. Her daughter's rumpled single bed was a mess of discarded hangers and clothes.

'Which one?'

'The blue one. You're sitting on it.'

Marion was in no mood to bend to her mother's neediness. Her head and heart were aching with the enormity of the King's death. She desperately wanted to be back in London, to bring reassurance to the Princesses and to the household. So much must be happening and it was vital that the girls were protected from all the emotional upset. The Duchess would need to know that life around her would carry on, to give her the time to soothe her husband in his grief and pick up the threads of public duty and royal continuance.

Her mother pulled the cardigan from under her and lifted it to her cheek, rubbing the soft wool on her skin.

'One of the nicest things I ever knitted for you.' She sighed and put her nose to it. 'It smells of you.'

Marion gritted her teeth in furious despair.

Maggie shot her an angry look. 'Can I not say anything to you? Do you speak to the Duchess the way you speak to me?'

Her stepfather came in bearing a tray of tea. 'I've put some sausages under the grill.'

Maggie wiped her eyes ostentatiously. 'The last thing I want is food. I couldn't keep it down.'

'Ah.' He put the tray down, assessing the situation. 'You two squabbling?'

Maggie sighed. 'I just don't know why she has to go back so soon.'

Robert took charge. 'Let's leave Marion to her packing. This is a very difficult time for her. Come downstairs with me.'

With space to herself, Marion collected herself and continued to pack, making a mental list of everything she had to do and would need to do once back in London. She also had to tell someone else that she was leaving today.

George.

George had spent Christmas day with them. Maggie's determination to matchmake was ironclad.

Marion had been dreading it.

At midday on Christmas day, George's car had driven onto the frosty drive, the boot laden with presents.

Maggie had made all sorts of fuss, welcoming him as if he were already a son-in-law.

'Marion, pour our guest a sherry. George, settle yourself on the sofa with Marion. Robert, I need your help in the kitchen.'

Excruciating.

Sitting next to each other, as decreed, George had admired the decorated tree in the corner and the cooking smells from the kitchen.

Marion was impelled to continue a conversation.

'Are you still helping your friend with the motor sales?'

'I am indeed. We met during the war. In France. Gordon Highlanders. The kind of friendship that is forged in battle. Brothers-in-arms, if you like.'

'Where were you in France?'

'Anywhere they needed us. We saw a lot of action. Lost good friends. Dreadful time.' He drained his sherry.

'And that's where you were given the rank of major?'

She saw embarrassment and modesty in his eyes before she asked, 'Would you like another?'

'No. No.' He smiled at her and she saw how his eyes crinkled at the edges. 'I want to appreciate your mother's lunch. So kind of her. It's a long time since I had a Christmas lunch with friends. Or indeed family.' He rubbed his moustache. 'Sorry. You don't want to hear my woes.'

Marion found that she actually did want to hear more, but as if on cue, her parents appeared.

'Marion.' Her mother smiled at her. 'Would you help me for a moment? And Robert, would you take George into the dining room? Luncheon is ready.'

'Well?' In the kitchen, Maggie whispered conspiratorially, 'How have you two been getting on?'

Marion refused to be drawn. 'Shall I take the dish of potatoes in?'

'Marion!' Maggie would not be shaken as she caught Marion's elbow. 'George is so nice, isn't he?'

Marion managed a brief smile, picked up the bowl of roast potatoes, and whispered, 'Mother, he's too old for me.'

George had brought with him a box of six crackers, and although his other gifts were stowed under the tree – not to be opened until teatime, a custom ordered by her mother years before – she did relent where the crackers were concerned and had laid one on each place setting, with the remaining two in the centre of the table.

'George!' She twinkled as she said, 'You are spoiling us.'

Robert picked his up and shook it. 'I didn't think you liked crackers, old girl.'

'She doesn't,' Marion added.

'It's not that I don't like them.' Her mother rubbed her hands nervously. 'It's just that the bang can be a bit unnerving.'

'Well, I tell you what' – George smiled at Marion sitting opposite him – 'you cover your ears, Maggie, while Marion and I pull the first one.'

He offered up the cracker to a hesitant Marion.

'Come on,' he said, waggling it in front of her. 'A cracker for a cracker.'

'Oh dear.' Maggie put her hands over her ears and squeezed her eyes shut.

Marion held the cracker and pulled hard. It snapped, leaving George with the winning end.

Marion tapped her mother's arm. 'It's done. George has won.'

George found the party hat inside the cracker and placed it on Maggie's head.

'I now pronounce you: Queen Maggie.'

'Oh!' Maggie giggled. 'You are a card. A real tonic.' She turned to Marion. 'Tell George about the Duchess's diamond tiara.'

George raised his eyebrows. 'What Duchess is this, then? I am intrigued. Do tell?'

Marion, mortified, remained silent.

'She's probably not allowed to tell you.' Maggie giggled again. 'But I can.'

'Maggie, no,' Robert said quietly.

'Why not? I'm proud of my daughter, even if you're not.'

Marion looked down at her clenched hands. Robert gave his wife a warning stare. Maggie ignored him.

'Marion is governess to Princess Elizabeth and Princess Margaret.'

'And who are they?' George asked, as if he had no idea.

'The King's granddaughters, of course. She works for the Duke and Duchess of York!'

George's mouth dropped open. 'You're having me on.'

'No, no. It's the truth. Tell him, Marion.'

Marion shifted slightly then said, 'It's true.'

'My word.' George sat back in his chair, then sat forward, saying earnestly, 'I would never have pressed you if I had known. Well, you have surprised me, in a good way.'

Robert pushed his chair back. 'I think we need another drink.' He stood and went to the drinks trolley. 'Whisky, George?'

George smiled. 'It *is* Christmas.'

Robert brought over two whiskies and two sherries for his wife and stepdaughter. 'A toast, I think. To Christmas.'

'To Christmas . . . and the King,' George said.

All four glasses were raised. 'To Christmas and the King.'

The atmosphere had shifted into something rather uncomfortable.

Robert made the first move. 'Right, then.' He rubbed his hands together. 'How about we open some presents?' He headed to the tree. 'And yes, Maggie, I know it's not teatime but today it's my rules.'

George's presents were thoughtful and generous. A bottle of five-year-old malt for Robert, a box of violet creams for Maggie and a pair of Fair Isle gloves for Marion.

'Oh, George, these are just what I wanted. I was only telling Mother the other day when we were shopping—' She stopped, seeing the conspiratorial wink between George and her mother. 'Have you two been talking?'

'A wee bird may have dropped a hint, aye.' George grinned.

Marion was touched. 'And you remembered? That's so kind, thank you.' She suddenly wanted to kiss him, to feel the warmth of his skin.

She looked away, and the moment passed.

Maggie, the effects of the sherry now evident, had opened her chocolates and was offering them around gleefully. 'George, you really shouldn't have. We don't have anything to give you.'

He looked around at all of them, resting his eyes on Marion. 'Your hospitality and company are the only gift I need. Since my parents have been gone . . . Well, let's just say Christmas has not been my favourite time of year.' His words, spoken in a soft voice, touched Marion. His eyes were still searching hers. 'Until now.'

As she searched for some words of comfort, Maggie's giggly cackle stopped her. 'You will come again, won't you, George? Marion is here for the whole of January, aren't you, Marion?'

'Mother, please. I am sure George will be busy. He won't want me foisted on him.'

George smiled broadly. 'There is nothing I would like more. Come to think of it, I have been offered tickets for a Hogmanay dinner dance; we could see the New Year in together, if you have no other plans?'

'Oh, she never has social plans, do you, Marion?' Maggie squawked.

Marion blushed with anger. 'Please, Mother.'

George got up. 'I'm sorry, I shouldn't have asked.' He checked his watch. 'I've overstayed my welcome. High time I should be going. Snow is forecast and my little motor might struggle a bit. Thank you all for a splendid day.'

In the hall, Maggie took his coat from the bannister and helped him in to it. 'Such a beautiful coat.' She stood back and admired it. 'Robert, this is exactly the sort of coat I have always wanted you to have. It reeks of quality and will last for years.'

George laughed. 'This old thing? It's done me for the last ten years and will do another ten for sure.' He took Maggie's hand and shook it. 'I really have had a wonderful time.'

Robert opened the front door and a wintry gust blew in a cupful of snowflakes.

Maggie gave Marion her coat from the hallstand. 'Go and see dear George off while your dad and I clear the kitchen.'

Marion's cheeks were burning. 'Mother!'

'Off you go.' Maggie pushed them both out onto the doorstep and shut the door behind them.

Out in the light snow, shame made Marion shiver. 'I am so sorry about my mother. It's the sherry. She's not used to it.'

'Och, she's a lovely woman, but you don't have to stay out here. Go on in, it's cold.'

Marion shivered again and pulled her coat over her shoulders. 'I should be wearing the lovely gloves you gave me.'

'I'm glad you like them. Well, goodnight.' He took the few steps to his car. 'This snow is settling.' He reached out and brushed a frosty layer from the car's windscreen. 'Another reason for me to remember such a special day.' He brushed his hands against his coat and opened the car door. 'Well, goodbye then.'

'George?'

'Yes, Marion?'

'It's not that I *can't* tell people about my job. It's just that . . .'

'Are you asking me to be discreet?'

'Would you do that?'

'Of course. I completely understand.'

'Thank you.'

George pulled his coat collar to his ears. 'I admire your loyalty.'

'Thank you again for my gloves.'

'My pleasure. And, look . . . if you do find yourself free on New Year's Eve . . .'

'I—' she began, but he stopped her.

'Think about it. I'll ring you up.' He looked at her and smiled, his eyes warm, his deep voice gentle. 'It would be my honour to escort you.'

She watched as he climbed into his car, his headlamps lighting the snowflakes as he drove away.

And in that moment, she knew she trusted him. He had bought her a thoughtful but not overly expensive gift. He seemed to like her but was gentle in his invitation. She knew he wouldn't tell anyone about her work, and there was just something about him that made her feel secure. She hoped he would ring.

Two days later he did. Her parents were out so there was no one to overhear their conversation. She had made her mind up to spend New Year's Eve with him, so when she picked up the receiver on the hall table and tugged it so that she could sit on the stairs and watch herself in the small hall mirror, she felt no nervousness.

'Hello, Marion Crawford speaking.'

'Hello, Marion?'

'Hello, George.'

'How are you?'

'Very well, thank you. And you?'

'Good, thanks. Erm, I was telephoning about New Year's Eve . . .'

'Yes?' She cradled the phone a little closer, his voice purring in her ear.

'Well, if you are not doing anything else, it would be my honour to take you out.'

'I would love to.'

She heard him draw breath, then his laugh of relief. 'Wonderful. I can pick you up at about six thirty?'

'That will be fine. Where are we going?'

'The Glen Mule. They are having a Hogmanay dinner dance. Can you dance the eightsome reel?'

'Of course. First dance my mother taught me.'

'I'll have to brush up then. By the way, I had better warn you, apart from two left feet, I'll be in my kilt.'

'Oh goodness, you will outshine me. I only have one long dress and I haven't worn it since goodness knows when.'

'Surely you are out at parties in London all the time?' She heard the teasing in his voice.

'Oh aye, me and the Prince of Wales are always out on the town.'

'Remind me to punch him on the nose the next time I see him.'

Marion laughed out loud. 'I'd lose my job!'

'Well then, I'll just stick my foot out and trip him up.'

She heard the engine of her father's car coming on to the drive.

'I can hear my parents coming back. I'd best go.'

'Six thirty. Don't forget.'

She hung up, then checked herself in the hall mirror, worried that her mother would spot a change in her face. Apart from two little bright spots on her cheeks, she looked the same.

She opened the front door for her parents and found Maggie gripping her coat with gloved hands. 'I hope you have lit the fire? Your dad and I are frozen.'

'Welcome back, Mother. How were the shops?'

'Busy. I would kill for a cup of tea.'

'You come in and sit down. The fire is lit and I'll make the tea.'

Maggie stopped shrugging out of her coat and eyed Marion suspiciously. 'What has happened to you?'

'Nothing. Let me hang your coat up.'

Maggie stopped her. 'Not before you tell me what's going on.'

'Mother, nothing is going on. Now go and sit down.'

'You have had a telephone call.' Maggie moved the telephone back to its rightful spot. 'I can tell. Who was it?'

Why did her mother have to know everything? 'If you must know, it was George. He is taking me out on New Year's Eve.'

Marion sighed now as she put the last of her clothes in the case, and sat on the edge of her bed. New Year's Eve with George had been lovely. He had behaved so kindly towards her. He had looked so safe and handsome in his kilt and had complimented her on the new dress her mother had made her . . .

As soon as Maggie knew George was taking Marion to the New Year's Eve Ball, she developed a spring in her step.

'Marion, we are going shopping.'

The haberdashers in Dunfermline was a quintessentially female shop. The scent of ladies' face powder and eau de cologne hung in the air. Three changing rooms were each hung with peach satin curtains and furnished with a large mirror and a petite armchair.

Mrs McGiver, small and plump like a tubby puppy, Marion always thought, welcomed them.

'Mrs Crawford. Do come in. And Marion, too. Home for Christmas?' She dropped her voice. 'The Duchess's dresses are divine. Where *does* she get the silk from?'

Marion didn't have to ask Mrs McGiver how she knew who she worked for. One look at her mother's guilty face told her. 'I am not privy to that sort of information, I'm afraid.'

'France or China, I would say. I have a few special silks in stock, myself.'

Maggie jumped straight in. 'Marion has a date. She's going to a Hogmanay Ball.'

Mrs McGiver's eyes lit up. 'And who is the lucky man?"

'Mother!' Marion's hushed warning fell on deaf ears.

'A major. So charming and you can see how fond he is of our lassie.'

Marion gave up any attempt to protest as her mother and Mrs McGiver discussed her.

'She would look lovely in dusty pink, with her dark hair and pale complexion.' Mrs McGiver was squinting at her. 'Or maybe scarlet?'

'I was thinking more of an opaque sea-green, to match her eyes?' Maggie proffered.

Mrs McGiver clapped her hands. 'You are right. I have a beautiful eau-de-nil satin. Come and see.'

While the two women stroked and critiqued several bolts of greenish fabric, Marion was sent to look through the pattern books.

'Nothing too revealing, Marion.' Maggie giggled. 'We don't want to show off all your assets too early, do we?'

Marion went pink, and turned to the section of patterns for evening dresses. There were so many different styles to choose. She picked a couple that looked very like the Duchess's style – frilly with long buttoned sleeves and a modest sweetheart neckline. She marked the pages with a ribbon. She flicked on, satisfied she had found something appropriate, until she came across an illustration of a slender woman, one long leg in front of the other. The dress clung to a small bust, jutting hipbones and ended at the ankle with a small train behind. The neckline ran in a sharp line across the throat, shoulder to shoulder, and the sleeves were puffed slightly at the top, then tight to the wrist. The reverse was pictured too. A swooping, chiffon cowl, exposing pale shoulder blades.

Much less Duchess, much more Mrs Simpson. Marion felt sinful just looking at it.

'Isn't that the thing?' Mrs McGiver was behind her. 'Mrs Crawford, your daughter has chosen exactly what I would have picked for her.'

Maggie was enraptured. 'Oh, Marion. For once your height and flat chest won't work against you! Simple and sophisticated. You will catch George yet.'

Those words 'catch George' got Marion wondering. Could she give up the Princesses, her work, her life, to marry a man like George? Could she stay as governess to the Princesses and still be a wife? If she let herself fall in love with George, what would happen? Was it possible to both be a wife and to keep working?

Three and a half yards of eau-de-nil crepe de chine were purchased, with a yard of wispy chiffon in the same colour for the cowl back, and many afternoons between Christmas and New Year were spent in the spare bedroom where Maggie set up her sewing table and machine.

'Fine feathers make fine birds,' she told Marion more than once. 'And don't move an inch while I pin this hem.'

When it was finished, she gave Robert the first viewing in the sitting room.

'What do you think, Dad?'

A big grin lit up his face. 'Beautiful. You look like a film star.'

'Thank you, Dad.'

Maggie came bustling down from upstairs, holding a large tissue-wrapped parcel.

'I was thinking you might be cold, and you don't want to wear your old coat over your new dress.'

She handed the parcel to Marion, who unwrapped it. 'Oh Mother! Your stole?'

'Real rabbit,' Maggie said.

Marion hugged her mother with true affection. 'Thank you. Thank you for the dress, and all your hard work and now your stole. I feel like Cinderella.'

'That's good.' Her mother squeezed her. 'Only you *are* quite a lot older than Cinderella was.'

*

When George arrived on the big night, he looked her up and down in admiration. 'If you don't mind my saying, you are a wee bobby-dazzler, Marion.' He produced a small box from behind his back. 'I hope you like this?'

It was a corsage of two white roses to wear around her wrist.

Maggie jogged out of the kitchen to the front door. 'George! You are wearing the kilt! I could never resist a man in a kilt.' She shouted over her shoulder, 'Robert, come and see what a gorgeous couple Marion and George make.'

When Robert appeared, he raised an eyebrow to George. 'Forgive her, Maggie's never seen a man in a kilt before.'

Maggie elbowed him hard in the ribs. 'Of course I have! But you haven't taken me anywhere I *can* see one for as long as I remember, that's all. Now, Marion, let me put your corsage on for you.'

Both parents stood on the doorstep as they watched George help Marion, wrapped in her mother's rabbit stole, into his little car, then waved until it was out of sight.

George drove the car skilfully, and Marion relaxed into the leather seat, allowing herself to feel a pleasure she was unused to. She glanced at George surreptitiously.

She hadn't noticed how strong his profile was until now. A good jaw, straight nose, bushy eyebrows. His hairline was receding a little which, she thought, was not a fault, more of a sign of maturity and reliability. And his moustache was rather dashing.

She had noticed that he was quite a bit shorter than her as he had walked her to the car, but then, she was very tall for a woman. Perhaps she shouldn't have worn heels after all.

He said very little as he drove, which she was thankful for, but as they arrived at the Glen Mule, he looked over to her, smiled, and took her hand. 'Forgive me, I am rather nervous. It's a long time since I have taken a lassie to dinner.'

It was a wonderful evening. The food and wine swept the cobwebs from serious, learned Marion, the Marion who could be shy and too sharp. That night she laughed at all George's jokes and stories and made him laugh with tales of her childhood.

'And do the Duke and Duchess know this about you?' he asked gently.

'Certainly not.'

'Do you have to be very stiff and proper around them?'

'Maybe at first, but I think they like me to be me. They enjoy having someone normal around them.'

'I'm sure they do. I would like to have you around more, too.'

Marion didn't know how to answer that. So she took a sip of her wine and changed the subject.

'Robert has been so good to us,' she said. 'My own father, John, died when I was three. I have a foggy memory of him – a feeling more than a memory, I suppose. Mother took it very badly and had what I think we would call now a nervous breakdown. Robert stepped in and has put up with us ever since.'

George lifted his glass of wine and took her hand across the table. 'A toast to your father John and to your stepfather Robert Crawford.'

'My two fathers.' They clinked glasses and drank.

The band struck up and George grinned at her. 'Come on, let's dance.'

They danced all the way to midnight and as the countdown began, balloons, party hats and streamers were released from a net hanging high above the dance floor.

'Happy New Year, Marion.' George caught a bundle of streamers which he hung around his neck, and a sparkly, crepe party hat, with a feather, which he placed with humorous courtesy on her head. 'I haven't had this much fun in a very long time.'

He returned Marion to her home at 1.15 a.m., insisting on walking her to the door. For a brief, anxious moment, she wondered if he was going to kiss her. It would be her first ever kiss and she was not sure what the protocol was.

She glanced anxiously up at her parents' bedroom window, which was open – she could imagine her mother's ears straining to hear what was going on.

'Goodnight, Marion,' he said simply, then took her hand and kissed it as he had done the first time they had met. She closed her eyes and hoped that he would kiss her cheek but he didn't. 'Thank you for a wonderful evening, Marion.'

'Goodnight, George. I had a wonderful evening too.'

He smiled. 'By the way, do you like winter walks?'

She laughed. 'Yes, I do.'

'Good. I'll ring you up.'

In the nineteen days since then, he had taken her on long frosty walks four times, and come for tea twice. Two days ago he had taken her to his place of work.

'Welcome to HQ,' he said, opening the main door to the motorcar showroom. And may I introduce you to the owner and my friend, Mr Christopher Bailey.'

A plump, red-haired man hurriedly took his feet from the desk where they were resting. He jumped up, his hand held out in welcome.

'Miss Crawford, I presume.'

'Good afternoon, Mr Bailey.' She took his small and damp hand. 'I have heard a lot about you.'

'Likewise.'

George grinned. 'Do not believe a word this blackguard tells you.'

Marion felt an unaccustomed shyness in this obviously male environment. She didn't know one end of a car from another, so when George asked, 'Shall I show you around?' she agreed with over-enthusiasm.

'That would be wonderful.'

Mr Bailey rubbed his hands together as his eyes travelled the length of her. She swallowed hard and turned her eyes to the showroom windows and the outside beyond. Supposing one of her parents' friends saw her here, alone with two men – what would they think?

'Marion?' asked George, angling his arm towards the biggest car there. 'Can I interest you in the elegant and noble Nine Monaco Riley in oxblood? Four doors and a top that folds back for those leisure breaks in the South of France?' He opened the driver's door. 'Hop in and get a feel for the old girl.'

'George, I don't drive.'

'Then this is your chance to get behind the wheel.'

She shook her head. 'You're not expecting me to try and drive it now, are you?'

Mr Bailey playfully scolded George. 'Don't tease her, old boy.' He shook his head and tutted, before turning back to Marion. 'Maybe the Riley is a bit too much to start with – how about I show you a smaller vehicle. Perfect for a woman?'

Marion saw Mr Bailey smirk at George. She had an awkward feeling that they were both laughing at her and wanted suddenly to leave.

She checked her watch. 'Oh dear, look at the time. I must be getting back. I'm so pleased to have met you, Mr Bailey.'

'Christopher, please.' He held his horrible hand out to her once more and she shook it quickly. 'George and I go back a long way.' He hesitated. 'I was hoping we could talk a little more, get to know each other a bit better, over a tray of tea?'

Marion declined quickly. She didn't like Mr Bailey. His pale piggy eyes below his bright red hair were too close and his mobile lips, when he licked them, made her uncomfortable. 'No, really. I'm so sorry to have to go. George, would you mind?'

She checked to make sure George didn't signal a raised eyebrow or a wink to Mr Bailey, but instead he appeared to understand her need to leave. 'Of course, my dear. Goodbye, Christopher.'

Marion was unsettled on the journey home. She was certain that Mr Bailey was not a friend of George's she'd like to meet again.

George was completely unaware and was whistling a cheery tune as he drove.

He glanced over to Marion, who was trying not to look or sound as brittle as she felt. 'What did you think of old Bailey then?'

She crossed her hands on her lap. 'Oh, you know . . .' she said with a vague smile.

'He's been a very good friend to me.'

'That's good.'

'He helped me through some very difficult times. I haven't told you this before but I was . . .' He took his right hand off the wheel and rubbed it over his face. 'I was married before.'

'Oh.' Marion was completely taken aback. In all her innocent, yet frequent imaginings of him, this was a scenario she had not thought of. Why hadn't she? He was an older man who must have had a past, but she had felt that he and she were the same. Uncomplicated. Unblemished by the dirtier side of life.

It seemed she was wrong.

'Have I shocked you?' He turned briefly to look at her before returning his eyes to the road.

'Not at all.' She raised her eyebrows with a quick smile. 'So you were . . . married before?'

'I should have listened to Bailey. He saw that she was wrong for me straight away. But I was foolish and the war had just ended. My parents were not the affectionate kind, and Ena – well, she was a ray of sunshine after the trenches. We were happy for a couple of years but I began to realize that she was a sick woman.'

'Oh dear,' Marion said, desperate to know more about this woman who had, out of the blue, cast a shadow over any future she might have with George. If she had a future . . . She felt angry, cheated and possibly jealous.

'Not physically ill – it was in her mind. Made her very diffi-cult to live with. And jealous. I couldn't go anywhere or see anybody without her throwing things at me when I got home. She accused me of all sorts. Women, drink, the lot. Then one day, I came home to find she'd put all my clothes outside the front door and locked me out. I went round the back, looked through the kitchen window and . . .' His voice began to waver and he coughed to clear it.

Marion remained silent and alert.

'She, er . . . she was lying on the floor with her head in the gas oven.'

Marion held her hand to her mouth. 'My God, how terrible.'

'I saved her, thankfully, but the doctors took her to hospital and after six months or so, they advised that she should stay there, for her own safety. And that I should divorce her, forget about her and find some happiness before I was too old.'

Marion was stunned. 'How dreadful.'

'I expect you think I was a coward.' He looked over at her. She had opened the small side window and the wind was pulling her hair.

'I think that must have taken a lot of courage,' she said.

'I shouldn't have just blurted that out but sometimes . . . it was just so awful and Bailey pulled me through it all. There was a time when I . . . I thought my life wasn't worth living. He saved me.'

'Oh, George.' Without thinking, she placed her hand on his leg. 'Your poor man.'

He took his left hand from the steering wheel and put it on top of hers, holding it tight.

'I'm sorry.'

Without hesitation she responded, 'Nothing to be sorry for.'

'Thank you. You are a wonderful girl, Marion.'

'George, let's stop for a drink before you take me home. I can't say goodbye to you without making sure you are all right.'

He turned his troubled face to her. 'I'd like that.'

They pulled in to the small car park of the Golden Fleece – a public house her dad didn't go to, so there was no fear of bumping into him.

George helped her out of the car and took her hand. Together they walked inside. Marion knew something between them had shifted with his revelation. To share his tragic story with her meant he trusted her. And to hold his hand and walk into this place for all to see made her feel a little giddy.

He settled her into a cosy table by the fire and she watched him as he walked to the bar and ordered. Although not a tall man, he walked with confidence and ease. As he chatted to the barman, he turned to look at her and smiled. Was this what it felt like to fall in love?

George brought their drinks over and sat close to her on the small banquette. 'To us.' He raised his glass.

'To us.' She was shocked by George's story and angry that his wife could have put so much strain on her marriage. She hadn't been well, so that wasn't her fault, but nonetheless, how could anyone be so awful to dear George? Fresh from the war and with uncaring parents.

He took her free hand again. 'I really am so sorry for pouring my woes out to you.'

'We are friends, aren't we?'

'I would like to hope we are.' He took another mouthful of his whisky. 'What must you think of me? Forty-three years old, divorced and with no family. I'm not much of a catch, am I?'

Marion looked into his eyes, then rested her forehead on his shoulder. Yes, she knew she was falling in love.

Chapter Sixteen

145 Piccadilly, 22nd January 1936

'Crawfie!' The little Princesses had been put to bed, but as soon as she opened their door they leapt out and ran to her.

'What are you two little monkeys awake for?' she whispered. 'Alah and Bobo are next door – they'll be cross with me for waking you up.'

'Then why did you?' asked Lilibet staunchly.

Marion put her arms round both girls, relieved to see them. 'I have missed you scallywags.'

'And we have missed you!' said Margaret, gripping Marion's legs tightly.

'Let's sit down before we all fall into a heap, shall we?'

She had arrived at 145 less than ten minutes ago and Ainslie had handed her a note from the Duchess. It read: *Don't let all this depress Lilibet and Margaret more than is necessary, Crawfie. They are so young.*

She sat in the armchair by the dying fire and held the hands of both sisters. 'How are you?' she asked gently.

Lilibet leant against the arm of Crawfie's chair, looking forlorn. 'We are all very sad.'

'Of course you are.'

Crawfie hitched Margaret onto her lap. 'And are you sad too?'

'Horribly,' Margaret said dramatically, before leaning on Crawfie's shoulder and doing her best to sob.

Lilibet put a comforting hand to her sister's back. 'Oh, Crawfie. I am worried for Granny. What will she do without Grandpa?'

'We can never play again!' Margaret wailed.

'Oh, hush the pair of you. Your grandfather loved you and the last thing he would want is for you or Granny or anyone else to be unhappy. Now, you two are tired and upset and you need some sleep. Tomorrow you will feel a lot better. Into bed, please.'

Marion tucked them up again and, saying goodbye, closed the door softly. She went to the nursery sitting room where she was sure she would find Alah and Bobo.

'I'm back,' she whispered, putting her head around the door.

Bobo immediately began weeping, but Alah, although she was pale with dark circles under her eyes, kept her upper lip stiff. 'Crawfie?'

'Yes. I came as soon as I could. How are you both holding up?'

Alah's face crumpled. 'We are fine. It's the girls . . .'

Marion stepped closer to the low flickering of the fire. 'Bobo, would you make a tray of tea, please?'

Marion felt a bit mean asking the poor girl to make tea, but she wanted to speak to Alah without the distraction of Bobo's sobs.

'I have just looked in on the Princesses,' she said, when Bobo was gone. 'They are worried for the Queen.'

Alah wiped her nose and sighed. 'We all are. What will we do without her and the King?' Tears ran again.

Marion, with more hope than belief, said, 'The Prince of Wales has been trained from birth to pick up the reins seamlessly. He'll be a wonderful King.'

Alah shook her head. 'But he doesn't have a queen. What will he do as an unmarried king? No children, no loving arms to come home to. The only child of the old King unmarried, and the very one that needs to be.'

'I am sure our Duke and Duchess, and the Princesses, will do all they can to help him,' Marion said. 'They will be wonderful.'

The damp hanky twisted in Alah's hands. 'The Duchess called us to her room this morning. She is still very weak from the flu, not well enough to leave her bed yet. The girls knew nothing of the King's death and the Duchess wanted to tell them herself. Dear little things thought they were going to get another chapter of *Right Ho, Jeeves*.'

Bobo returned, bumping the door with the heavy tea tray. Marion gestured to her. 'Just pop it all on the table here. Alah is telling me about this morning.'

Bobo's little face fell glum again. 'I still can't believe it.'

Marion gave her a small smile. 'Pour the tea, and let's listen to Alah a moment.'

Alah sighed again. 'The Duchess, so pale but still so pretty, had Dookie on the bed with her and the girls dived on to him, laughing and making the damn thing bark. But after the Duchess explained about the dear King . . .' A tear ran down the older woman's face. 'And Lilibet, not even ten, immediately comforted her mother. You know how she is. So stoic and so . . . grown up. She asked how the Duke and Queen Mary were and then said "*Poor* Uncle David. Has he got to be King?"' Alah's tears flowed freely. Her body collapsed in on itself.

Marion could picture the heartbreaking scene, and swallowed the lump in her throat. 'I think you can pour the tea now, Bobo.'

Sandringham, 22nd January 1936

The day had been long and heavy with grief. Tommy was grateful that he had not had to deal with the undertakers who prepared the King's body for the first stage of his return to London. Instead, he had the job of relaying messages across the Commonwealth.

No matter how much preparation was put into a state funeral, the rehearsals for the procession of horses, carriages and servicemen, there were always crowned heads and presidents, admirals and generals who needed to have the schedule in order to organize their own. There were telephone calls between number ten, the palace and Sandringham that needed to be joined and minuted.

And here was the emotional wreck that was the new King, Edward VIII. He drank and smoked and cried and the Queen comforted him as best she could, but her own heart was broken.

More than once the King had begged Tommy to arrange for Mrs Simpson to join him, so much so that he passed the receiver over to Tommy while Mrs Simpson was on the line.

'Please let her come. I need her,' wept the King.

Tommy took the receiver calmly. 'Mrs Simpson? Tommy Lascelles here.'

'Tommy,' she said, using her saddest American drawl, 'I am really worried about David. He is so upset and wants me by his side, but I just can't come. It would be too difficult for the Queen and everyone. Can you please help him to understand? I am waiting in London and will be here when he returns.'

Tommy controlled his relief at this turn of events. 'Of course, Mrs Simpson. I understand, and so will the King.'

The King was not pleased and drank steadily until his father's body was taken to the small church where the family worshipped.

Then at last, and totally drained, Tommy wrote to Joan.

Joan my darling,

It is very late, but I will not be able to sleep without getting the events of the day down on paper. Forgive me for unburdening myself to you.

Tonight the King lies peacefully in the little church, St Mary Magdalene, at the edge of the garden. We left the house, with the Queen and the family, no more than a dozen of us, following the small, wheeled bier which was flanked by a few towering Grenadiers and led by the King's piper playing a lament. It was dark and rainy with gusts of icy wind tearing through us. Turning a corner, we saw the lychgate of the church, lit brilliantly, with the rector, Fuller, waiting for us.

The guardsmen carried the coffin from the bier and let it rest in front of the altar for a brief but desperately moving service. The Queen said nothing, but what must have been going through her mind? I only hope she will remember this dignified, private moment, when the clamour of the state funeral dins her ears.

The Prince of Wales, paler than I have ever seen him, even after a day of drinking, stood forlorn by her side. I suppose I shall be thrown back into service with him. Junior members of the household cannot walk out on a new king simply because they disapproved of him as Prince of Wales.

The old King is now to be watched for a vigil of thirty-six hours by the men of the Sandringham estate: gamekeepers, gardeners, faithful retainers, all guarding their beloved squire.

Tomorrow we will accompany him to London by train, and all the inevitability of a state funeral will follow.

When we got back to the house tonight, I am not ashamed to say that the Duke of York and I shared a couple of glasses of whisky. What a decent man he is.

Yours,

Tommy

145 Piccadilly, 22nd January 1936

Marion watched as Alah fumbled for a handkerchief and wiped her eyes then the corners of her lips. Then she held the square of cotton over her mouth, stifling her grief.

A flood of compassion for the older woman flowed through Marion. 'Do we know any of the plans for the . . . arrangements . . . for the King yet?'

'Not yet, but Lilibet will go to the lying in state at Westminster Hall. It is her duty.'

Marion felt her heart sink. 'That poor little girl. Perhaps I could chaperone her?'

Alah was quick to reply, 'The Duchess has already asked me to accompany the Princess Elizabeth.'

'But I should so like to pay my respects to the King. He was a great support to me.'

Alah set her lips firm. 'I am the one who has known Lilibet from birth, therefore I am the person the Duchess wants.'

Marion was tired after her long journey, exhausted by her mother's interferences, anxious that she had been unable to get hold of George to tell him where she was – and now Alah was pulling rank on her, as she had been doing recently. Marion had had enough. Anger murdered her compassion.

'Alah, you and I are not in competition with each other. For goodness' sake, do we always have to bicker?'

'Bicker? I accommodated you when you first arrived, showed you the ropes when you knew nothing – but you forget all that now. You have got a bit big for your boots, young woman. Yes, I see you watching the Duchess, copying her manner and style as best you can, thinking you're best friends with the family. Well, you're not. You and I are paid servants. We are needed and useful, but we are not their friends. You would do well to remember that.'

Marion felt the sting of Alah's words.

'I am sorry you feel that way.' She stood up, towering over her colleague and her pettiness. 'I shall ask the Duchess myself. I am sure she would be grateful to have both of us accompany Lilibet.'

Chapter Seventeen

Buckingham Palace, 23rd January 1936

Tommy was on the phone to the Duchess of York, who was calling from her sickbed. 'I shall deal with that immediately, ma'am.'

'Tommy, dear, thank you. I know you have a lot to deal with over the ensuing week, but one of your quiet words would help me enormously. I don't want to worry the Duke just now.'

'Understood, ma'am.'

Tommy replaced the receiver in its cradle and cupped his tired mind in his hands. 'Dear God.' He sighed, then buzzed P-T, his secretary.

'Yes, sir?'

'Would you ask Miss Clara Knight and Miss Crawford to pop over from 145 and come to my office please?'

'Yes, sir.'

'And a tray of tea for three may be in order.'

'Of course, sir.'

Thank God he had P-T – calm, efficient, never wasted words. He got up and walked to his window, surveying the neat yellow gravel within the palace gates and the traffic on Constitution Hill beyond. The past forty-eight hours had been a non-stop melee of meetings, orders and arrangements. He would give anything to take a walk up to Wellington Arch, along Piccadilly and into the civilized realms of Fortnum's for a reviving lunch. Perhaps a fillet of Dover sole with slices of thin bread and butter, or an Omelette Arnold Bennett with a glass of chilled Pouilly-Fuissé? In the last few days since the King had died, meals had been scant and unpredictable.

His insides were feeling the lack.

He hoped P-T would show her usual foresight and bring some biscuits with the tea. In the interim he gave himself a swift pace around the room, then sat down to reread and absorb the complicated arrangements for the funeral.

P-T knocked and entered, bringing with her his two guests.

'Sir, Miss Marion Crawford and Miss Clara Knight. Tea is on its way.'

Tommy stood, smoothing the strips of hair either side of his balding head. 'Ladies, do take a seat.' He indicated the two chairs in front of his desk. 'Thank you for coming, and forgive me if I have interrupted your morning routine.'

The two women sat, looking equally composed – but, he noted, not at each other. This would clearly require all his diplomatic skills if no feathers were to be ruffled.

He plucked at the knees of his trousers and sat down.

'As you know, the King is now lying in state at Westminster Hall. Princess Elizabeth is expected to attend so that she may pay her respects to her beloved grandfather, and also to see and understand the royal protocol surrounding such occasions.'

Miss Knight bent her head in agreement, then glanced sharply at Miss Crawford. She looked ahead, listening intently. The elder woman spoke. 'The Duke and Duchess both agree that the Princess is old enough to attend. It is my duty and my pleasure to accompany the Princess.'

Tommy dipped his chin in agreement. 'Yes, quite so. A car will take you and the Princess Elizabeth this evening, when the crowds will be thinner. It will be a special memory for her – she will go during the twenty minutes when her father and uncles will be holding their own vigil at their father's coffin. The Duke of York,

King Edward VIII, the Duke of Kent and the Duke of Gloucester, will attend in full uniform and swords reversed, as is the custom.'

Miss Knight was triumphant. 'Thank you, sir.'

There was a tap at the door and P-T nudged it open with a hip. She bore the tea tray in her hands, and Tommy was cheered by the sight of bourbon biscuits.

P-T smiled. 'Here you are, sir. Tea, as ordered. Shall I pour?'

'Just leave it on the side table, please.'

When she'd gone, Tommy poured three cups and offered the women the bourbons. To his delight, they politely declined.

Miss Crawford managed a warmish smile for Miss Knight.

Tommy stirred his tea three times clockwise, as he always did, before saying, 'I hear, Miss Crawford, you would like to pay your respects to the King, yourself. Is that correct?'

She looked up. 'It is, sir, yes, and I was wondering if I could—'

He raised a hand to stop her. 'I am going myself today, after luncheon, and the Duchess has given permission for you to take the afternoon off to accompany me if you so wish? No point sending two cars when one will do, eh?'

Miss Crawford beamed as she accepted the invitation. 'Sir, I would be honoured.'

'Good. I am glad that is settled. Meet me here at two o'clock sharp.' He drained his teacup and walked to the door. 'Very nice to see you again, Miss Knight, and also to meet you, Miss Crawford.'

He saw them off with a charming smile. As they disappeared down the corridor, he shut the door and breathed a sigh of relief.

That, Tommy old boy, he said to himself, *is diplomacy in action.*

At 2.00 p.m. sharp, Crawfie returned to Buckingham Palace and was met by Tommy's secretary. 'Sir Alan will be with you in just a moment,' she said. 'Do take a seat.' She proffered a choice of three chairs in the corridor.

'Thank you.'

'He shouldn't be too long, Miss Crawford.'

'Forgive me, but I don't believe I know your name.'

'Oh golly, sorry. It's Jane Pepper-Thynne, but everyone calls me P-T. So much easier.'

'We all seem to have nicknames, don't we? Mine is Crawfie.'

P-T relaxed, leaning back against the wall. 'Oh *you're* Crawfie! How lovely to meet you. I hear you are working wonders in the schoolroom. And how are the terrifying Alah and dear Bobo?'

Crawfie smiled carefully; she didn't want to be reported as a gossip. 'Delightful.'

'Really? That's not what I have heard.' P-T laughed. 'Sir Alan shouldn't be too long now. You know even he has a nickname, don't you?'

'No.'

'Everyone calls him "Tommy" – but only when he gives them permission. For now, call him Sir Alan. Ah, here he is.' Tommy stepped out of his office carrying a heavy coat and his hat. 'Miss Crawford is here, sir.'

'Good.' He smiled at Marion. 'As you have a warm coat on, I think we shall walk to Westminster Hall. I could do with some fresh air.'

In silence she followed him from his office, down a short, red-carpeted flight of stairs, along the corridor, past the painting of Queen Victoria's coronation and out through the door that took them to the front of the palace. The cold was fierce, and Marion pulled her coat firmly around her.

Outside the gates, they pushed their way through the growing crowd of mourners. They were clustered in groups around the gates, looking up at the royal standard that hung limply against the January sky.

'I don't know what they hope to see,' murmured Tommy as he carved a path to the right. 'The Queen isn't going to come out for a chat, is she?'

Marion was surprised by his lack of heart, but thinking this might be another test of her loyalty, she said nothing.

'How is everyone at 145?' he asked, striding out so that she had to increase her pace to keep up with him.

'We are all pulling together. Of course we feel deep sorrow for the whole family.'

'And the Duchess? The Duke tells me she is beginning to feel a lot better after her nasty flu.'

'I believe so, sir.'

'And the girls?'

'Bearing up, sir.'

'Good.' As they crossed the road heading for Birdcage Walk, Tommy wondered why the old King had spoken so highly of the young woman by his side. He had said that she was intelligent, thoughtful and brought a breath of fresh air into the fusty old schoolroom – nothing like the expressionless, monosyllabic and rather dour Scottish woman now presenting herself.

He tried again. 'How long have you been with us now, Miss Crawford?'

'Four years, sir.'

'Ah, four years. Goodness.'

'Yes.'

He gave up further conversation, but was pleased to notice she could walk as fast as him and with little effort. That showed good Scottish stock of which he approved. She was tall; Tommy was over six foot himself but she wasn't much under that.

They carried on in silence down to Parliament Square and to the gates of Parliament itself.

A uniformed police officer held his hand up to stop them.

'Good afternoon, Sir Alan, madam.' He smiled, touching the brim of his police helmet. 'The lady is with you, sir?'

'Yes, I can vouch for her. She works in the household.'

'Very good, sir, madam.'

'Is it busy, constable?' Tommy asked.

'Yes sir, but fortunately the queue is a little shorter than it was this morning.'

'Ah yes, the after-luncheon pause.' He turned to Marion. 'Come along, Miss Crawford, while we can still visit in relative calm.'

Together they crossed New Palace Yard, heading right towards the imposing steps of the great Westminster Hall.

Marion was immediately aware of the darkness within. The lofty beamed roof soared above an enormous catafalque on which the King's coffin rested. A long and quiet queue was winding slowly past the departed monarch.

Tommy whispered something to another policeman who was keeping the queue orderly, and in moments he and Marion were escorted past the waiting people to the funerary casket itself.

The crowd made way for them, respecting the wing-collared, frock-coated Tommy and his companion.

Marion was overawed by the devotion of the mourners: men holding their hats to their chest, some with unstopped tears, the women pale and shocked by the incontrovertible truth that their King was gone. The echo of hushed voices and the overpowering scent of lilies, incense and melting candlewax clung to everything and everyone.

An involuntary gasp escaped as she fumbled for her handkerchief.

Tommy took her elbow gently, saying nothing, but lending support.

'I'm all right,' she whispered. 'Thank you.'

The line shuffled forwards. At the sight of the flower-covered bier, the splendour of the royal standard draped over the casket, and the glimmering jewels of the imperial crown resting on top, Marion was overwhelmed again.

'How will Lilibet manage this?' she whispered to Tommy.

Tommy's eyes were fixed on the crown above him. 'Because she must.'

At each corner of the coffin stood members of the household troops and the yeoman of the guard, maintaining a constant, motionless vigil.

Tommy and Crawfie walked slowly around the exhibited King. As they got to the last corner, Tommy made a smart, respectful neck bow inviting Crawfie to do the same.

'God save the King!' shouted a woman behind them, before being shushed.

And suddenly they were outside again, blinking in the brightness of an overcast sky.

Tommy turned up the collar of his coat. 'Right. I think a cup of tea is in order. Will Fortnum's do you?'

Marion was surprised by the invitation, but grateful. 'Thank you, yes.'

The twenty-minute walk to Fortnum & Mason Piccadilly was a quiet one. Tommy hummed to himself as he mulled over a choice between cucumber sandwiches or a cheese scone.

Marion could think of no conversation. She was still shaken by the power of witnessing a dead king lying in state for the world to see.

How would Lilibet react when she saw it all, the pomp and silence and sadness? And, more worrying, how would Alah cope? Lilibet's youthful resilience would carry her through. But Alah? Marion made up her mind to clear the air with her that evening. As irritating as the older woman could be, Marion had become fond of her over the last four years, and she knew Alah deserved her respect. Marion had thought over what she had said, and while not agreeing with all of it, she accepted that maybe she did want to be closer to the family than any other servant. And that was wrong.

In Fortnum & Mason, Tommy, with his air of complete superiority, swept Marion through to the tearoom. The room was light and airy, painted in a subtle duck-egg blue with highlights of petal pink and primrose yellow – the utter antithesis to the solemnity of Westminster Hall. Marion took in all the grandeur.

'Are you cold?' Tommy asked her, his eyes scouring the busy room for a table.

'I'm fine, thank you.'

'My wife, Joan, has made me perfect the art of finding a table without a draught. She feels the cold.' He attracted the attention of a waiter. 'Table for two.'

'Certainly, sir.' The waiter smiled and steered them towards a discreetly prominent table. 'You like this one, sir.'

Tommy nodded.

Several of the surrounding tables couldn't help but stare as the two of them walked past. Women dressed in fur stoles and hats peered round, and men, some like Tommy in wing collars, looked over. Tommy was quite obviously well-to-do – tall and handsome in the way privately schooled boys tended to develop. And his companion? Also tall, rather ungainly. No beauty. She was neatly dressed, which was acceptable, but she looked less than wealthy, which was not.

They settled at the table which overlooked Green Park to Marion's right and the room with its inquisitive tea drinkers to her left.

Tommy ordered without asking her opinion. 'Two teas, please, with cheese scones and butter.'

The waitress departed and Tommy spotted someone he knew across the room and waved. Marion looked over her shoulder to see who: an older woman with scarlet lipstick swiped above and beyond the outline of her lips (and with a lot of it tinting her teeth) was grinning at him and beckoning him over.

Tommy shook his head, tapping his watch and mouthing, 'No time. Sorry.'

The tea and scones arrived. After the waitress had left, Tommy bowed his head a little and bent towards Marion, whispering, 'Frightful woman. An American journalist, Mrs Beatrice Gould. To be avoided at all costs. How's your tea?'

'Very nice, thank you.'

'Wait until you taste the scones. Heavenly. Joan and I come here whenever we feel the need to be bucked up. She's in the country most of the time. West Sussex, place called Bepton. London is no place for the children.' He stopped buttering his scone and looked up at her. 'Unless you are a princess, eh?'

Marion had just taken a bite of scone and was unable to reply. Tommy carried on. 'How is it going in the schoolroom?'

She swallowed and took a sip of tea to help wash down the delicate crumbs. 'Very well, thank you.'

'Not too much interference from their mother?'

'She is very supportive,' Marion answered carefully. 'Why do you ask?'

Tommy wiped his neat moustache with his napkin. 'Don't worry, I'm not trying to catch you out. It's the Queen who tells me how frustrating the Duchess can be. No regard for your timetable, I suppose?'

'We have mornings in the schoolroom, then in the afternoon we play in the garden, or sometimes the Duchess takes them out.'

Tommy put his teacup down. 'I applaud your diplomacy, Miss Crawford. Many others would – and have – been gossiping with me by now.' He held his hand up to stop her protestations. 'I promise I have not brought you here to test your loyalty, but if I had, you would have passed the test.'

Marion didn't answer.

He pressed her. 'So, why did you come to work for the family?'

No one had really asked her this before, so her answer was unprepared. 'It was all rather odd really,' she said. 'I had a place waiting for me at Glasgow University to study child psychology. There is a lot to learn. The importance of a decent diet, good education and nurture cannot be underestimated in the development of the brain. We have many children living with little food, love or education in Scotland. Without those basics, their futures promise little.' Marion stopped, embarrassed suddenly by her own passion. 'Sorry.'

Tommy raised his eyebrows. 'Whatever for! Tell me more.'

'My own upbringing was happy, but hardly wealthy. I needed to earn some money to pay my university fees, so I took a summer job looking after the children of the Earl of Elgin, in Scotland.'

'Ah, the marbles' thieves.' Tommy smiled. 'Are the marbles actually in his house?'

'Yes. Some. In the hall actually.'

'Really? What a rascal. Continue.'

'I had no idea that the Elgins were related to the Duke and Duchess of York until they came over for tea with the little Princesses. I was not expecting to be introduced to them but they seemed so friendly and kind, and the girls so well behaved that they made me feel at ease and asked me all sorts of questions about my work. A few days later, I had a letter asking me to come to London.'

'And you went? You gave up your desire to be a child psychologist?'

'Not at all. I thought it would be for the summer only and that I would be back in Scotland for the start of the autumn term.'

'But you decided that you liked London and royal life.' His tone as he said this was dismissive, as though almost disappointed in her.

'Not at all.' She was maddened by his assumption. 'Once I was here and time was ticking on, I spoke to the Duchess about going back to Scotland, but she said not yet and *kept* saying not yet, and so, I stayed.'

Tommy leant back with a bark of laughter. 'Sounds as if you were snaffled. Typical behaviour of our glorious royals. No one can say no to them. But why on earth did you come to look after two of the most fortunate children in the world, when the sort of children you had originally planned to assist still need your help?'

Marion was shocked. 'I consider it an honour to work for them. The Princesses may not lack food, love or education, but they have other limitations. They have few friends, and there is no chance of a train ride to Brighton for the day to spend some money on the pier and paddle as ordinary children do. The kind of secluded childhood they have can do as much harm as any other. I see it as my duty to show them the world as the rest of us see it, and I thank God that they are not the daughters of a king so they will never have to face the rigours of life as a senior royal. They can fall in love, marry, have children and live a peaceful, private life. I see first-hand how hard the Duke, as the King's second son, and the Duchess, as his wife, work to fill the engagements that the Prince of Wales' – she stumbled, unused to the new name – 'I mean, King Edward, cannot do until he marries and has his own family.'

'My, my.' Tommy smiled wryly at her. 'Another fully paid-up royalist in the ranks.'

Marion frowned. 'But you must feel the same?'

'To be honest,' he said, lowering his voice, 'I don't altogether. I worked with the Prince of Wales as his assistant private secretary for several years. In the end I resigned, unable to continue mopping up after him. He took every ounce of privilege he could gather, and more. He is a drunk and a womanizer – in short, a man with no solid foundations. However, he is our King and I would rather die than see the Crown humiliated. My job is to make them look irreproachable, even when they're not.'

Marion couldn't believe this lack of respect.

He continued, amused, 'You look shocked, Miss Crawford, but everything I say is true. My advice to you, if you wish to stay in your job, is to continue to do it well, but do not sell them your soul. I have enormous respect for the institution of the monarchy, but remember, we are just staff. We are a kind of cannon fodder, used until we are no longer useful. Trust me.'

Marion picked up the napkin on her lap and folded it more times than was necessary. 'I have only recently been given this argument by another member of the household,' she said at last. 'I was appalled then and I am appalled now. I see the royal family as humans, people who have not chosen the life they have been given but must make the most of it under the most extreme pressure. We, who have a life of anonymity, must help to keep them abreast of the real world. We must show them kindness, loyalty, give them a chance to be normal in their abnormal life.'

Tommy looked at her carefully. 'I have upset you.'

'Surprised me, certainly. I had no idea that we would be so opposite in our thoughts. Thank you for taking me to Westminster Hall, and for this delightful tea, but now I really must be getting back.'

'Wait, I'll walk you to 145.'

She stood up. 'No need. Goodbye, Sir Alan.'

Tommy watched her walk purposefully out of the tearoom. She had spirit and he sensed an authenticity about her that was unusual in his experience. The family, he concluded, were lucky to have her.

Chapter Eighteen

145 Piccadilly, 23rd January 1936

Alah and Lilibet arrived home in sombre mood, their black clothes covered in rain and smelling of the dark winter evening. Bobo welcomed them in. She had been worrying over the lateness of the hour.

In the nursery, the curtains were drawn against the cold night. The fire glowed warm and the clock on the mantelpiece above stood at past nine o'clock. Lilibet yawned, shaking raindrops from her new black tam-o'-shanter, chosen specially for the occasion.

Bobo fussed around them. 'Let me take your coats. You're soaking wet.'

'My socks are wet,' Lilibet said, unbuckling her black shoes, 'and I would like to warm my feet up, please.'

Bobo took the shoes and caught Alah's coat, as the older woman dropped into her armchair by the fire.

'How did it go?' Bobo asked her, in a lowered voice.

Alah unpinned her hat and let it fall beside her. 'Ask Lilibet,' she said wearily.

Bobo collected Lilibet's coat and velvet tammy, then passed her a towel for her hair and warm slippers for her cold toes. 'So, my darling, what was it like at Westminster Hall?'

Lilibet sat down in the other armchair and wriggled into her slippers, while Bobo passed a crocheted blanket for her knees. 'There were heaps and heaps of beautiful flowers,' she said.

'So high I couldn't see where Grandpa was. And do you know, lots of people were there. They can come whenever they want, even at night. The policeman who took Alah and me in said that a million people will have visited Grandpa before he is buried. Isn't that lovely? I said a prayer for Grandpa and then I saw Papa, Uncle David, Uncle Harry and Uncle George, all in full dress uniform, standing guard around the King. Do you know, they never moved at all, not even an eyelid. And everyone was whispering and quiet as if the King was asleep.'

Staring into the flames of the fire, Alah agreed. 'Those poor boys. They did their father very proud tonight.'

'I smiled at Papa, but he didn't smile back. And then Big Ben chimed nine times and it was so noisy. The floor shook under us and made my ears hurt a bit.'

'Oh my.' Bobo could picture it all. 'And are you glad you went? It wasn't too frightening?'

'It was just very sad.' Lilibet looked into the fire. 'I wish I could have said goodbye to him properly, but we are not allowed to open his box.'

Alah stopped this line of conversation immediately. 'Now, young lady.' She pointed at Lilibet. 'It's way past your time for bed, so off you go, please. Bobo will take you.'

'Good night, Alah.' Lilibet yawned. 'Thank you for taking me. Bobo, may I have some warm milk?'

'As long as you don't wake your sister.'

'I won't, I promise.'

Crawfie was in her room just across the nursery landing when she heard Bobo taking Lilibet to bed. She stepped out of her room and went to check on Alah. She found her sobbing quietly in her chair by the fire.

'It's only me,' she said softly. 'Are you all right?'

'Oh Crawfie, dear . . . I'm glad to have seen it, but it was all so final. I kept thinking about him waving across the park at us from his office, about how much he loved Lilibet and how the Queen must be feeling so lonely.'

Crawfie took Alah's hands. 'I felt exactly the same way. But we went, and we said our goodbyes, and the world moves on. Let me make you some cocoa.'

'Thank you. That would be very nice.'

'And Alah, I am so sorry about last night. It was wrong of me to think I could take Lilibet today. And some of the things you said I have thought about, even though they hurt. We both want the best for the family, and that is all that matters.'

Alah looked up at her and smiled through her tears.

PART TWO

Chapter Nineteen

Crawfie was looking for Ainslie, butler to the Duke and Duchess of York. She found him in the neatness of the post-breakfast kitchen, reading *The Times*.

'Good morning, Ainslie.'

He closed the paper and folded it quickly. 'Morning, Miss Crawford. May I be of help?'

'The Princesses will have lunch in the nursery today, please, and I wonder if the post has arrived?'

'I shall let Cook know. The post has indeed arrived, but there is nothing for you today.'

A frown crossed Marion's face. She had written to George weekly since her return to London in the New Year and, at the start, he had replied at the same rate. He wrote lovely, fond letters, full of funny stories about the customers at the motorcar showroom, or how he and Christopher Bailey were happily banking the money that came from a sale. But over the last couple of months his letters had become less regular and certainly shorter. The last one had arrived almost three weeks ago. She did have a telephone number for him, but it was for the showroom and she was nervous that Christopher Bailey would answer. She couldn't bear the thought of him making jokes about her. But what had happened – why wouldn't he write? Was George getting bored with her? Had she read too much into the affection he had shown her at New Year? London

157

was such a long way from Scotland, and there were girls far prettier than her who would be attracted to a handsome man like him.

If this was love, it hurt like a burn.

'Are you expecting something important?' asked Ainslie.

Marion brought herself back from her thoughts. 'I haven't heard from my parents for a while,' she fibbed. 'That's all.'

'I thought you received a letter from them two days ago?'

Crawfie flushed. 'Oh yes, but, you know how it is.'

Ainslie knew exactly how it was. He'd seen Crawfie's reaction to envelopes written in a hand that was not her mother's. 'If anything arrives for you from your family or . . . a friend, I shall have it delivered upstairs immediately.'

She smiled at him. 'Thank you.'

He got up and went to the range. 'I'm making some coffee, if you have time.'

'Thank you.' Marion reached across the table and picked up the discarded *Times*. 'They won't miss me for ten minutes.' She flicked through the pages. 'Very nice photograph of the Duke and Duchess here. Did you see it?'

'Yes.' Ainslie reached for two coffee cups as the kettle boiled. 'Dinner at the Ritz, wasn't it?'

'I'd love to dance at the Ritz.' Crawfie leant her chin on her hand. 'The last time I danced was Hogmanay. It was such fun.'

'Then you'll love the Ghillies Ball if you ever get to Balmoral.'

Crawfie began reading aloud the short paragraph beneath the photograph: '*Their Royal Highnesses the Duke and Duchess of York attended a private dinner in Mayfair last evening. The Ritz Hotel is one of the Duchess's favourite places to dine. Looking splendid in rose satin and diamonds, the Duchess charmed everyone she met. The Duke thanked all those who had made their evening so entertaining.*

'They are wonderful people, aren't they?' Crawfie said affectionately.

Ainslie brought the coffee and sat down beside her. 'Well, let's put it this way, I would rather work for the Yorks than his brother the King.'

Crawfie put the paper down. 'Poor man. He must be feeling so lonely and wretched. Bereaved and preparing for his coronation and the rest of his life in service to the country.'

'That's not in question.' Ainslie pursed his lips. 'It's his private behaviour he needs to be careful with . . .'

Marion stared at him. 'What do you mean?'

'Come, come, Miss Crawford, you aren't deaf. You must have heard the gossip.'

She had, but she was trying not to listen to it. 'Well, of course he has close friends, and some are married women,' Crawfie scoffed.

'Exactly. A married woman is safe.' He raised his eyebrows pointedly. 'One would assume.'

Crawfie shook her head. 'He is not that sort of man.'

'I fear he is exactly that sort of man, Miss Crawford. And some men are the sort who would lay down their wives for their King.'

'That is a shocking thing to say!' Crawfie's mind was still fresh with the idea that George might have forgotten her for some other woman, and Ainslie's words stung her.

Ainslie's chin tucked itself into his neck. 'I hear that the King is bringing his special friend, Mrs Simpson, to dine with the Duke and Duchess at the Royal Lodge this Saturday.' He paused. 'Without Mr Simpson.'

Marion was stout in her reply. 'Perhaps Mr Simpson is busy.' She stood and headed for the door, adding, 'One o'clock luncheon in the nursery, please. Do have a footman bring it up.'

Crawfie was very aware of the household gossip surrounding the King and Mrs Simpson. Her schoolgirl crush on him had never really waned, and she was still deeply embarrassed to think about her fainting fit in the hall at 145 Piccadilly. He had been very kind about it, but what must he have thought of her privately?

Of course, she reminded herself, he probably thought nothing of her at all.

He hardly visited his brother and sister-in-law at 145 Piccadilly nowadays, and she did her best to disappear when she knew he was coming. She knew the girls missed their uncle very much. But, she told herself, his absence was due to his great responsibilities and not because he was louche.

Whispers and rumours were often reported by Bobo, who had a couple of housemaid friends in the palace. Alah and Crawfie listened with distaste.

In the past week, Mrs Simpson's name had appeared in the Court Circular, as attending a West End theatre play with the King.

The thought of the King having a love affair with a married woman was beyond Crawfie's comprehension. Only the worst kind of men did that, surely? And the King was so handsome and amusing – why should he seek the unattainable when so many beautiful young, single women, were there for his choosing?

No, it was ridiculous. Really, people had more time than sense to be gossiping about such things.

On Friday afternoon, as was their custom, the Duke, Duchess, and Princesses left London and headed to Windsor, to spend the weekend at Royal Lodge. Crawfie, Bobo and Alah travelled together in a car full of all the essentials that could be required by the girls.

By Saturday morning, the Royal Lodge was humming with nervous excitement. The King and his guest, Mrs Simpson, were to arrive at 7.00 p.m. They were staying at Windsor Castle, of course, but were coming to the Royal Lodge for dinner that evening, and for Sunday lunch the following day.

Crawfie kept herself very much away from anything that was not part of her duties. She was still keeping her distance from Ainslie, irritated by his words the other day.

Over breakfast with the girls, she suggested an outing into Windsor Great Park. 'It's going to be a beautiful day. Who would like to cycle up to the Copper Horse and have a picnic?'

'Me!' and 'Me!' came the replies.

Crawfie sent Bobo down to the kitchen to order the picnic, so that she could avoid Ainslie. Then she made sure that the two detectives allotted to the Princesses would be free to accompany them.

Towards lunchtime, with sunhats on and bicycles ready, the party of five set off for the short ride into the park.

The Princesses always enjoyed seeing other children playing, and today there were many – some running, others skipping or playing catch – and all with beaming smiles.

'Did you bring a ball, Crawfie?' asked Lilibet, who was cycling beside her.

'I did,' said one of the detectives. 'Can't have fun without a ball!'

'Well done, Mr Brown,' Lilibet said with approval.

'Can I play?' asked Margaret.

Lilibet frowned. 'But you still can't catch very well.'

'But how can I practise if you don't let me play?' At this, Margaret looked as if she were on the brink of a tantrum, so the second detective, Mr Williams, nipped her tears in the bud. 'You and I can be a team and we'll beat the others.'

'Hooray! We're going to beat them, we're going to beat them,' Margaret sang.

Crawfie laughed.

'In that case,' said Mr Brown, pedalling harder, 'last one to the Copper Horse gets a tickle!'

*

It was less than two miles to the statue of George III upon his Copper Horse, and they arrived panting and laughing with Mr Williams at the rear. The girls hopped off their bicycles and dropped them to the grass. Shouting 'You are last!' they jumped on top of the defenceless detective and began tickling him.

'Help me, help me!' he cried, laughing while Crawfie and Mr Brown got on with spreading two blankets and setting up the picnic.

'Come on now, you three. Lunch is ready.' Crawfie watched fondly as the girls peeled themselves off poor Mr Williams and wiped their sweaty hands on their dresses. 'I expect you're thirsty. Let's all catch our breath for a minute.'

It didn't take long before the two young girls, chatting away together, had abandoned their lemonades and meat paste sandwiches and were sitting amongst the grass in deep concentration, creating long daisy chains.

Crawfie sat a little apart from the detectives, who were keeping an eye on the girls from a distance and chatting quietly together.

'So, Mrs Simpson is visiting tonight, then,' Brown said, through a blade of grass he was chewing.

Crawfie, despite herself, pricked up her ears and listened.

'Poor blighter doesn't know what he's getting into there, does he?' replied Williams.

'What do you make of her?'

'I shouldn't like to use the word my missus does, but with all those women he could choose, why has he gone for her?'

'Maybe he feels sorry for her.'

'I feel sorry for her husband.'

'Which one? She's had two.' They sniggered like schoolboys.

'The first one took her to China with him. He liked to take her to the bawdy houses to watch him with the, er . . .' Williams looked up to check that Crawfie wasn't listening and she sipped her lemonade, pretending to be occupied watching the girls as he lowered his voice. 'With the working girls.'

'Blimey.'

'Rumour says she learned a few party tricks in the bedroom department.' Both men chuckled.

'No wonder she's hooked the King.' The two men laughed again. Then Brown said with fondness, 'I liked Mrs Dudley Ward, though. She was always pleasant. Without her, Fort Belvedere would still be a broken-down ruin. She was the one who got the work in the house and garden done. She must kick herself now, introducing Mrs S to the King like she did.'

Crawfie had heard enough. She got up and brushed the grass from her skirt. 'Lilibet, Margaret, who's for a game of catch?'

The detectives glanced at each other quickly, hoping she hadn't overheard anything. Both scrabbled for the tennis ball. 'Come on, ladies,' Williams shouted, 'who's going to play catch?'

The girls darted and shrieked and tumbled as Williams threw the ball high and let the Princesses run for it.

Crawfie, watching them, began to fold the blankets and collect up the greaseproof-paper wrappings that the sandwiches had come in. She emptied the beakers onto the grass and tucked them around the napkins, then stowed everything between the five bicycle baskets.

She was working as an automaton, still shocked by what she had heard. Her body did what it knew it had to do, while her brain was filled with the disgusting conversation she had listened to. She only knew the theory of the sexual act, and that rather patchily, but had always imagined it as loving, precious and private. She had always liked Mr Brown and Mr Williams, but what sort of men would idly discuss it and laugh?

She thought of George and the unformed fantasies she had about him. And why hadn't he written for so long? Had she done something wrong? Perhaps he was ill, or something terrible had happened.

She made up her mind to write to him tonight once all her work was finished. This thought alone made her feel a little better.

Above her, a blanket of clouds was moving over the sun, and she shivered in the light breeze.

'Ladies,' she called. 'Time to go home, before it rains.'

'Can we cycle down the Long Walk and find conkers?' Lilibet asked. 'Please?'

Crawfie checked the sky and her watch. 'All right, but just for ten minutes or they'll be wondering where we are.'

They got back to Royal Lodge just as the rain was starting. Williams and Brown took charge of the bikes and wheeled them back to the stables and Crawfie was relieved to see them go.

The Duchess was waiting for them in the hall. 'My darlings.' She hugged them. 'Have you been good girls for Crawfie?'

They looked at Crawfie for the answer. 'Have we?'

She smiled. 'Yes. Very good.'

'Excellent.' The Duchess turned back to her daughters. 'Guess who is coming to dinner tonight?'

Margaret was thinking. 'Hmm.'

Lilibet put her hand up. 'I know.'

Margaret, desperate to answer first, started jumping up and down. 'I know! It's Peter Pan and Wendy.'

Lilibet frowned. 'You're being silly.'

'Now, now, darlings.' The Duchess intervened. 'It's Uncle David. And he's bringing his friend, Mrs Simpson.' She looked at Crawfie. 'Would you ask Alah to bring them downstairs after their dinner? At quarter past seven, just for a few minutes. In their nightclothes will be fine.'

'Yes, ma'am.'

Up in the nursery, Alah was fighting a summer cold. She was wrapped up by the fire, while Bobo made her warm lemon and honey.

'You look tired, Alah,' Crawfie said with concern.

'She's quite poorly,' Bobo answered, handing over the steaming beaker. 'I think she should go to bed as soon as the girls do.'

'Alah, the Duchess has just asked if you would take the Princesses down at quarter past seven, to say goodnight to the King and . . . Mrs Simpson,' Crawfie told her. 'Would you rather not?'

'To be truthful, I don't think I can.' Alah coughed. 'I wouldn't want to give this to the rest of the household.'

Bobo looked up. 'I can feed and bathe the girls if you would take them down, Crawfie?'

Crawfie frowned. She did not want to put herself in the position of seeing the woman of whom she did not approve. 'Oh but Bobo, don't you want to see the King? We haven't seen him here for a long time.'

'Oh, I couldn't.' Bobo nervously twisted her hands in her apron pockets. 'I wouldn't know what to say.'

'You'll take them, won't you, Crawfie dear?' Alah said limply.

How could Crawfie refuse? As much as she didn't want to see the King with Mrs Simpson, her very human curiosity was fighting back. To see first-hand how close their relationship was, and to decide for herself what she thought of Mrs Simpson, was too tempting. It would only be for a few minutes, after all.

'Of course I will. You rest, Alah.'

Chapter Twenty

Royal Lodge, August 1936

While the Princesses were being readied to greet the King and Mrs Simpson, Crawfie used her free time to start a letter to George. The wastepaper basket under her neat writing table already contained two discarded drafts. She was having difficulty in getting the tone right; it must not come across as hectoring, hurt, demanding or emotional. She had fallen in love with him – she could not deny that – and she was almost sure that he had feelings for her. But it would be a terrible mistake for her to confess her own feelings or question his. The letter must be friendly but dignified and light, neither asking too much or too little about what he had been doing – or, and this would be hard, why he hadn't written.

She stared out of her window above the garden. The sun was slowly setting and the rain showers had given way to a beautiful evening.

There was a knock at her door. 'Come in.'

The Princesses, clean and shining in their dressing gowns, rushed in, with Bobo behind.

Crawfie smiled at them. 'Hello! And who are these two little rascals?'

'It's us, silly Crawfie,' giggled Margaret, spinning round on the spot. 'Look at me!'

'And what did you have for your dinner?'

'Cottage pie,' Lilibet answered, while trying to catch her dizzied sister, 'and if Margaret doesn't stop spinning, she'll be sick!'

A grey-faced Alah appeared at the door. 'I have just received a message from downstairs. The King is running late. Cook is worried about her soufflés and Ainslie is concerned his wine is being left to breathe too long. The Duchess would like you to take the girls down now to say goodnight.'

'Will we not see Uncle David, then?' asked Lilibet.

'I think not,' Crawfie replied. 'But never mind. When we come back upstairs, you can hop into bed and we can start the new Agatha Christie you have. How does that sound?' She took in the girls' smiles. 'Now, let's go downstairs.'

The drawing room was looking very beautiful. Vases of cut delphiniums, peonies and roses scented the air. The mirrored cocktail trolley, with its ice bucket, glasses and bottles, twinkled in the last rays of the sun as it crept through the large windows.

Looking out on to the golden parkland were the Duke, smoking, and the Duchess, with a glass of Dubonnet and gin her hand.

'I really don't see what he sees in' – the Duchess dropped her voice – 'a certain person.'

The Duke sighed. 'We must give her a chance.'

'But I cannot like her.' The Duchess shook her head. 'She is so very superior to us mere mortals.'

'Darling, we must make the effort.'

'But why?' She sipped at her gin, the ice clinking as she tipped the glass to her mouth, 'He makes no effort for you. Or me. We three used to be so close.' She lifted her gloved left hand to her forehead, remembering happier times. 'Lady Furness was much better for him. We all had so much fun.'

'He does seem to be enchanted by married American women.'

'But she was so very different. Remember how she got David and us together as a working party for the gardens at Fort Belvedere? It was a jungle before she tackled it.' She paused, thinking. 'And the Fort itself – it was in a dreadful state until she took it in hand. I don't think anyone had touched it for two hundred years. Goodness knows why he had to have it. Like a small boy wanting his own toy castle to play with, I suppose.'

The Duke put his cigarette to his lips and inhaled deeply. 'I felt rather badly for him. I mean, you and I have this glorious house, much more fitting for the heir to the throne.'

The Duchess put her hand on her husband's arm. 'But darling, he has York House, too – perfect for his tailor in St James's.' She laughed wickedly. 'I don't mean to poke fun at him but sometimes he needs it. A certain person will be soothing his sensibilities at every turn. Thelma Furness would have been different. She could laugh at herself and him, and he enjoyed it. She was *one of us*. She knew the score and she had perfect manners. So did her husband, bless him. But look how David treated her when a certain person arrived on the scene – and how Thelma backed off graciously. I do miss her.'

A cough from the door made them turn.

Crawfie stood in the doorway, the Princesses by her side. 'Good evening, sir, ma'am. The girls would like to say goodnight.'

Husband and wife moved quickly from the window and put their arms out to greet their daughters.

'Have you had a good day, my darlings?' the Duke asked, embracing one in each arm.

'We have, thank you,' said Lilibet. 'Can we wait for Uncle David?'

'If he's here before eight o'clock, of course you can,' their father said.

The Duchess laughed. 'Such spoiled girls! Shall we have a quick game of Happy Families while we wait? I was expecting Alah, Crawfie, but perhaps you would like to play?'

'I would like that, thank you,' she answered. Despite herself, she really did want to see Mrs Simpson.

'I will get the cards,' said Princess Margaret bossily.

'And I will shuffle them,' replied Lilibet.

*

By eight o'clock – after several furious rounds of cards – there was still no sign of the visitors. The girls reluctantly said their good nights and headed for the stairs, a disappointed Crawfie chivvying them along.

As they crossed the hall from the drawing room to the stairs, the powerful roar of a motorcar speeding its way up the drive stopped everyone in their tracks.

'It's Uncle David!' screamed the girls.

Ainslie appeared from nowhere to open the front door, where a huge and sleek American motorcar stood on the thick gravel.

'Halloo!' called the King, as he bounded out and around the endless bonnet, before helping Mrs Simpson to disembark.

The girls ran out to greet him, but stopped when they saw the elegant woman stepping out. She was clutching a small handbag and had a large diamond brooch on the shoulder of her effortless cocktail dress. She walked towards them in very high heels, clutching their Uncle David's arm.

The Duchess stood inside the open portico of Royal Lodge and went no further. Crawfie noticed the charming smile arranged on the Duchess's lips, but her eyes, usually so blue and twinkly, were carefully fixed on Mrs Simpson

'Darling Elizabeth.' The King, who had always been fond of his brother's wife, took the steps two at a time to reach her. 'Long time no see.' He kissed her hand and her cheek, then turned to Mrs Simpson who was hanging back a little. 'Wallis has been dying to see you again, haven't you, my love?'

Crawfie saw the imperceptible curl of Mrs Simpson's carmine lips as she answered, 'Gosh, yes,' in her East Coast American drawl.

The Duchess bent her head graciously but said nothing

The Duke stepped forward and shook her hand. 'W-welcome to Royal Lodge, Mrs Simpson. Now, come on in, both of you. The ice in the cocktails is melting.'

His stammer was a little worse tonight – a sign of his anxiety.

Crawfie stood back in the shadows of the staircase, watching the scene. Not one of them seemed to notice her.

The Duchess made her way to her husband and held his arm. 'David,' she said, 'you are very naughty keeping Cook waiting.' She said this with a tinkling laugh, but underneath it lay annoyance, Crawfie could tell. 'I imagine you'll be late for your coronation!'

The King shrugged his shoulders and swooped on to his two nieces. Mrs Simpson looked as if she were in the presence of zoo animals, as she watched the King tussle and wrestle with the giggling girls. Putting them back on their feet, he adjusted his jacket sleeves and waved his hand towards Mrs Simpson. 'Girls, you remember Mrs Simpson. Say hello to her.'

Crawfie saw the Duchess's eyes tighten.

'Hello,' they said politely.

The King lit a cigarette. 'My new car, and Mrs Simpson, are both from America. Do you like my car?'

'Yes, but it's jolly noisy,' said Lilibet.

'But that's the part you will like when you come for a ride with your Uncle David and Aunt Wallis.'

The girls looked at her shyly. Uncle David's friends were always very smart and pretty, but this woman had none of the curves and comfort their mother had. Her perfume was overpowering and body too angular.

'Give her a kiss then,' the King told them.

They did so. All three of them looking stilted and uncomfortable.

'Well, now.' Their mother smiled – satisfied, Crawfie thought, that her daughters would not take to the American interloper. 'Time for bed, girls.'

*

Upstairs, as Crawfie helped Bobo to tuck them in, Margaret whispered to her, 'I still don't like Uncle David's friend. Her dress is so tight you could see her bones.'

Lilibet whispered back, 'I don't think Mummy likes her either.'

'Now, now.' Crawfie reached for the new Agatha Christie. 'She is a lady a long way from her home, so we must be kind.'

Crawfie went to bed that night without once thinking about George, or the letter she should write him.

Chapter Twenty-One

Royal Lodge, August 1936

Tommy came up on the early Sunday morning train from London to Windsor. He had planned to go to West Sussex for the weekend; his family home was in the small village of Bepton, at the foot of the Sussex Downs, and it had been a couple of weeks since he'd seen his wife Joan and their three children. How he longed to be back home. He could do with a damned good walk as much as anything. The South Downs Way always cleared his mind of the clutter of state.

When in London he lived and worked at Buckingham Palace, which Joan didn't like. He frequently attempted to soothe her anxieties, persuading her that she and the children were better off out of the capital, which of course they were. They could lead a perfectly normal life with perfectly normal hours, rather than constantly wondering where he was, when would he be home and whether he had eaten. But that didn't mean he didn't miss her. He loved to take her out for lunch in Chichester, or go swimming at the Witterings, or do the gardening together.

Simple things, but all his plans were currently dashed.

The Duke and Duchess of York had invited the King to a family lunch at Royal Lodge. Alec Hardinge, the King's private secretary, and therefore Tommy's boss, could not attend; thus, as assistant private secretary, Tommy was obliged to show his face.

Joan had been disappointed but understanding.

'Will Mrs Simpson be there?' she had asked.

'I have no idea,' he had replied.

'Well, if she is, I want you to tell me all.'

He climbed out of the car that had been sent to collect him from Windsor station and stood for a moment, surveying the large and beautiful house and garden. A pleasant breeze brought with it the smell of newly mown grass. The flower beds were rather ordinary, shrubs mostly, but there were a few good roses too. He must remember to ask Joan how the roses were doing in Sussex.

Taking a preparatory deep breath, he turned back to the house and climbed the steps to the door.

'Good morning, Sir Alan.' Ainslie seamlessly took Tommy's summer coat and panama hat.

'Hello, Ainslie. Is the King here yet?'

'No, sir, I believe he is still at the castle. There was a rather late dinner party last night. We are not expecting His Majesty and his guest for another hour.'

'Hmm. And his weekend guest is?'

'Mrs Simpson, sir.'

'Hmm,' Tommy said again.

Ainslie blinked, but did not comment. 'Their Royal Highnesses are waiting on the terrace.'

Tommy followed Ainslie across the hall, through the drawing room and out on to the beautiful terrace overlooking Windsor Great Park.

Ainslie announced him. 'Sir Alan, ma'am.'

The Duchess was sitting under a vast parasol, watching the Princesses, who were sitting on the lawn, counting with their eyes closed.

Tommy addressed the Duchess. 'Good morning, ma'am.' He inclined his neck in the perfect courtier's bow.

'Ah, Tommy. Would you like a drink before lunch?'

'A small gin and tonic would be just the ticket, thank you.'

'Very good, sir.' Ainslie withdrew to the drawing room.

The Duchess looked across the lawn. 'The Duke is playing hide and seek. He's awfully good. Can you see him?'

Tommy peered into the sun. In a small copse of five silver birches, he caught a flash of a royal trousered leg dangling from a branch.

'Ah, I may have caught a glimpse but mum is the word.'

The Duchess laughed. 'We had rather a late party last night.'

Ainslie appeared with a clinking gin and tonic and withdrew once more.

Tommy kept his eyes on the garden. 'Oh yes?'

'The King and his friend Mrs Simpson were here.'

Tommy's eyes didn't waver. 'Ah.'

The Duchess looked closely at him. 'Thank you for joining us today. I hope it hasn't mucked up any plans you may have had?'

He sipped his drink. 'Not at all, ma'am.'

Shouts of 'Coming to find you, ready or not!' came across the garden.

The Duchess waved and smiled, then said, 'How is it, working with the King?'

'It's an honour to serve, ma'am.'

Her girls had found the Duke's hiding place and were now being chased by him.

The Duchess said, 'I recall you actually resigned from his service, when he was Prince of Wales.'

Tommy looked into his glass without an answer.

'I believe you disapproved of his lifestyle at that time. What do you think of it now?'

'Ma'am, I serve our King. I do not judge him.'

The Duchess laughed. 'A courtier's answer, if ever I heard one.'

The Duke came across the lawn, wiping his brow. 'I could do with a drink – where's Ainslie? Ah, hello Tommy. You need a top-up, by the looks of your glass.'

Ainslie reappeared, took the orders and disappeared again.

A pleasant hour idled by, as the conversation flitted between roses, cricket and a Beethoven concert that had been on the wireless. The Princesses were charming and polite. They greeted Tommy, then retreated to a blanket under the shade of the birches, reading their books and pouring glasses from a jug of lemonade.

Tommy felt himself getting drowsy, and the Duke looked as if he had already fallen asleep. It was a perfect English summer Sunday.

But idylls did not last, and this one was abruptly ended by the arrival of a hungover King and his immaculate female friend.

The Duke and Tommy got to their feet and bowed to their sovereign, while the Duchess performed a perfect curtsey. Mrs Simpson ignored it all, heading to a chair under the shade of the parasol.

The King, in dark glasses, was ordering a drink from Ainslie.

'A Bloody Mary – large.' Stubbing out his cigarette, he lit another and sat down in the chair Tommy had just risen from. 'And a dry martini for Mrs Simpson.' He rubbed his head. 'I have a headache.'

After a slow train journey, Tommy was back in London, in his rooms at Buckingham Palace. He divested himself of his clothes and put on his dressing gown, a gift from Joan. He missed her and the children dreadfully, but he also prized the solitude of life he led without them. He often felt torn between the two.

Sitting at his desk, he pulled out a sheet of headed note paper and began to write.

Darling Joan,

I have just returned from Royal Lodge. Excellent lunch as always – poached salmon and new potatoes, then summer pudding. The Yorks were charming.

However, the garden was a disappointment, the lawn suffering without water. I found myself wanting desperately to be back in West Sussex. By the way, how is the Dahlia v Earwig contest going?

But you won't want talk about earwigs. You want to hear all about 'a certain person', as she is known at BP.

The King was hungover and chain smoking. Nothing new there. He was pleasant enough and his family appeared happy to see him, but I detected several degrees of concern. He is very thin and tired-looking. He ate very little of the excellent food and smoked throughout lunch.

The Duchess was warm and amusing – you know how engaging and supportive she can be – but I saw one or two expressions of disquiet cross her pretty face. There is a tough woman behind her soft exterior. She remained cool, hiding her emotions admirably.

The centre of attention was, of course, Mrs Simpson. She was totally at ease, so much so that she took the hostess's chair, at the head of the table.

The Duchess, with perfect manners, did not turn a hair as she took Mrs S's allotted seat. Ainslie, poor man, was puce with anxiety about where the King would sit. To Ainslie's relief, he did not take his brother's seat but settled where he had been placed.

I had the feeling that Mrs S's faux pas was no mistake. She is very slender with a sharp face and dark hair pulled back to reveal hard eyebrows, rather pained eyes, a large nose and a thin, lipsticked mouth. Her jewellery, however, was exquisite: a gem-encrusted bracelet, three rows of very good pearls and diamond drop earrings. I have no doubt they have been gifted to her by the King.

At one point she looked out on to the garden and the hill beyond and said to the King, in full earshot of the Yorks, owners of the said garden, 'Don't you think, David darling, that the view could be improved by moving a few of the trees and flattening part of the hill?'

The Duchess remained the very distillate of unruffled. If the remark was designed to irritate, the very opposite appeared true. The Duchess smiled and even managed a light joke. 'Goodness. Our weekends would be busy.'

As we were leaving, we all had to admire the King's new American station wagon car, a huge boat of a machine.

'Isn't she marvellous?' the King said.

The Duchess said it was delightful.

Mrs Simpson replied, laughing all the while (and I still cannot believe she actually said this): 'I am left with a distinct impression that while the Duchess is sold on an American car, she is not so sold on the King's other American interests.'

How does one respond to that?

In short, my darling Joan, I fear the woman is unsuitable company for a King to keep. He reminds me so much of Mr Toad from The Wind in The Willows, always looking for the next great excitement.

Talking of which, plans for his coronation are coming together for next spring. Definitely good reason for you to go hat shopping.

And don't forget to let me know re dahlias and earwigs.

Your

Tommy xxx

While Tommy signed and sealed his letter in London, Crawfie was at her desk in Royal Lodge, writing a letter to George.

She had procrastinated for too long. She was going back to Scotland very soon for her summer break and it was only good manners to let him know of her return, in case he wished to avoid seeing her. She had agonized over the wording, but finally decided that she had better be short and to the point.

Dear George,

I do hope you are well. I am coming back to Dunfermline next week and will be staying with my parents. I shall be home until early September. I hope you might be free to meet. It would be very nice to hear all your news.

I quite understand if this does not suit.

Yours truly,

Marion

Chapter Twenty-Two

Marion felt the chill of the Scottish evening as she stepped off the train at Dunfermline station. In London, she had left behind a sweltering August, and even though she'd brought a coat, she was rueing her decision not to wear a cardigan as well.

She carried her bags to the small taxi office, hoping that they would have a car available. She found him sitting behind his glass window, smoking a pipe.

'Mr McGregor?'

He looked up and grinned. 'Ah, Miss Crawford. Back home again. What is our new King like? Have you met him yet?'

She ignored the question. 'Do you have a wee car to go?'

'I thought you'd be wanting a carriage and fine horses?' He moved the pipe from one corner of his mouth to the other, laughing.

She smiled politely. 'Just a wee taxi, please.'

She heard footsteps behind her, but kept her focus on Mr McGregor, who was running his finger down a notebook with that evening's bookings. 'Maybe in about twenty minutes. Jim is dropping at the hospital just now and Robbie has just gone home for the day.'

The footsteps behind her were getting closer. A man's voice said, 'Marion. Your chariot awaits if you'd care to hop in?'

She spun round in delighted surprise. 'George!'

'Hello.' He smiled at her. 'I hope you don't mind, but Robert told me which train you were on. How could I leave you stranded?'

Mr McGregor sat back in his old wooden rotating chair. 'Do you know this gentleman, Miss Crawford?'

'Oh, yes, thank you, I do.' Marion was flushed with pleasure. 'George, this is Mr McGregor, and Mr McGregor, this is George Buthlay. A . . .' She wasn't sure how to introduce him. 'A friend of the family.'

'So, you won't be needing a car?'

'No. I am fine now, thank you.'

As they walked towards George's motorcar, George carrying her luggage, she said, 'Funnily enough I wrote to you yesterday.'

He placed her bags in the boot, and turned around with a sheepish smile. 'I must apologize for my lack of letters. I have been very busy with the garage and I have moved. I meant to send you my new address.'

He opened the car door for her and waited as she settled herself. As he walked round to get into the driver's seat, she allowed herself to relax in the face of his simple explanation. He had been too busy and he had moved. There was nothing so very terrible in that.

'Where have you moved to?' she asked, as George got in and started up the engine.

'A nice little house in between here and Stirling.' He manoeuvred the car out of the station car park and set off towards her home. 'I am closer to work, and it will still be a short drive to visit you. You remember Christopher, from the garage?'

She did, and not favourably. She nodded.

'He and I are sharing the place. Decent rent and a little garden. You will have to come and see it.'

'I would love to.'

'Hardly a palace, though – it's not what you'll be used to.'

'George, please don't say that. Whenever I come home, people expect me to be . . . oh, I don't know . . . grand or something? But I am a proper Scots lassie, nothing else.'

He looked at her and smiled, his eyes crinkling with fun. 'I have missed you.'

Her heart did a flip. 'Don't talk nonsense.'

The six weeks that followed were something that Marion had never experienced before. She was *romanced*.

George gave her his constant attention. During the week she hardly saw him as he was so busy with Christopher selling cars, but at weekends they shared walks and picnics, quiet pubs and dinners.

Her mother was relentless.

'You will never find another man like George. He's so kind and thoughtful, exactly the sort of husband I would choose for you.'

And after one particularly excruciating Sunday lunch at home, she asked across the dining room table, 'I can't believe you have never married, George. But then, maybe you haven't met the right girl.'

Marion's embarrassment was obvious, but George took the question in his stride. 'Actually, Maggie, I was married once, a long time ago. I am divorced.'

'Oh,' Maggie said, taken aback. 'Any children?'

'No.'

Maggie rallied. 'Well, that's a blessing.' Then added hurriedly, 'That is, did you want a family?'

He furrowed his brow and he said with sincerity, 'I would dearly love a family, but who would want a man like me? I'm in my mid-forties and I know I have very little to offer a woman who is young enough to have children.'

'Robert and I would so love to be grandparents.'

Robert was as uncomfortable with this conversation as his daughter and drew a line under it. 'Why don't we clear the table, Maggie, and make some tea?'

Left on her own with George, Marion apologized. 'I wish mother wouldn't talk so freely about things she shouldn't.'

'Why shouldn't she?' George asked her. 'She wants the best for you.'

'Well, I hate it.'

He was quiet for a moment, looking at her across the table. 'Do you want to be married?'

She flushed. 'Goodness, what a question.'

'I think you would make a wonderful wife and mother.'

Her heart jumped in her chest. What was he asking?

Before she could think of a response, he said, 'I know how fond of you the little Princesses are, but don't you ever think about looking after your own children, rather than someone else's?'

She glanced towards the kitchen, terrified her mother would be listening in. Then she looked back at him with pleading eyes. 'Please, George, can we change the subject?'

'I know I'm sixteen years older than you, but we are friends . . . I hope?'

'Yes.'

He took her hand. 'You see, there's something I want to ask you.'

Was this it? Was he going to propose?

She had thought about this moment many, many times, so why was she frightened? She knew she loved George, but this was unexpected, too sudden. She wouldn't know how to answer him. It was all too soon and not how she had imagined, and anyway how could she stay in London if she said yes? Her life would change irrevocably and she wasn't ready. She felt suddenly hot and sick. The timing was all wrong. She thought she might throw up.

'George, I am sorry, but I'm not feeling very well.'

His eyes were full of concern. 'I have upset you.'

She took her hand from under his and stood up. 'It's not you. I just need to lie down.'

She needed to leave before she was sick in front of him.
'Sorry.'

She ran upstairs to her room and closed the door behind her. What had just happened? Adrenaline was gushing in her veins. The pit of her stomach was cold. Her breath was coming fast and shallow. Feeling faint, she went to her open window. It was a hot day with barely a breeze, but the air felt good in her lungs. She sucked in as much as she could, until calm was regained and the nausea abated.

Had George been about to propose to her? Or was he teasing? Or did he really think he was too old for her? She didn't think he was.

She lay down on her bed, not wanting to go back downstairs, not wanting to face him.

After a little while, there came a quiet knock on her door, then it opened an inch. 'Marion?' It was her mother. 'What happened?'

'I came over a bit faint. I think maybe I have had too much sun.'

'George has gone. He said to tell you he'll call tomorrow. He's worried you aren't well.'

'I'm fine.'

Maggie stood at her daughter's bedside and took her hand. 'Was it my fault? Your father has already had words with me.'

'Mother, I just need to sleep. Let's speak tomorrow.'

George rang up the next day, but Marion told her mother that she wasn't feeling well enough to come to the telephone. She said the same for the next three days.

On the fourth day, he didn't ring.

On the fifth day, she felt safe enough to leave the sanctuary of her room and venture out into the garden.

Her parents were outside, sitting in the shade of her father's prize rose – a peach-coloured and heavily scented climber, his pride and joy.

Her mother, mending basket on her lap, shaded her eyes with a cupped hand and looked her up and down. 'So, you're up.'

Her stepfather was more sympathetic. 'How are you feeling, lassie?'

'I'm all right.'

'Come and sit in the shade.' He got up to give his seat to Marion. 'I'll get you a cold drink. Would you like a sandwich? You've hardly eaten all week.'

'A drink would be lovely. Thank you, Dad.'

As soon as he had disappeared into the kitchen, Maggie started. 'Are you going to tell me what happened between you and George?'

'I don't want to talk right now, Mother.'

Over her reading glasses, she gazed at Marion. She asked quietly, 'Was he inappropriate with you?'

Marion frowned. 'No!'

'Did he want you to do something you didn't want to do?'

'Mother! No.'

'Then what?'

'He . . .' She took a deep breath. 'I thought he was going to ask me to marry him and . . . it scared me.'

'Oh my God!' Maggie's jaw dropped into a wide grin. 'He was going to propose?'

'I thought so, yes.'

Maggie smiled. 'Congratulations. You did the right thing to keep him in suspense.'

'Mum . . .'

'It's always best to think about these things.'

'I don't know what I'm thinking. I don't know what to do.'

'Well, do you like him?'

'Yes, but—'

Maggie was gentler. 'He is quite a bit older than you, I know, but that means he's matured. He obviously thinks the world of you or he wouldn't be paying you so much attention.'

Marion looked sad. 'But now he hasn't rung up for two days.'

'He'll try again.' Maggie laughed. 'And when he does, you'll agree to see him.'

'But what if he actually proposes?'

'Could you love him?'

This was an awkward question. 'I have sometimes thought I loved him, but . . . If I love him, why was I so scared?'

Her mother tutted. 'Marion, you are ready to marry. You're at the perfect age and he is a lovely man. Do you respect him, trust him?'

'I do.'

'Good. The rest will follow. Say yes and make him happy.'

'But what about my work? I don't want to leave the Duchess or the girls.'

Maggie patted her arm. 'You don't now, but when you are married, with your own home and children, you will feel very differently.'

She didn't think she would. Not unless . . . unless she could stay in London and do her job, even after she was married. Governesses and teachers gave up their careers as a rule when they married, but Marion's situation was surely unique. How could she just leave the York household? They needed her and, in a way she couldn't put into words, she needed them.

Perhaps George would come to London? That would be the perfect solution. But could he leave Scotland? He didn't have family that she knew of, so there wasn't anyone standing in his way, but she knew he liked his work with Chris.

She shook herself.

No. He'd stopped ringing her because she had behaved like a fool on Sunday, and she would probably never hear from him again. Indeed, she would be too horribly embarrassed to ever see him again.

She was worrying without need. The moment had passed and she could carry on with her job unchallenged. It was a narrow escape if ever there was one.

*

The next day was Sunday, and her parents were out at church when the telephone in the hall rang. She was almost too afraid to answer it. If it was George, what would she say? If he asked her again, she wanted to say yes – but only if he would come to London with her.

She steeled herself, and picked up the receiver. 'Hello.'

'Marion? It's me. George.'

She felt her legs weaken and she sank onto the bottom stair. He was anxious. 'Marion? Are you all right?'

'Yes. I am fine, George.' Her voice sounded tinny.

'I have been expecting you to never want to speak to me again,' he said quickly. 'I am so sorry about last Sunday. It came out all wrong. Would you please accept my apology?'

Marion felt far from comfortable with this. She had no idea how to deal with personal situations. And what did it mean, that he was apologizing? That he hadn't meant it, that he hadn't been able to propose after all?

'Nothing to apologize for,' she heard herself say. 'I was suffering from the heat and had to lie down. That's all.'

'I rang you in the week. Several times. But your mother said you were resting.'

'Yes.'

'And are you feeling better now?'

'Yes. I am so sorry about dashing off the other night.'

Marion held the phone, breathing hard, desperate for him to speak again. Was this the moment her life would change forever? When friendship became intimacy?

'Marion, are you busy this evening?'

'No.'

'I could pick you up at five and have you home by seven. Maybe a little fresh air? We could stop at that little pub we like, the one that does jugs of Pimms. Remember?'

She held her hand to her throat. He had said *we*. The pub *we* like. She smiled. 'Yes, I remember.'

'Then you'll come?'

She closed her eyes and took a leap into the unknown. 'Yes, I will.'

Chapter Twenty-Three

Buckingham Palace, mid-September 1936

Darling Joan,

I am in a jam. Alas, I shall have to postpone my trip to join you for John's fourteenth birthday celebrations. I will ring up on Saturday morning to wish him many happy returns. I am sure he won't even miss me. You are so good at organizing parties and such like, he will hardly notice I am not there. I will put a postal order for £2.00 in the post.

Things have got a little heated here.

The King has announced privately that he wishes to marry Mrs Simpson. There are many reasons why he cannot. She is still married to Mr Simpson, for one thing, and even after a divorce, the King would be her third husband. It is unlikely that she would bear children and therefore any line of succession to the Crown would be impossible. And more pertinently, I believe the country would not take to her. Marriage to her would be disastrous for the country.

The Prime Minister, Mr Baldwin, came for a private luncheon yesterday to which I was also invited. The purpose was to discuss the King's coronation and gauge his ability and sense of duty for the job. I also had the opportunity to watch Mrs S and scrutinize her motives.

She is smart, attractive and friendly, with a keen interest in the King's future, but has a side to her that is too sharp. She and the King behaved very badly in front of the Prime Minister, me and the attendants serving our lunch. She laughed as she shared her opinion of the Yorks. She thinks the Duke dull and the Duchess plump and dowdy, calling her 'Cookie' and sneering at her taste in décor and clothes. The terrible thing is the King laughed too. And he used to be so close to his brother and sister-in-law. The King, I fear, is as weak and spoiled a man as he was when I worked with him as the Prince of Wales.

I felt I must defend the Yorks, and from across the table I laid my opinion bare. 'They are people to admire,' I said.

Her reply was astonishing. 'They don't like me, so I don't need to like them.'

Poor Mr Baldwin is, like me, very fond of the Yorks, and was horrified, but he said nothing.

The upshot of all this is that Mr Baldwin has called for a meeting this weekend, in an attempt to seek some order in this chaos.

I can't help thinking that if we could simply remove the King and Mrs S and replace them with the Yorks, the monarchy would be in very safe hands. They have a stable marriage and two charming little girls. Of course the Duke's stammer would need to be addressed, and the Princess Elizabeth would need to bear the weight of being a future Queen, but it would be much the easiest solution.

I know I needn't tell you that this is all strictly confidential and I should not be letting you know the situation. It's all rather shocking and I would be in a frightful pickle if anyone but you read this letter.

I miss you dreadfully. How about you come up to town next week? I need to take my wife to lunch!

Your
Tommy

The Good Servant

Marion was in a state of agitated excitement. George was arriving that evening and she was to meet him at the Lyons' Corner House at Leicester Square. It was now three weeks since he had taken her to the nice pub that served Pimms, and she was still taken aback by what he had had to say.

He had carried the tray with the jug and glasses out into the beer garden. There was a small wooden table in a secluded corner, with a bower of peach roses hung above it. Their scent on the cooling evening air settled around them.

'Are you comfortable, Marion? Would you like my jacket?' he had asked.

Marion looked over the fields towards the purple hills beyond. She knew she would look back on this in the years to come as the most perfect moment in her life. 'Yes. Thank you,' she said.

They sat in peaceful silence sipping their drinks, while George gathered his words.

'Marion.'

She took a breath. 'Yes?'

He ran a finger over each side of his moustache. 'I don't have much in the way of savings, and so I am thinking of looking for a new job. I have decided to look for work in London.'

Her heart skipped for a moment. He wanted to come to her, so that she need not return to Scotland? Her prayers were being answered.

'Why?' she asked.

'I need a decent income, and I have applied for a post in a bank.'

'A bank!' Her mother would be satisfied.

'Yes. I have an interview in September. And I wondered if you might know anywhere I could stay?'

She smiled. 'There are plenty of affordable guest houses.'

'Oh, that's good. Could you look one out for me? I mean, you actually being in situ, you would be better placed.'

She hesitated. He was asking her to look for a place for him – one that she could visit? She felt nervous again. 'Yes . . . I could.'

'Oh, that is a weight off my mind. I haven't been to London since the war and I expect it has all changed so much.'

'Is that what you wanted to talk to me about?'

'Aye.'

Crawfie's heart dropped into her abdomen. He wasn't going to propose? She picked her disappointment up quickly. 'No problem at all.'

'And maybe—' He halted.

Her hopes lifted a little. 'What?'

'Maybe I could take you out for dinner to thank you when I get there.'

She became brisk. She didn't want to show any signs of dismay. 'That would be very nice. Goodness, look at the time – I really must get home.'

She had wanted to renege on the decision to find him a place to live. Why should she wear her shoe leather out? What did he actually want from her? To use their friendship for his own ends, for convenience?

Her mother, when she heard what had happened, could only see his actions as noble. 'Marion, he is obviously keen. Why wouldn't he want to gather some savings ready for married life? And a bank! He has ambition and drive – both very good things. I foresee that this time next year you will be married, or at least engaged, and he will be doing very well and you will have no need to work. Don't look a gift horse in the mouth. He's taking things slowly so as not to scare you off. Now, you start searching for a nice guest house for him and make sure it's close enough for you both to see each other easily while he's in London.'

Marion had found a clean and homely guest house off Kensington High Street, run by a tiny woman, a Scot as it happened, widowed by the war. Mrs Bridie was warm, chatty and happy to take in a respectable fellow Scot.

'The thing is,' Marion explained, 'I don't have a firm date for his arrival yet.'

'Nae bother, lassie. You write down his name for me so I know who to expect. Around mid-September you say? I always keep my back room free in case of last-minute guests. I hate to turn anyone back to the streets; I think of my husband, given shelter by French farmers during the war. He wrote to tell me how lovely their cheeses were.' She smiled sadly. 'But they couldn't save him from the fighting. Only twenty-eight when he was killed.' She appeared to shake the memory away. 'I was in service. Big house in Regent's Park. But I had saved a bit and bought this wee house to do for others what others had done for Bill. Here's my telephone number. Just ask him to ring up and we'll make the arrangements.'

She passed Marion a piece of paper with her number written in pencil.

She had written to George, sending him the number and the address: *The Highlands Guest House, Church Street, Kensington.*

And today he was arriving in London.

'Crawfie dear, may I ask why you wish to leave your duties a little earlier tonight?' The Duchess smiled, a particular smile that Marion knew preceded a change in mood. Her lips had tightened and her eyes were steady and intent on Crawfie's own. 'Only, it is of great inconvenience to the Duke and me this evening.'

Crawfie knew from asking Ainslie earlier, that the royal couple had no engagements and would be dining alone at home. She had fully hoped that she would be given permission to meet George.

'Of course, ma'am. I was going to meet a friend, but I can do that another time.' How else could Crawfie reply?

'Thank you.'

Crawfie was dismissed.

She left the room and returned to the nursery, where the Princesses were diligently working on the assignments she had left with them.

Alah looked up from her darning, noticing Crawfie's glum face. 'She said no?'

Crawfie nodded.

'Who said no?' asked Princess Margaret.

Lilibet gave her a frown. 'Don't ask personal questions. It is rude.'

Margaret stuck her tongue out at her sister. 'It's not rude to ask questions. Crawfie always says that asking questions helps us to understand things. Isn't that right, Crawfie?'

Alah ignored her. 'The girls have almost finished their work and I promised them a walk in the gardens when you got back.'

Crawfie looked at the clock on the mantel. It was four now and she was due to meet George at five thirty, but she wouldn't finish her duties until six thirty. Would George wait for her? There was no way she could get a message to him to let him know what had happened.

'I think there will be lots of conkers to collect,' Lilibet said.

Crawfie was pulled back to the present. 'Conkers?'

'Yes.' Margaret joined in. 'Bobo said she would have them baked hard by Cook in the oven. Then we can beat Papa. You said you would take us.'

Crawfie put her anxiety to one side. She could think about this later. 'All right then, girls. Put your work away neatly and get your coats on.'

When they had gone to collect their outdoor clothes, Alah whispered, 'What time are you meeting your friend?' She had managed to get as much as she could out of Crawfie, which wasn't much, but she did know that a gentleman friend was on his way from Scotland to meet her at the Leicester Square Lyons' Corner House. Crawfie shook her head. 'Five thirty, but there's no chance now.'

'Look, you have the Princesses back here by five and nobody will know if you slip off. I'll be telling no one and Bobo will not dare.'

'But suppose the Duke and Duchess come looking for me?'

'Then you'll have a headache and be sleeping soundly. I'll tell any callers that you are not to be disturbed. Now get your coat and collect some conkers.'

Just after five, Crawfie delivered the Princesses back to the nursery, their pockets bulging with shiny conkers, some still in their spikey green armour.

'Oh dear, dear!' Alah said in front of them. 'Poor Crawfie, you look awful pale. Have you got one of your heads?'

Crawfie blushed at the lie. Alah's subterfuge was so kindly meant, but it made her feel a fool. She managed an embarrassed, 'I think so, yes.'

'Then you'd best get to bed. Off you go. Bobo and I will see to the young ladies.'

Nervously, Crawfie slipped out of the below stairs door next to the kitchen unnoticed. She calculated that it would take her about twenty minutes to get to Leicester Square, so she set off with a brisk stride and her head down, hoping that Ainslie or Cook didn't spot her.

The September afternoon had the scent of autumn about it. Yellow leaves from the plane trees were scuttling on the roads, and the pavements were crowded with hurrying, sidestepping office workers leaving for their train home. She dodged round them, pulling her coat tightly around her. At last she reached her destination just as a nearby church clock chimed five thirty.

The place was filling up with workers meeting up with friends, planning the evening ahead of them. Marion scanned the room. A waitress approached her.

'May I have a table for two, please?' Marion asked and was shown to a small table in the centre of the room.

'What will you have?' the woman asked, with the pen and notepad ready.

'May I wait a few minutes? My friend hasn't arrived yet.'

Ten minutes went by. The train was probably late arriving at King's Cross, Marion thought to herself. At least she could sit and compose herself, plan what she would say to him. She would be open and friendly, tell him not to worry that she had waited. After all, she was in the warm.

Another fifteen minutes went by and Marion decided to order a pot of tea and a teacake.

By six o'clock, she began to worry. Had she given him the right address? Had there been a train crash? Was he lost somewhere on a bus? Had he gone straight to Kensington? She had sent him the address, so perhaps he was now being shown around his new home by the landlady.

She'd give him another ten minutes.

Then another five.

At half past six, the afternoon crush around her had dissipated. She felt exposed, sitting in the middle of the emptying room. She saw a couple of women look at her and nudge each other, giggling as they left.

'Can I get you anything else, miss?' the waitress asked again.

'No, thank you. I am afraid my friend must have been delayed. I wonder, if a man called George Buthlay comes in, medium height with a moustache, carrying a suitcase – would you tell him I waited but that I have now gone home?'

'Of course, miss.'

Marion paid her bill, leaving a good tip for the waitress who had been so kind, and walked out into the darkening night. There was rain in the air and smartly dressed people were hurrying to the picture houses, theatres and restaurants. She walked all four sides of Leicester Square hoping to see George, maybe getting out of a taxi, flustered and worried.

But there was no sign of him.

Chapter Twenty-Four

145 Piccadilly, mid-September 1936

When Marion returned to 145 Piccadilly, Alah and Bobo were waiting. Bobo was goggle-eyed with curiosity, and though Alah managed to keep her inquisitiveness under control, she was nonetheless desperate to gather news. Alah was a shrewd woman who could read a person's face easily – it was what made her a successful nanny – and she had read Crawfie's mind without difficulty. The dear lass had her heart set on a man.

Romance was not something that often troubled the nursery floor and Alah noted the presence of it with interest.

'Ah, you're back,' Alah said. 'Bobo, put the kettle on and put another lump of coal on the fire as you go.' She turned her attention back to Crawfie. 'Is it cold outside, dear? Come and sit down.'

'A bit chilly.' Crawfie shook off her coat without looking at Alah. 'I need to hang this up and get a jumper from my room. I'll be back in a minute.'

Alah watched the young governess as she went into her room. She was not herself, to be sure. No cheery hello, no smiles, no eye contact.

Something was very wrong.

Alah covertly checked that Bobo was still occupied in the small nursery kitchen, before tiptoeing across the landing and putting her ear to Crawfie's door. If she really was putting her coat away, Alah would hear the clang of a hanger in the wardrobe.

What she heard was sniffling, whimpering and nose blowing. Crawfie was crying.

A few minutes passed before Crawfie returned to the nursery sitting room, wrapped in a navy cardigan. Alah was sitting in her chair by the fire as if she had never left, but she noted the swollen eyelids and cheeks pinkened by the undoubted splashing of cold water. She mentioned neither.

'Feeling a bit warmer, dear?'

'Yes, thank you.' Crawfie's voice and eyes were low.

The two women drank their tea without speaking. The fire crackled and the mantel clock ticked pleasantly as the evening traffic droned by beneath the nursery window.

Alah broke the silence. 'Have you had anything to eat? Bobo is making scrambled egg with a little toast. Will you join us?'

Crawfie put down her half-drunk cup. 'I feel a bit of a head-ache coming on. I think I might just get an early night, if you don't mind.'

Alah knew a lie when she heard one. 'Why would I? Get some rest.'

As Bobo brought the tray of scrambled eggs round to the nursery sitting room, she saw Crawfie disappear into her room and close the door firmly behind her. She was filled with disap-pointment.

'She hasn't gone to bed, has she?' she asked Alah.

'A little under the weather. She will be fine in the morning.'

Bobo put the tray down. 'Did she tell you anything about . . .'

Alah held her palm up as a stop sign, and Bobo was quietened. 'I believe Sandy Powell is on the wireless tonight. Shall we listen as we eat?'

Crawfie spent an anxious night.

The moment she had turned off her light, the anxiety and worry that had gnawed at her brain exploded. Why hadn't George come? He might be injured or, God forbid, dead. No one in

London knew him. How would they identify him? Who would the hospital contact?

Or had he even come to London at all? Maybe he had missed the train. Or cancelled his ticket. Perhaps he'd changed his mind about coming at all. The more she thought about what might have happened, the more anxious and mystified she became.

A horrible thought chilled her. It was her fault. She had so stubbornly stuck to her determination to care for the Princesses that she hadn't made enough room for George in her life. When he had said he was looking at jobs in London, had he expected her to offer to stay in Scotland? How must he be feeling? He must see her as cold – unfeeling, unavailable, uncaring. He must think she wasn't interested in him, that she was a selfish, work-obsessed woman. The kind who emasculated men.

For all the time she had known him, more than a year now, she had never once put him first. She remembered the night of the non-proposal with shame, and how the thought of being married had terrified her. What kind of person was she, that she was so afraid of marrying a man she loved?

All these thoughts agitated until eventually she fell into a fretful sleep.

At 2.00 a.m. she woke filled with powerful indignation. How could he just leave her waiting for him? It was a shabby thing to do and he must know how much she was worrying.

By 4.45 a.m. the flames of anger licked in her lower gut. How dare he? How could George treat her like some lackey? He had used her to find him a place to stay. He had humiliated her.

Well, he wouldn't get a second chance. How could she have been so gullible and foolish? If she ever saw him again, she would tell him exactly what she thought of him. Nobody would ever take her for a fool again.

As the glimmer of dawn began to lighten the London sky, Crawfie's thoughts and emotions had gone full circle – back to the certainty that George must be lying injured in a hospital bed. He had amnesia and couldn't tell the kindly doctor and nurses who were quietly checking his pulse and attending to his bandages who he was or where he had come from. She would have to find him. She didn't care if the Duchess wouldn't let her go. She would go anyway. She wiped the tears from her cheeks and then jumped at a knock on her door. Was it the police? Had they found him?

She pulled her bed jacket around her and called out, 'Who is it?'

'It's Alah.' The door opened and a hand appeared holding a cup of tea, followed by Alah in her dressing gown.

'I wanted to see how you are and thought you might like a cup?'

This kindness provoked a sudden outpouring of Crawfie's tears.

'Now, now,' Alah said gently, 'What on earth has happened?'

Crawfie told her everything, Alah's lips getting tighter with disapproval as the story progressed.

Crawfie wiped her eyes and sniffed. 'So, you see, anything could have happened to him. I am so worried.'

Alah thought carefully before saying, 'Now, dear, if I know men, they always fall on their feet. A pound to a penny he'll turn up sooner or later. Why, at this moment, he's probably reading the morning paper and eating a full English somewhere. Mark my words.' She patted Crawfie's hands. 'I think it's best we keep this between ourselves.'

Crawfie agreed. 'Please don't tell Bobo. She's a dear but . . . well, you know.'

'She'll hear nothing from me.' Alah patted her hand again.

Crawfie was exhausted and empty of further tears. She asked pitifully, 'But what shall I do? Should I report him missing?'

'Maybe in a few days but not now. No news is good news, isn't it? You're bound to hear from him soon.'

'I suppose so.'

'Now, you get yourself up and dressed and ready for the schoolroom.'

'Good morning, Crawfie,' the two Princesses chimed as they entered the schoolroom, followed by Dookie the corgi.

'Good morning, girls and Master Dookie.' Crawfie bent to tickle the dog's ears. 'And how are you with a paint brush, young sir?'

The Princesses giggled. 'He can paint muddy paws up the stairs,' Margaret said.

Lilibet crouched down to pat him. 'He's very good at that. *And* getting fur on Alah's favourite chair.'

'Well, he'll have to be a very good boy if he is to stay for lessons today.' Crawfie straightened up, her head suddenly swimming with the rush of blood to her head and lack of sleep.

'Why?' asked Margaret.

'Because I don't want him dipping his tail in the paint pot.'

The girls laughed again. 'He will be good, we promise.'

Dookie skulked under the girls' desk and flopped down with a sigh. 'See?' said Lilibet.

Crawfie didn't usually encourage Dookie to visit the schoolroom, but she didn't have the mental energy to throw him out today.

'What are we painting?' Margaret asked.

'I hope it's a horse,' said Lilibet.

'Well, yes, it is.' Crawfie went to the large book on her desk and turned to the page she had marked with a strip of paper. 'It's a painting of a horse called Molly Long Legs. She was a famous racehorse and here is a picture of her with her jockey.' She held the book up in front of the girls, who were instantly enraptured. 'She's a brown horse.'

Lilibet interrupted. 'You mean she's a bay. That's what a brown horse is called.'

'Ah yes. A bay. Well done,' Crawfie said. 'And she has a very short tail. Do you know why?'

Lilibet's arm shot up but Margaret shouted out, 'So that it doesn't get caught up in the rigging of a carriage.'

Lilibet, not to be outdone said, 'And it's called docking. I know because Grandpa told us all about it when we were little.'

'Very good. Now this painting is by a man called Mr Stubbs. George Stub—' Crawfie stopped. She had successfully put George from her mind for just a few seconds but now, saying his name in another setting brought fresh anguish.

Margaret pulled a face at her sister and chattered on, 'Mummy likes his paintings.'

'She has two in her drawing room,' Lilibet added. 'And don't stick your tongue out at me, Margaret, it's rude.'

'But *I* wanted to tell Crawfie that bit. You are showing off.'

'I don't show off.'

'Did!'

'Didn't!'

Dookie ran out from under the desk and started barking, running in small circles from one girl to the other.

Crawfie banged the book shut. 'QUIET.'

Lilibet blushed and said quietly, 'Sorry, Crawfie.'

Margaret, in shock at the sudden noise, began to cry.

Crawfie grabbed Dookie, who immediately nipped her hand, and hauled him out of the room and into the corridor. A footman was approaching. 'Take this dog away from my schoolroom,' she ordered.

'Where shall I take him?' he asked, grabbing the dog by its scruff.

'Anywhere but here.' Crawfie was shaking. Two fingers of her left hand had deep teeth marks and were starting to bleed.

'Are you all right?' the footman asked. 'You might need some iodine on that.' He frowned, scooping Dookie into an armlock.

'Oh and I've got a note for you, miss.' He handed over a small white envelope, marked only with her name.

She knew the handwriting. Tears pricked her eyes.

The footman was wrestling with Dookie. 'Stop your fighting or you'll get my boot up your backside, you horrible little mutt.'

'Thank you.' Crawfie stood watching as dog and footman walked away. 'And I am so sorry to be so snappy,' she called after him. 'I didn't sleep very well.'

'That's all right, miss,' he said over the head of the struggling Dookie. 'I've had much worse from the boss.'

The unopened letter from George was still in her hand. He was alive, then. Where was he – down in the kitchen, charming Cook into making him a cup of tea? Or was he talking to Ainslie? The whole household would see him. Were they gossiping in the pantry about him . . . and her?

'Crawfie?' Lilibet's voice startled her. She was peering around the doorway. 'We are very sorry. Can we paint our pictures now, please?'

Crawfie stuffed the envelope into the pocket of her cardigan. She took a deep breath and, steadying herself, said with authority, 'Yes, but no more Dookie in my lessons.'

Chapter Twenty-Five

145 Piccadilly, mid-September 1936

The letter burned in her pocket all morning. The lunch hour couldn't come quickly enough. She delivered the Princesses to the dining room with haste, desperate to return to the privacy of her bedroom to read George's message. But as she made to escape, the Duchess called her back.

'Oh, Crawfie, dear.'

Crawfie stopped. 'Yes, ma'am?'

'Queen Mary is taking a day away from mourning tomorrow to visit Southampton. She has been invited to lunch on RMS *Queen Mary*. She hasn't seen the ship since she launched her back in May and she needs cheering up so she would like the Duke and me, and the girls too, of course, to join her.'

Crawfie's mind was immediately working on a plan for this unexpected day off. She would find George and get to the bottom of his disappearance. 'How wonderful. The girls will enjoy a family day out.'

Margaret bounced on her dining chair. 'Are we going to the seaside? Can we have ice creams?'

Her mother laid a hand on her daughter's arm. 'We'll see, won't we? It's such a beautiful ship.' The Duchess smiled dreamily. 'We'll have lots of fun and it's very educational.'

'I am sure it is,' said Crawfie. 'You will have a wonderful day indeed.'

The Duchess smiled. 'Oh, we will. Now, join us for lunch and we can discuss the arrangements.'

Crawfie had lost the chance to read George's letter. Smothering her frustration with as neat a smile as she could manage, she sat at the place Ainslie had hurriedly laid.

Unfolding her napkin and spreading it on her lap, she asked, 'What time tomorrow morning would you like me to have the girls ready for Southampton?'

The Duke spoke. 'We shall leave at 09.00 hours. Back to London by 18.30. Function at the Guildhall tomorrow evening.'

The Duchess smiled. 'My husband still talks like a sailor.'

Crawfie did some mental arithmetic. She would have over nine hours free of her duties: time enough to find George and let him know how much he meant to her

The Duchess was still chatting away. 'I have never been aboard the *Queen Mary*, but I hear she is quite splendid. The Queen is very fond of her, and her captain. He telegraphed Buckingham Palace this evening to invite her aboard. Wasn't that thoughtful? The ship is on its way back from New York and will dock in Southampton late tonight. Tomorrow she will refuel and replenish her food and drink stocks before the new passengers arrive. We shall have the whole boat to ourselves for the day!'

'Ship, darling,' said the Duke. 'It's not a boat.'

The Duchess laughed. 'The passengers don't get on until the evening. Won't it be fun?'

'Embark,' muttered the Duke.

'Yes, yes, embark.' The Duchess flapped her hand. 'Now, Crawfie, I suggest you pack a waterproof coat, sensible shoes and a cardigan in case. Being near water one always feels the wind.'

Crawfie's heart plummeted. She was expected to join them? No free day to find George?

The Duchess grinned. 'What a wonderful day we shall have.'

*

The afternoon in the schoolroom dragged frustratingly slowly. George's letter still begged to be read and Crawfie was constantly aware of it within her pocket. Supposing he had decided that their friendship was over, that he had found someone else? What if he had simply realized that she, Marion, was not the woman for him after all?

She looked at the little Princesses, their heads bent over a huge book about RMS *Queen Mary* that the Duke had had fetched for them from his library. This was her job and her duty: to educate the royal children, to give them security, routine and happiness.

She stoically pushed her own desires aside.

'Look, Crawfie.' Lilibet was pointing to one of the photos. 'There's Granny launching her boat!'

'Ship,' said Crawfie unconsciously.

The girls pored over the pictures. There were shots of the gentlemen's Turkish Bath, a swimming pool and, best of all, the children's play area with slides and a toy piano.

At last the school day came to its close, and the girls were collected by Alah and taken up to the nursery.

Crawfie, turning down her usual cup of tea with Alah and Bobo, slipped into her room and locked the door.

The envelope opened with ease, having been stuck down carelessly. The one sheet of paper within was plain, the note itself short:

My dear Marion,

Forgive me for delivering this by hand, but I did not know how else to get this message to you as quickly as possible.

You must think me an awful heel not turning up at the teashop. You see, I got into London on an earlier train as my interview with the bank had been brought forward and they wanted to see me that afternoon. They kept me waiting for two hours and by the time the meeting was finished, it was after six. I had hoped you might wait, but the café was shut by the time I got there.

*Would you meet me so that I can explain? I shall be in
Kensington Gardens by the Peter Pan statue on Saturday at
10.00 a.m.*

Please come.

George

Marion reread the note with joy. Of course he wouldn't ever let
her down – not in the way she had let him down by being so
absent. She should and would make herself more available to
him, make him see how important he was to her. She resolved
to make more time in her life for him. She wasn't quite sure how,
but she would.

That thought was immediately dashed by the realization that
she would be in Windsor at the weekend and wouldn't be able
to meet him in Kensington Gardens. She could hardly do
anything about that now.

She would have to write to him, at Mrs Bridie's Highlands
Guest House, and explain. Perhaps he could come to Windsor
to meet her? It would have to be Sunday morning while the
family were at church, but she could find an excuse not to join
them. Telling the Duchess the truth would cause a fuss – the
Duchess was not fond of her staff changing plans at the last
minute. She wasn't an unkind woman, but Marion suspected
that the Duchess would not appreciate the need to see one's man
friend as important enough to miss church. The only option
was to fib a little.

She reached for her pen and notepaper and scrawled a quick
note:

Dear George,

*I shall be in Windsor for the weekend. Could you come to
Snow Hill, in Windsor Great Park, and meet me by the statue
of the Copper Horse? Same time, 10 o'clock? I will be there, but
only for an hour while the family are at church.*

So sorry to be a nuisance. I hope you can be there.
I am so looking forward to seeing you.
Marion

She hurriedly folded the sheet into an envelope, hoping to catch the house post which left at 5.15 p.m. every day. She reached for her little box of stamps but caught it awkwardly so that the lid flew open and her stash of stamps jumped out of the box and onto the carpet beneath her desk. Kneeling to pick them up, she banged her head on the open drawer of her bureau. She crumpled in despair.

Rubbing her sore scalp with one hand, while picking up stamps with the other, Marion was close to tears. She would have thrown herself on the bed for ten minutes of pure self-pity if she had had the time. She could hear her mother's voice: *more haste less speed, Marion.*

'Oh, shut up! Just shut up,' she said to the empty room. She stuck a stamp on the envelope and pulled herself together. 'Right, Miss Crawford. Stop your mewling and damn well get on with it.'

She stared at herself in her long mirror, pricked with age spots spreading like lichen across its silvery glass. Her reflection looked back at her: tired eyes, tired hairstyle, tired cardigan and blouse. What would George think of her?

'No time for vanity, Marion,' she told herself briskly. 'He either likes you as you are, or not at all. It can't be helped.'

She caught the house post, thanks to Ainslie, who called the footman back as he was leaving with the small pile of envelopes.

'Mr Jordan, Miss Crawford has a letter.'

'Thank you. Thank you so much.' She flushed as Ainslie caught sight of the addressee. 'A friend I haven't seen for a while,' she said hurriedly. 'Just catching up.'

Ainslie was no fool, but he said only, 'Very good.'

*

The evening was spent darning her best pair of stockings and ironing her good blouse for tomorrow's trip. The routine and rhythm of these small domestic tasks soothed her frayed emotions and by bedtime she was feeling calmer. She said a prayer of thanks that George was fit and well as she got into bed. There were just three days until Sunday and it would not do to arrive at the Copper Horse in a state of tearful agitation.

Chapter Twenty-Six

145 Piccadilly, mid-September 1936

Dear Mother and Dad,

Today I went aboard RMS Queen Mary! My first time on an ocean liner and it is the greatest ship in the world. I was in good company: Queen Mary, the Duke and Duchess, the girls and ME!

Remember how, as a child, I read avidly about the sinking of the Titanic? RMS Queen Mary is a descendant of that fated ship and I must admit I was as excited to see her as any of the royal party.

We took the royal train from Waterloo to Southampton this morning. I had never travelled on a train of such splendour before. It's like an hotel on wheels! Queen Mary insisted that I sat in the same carriage as them all and I marvelled at the comfort of the seats; we each had our own armchairs, and refreshments were served to us. We enjoyed the delicate sandwiches, cakes and tea as the countryside whizzed past us. Dear Queen Mary encouraged us all to 'tuck in'.

She is so kind and was grateful, I think, that she was accompanied by us all.

The Duchess is very fond of her mother-in-law and I must admit I continue to admire her very much. The girls constantly asked her questions about her ship: 'How big is it? How many passengers does it hold? Will it sink like the Titanic?' All these she answered until, needing some peace, she asked me if the girls had books they might read quietly?

I pulled from my bag Lilibet's Black Beauty *and Margaret's* Babar the Elephant; *I had thought it best not to pack Agatha Christie.*

Technically, Margaret is rather too old for Babar but she loves the story and enjoys the wonderful illustrations. Also, it keeps her quiet!

With the girls occupied and the gentle rocking of the train, I gave myself permission to close my eyes. The Duke was fast asleep across the aisle from me, snoring gently.

The Queen and the Duchess must have imagined I was asleep, too. They were talking quietly to avoid waking the Duke and to keep their talk from the girls, but I couldn't help but overhear. Please, please never tell anyone about what I am about to write, but it has really unsettled me and may have repercussions for the whole country. I shouldn't write any of this, I know, but I need to tell someone and who can I trust better than my own parents?

You will find this as shocking as I did.

'The thing is,' the Queen said in a low voice, 'I am so afraid he may ask me to receive her.'

I opened my eyes a crack, and saw two bright spots of crimson burning on her cheeks. I shut them immediately, but by now my hearing was horribly alert.

'He gives her the most beautiful jewels.'

The Duchess spoke. 'The whole situation is horribly complicated. I do not feel I can make advances to her or ask her to my house again. I am so unhappy about it. I am sorry for being so indiscreet but there is no one I can talk to. Dear Bertie and David have been such friends and now all is strained. We live a life of conjecture, never knowing what will happen tomorrow.'

The Queen replied, 'I am more worried than I can say. The tension, sorrow and loneliness are unbearable. The King, if he were still alive, would surely talk sense into David. What a mess we have got into, and all for such an unworthy person!'

The Duchess lowered her voice still further and what I heard next I couldn't believe. 'How can David contemplate such a step as abdication? It puts Bertie and me in such a horrible position.'

Yes, that's what she said. Abdication. I had no idea that this could even be allowed. Is the new King, Edward VIII, really discussing the possibility of giving up his birthright for Mrs Simpson? It doesn't seem possible. This is 1936, not the dark ages. Surely a man can marry the woman he loves, whatever her background?

'I shall write to him,' the Duchess continued. 'I will ask him to be kind to Bertie. We love David and want him to be happy, but I am so terrified for my husband, and for us all. I will ask him not to tell Bertie that I have written. It would only upset him further.'

Mother, I wish I had not overheard this conversation. The King cannot, must not, abdicate. Perhaps – and forgive me for saying so – perhaps he can marry a respectable girl, one the nation can love, one who can bear the children he must produce, and then keep Mrs Simpson as a friend of whom he is very fond? That must surely be a way forward. Which king hasn't had a favourite? A way must be found.

Otherwise, the Crown will go to the next son and his wife: the Duke and Duchess of York. Icy fingers grip my heart at the thought of dear Lilibet becoming the heir to the throne.

She wants a life in the country with horses and dogs. She and I have imagined that often enough.

'I want a stable full of horses to look after and lots of dogs to go on long walks with,' she told me, only a few days ago. 'And a nice husband and some children.'

The Crown would change her life forever.

Abdication?

It can't happen.

It's a storm in a teacup.

*Not the first one either, but the Prime Minister and the King
will make sure the waters are soothed, I am sure.*

*We will all get through this the same way we got through the
Great War. Bravery. Trust. Strength.*

*Dear Mother and Dad, thank you for reading this and
allowing me to get it all off my chest. I feel a lot better for it. I
am finding increasingly that life in the royal family – indeed life
for any adult – is all about training oneself to deal with all and
any unpalatable dilemmas.*

Yours fondly,
Marion

PS The RMS Queen Mary *really is a very wonderful ship, truly
the greatest liner the world has ever seen and a testament to the
Scottish shipbuilders of the Clyde.*

Marion laid down her pen. It was late, and 145 Piccadilly was at
rest. In the knowledge that all its inhabitants were sleeping,
Marion reread her letter, folded it carefully in four, and walked
to the grate with its still glowing ash.

Tearing the letter in half, she threw it onto the embers and
watched as it slowly smoked, then caught. Its edges curled in
the flame. She watched until it was unreadable, fragile, charred –
irrevocably changed from the letter it had been minutes ago.

It was a letter she had needed to write, but a letter that could
never be sent. It was the work of a traitor and she knew her
mother could not be trusted to stay quiet.

She stirred the final remains with the small poker, feeling her
emotions relax. There could be no abdication. Life would
continue. She would never, ever tell a living soul what she had
heard that day.

Chapter Twenty-Seven

Windsor, late September 1936

'Good morning, sir, ma'am.' Crawfie brought the two little girls, in their Sunday best, down for breakfast.

'Good morning, Crawfie.' The Duchess was looking very beautiful in a soft apricot gown with chiffon sleeves and a row of pearls at her neck. 'We shall leave for church at nine forty-five, if you would like to meet us at the door?'

'Ma'am, I wonder if I may be excused? I would like to use the time to write up the lesson plans for next week. The wonderful trip to Southampton has given me some ideas for a history topic.'

The rehearsed lie was told – and believed. No objection was made to their governess, who they thanked for her diligence. Marion felt a small rush of guilt, but it was not strong enough to make her come clean.

The gardens of Royal Lodge were gently misted with an autumn dew as Marion slipped out of the back door. The sun was bright with a pleasant warmth and her walk into Windsor Great Park, heading for the Copper Horse, gave her a chance to calm the butterflies in her stomach. She took deep breaths of the sweet air and her long shadow, following beside her, comforted her.

The September sun was low in the sky and its rays bounced off the Copper Horse on the horizon. She shaded her eyes from the glare and squinted. Was George there already? As far as she could tell there was nobody there at all. But it was not quite ten o'clock.

She had been imagining this meeting for days. George had sent no reply to her letter, but she was certain he would come. She had no doubt that Mrs Bridie would have put the letter in George's hands, and she trusted him. In a way, she was glad he hadn't written; a letter delivered to her always brought with it some innocent curiosity from the downstairs staff. Ainslie, she felt sure, had begun to recognize George's handwriting after the few letters he had sent in the spring.

The Copper Horse was now maybe one hundred yards away. No sign of George yet, but there were still a few minutes in hand.

What would they say when they saw each other again?

She walked with purpose, her breathing increasing with every step.

Fifty yards.

Ten yards.

Five yards.

She reached the base of the monument.

He wasn't there.

Well, she told herself, she *had* left early and walked quickly.

A movement to her left caught her attention and as she turned, a pair of hands clamped themselves over her eyes.

She gave a little yelp. 'George?'

'Aye.' His familiar deep voice was as sweet as Scottish air.

She laughed. 'Let me see you.'

He stood before her, dressed in good tweed trousers and his familiar overcoat and trilby hat. He put his hand into one of his pockets and brought out a sprig of white heather tied with a tartan ribbon. 'From near home – picked specially to remind you of home and to bring you . . . us . . . luck.' He handed it to her with a courtier's bow

'Oh, George!' She lifted the flowers to her nose; they smelt of the Scottish hills.

He asked, 'Do you forgive me for missing you at the tearoom?'

'I was so worried.'

'How do you think I felt when you weren't there?'

'I was there until closing time. The waitress told you.'

'I am only kidding you. I am so sorry I had to wait for the interview at the bank. However . . .' He grinned. 'I have good news.'

She gripped the heather, not noticing the prickles in her palm. 'You got the job?'

'Aye.'

'How wonderful. Does it mean you'll be working in London?'

He looked around them. 'Is there anywhere we could go to talk comfortably? Maybe get that cup of tea at last?'

Marion checked her small watch and sighed. 'I don't have much time. Can't we just sit here? It's such a lovely day.'

'But the grass is damp.'

'Oh, I don't mind.'

'Well, we can sit on my coat. I wouldn't want you to get your skirt damp.'

Marion watched as he spread his coat. It seemed such a romantic gesture, and she felt her heart swell. He took her hand and helped her to sit down comfortably on the bottle-green coat. It still held the warmth of him.

'There now.' He lay, propped on one arm. 'Tell me all your news. You don't write as much as you used to. I miss your letters.'

'When I hadn't heard from you for a while I thought maybe you were bored by them. By me.'

'How could I be? And it's not just the letters I have missed.' His deep brown eyes wandered over her face. 'How are you, Marion?'

'I'm happy to see you.' He was here in front of her at last. She was floating somewhere above herself, looking down on them. She swallowed hard, tried to bring herself back to the moment. 'I can't believe you are really here.'

He lifted her hand to his lips and kissed it. 'I feel the same.'

For a moment, Marion thought he was going to kiss her lips too. It would be heavenly, she was sure – though it would be too awful if anyone saw them. She breathed in, waiting, her mind whirring, but George didn't move. The moment passed, and he let her hand drop as he fumbled in his trouser pockets for his cigarettes and lighter.

'Tell me about the job,' she said.

George lit his cigarette and blew a perfect smoke ring. 'It's rather good, actually. A private bank in the city. Drummonds. Small and discreet, which makes it attractive to people with a lot of money. We give each customer a personal service and they can rest assured their money is in safe hands.'

'You will be living in London, then?' What did she say that for? She snatched at a long blade of grass to hide her embarrassment.

'In time, yes, but I shall be mostly at the Aberdeen branch for a while.' He stubbed his cigarette out. 'Running it, actually.'

'The manager?' Marion was thrilled. To think that she had a bank manager as a suitor! Her mother would be beside herself with the very idea . . . If she found out, that was – which she wouldn't. Not yet anyway.

And yet Aberdeen was such a long way away.

'Something like that, aye.'

'So how often will you be in London?'

'To start with? Once a month.'

Marion hid her disappointment. 'Oh, that's wonderful. It will be very nice to see you more often.' She felt herself flush.

'I might be down more often, as the job progresses.' He smiled. 'And by the way, Mrs Bridie at The Highlands? She's very nice, but the woman can't stop talking. And all that tartan! And the stuffed animals! In the bathroom there is even a painting of Nessie – terrifying when you get in the bath!' George laughed heartily. 'Well, there's only so much haggis and porridge a man can take at breakfast.'

Marion immediately felt foolish. She had thought the place perfect and Mrs Bridie a dear. How could she not have seen that tartan was indeed everywhere? She'd only seen one stuffed rabbit, dangling from the jaws of a rigid fox in the sitting room. It had seemed very like the decorations of Balmoral but on a smaller scale. She had actually liked it.

'Oh dear. I'm sorry.'

'Aye well. No harm done. You weren't to know about Nessie, but did you not see the rest of it? The place gave me a laugh, but I can't stay there again.'

'I suppose not.'

He laughed. 'Och, you weren't to know.'

She quietly berated herself. She felt she'd let him down.

'What's the worried face for?' He smiled at her. 'You did your best. Don't be silly.'

She checked her watch. 'I'll have to go in a minute.'

'Duty calls, eh?'

'Yes.'

He took her hand again. 'Just stay a few more minutes. I haven't seen you for so long and they see you every day, the lucky devils. What do you say, just ten more minutes?'

Marion wished she could stay, but she knew it was impossible. She began to gather herself and stood up. 'Oh George, I hate not seeing you. I wish I could see you every day.'

'Do you?'

'Yes, I do. But this is my job for now.' She hesitated. 'It won't be forever.'

'When will you leave?'

Marion swallowed hard. 'Well, I . . . I have to stay until the Princesses finish their education.'

George picked his coat up and looked at her, shaking his head. 'That must be another eight or ten years at least.' He held his arms wide. 'Look at me, Marion. I will be an old man by then. Can you not see? I want to be with you, Marion. I am doing my best. I've taken the job at the bank so that I can come to London more often, just to be closer to you.'

'Oh, George.' Marion did not know what to feel; she was flattered, anxious, torn. 'I am doing my best, but . . . I can't leave them in the lurch just now.'

George put on his coat and began to do up the buttons. 'At least I know where I stand.'

'It's not that . . .' Marion felt wretched. 'George, where do *I* stand with *you*?'

'Would it make any difference? Marion, you have to work out what you want.'

'George, I am so sorry.' She quickly glanced at her watch. Time was running out and she had to be back soon.

He saw her and sighed. 'There you are, you see – needing to be gone. I have to be off, too. I am on the afternoon train back home.'

Marion didn't know how everything had gone so wrong. 'I thought perhaps you might be here for a few more days? We need to talk. You are cross with me. George, you mean so much to me. Please stay just for a couple of days longer and I will find the time. We could have dinner and . . .'

'I'll let you know when I'm coming back. In the meantime, you look after that piece of heather. Every time you look at it, remember that I will be thinking of you.'

'Oh George . . .'

He smiled at her, though the brightness didn't reach his eyes. 'Off you go like a good girl. I don't like goodbyes. And don't look back – I will be watching you until you disappear from sight.' He put both hands on her shoulders. 'I mean it. Now go, before I stop you.'

He did stay to watch her go, but she didn't turn round. She didn't see the old woman either, carrying a flat wicker basket full of heather that she was selling to the young couples and families taking an autumn stroll. She didn't hear her telling them, 'Genuine lucky heather. Ha'penny a bunch.'

She recognized George as he walked past, 'Hello again, sir. Did your young lady like the bunch?'

He raised his hat to her. 'She did indeed.'

Marion felt his loving eyes watching as she walked away to Royal Lodge.

She was in love, she knew, and in his thrall. His order not to turn back made her feel safe and cared for. But she had hurt him, she knew. Of course he must feel that she had neglected him – and she believed she had. How could she have got into such a difficult situation? She should have told him that she loved him, that she wanted to be with him. But what then?

She twisted the sprig of heather between finger and thumb, certain that he would be thinking of her.

What a fool she had been, expecting that something so parochial as The Highlands would have suited him. He must think her an absolute dolt. Unsophisticated and unworldly.

She would have to pay better attention to his likes and dislikes, so that when – *if* – they married, their home would be exactly how he liked it. She would focus on the subtleties of what was considered socially correct: the right colour of crockery, the correct weight of cutlery, how to decorate a house.

From now on she would do her best to please George. She would have to make more time for him, write more often, find ways to see him whenever he was down in London. She must find more space in her life for George. For the man she now knew she wanted to marry – should he ever ask her.

Chapter Twenty-Eight

145 Piccadilly, October 1936

Crawfie was on an outing to the Tower of London with the Princesses when first she saw a photograph of Mrs Simpson on the front page of a newspaper. The car in which they were travelling stopped at traffic lights along the Embankment, and on the pavement a newsboy was doing good business, waving the early edition of the *London Evening News*. 'King and Mrs Simpson. Read all about it!'

Crawfie was horrified. Thankfully the lights changed and the car moved off before the Princesses could become aware of the unpleasant sight.

The driver, however, young Jackson, caught her eye in the rear-view mirror and raised his eyebrows knowingly. Flustered, she looked away. Gossiping between servants must be discouraged, now more than ever.

As they pulled up to the Tower, she decided not to think about the unsettling incident and concentrate on the job in hand.

'Come along, girls.'

Stepping out of the car, they were met by a Yeoman of the Guard in full scarlet and black regalia. He swept off his hat and bowed. 'Good morning.'

'I know who you are,' Lilibet said.

'So do I,' chirped Margaret. 'You're a Beefeater. Is that all you eat?'

'Don't be silly,' Lilibet admonished her. 'I expect he eats all sorts of things. Don't you?' She looked at the yeoman.

'Yes, Your Royal Highness, that is correct. Beefeaters get a ration of beef every day, thanks to old King Henry VIII. But I eat all my greens as well.'

'Even cabbage?' asked Margaret.

'Yes, ma'am.'

'Eugh. Pooey.' Margaret held her nose between her fingers.

Crawfie took immediate action. 'Apologize at once, young lady. That is very rude.'

Sullenly, the little Princess did so.

The yeoman laughed and introduced himself. 'My name is James and it is my great pleasure to be escorting you ladies through the Tower today. I'll give you a bit of a history lesson as we go. Are you ready?'

'Ready,' said Lilibet excitedly.

'Follow me,' said James. 'Now, if you happen to see one of our ghosts, will you let me know?'

'Are they scary?' Margaret asked quietly.

'She's only six, so she gets frightened,' Lilibet told him. 'I'm ten so I am quite brave.'

'That's good to know.' James smiled at Margaret. 'It just depends how the ghosts are feeling today.'

Crawfie smiled at the girls, who were looking worried. 'Don't you worry. I am not afraid of ghosts.'

'All right,' the girls chimed uncertainly.

'You can always hold my hand,' Crawfie said.

As they set off to follow James, Crawfie soon felt two little hands steal into hers.

In some of the darker rooms, the girls didn't want to stay for too long. James's talent for telling creepy stories was excellent, but the tales of murdered young princesses did not go down too well.

The armoury was more of a success. Standing in front of the huge armour worn by Henry VIII, the girls chuckled and pointed at the large metal codpiece attached to it.

James caught them. 'Well, he wouldn't want his winky shot off with an arrow now, would he?'

The girls were in gales of laughter until Crawfie asked them to stop. 'That's enough, thank you, ladies.'

James was seamless. 'Who wants to see the world's biggest diamond?'

The Princesses and Crawfie stared in silent awe through the toughened glass.

'You see the sceptre there?' James pointed. 'Every monarch since Charles II has held that at his or her coronation. The diamond in the top is the world's largest – the Cullinan, found in 1905. And you see the empty velvet cushion next to it? That is where St Edward's crown usually rests, but it is at the jewellers being cleaned and resized to fit His Majesty King Edward VIII at the moment, ready for his coronation in the spring.'

James moved along to another display, while the girls chattered beside him, excited to be so close to the twinkling treasure trove.

Crawfie heard Lilibet say, 'Mummy has worn those earrings. I saw them on her dressing table.'

'I've seen her wear her crown,' Margaret said.

'No you haven't,' Lilibet scoffed. 'She has a coronet. She can't have a crown because she's not a queen.'

'Not just queens wear crowns.'

'Oh, do be quiet and *listen*,' huffed Lilibet.

Crawfie stayed where she was, consumed by the sight of the empty cushion. If the King were to be crowned, he would have to postpone his marriage to Mrs Simpson until it was deemed respectable. But how awful it seemed for two people to be in love and not be able to marry. How could anyone want to stand in the way of love?

Her own heart was suffering from the absence of George. She hadn't seen him since the Copper Horse meeting – she liked to call it that in her mind; it sounded so romantic – and the weeks apart from him were causing her pain. They had been writing to each other since then, but his letters weren't as easy as they had been and when he mentioned her work he seemed to do it grudgingly. She did her best to write cheerful, newsy missives, but the very real problem of when she would leave the royal family and commit herself to their friendship (she daren't call it a relationship) was not discussed and he seemed to have withdrawn from her. Unfortunately, his work at the London office of Drummonds bank was postponed until the following spring, and he would be in Aberdeen continually until then.

But she was definitely going home for Christmas. She hoped George might make his intentions clear by then, so that she knew for certain where her future lay.

Lilibet's voice broke into her thoughts. 'James says we can see the Ravens. Come on, Crawfie!'

Eventually, the history tour was over. Outside, Jackson slid the car towards them, hopping out to help them in.

'Got something for you, Miss Crawford.' He passed a folded newspaper to her. 'Thought you might like it.'

She glimpsed the photo of Mrs Simpson on the front. 'Thank you, Jackson,' she said sharply. 'I am sure Alah would like to read it.'

Buckingham Palace, October 1936

Tommy stood in his office, clenched fists by his side, the newspaper on the desk in front of him. The details in the later edition of the *London Evening News* were worse than the earlier one.

'Where the hell did they get that photograph?' he exclaimed. 'And who is leaking this stuff to the paper? The entire situation needs to be handled with extreme diplomacy if the King has a hope in hell of marrying her. It could take years. But of course, he has always wanted things now. Always now.'

P-T, the only other person in the room, knew to let her boss expend all his anger before offering him a cup of tea.

'I need a whisky. Large. Ice and soda.'

When she returned with his drink, she found him smoking his pipe furiously. She handed him the whisky.

'Sir.'

'Yes?'

'The King has asked to see you.'

'What does he want? Other than to finish me off before my time?'

'Apparently there is rather a flap on in Downing Street.'

He snorted. 'Oh, you do surprise me.'

'Yes, sir. The PM wants to speak to you.'

'Before or after I see the King?'

'Now, sir. He's on the line.'

'Let me finish this drink and then put him through.'

Tommy was unsurprised to find the Prime Minister furious. 'The man has no sense,' he said down the telephone. 'He *cannot* marry that woman.'

'Yes sir, I do agree, sir.' Tommy put a finger underneath his winged collar.

'He is blackmailing the government, and the country, by threatening to abdicate if he cannot marry Mrs Simpson.'

'I concur, sir.'

'Can he not do what his forebears have done for generations and set her up in a country house where they could get up to whatever they liked, in private? He *cannot* give up the throne.'

'No, sir.'

'Can you talk to him?'

'He is expecting me now, sir.'

'Good. Let me know if he is sober.'

Seventeen minutes later, Tommy was ushered into the King's presence. The King was relaxing in an armchair, smoking. Mrs Simpson was pacing by the window with a cocktail in hand.

'Ah, Tommy.' The King waved at the paper on the table by his side. 'Have you read that?'

'Yes, sir. I have.'

'What are we going to do about it?'

'What do you want to do about it?'

Mrs Simpson snapped, 'Oh, for Christ's sakes. *Stop* them writing about *me!*'

Tommy inclined his head. 'Unfortunately, that is rather, as we Brits say, shutting the stable door after the horse has bolted.'

She fixed her flinty eyes on Tommy. 'Listen to me. When I fell in love with David, I had no idea that it would be anything like this. It is not just that they are attacking me, or their King. They are attacking their own monarchy.'

'Yes indeed.' Tommy couldn't bear this sort of woolly patriotism, especially when it came from an American. 'But, you see, Mrs Simpson, we do have rules and protocol to follow. Blame Henry VIII. He broke with Rome, created the Church of England and called himself Defender of the Faith who had the divine right of Kings. In effect, the church would tolerate divorce but frown on remarriage, and—'

'I don't need a damn lesson in British history. I need you to *stop* them attacking me.' Mrs Simpson threw the newspaper at him. He stood respectfully as the pages showered down around him like very large snowflakes.

'Oh, darling!' cried the King. 'Poor Tommy.'

She ran from the room.

The King looked sorrowfully after her, then rang the bell, presumably for another cocktail. 'So, Tommy, the thing is,' he said, 'we have a problem. Wallis and I love each other and wish to be married. If the archaic rules of old Henry remain, I shall abdicate.'

'Ah, sir,' Tommy replied. 'I think that is rather what the PM is worried about.'

The King set his jaw. 'Bloody Baldwin can go and boil his bloody head. You can tell him that. You may go.'

Tommy did go. Straight back to his office to do what he always did in crisis: write to his wife.

Dear Joan,

God, how I long to be home with you. How is the garden looking? Have you lifted the dahlias yet?

Rather larger problems here. The King is insistent that he wishes to plant Mrs Simpson at the centre of the monarchy by marrying her. He's mad with love, apparently. Why does he have to marry her? Why not keep her as a mistress? He's had enough practice. I suppose she wants to be Queen, but I cannot see the country swallowing that.

Poor Baldwin is apoplectic. The King must not marry a divorcee. Besides, we all know the divorcee in question would make an appalling Queen and has no love of children. She pretends with the York girls but it's clear she has no interest in them. She is furious that the British press now have the story (I don't know how we stopped them for so long – the foreign press has been running it for months) and the King is threatening abdication. It's a poor threat.

God knows what this is doing to his mother. The respect Queen Mary has within the royal household and among the people is second to none.

Does the King really think Mrs Simpson could live up to that?

Presumably he cannot bear to be out of the company of his American friend for more than twenty-four hours. I hear he has given her £50,000 of jewellery which has been in the royal family for several generations. Unfortunately, somebody told the Queen this, and she has showed her displeasure by being distant and cool towards him. Both commendable and proper.

All those years I spent in service to him when he was Prince of Wales, I witnessed such disgraceful behaviour. He was always late, keeping dignitaries waiting, arriving smelling of the previous evening's excessive drinking and, on one occasion, unshaved. Unforgiveable.

I was right to leave him when I did. I had hoped that, returning to work with him after more than a decade, I would find some maturity in him. He has never said an unkind word to me, but I find his character as appalling as ever.

My love to the children, and perhaps you could make a trip to London soon, and allow your old husband to take you to lunch?

With my fondest love,
Tommy

Chapter Twenty-Nine

Windsor, 11th December 1936

The worst had happened.

Sitting at his desk, staring across the room, Tommy's head was clear and focused.

The Prime Minister had done all he could to dissuade the King from abdicating, but the King insisted he could not sit on the throne without the woman he loved by his side.

This impasse had gone on for weeks but now the final blow had fallen. The King was to be forever severed from his birthright.

The end had come.

Tommy had been witness to one dreadful conversation where the Prime Minister almost begged the King. 'Think of the country, sir. Your father. Your mother. There is time to change your mind.'

But the King was determined. 'The answer is the same, Mr Baldwin. No marriage, no coronation.'

Mrs Simpson had been distraught. Finally she understood that she was the one responsible for the situation. Tommy did not doubt that there were strong feelings between her and the King, but she did not wish to be the most hated woman in British royal history. She wrote a statement declaring her wish to 'withdraw forthwith from the situation'. Was it gallantry or cowardice? Tommy couldn't be sure, but the blithe, quick, gay and unconquerable Wallis had fled that night from England's shores to await her divorce in France.

In all of this, Tommy was a mere servant. His job was to serve the monarchy, smooth stormy waters, to apply all the smoke and mirrors of diplomacy he had at his disposal and to present this disaster as a mere blip.

With a sigh, Tommy picked up his pen.

Dear Joan,

The inevitability of the situation we have found ourselves in is worse than one could have imagined. The King will be the most tragic 'might have been' in all history. He could not have his cake and eat it, so he ate it.

I have spoken to the Duke of York, who is in a state of shock over what has happened. But he accepts the role he must now take on.

Earlier today a meeting was held to explain how the machine of state would proclaim him King on Saturday.

He listened attentively and solemnly to the briefing, after which, when we were on our own, he offered me a drink. I felt he wished to get things off his chest. And my word, he did.

The King had taken the draft Instrument of Abdication to his mother, and had wept on the Queen's shoulder for an hour. What was in his mother's heart as she held him, we will never know. Maybe she always knew he would not, could not, face the ultimate price that kingship requires.

I feel so much for her. In one year she has lost her husband, her position, and now her son.

Apparently the King gave his final dinner party at Fort Belvedere, his beloved home, two nights ago. A party of nine included Mr Baldwin, the Duke of York, and others. The King made sure they talked of everything other than the problem at hand. And his younger brother made no mention of the fact that he would soon be King.

The following day all three younger brothers – the Duke of

York, Duke of Gloucester and Duke of Kent – arrived at the Fort to witness the signing of the abdication document.

We are now in uncharted waters. May God guide us.

Our ex-King went to his room to continue packing. The Duke of York joined him. The sofa was cluttered with personal belongings and clothes but the ex-King made space for him. I heard him say, 'You are not going to find this job difficult at all. You know all the ropes.'

The Duke's stutter was amplified by the circumstance, but he managed to say, 'The first act of my reign will be to create you a Duke with the family name Windsor.'

One can only imagine the level of emotion between the two.

The Duke of York then left the Fort and returned to Royal Lodge alone. The Duchess is unwell with a bad attack of flu and had remained in London with the Princesses. The Duke sat by himself and listened to the King's radio broadcast of abdication.

At midnight the old King was packed and ready to leave the Fort without a look back. He got into his waiting car and asked the driver to take him to Royal Lodge for a final adieu to his successor, his brother.

I hear the new King George VI was surprised by the visit and almost wept as his brother bowed to him as his subject before taking his leave.

He is headed to the continent, bound for Austria, where he will stay with friends. They say Mrs Simpson will remain in France until her divorce is finalized.

So, the King is dead. Long live the King.

The British public will be devastated, naturally. But we must present the new King as a phoenix from the ashes. Capable and respected. Strong and just. A family man with a good woman at his side and two beautiful daughters.

Prince Albert, Duke of York, second in line to the throne, is now King George VI.

Has there ever before been a year of three Kings?
I shall telephone you when I can, my darling.
Fondly,
Tommy

PS I think the idea of enlarging the new kitchen garden is an
excellent one. Give Jennings the go ahead xx

145 Piccadilly, 12th December 1936

The nursery was in shock. Alah, Bobo and Crawfie had sat huddled around the wireless the previous day, listening to the King's abdication speech.

Today, the entire household ran as usual, as if on rails, but in stupefied disbelief.

The Duchess had taken to her bed, struck down by the flu she was so susceptible to. She had not been in Windsor as her husband had witnessed the final hours of the King's reign.

This morning she had woken as a Queen.

After breakfast, Crawfie took the Princesses to see her. Her bedroom curtains were half drawn, allowing the weak December daylight to creep across the carpet.

'Good morning, Your Majesty,' Crawfie said with respect and a deep curtsey.

'Good morning,' the new Queen croaked. She looked sallow against her peach pillows.

'How are you, Mummy?' Lilibet was all solicitude.

Margaret ran and jumped onto the bed, planting a kiss on her mother's face. 'Daddy's going to be King.'

'Yes, darling. I know.'

'He telephoned and told us last night,' said Margaret.

Lilibet sat on the edge of the peach-quilted counterpane. 'I think he sounded a bit sad when he told us.'

'Yes. I think he is a bit sad,' the Queen agreed.

'Why?' asked Margaret.

'Because he wanted Uncle David to stay as King.'

'Why couldn't he?'

Lilibet frowned at her little sister. 'Because he loves Mrs Simpson.'

The new Queen lifted herself limply further up her pillows. 'Darlings, this is all so difficult for Daddy. He needs us three to be good and look after him.' She looked at Crawfie, who was waiting to be dismissed. 'Isn't that right, Crawfie?'

'Indeed, ma'am.'

The Princesses snuggled up on either side of their mother. 'Margaret and I will look after you, Mummy. And Crawfie too,' Lilibet told her.

'Yes.' The new Queen stroked Lilibet's hair gently. 'You know, Crawfie, I started the year as a King's daughter-in-law, then a King's sister-in-law, and now I'm finishing the year as a Queen.' She kissed Lilibet's head. 'The future looks so different for all of us.'

Crawfie knew exactly what the Queen was thinking: her precious elder daughter would never have the life she wanted. No house in the country with dogs and children and horses.

Her future would one day be as Queen herself.

Chapter Thirty

King's Cross Station, 22nd December 1936

The train hissed and squealed as it began to pull out of King's Cross Station and Marion knew she would be using the long journey to process the last few days.

She had almost decided not to come home for Christmas. She had not wanted to leave the young Princesses at this critical and shocking time, but the Duke and Duchess – Their Majesties, she corrected herself – had persuaded her.

'Darling Crawfie, you are an absolute brick, but you must have your holiday. We shall need you to be fit and strong in the New Year.' The Queen had patted Crawfie's arm and smiled warmly.

'But you are still recovering from the flu, ma'am,' Crawfie protested. 'I am happy to look after the wee Princesses while you recover. You must rest.'

The Queen shook her head. 'Alah and Bobo always come to Sandringham for Christmas with us. The girls shall be looked after very well. Besides which, your parents must be longing to see you. In the new year, there will be a lot of change. You will have to move the schoolroom into the Palace.' The Queen sighed. 'So much to do.'

'If you are sure?'

'Absolutely. And the King agrees with me, don't you, Bertie?'

They had been in the drawing room at 145 Piccadilly, the King sitting in his armchair by the window, smoking. He had lost weight, Crawfie knew, and his skin was grey. 'What am I agreeing to?'

'Miss Crawford must go home for Christmas. We shall need her fit and rested for January.'

'Oh, good Lord, yes.' The King had tapped some ash from his cigarette. 'Crawfie, we are depending on you to do your bit in keeping the family on an even keel. If the Princesses are happy, the Queen is happy. And if the Queen is happy, the King is happy. And if the King is happy, the Country is happy . . . You see what I mean?'

Marion's train was full of people going north for Christmas. She could sense the joy of her fellow passengers as they came aboard, searching for spaces in the racks above the seats into which they could push their suitcases. She sat quietly by the window, her eyes tracking drips of condensation as they rolled down the glass.

Marion's compartment was full. A young couple were sitting beside her, while an older couple with two children – a son of about seven she guessed and daughter a little older – sat opposite. Marion was in no mood to talk. The last week had been nothing but talk. The gossip amongst the household staff and servants' quarters had taken on a life of its own.

All week photographers and reporters had been camped outside the front door of 145 Piccadilly, day and night. Flash lights popped, catching the startled expressions of cabinet ministers, clergy and the Prime Minister as they climbed from their official cars.

And there were also a determined few who hung around the basement door of the house, offering money to household staff for a story.

Ainslie had called a below-stairs meeting.

'If I catch anyone,' he had told his assembled team, 'speaking to a reporter, passing a note to a reporter, or receiving money from these grubby Fleet Street vermin, I shall see to it that they are sacked immediately without reference. Everything you hear or see that is said or done in this house is top secret. Do you understand me?'

There was a shuffling of feet and a murmured, 'Yes, Mr Ainslie.'

'The King and Queen must trust us. That is our duty. This is their home, their sanctuary, away from public interest.' Ainslie had swept his eyes around the room, searching for any guilty faces. 'If you have even the slightest suspicion that someone in this household is passing information to reporters, I am asking you to come to my room, at once, and give me that person's name.'

'You're asking us to snake on our friends?' exclaimed the under-cook.

Ainslie straightened his ramrod back further. 'I think you will find that anyone prepared to betray Their Majesties is not your friend, or mine. Anyone with information will remain anonymous and the accused will be given a fair examination. But if the evidence is too strong to be refuted' – he gave them another sweep of his steely eyes – 'may God have mercy on their souls.' He paused, then added, 'God save the King!'

Closing her eyes, Marion gave herself up to the lumpy springs of the scratchy woollen seat. She wanted to make clear to her travelling companions that she didn't wish to be spoken to.

Now the train had left the station and was in steady motion, the older woman opposite her pulled some knitting from her bag and turned to the young couple. 'Off home for Christmas?'

'Yes,' said the young man.

'Work in London, do you?'

'Yes. We both do.' He turned to the young woman next to him and squeezed her hand. 'My fiancée and I.'

'Fiancée!' The woman sounded thrilled. 'When is the happy day?'

'Well, Florrie and I have to tell our parents first.'

'It's sort of their Christmas present.' Marion did not open her eyes, but assumed this information came from Florrie.

'How exciting.' The woman had a pitch to her voice that was extraordinarily irritating. Marion thought she could sense one of her headaches coming on. 'You are not going to elope then?'

'My mam and dad would kill me.' Florrie again.

'But so romantic.' The woman's knitting needles were clacking at an irritating pace. 'I reckon Mrs Simpson and . . .' She stopped knitting for a moment. 'What's the King's new name?'

'Duke of Windsor,' her husband said.

'That's it. I reckon she and the Duke of Windsor ought to have eloped. They could have come back to Buckingham Palace and told everyone, too late to abdicate then. That's what I said, didn't I, Ronald?'

'Yes, dear.'

Marion fidgeted involuntarily at this ridiculous thought.

'Are we disturbing you?' the woman asked, leaning over and patting Marion's knee.

Marion opened her eyes a little. 'Not at all, it's just that I do have a rather bad headache coming on.'

'Oh dear.' The woman began to rummage in her handbag. 'I have some smelling salts here somewhere. I find they are wonderful at curing my headaches. Don't I, Ronald?' She didn't wait for an answer, just handed over the small bottle of salts to Marion, who was now obliged to open it and take a sniff. The ammonia and eucalyptus made her eyes water and she coughed.

'That's it. Take a good sniff.'

Marion knew the woman meant well, but this was all still a nuisance. She returned the bottle and searched for her handker-chief to wipe her nose. 'Thank you.'

'I just hope the poor new Queen has a bottle of these with her at all times. What a shock all the abdication business must have been. And her poor husband, with his stammer, having to take over. Not to mention those little girls. I suppose the older one will be Queen now, if they don't have a son. Dreadful business. I still don't understand why his brother couldn't just marry Mrs Simpson and be happy! People think being royal is easy, but I think it's cruel. Imagine not being able to marry the one you love.'

'I think Mrs Simpson is a very stylish woman,' said Florrie.

'Oh, I don't know,' her betrothed answered. 'Not as pretty as you.'

Florrie giggled. 'Oh, Frank, that's so sweet of you.'

Marion wanted desperately to escape, but didn't know how. It would be too rude to just get up and leave, and it was so busy today that there might not be another seat left on the train.

At last, rescue came in the shape of the guard.

'Next stop in five minutes. Five minutes to next stop.'

'Is this us?' asked the woman.

'Yes,' Ronald answered.

The two children, who had been quietly reading, were given their coats. The suitcases were retrieved. The woman couldn't resist a final 'Goodbye. Nice to meet you. Happy Christmas and good luck with the wedding.'

The train jolted to a stop, doors were opened and slammed, a whistle was blown, and the carriage was silent once more.

Marion closed her eyes.

'How is your head?' Florrie asked sweetly.

'Can I get you something from the buffet car?' That was Frank.

Without moving either closed eyelid, Marion said, 'I think I may be sick.'

'Oh dear.' Frank sounded concerned. 'Can we get you anything?'

She shook her head.

'We'll leave you in peace then.'

The compartment door closed, leaving her to herself. Marion sighed with satisfaction. She was tired and more than a little frayed by the recent goings on at 145, but now she would be at home for four long, peaceful weeks – and George was waiting for her at Dunfermline. Dear George, whom she hadn't seen for three long months. The heather he had given her was her talisman, proof that he cared. She carried it with her always.

She relaxed back on her lumpy seat and smiled to herself. She really needed to be home, back in the real world. This Christmas was going to be perfect.

Chapter Thirty-One

Dunfermline, late December 1936

George was there, waiting for her. He looked well and pleased to see her, fussing around, collecting her case and helping her into his car. The night was cold and a frost was starting to rime the dark pavements. The heavens were clear and the stars glinted above them as they drove to her family home.

'Oh, George,' she breathed, turning to look at his familiar profile – hair brushed straight back off his forehead, his eyes on the road, his moustache clipped neatly. 'I have missed you.'

'Have you?' He smiled. 'I've missed you, too.'

Christmas with her mother, stepfather and George had been the most joyful Marion could remember. Her parents had kept to their promise not to invite the neighbours round, as they would inevitably want all the gossip surrounding the abdication.

'I cannot say anything,' she'd told them all.

George took her on long walks and out for pub lunches and suppers. His work in the bank in Aberdeen was going well, and he hoped that he would be coming to London more often by the spring.

He grinned. 'I might get there for the coronation.'

'Could you? That would be marvellous.' Marion's heart lifted. 'I don't know if I could meet you on the day, though. I will be needed.'

A small frown creased his eyebrows.

'I'm sorry.' She reached for his hand. 'It won't be forever.'

That was the only moment where the atmosphere between them cooled, and it passed very quickly.

'Marion?'

'Yes, George?'

'New Year's Eve.'

'Yes?'

'Can you believe it's a year since the last one?'

She laughed. 'Yes, I can. They tend to come round roughly every 365 days.'

'You know what I mean.' He squeezed her hand. 'Last year was so much fun. Shall we do it again?'

She gave him a look of such tenderness. 'Yes please. I should love it.'

She wore last year's eau de nil silk, but with some alterations.

'You've lost more weight, dear.' Her mother tutted with a mouth full of pins as she took in the extra fabric at Marion's waist and hips. 'I have a piece of pink velvet I think might look nice with this – dusty pink, it's called. I could make it in to a stole if you like it? Hide your bony shoulders.'

Marion took a calming breath.

'That would be very nice, thank you.'

'You going to the same place as last year? The Glen Mule, was it?'

'Yes.'

'My, but he looked charming in his kilt, didn't he? I wonder if he'll be bringing you a corsage again.'

'Mmm.'

'And do you think you should wear heels? Only, you are quite a bit taller than him.'

Why did her mother always find something about Marion to criticize? 'Only a bit taller,' Marion muttered.

On New Year's Eve, George picked her up at 6.30 as arranged. Marion opened the door to him, then had to hide her disappointment. He was not in his kilt. He was wearing ordinary trousers, tie and jacket. He certainly didn't have a corsage in his hand.

'Am I overdressed?' she asked him anxiously.

'Goodness!' he said, taking in her full evening dress. 'You look beautiful. But did I not tell you we are going to a little pub I know?' He hesitated. 'Do you want to get changed?'

Her mind raced. He hadn't actually said they were going to the Glen Mule but hadn't he implied it?

'Oh dear. I assumed . . . Just give me two minutes.'

The pub was on the Stirling Road, and from the outside didn't look particularly festive or welcoming.

'Right. Here we are.' George got out of the car and left her to get out by herself – something he had never done before.

The pub was dark and noisy. Crowds were bunched by the bar, drinking, smoking and laughing loudly across each other.

'What will you have, Marion?' George was not looking at her as he scanned the bar. He seemed to be searching for someone.

'A sherry, please.'

He headed towards the bar and Marion was left standing on her own in a sea of small tables and chairs. Women were gathered around them, just as the men were at the bar.

She was grateful that George had asked her to change her clothes. This place was certainly not the Glen Mule.

A band was playing from one corner of the room: a four-piece with drummer, fiddle player, flute, accordion and a singer who at that moment was giving his all to a big ballad.

Nobody seemed to notice Marion. Feeling exposed and uncomfortable, she looked over to the bar to see if George had managed to get their drinks yet. He was there, drinking a pint in jolly conversation with a man she recognized: Christopher, his old boss from the garage.

Mustering confidence, she strolled towards them.

'Oh, Marion.' George smiled. 'Look who's here. You remember Chris?'

'Of course. Hello, Chris.' She held out her hand. Chris took it, but pulled her to him so that he could plant a damp kiss on her cheek, as close to her lips as possible.

'Can't forget you, Marion, hen.' He wiped his mouth. 'Can't believe you're still knocking about with this rogue.' He cuffed George's cheek. 'What are you drinking, Marion?'

'George is getting me a sherry.'

George was sheepish. 'I was just about to when Chris arrived.' He signalled to the barmaid – a pretty woman, in her forties, Marion guessed, with brown hair and very red lipstick. Her white lace blouse had one too many buttons undone.

'A sherry for the lady,' Chris said, with his eyes firmly on her cleavage.

George put his arm protectively around Marion's shoulder as the barmaid poured a schooner of cream sherry. She put it down on the bar, took a few coins from Chris, then looked round at Marion, giving her a friendly once-over. 'You're a new face round here.'

Marion bristled. 'This is the first time I have been in here, if that's what you mean.'

'Aye. And which of these two boys have you come with, George or Chris?'

'George.'

She raised her eyebrows, sliding her smiling eyes to George. 'What's a nice girl doing with a man like you, George?'

Chris laughed, showing too much teeth, enjoying George's clear discomfort.

Marion didn't like the woman, and felt unsettled that she seemed to know both George and Chris so well. 'George and I are old friends. This is our second Hogmanay together.' She held out her hand. 'My name's Marion.'

'And I'm Evie. Good to meet you, Marion.' She leant a little closer. 'I'm going on my break now. Would you care to go outside? We can leave the boys to their beer. It's so noisy in here.'

George tried to stop her but Marion was feeling riled. She found herself saying, 'I'd love some fresh air.'

Evie poured herself an orange juice, then led Marion out to the back of the pub. They sat down on a wooden bench in the dark, looking up at the sky. A waxing moon shimmered behind a thin cloud. It would be a frosty night for certain.

'Would you care for a smoke, Marion?' Evie took a packet of cigarettes from her skirt.

'No, thank you.' Marion sipped her sherry. She was surprised that she had agreed to come outside with this woman she didn't know and didn't think she much liked. Some kind of instinct must have guided her. She came straight to the point. 'How do you know George and Chris?'

'I was at school with them both. Right pair of cheeky boys they were. George was a charmer, all right. He could twist any situation to his advantage, which meant Chris got the blame for everything.'

Marion took another sip of her sherry. 'Like what?'

'I'm no snitch.' Evie chuckled. 'Still, Chris has done all right for someone who wasn't very good at school. He has a car business.'

'Yes, I know'

'Do you? And he hasn't had any more trouble?'

Marion asked sharply, 'What trouble?'

'Oh, something and nothing.' Evie shrugged. 'A mix up. The police investigated but I don't think they found anything.'

'What were they looking for?'

Evie shrugged her shoulders. 'Och, they said he was laundering money. I mean, *really*. He's just not clever enough. Now, if it had been George they wanted to talk to, I could have believed them.'

'George is an honest man,' Marion said primly. 'I would trust him with my life.'

Evie laughed. 'Lord love you. Did your mother not tell you not to trust any man?'

Marion said nothing.

Evie took a last inhale of her cigarette, then ground the butt beneath her shoe. 'You're the girl he talks about, aren't you?'

'Am I?' Crawfie was tight-lipped.

'Aye, you are. He's always talking about you.'

So, George did think about her when they were apart. That was good to know – but it was also very bad that he was airing their personal life in public houses. Marion felt a little queasy.

'You're Marion Crawford,' Evie said matter-of-factly. 'You're governess to the two Princesses, and George likes everyone to know it.'

Marion flinched. 'He cannot possibly have told you that.'

Evie stood up, collecting her cigarettes and matches. 'A few years ago I would have thought the same, but I know him – and I think you should get to know him better.'

Marion was furious. 'What on earth do you mean?'

Evie laughed. 'Listen.' She put her head to one side, with her eyes closed. 'I swear I can hear wedding bells.'

The pub was crowded when they went back in. The band were playing loudly, and several people had stood up to dance. Tables and chairs were being pushed to the edges of the bar, and before Marion had a minute to find George, a man took her arm and whirled her into a Gay Gordons. He shouted into her ear, 'This is my song! My name is Gordy. Do ye get it? It's the Gay Gordons and my name is Gordy! What's your name?'

'Marion,' she muttered, keeping her nose clear of his beery fumes.

'Right, Marion. Let's show them what we are made of.'

Marion tried to pull away, but Gordy refused to let her go. They reeled and jigged for what seemed like an eternity, until he needed a fresh pint, and left her. Marion made her escape. She had been trying to catch George's eye each time she was whirled past the bar, but he was still in deep conversation with

Chris and Evie. Now she pushed her way through a bundle of drunken, sweating bodies and finally reached George.

'There you are.' George put his arm around her waist – something he'd never done before. 'Where have you been?'

'Dancing. With someone called Gordy.'

'That big lummox? Did he try anything on?'

'I was hoping you might come to rescue me.'

'I don't have to take him outside, do I? I would, you know.'

Marion realized George was a little drunk. 'I would like to go home,' she said, as firmly as she could.

'What? It's not midnight yet.'

'Does it matter?'

'Of course it matters.' He leant into her and whispered loudly in her ear, 'I have something to talk to you about at midnight.'

Marion's heart jumped. What did that mean? Was he going to propose? No, the last time she thought that she'd felt a fool. And even if he was going to propose, she didn't want it to be in front of a bunch of drunken strangers. There was what Evie had said, too, which she couldn't get out of her head. She wanted to ask George exactly what he'd been telling people about her.

'We could be home by midnight.' She wriggled away from him. 'We can talk at home. It'll be quieter.'

Extricating him from the crowd took a little while. He had to say goodbye and Happy New Year to everyone, some of them twice. Evie waved to her from across the room, raising her glass to Marion. Marion pretended not to see the wave and eventually got George outside.

As soon as George hit the cold air, he swayed and stumbled into Marion.

'George, shall we call a taxi?' she asked.

'Whatever for? The bloody car is right here.'

Marion did not like swearing at the best of times, even though she had heard worse in the royal kitchens and even from the King himself.

She took George's arm in an attempt to steady him as he wobbled to his car.

Once inside, he seemed to have control of himself again, and they soon sped off along the dark road which took them over the hills and valleys towards Dunfermline.

'That was a nice evening,' she said lightly, hoping to keep him awake.

'Light me a cigarette, would you?'

He lifted his left arm without taking his hand off the steering wheel, and she delved into his coat pocket.

She had never smoked, but had watched the King often enough to know how to light it. 'Here you are.'

He took it and, turning to look at her, said, 'You're a good girl, Marion.'

With both their eyes off the road, neither saw the left-hand bend looming, and the little car ran straight on, across the road and into a hedge.

Marion's knees hit the small metal glove compartment as she braced herself against the tiny dashboard. For a moment the world spun, and then she managed to get a hold of herself, to turn and look around her.

George lay still, humped over the steering wheel.

'George! Are you all right?' She reached over and shook his arm. 'George?'

He coughed and pulled himself upright. 'Winded myself.'

'Thank God you are all right!' Relief swept through her. 'I thought you were knocked out.' Tears constricted her throat. 'Or worse.' Her breathing was sharp and shallow with shock. 'Is anything broken?'

'Stop fussing, woman. I'm fine. You'll have to get out and push from the front.'

'But my knees and wrists are bruised. I don't think I have the strength.'

'Well, unless you know how to drive a car, you'll have to.' She heard the sharpness in his tone, and it stung.

'But George—'

'Well, I can't push, because I have to drive.'

Marion heard real anger in his voice now. She tried to tell herself that he was probably in shock, probably still drunk – and besides, she didn't want to start a row.

So she opened the door and stepped out onto long, frosty grass, into mud that, although frozen, broke as her heels cracked it. She felt the cold water seep into her best shoes and her new stockings.

She managed to get round to the front of the car, where the bumper was bent and wedged into the gate.

George wound down the window. 'When I say push, push.'

The engine had stalled on impact but the headlights were still on, bright in her face and eyes, meaning she couldn't see George or where she was pushing to. 'I don't have enough space to get all the way to the front of the car,' she shouted.

In answer, George fired up the engine again and yelled, 'Stand by!' He revved the engine. '*Push!*'

The car moved back just enough for her to get some purchase on the radiator grill. 'I'm pushing.'

'*Puuush!*'

'I am!' She put her shoulder to the metal, and with her limited weight behind her, pushed and pushed, until the little car shot out from the hedge and she fell flat on her hands and knees. Fresh pain shot through her throbbing knees and hands.

'Good girl!' George shouted. 'In you jump.'

In the light of the headlamps she got to her feet and examined herself. She was cold and muddy and she could see faint bruises above her wrists and on her palms. She limped towards her side of the car.

'What's the matter with you?' George yelled. 'Get in.'

She climbed in and for the rest of the journey she said not a word, but her inner dialogue was at full volume. Drink had brought out another side to George and she was frightened by it. This wasn't the man she knew at all.

And what had Evie meant about not trusting him? Could it really be true that Christopher Bailey, George's best friend, had been in trouble with the police? Marion didn't want to believe Evie. There might be another explanation, of course – jealousy could make women say terrible things.

She would have to ask him about all of this tomorrow – if they got home in one piece, that was.

He dropped her off just after midnight. Whether he had forgotten what he wanted to talk to her about or whether he was too angry and out of sorts to discuss it, she didn't know, because he drove off as soon as she had closed the car door.

She walked up the front path, miserable and confused, and her mother scared her by throwing open the front door before she reached it. 'You're early. Did you have a good time? Happy New Year, Marion. Where's George? Your dad's waiting up with a lump of coal hoping George would be our first footer . . .' The light from the hallway had fallen on Marion and her mother saw the bruises and holed stockings. 'Whatever has happened to you? Your knees are bleeding.'

It had all been very embarrassing. Robert thought George must have assaulted her, and wanted to call the police.

She had to explain the car accident, but she did not mention that George had had too much to drink, or that the whole evening had not been what she had hoped. George had not been his usual charming self at all, and she worried about this other side to him.

George turned up mid-morning the next day to check on Marion's bruises and apologize profusely to her parents.

'It was the deer running across the road,' he told them. 'A young buck. I didn't want to hurt him, so we ended up in the hedge. You saw him, didn't you, Marion?' Sitting next to her on her parents' sofa, drinking tea, he nudged her with an elbow, smiling his usual charming smile. 'If you could drive, I would have pushed the car out myself, but . . .' He fixed his soulful eyes on her stepfather. 'I wanted to get her home safely, Robert. I knew you'd be worrying. If we had stayed out until midnight there would have been a few people driving their cars in no fit state and I didn't want that.'

Maggie was full of sympathy. 'You did the right thing, George. Marion only scraped her knees and has a small bruise on her palm. It could have happened to anyone. Thank you for being so thoughtful. Will you stay for your tea?'

Marion was confused by his lies. He had exonerated himself with her parents, but not with her. She did her best not to address him, and said little throughout the meal.

Tea eaten and the wireless evening news listened to, Maggie and Robert were clearing up in the kitchen. As Marion brought some glasses in from the other room, she overheard her mother encouraging her dad to have an early night. 'Marion and George need to have a little time on their own, Robert.'

'But why?'

'Why do you think? Have you forgotten how hard it was when we were courting?'

Robert laughed. 'Aye, Marion was such a nosy little bairn. Always pushing herself between you and me when we were sitting on the sofa.'

'Exactly! So, let's leave them alone for now.'

Marion swallowed hard and went back to the sitting room.

'Goodnight, Marion,' her mother called through the half-open door. 'Goodnight, George.'

'Goodnight, Maggie. Thank you for tea.'

Marion sat down uneasily beside George. She was still dumbfounded. He had lied to her parents and she hadn't said a word. She looked down at her folded hands in her lap, at the bruise curling around the bottom of one thumb. The accident had not been caused by a deer. She didn't know what to say.

George stood up and gestured to the small drinks cupboard. 'Do you think Robert would mind if I had a wee Scotch?'

She stared at him. 'Why did you say there was a deer on the road? You know that's not true.'

He measured a finger of Scotch before answering. 'Look, Marion, I was embarrassed. I am so sorry about last night. I will never behave like that again. I promise.' He sat next to her again, his anguished eyes locked on to hers. 'The evening was not what I had planned at all. I had booked us a table at a smaller place down the road from the pub, but I thought we could pop in to see if Chris was there. You know, have a quick drink with him, wish him a happy new year. He hasn't been having any luck recently and . . .'

'Yes, Evie told me.'

He blinked twice in surprise. 'Evie told you what?'

'That Chris had had some trouble with the police?'

Did George relax slightly? 'Oh, that. That was nothing.'

'So how has he been unlucky?'

'A couple of business deals fell through. The bank I work for is trying to help him.'

'I see.'

'I didn't realize how upset he was about it all. He needed to get it all off his chest and I couldn't just leave him. He kept buying drinks and—'

'And all the while, you forgot to bring me my drink, and you left me in the midst of strangers. I was grateful to Evie for taking me outside for ten minutes and making me feel less on my own. Did you even notice I wasn't there? And then I was forced to dance with another man.'

'Who was that?'

'I told you, his name was Gordy or something – it doesn't matter. I tried to catch your eye but you didn't even notice. You didn't look for me once.' She was shaking, amazed that she was saying all this out loud. 'George, you were drunk when you drove me home and you know very well that is why you crashed the car.'

'Marion.' He took her hand. 'I am not a liar, but I just couldn't face telling your wonderful parents that I had crashed the car with you in it, that I had had too much to drink, that I had been that reckless. Can you ever forgive me?'

'I did not like the way you were last night. You – well, you weren't yourself. And I didn't like that.'

George looked at her with pleading eyes. 'I will make it up to you. We need to talk about a lot of things. Don't break my heart, Marion. Please. Will you forgive me?'

He looked so forlorn that she couldn't help but trust him. 'All right,' she said at last, and managed a weak smile.

And so Marion persuaded herself that George had been a good friend to Chris last night. It was all Chris's fault that George had had too much to drink. He wouldn't have crashed the car, or acted as he had done, if it hadn't been for that. He had been too much in shock to make sure she was all right after the accident. The lie he had told her parents was his way of protecting her. It was just one big mistake and he felt very guilty. She knew that.

She trusted him. She was certain it would never happen again.

Chapter Thirty-Two

Dunfermline, January 1937

In the end she told a white lie herself – to her parents, and to George.

'I have to get back to London,' she said, late on New Year's Day.

Maggie turned around in surprise. 'I thought you had another couple of weeks with us?'

'I have been thinking about all the things I have to pack up from 145 Piccadilly to take to Buckingham Palace. The schoolroom to start with, then my own things – and I will have to help Alah and Bobo with the nursery. It's best I make a start while the family are still at Sandringham.'

She left Scotland without seeing George, but she did write to him, apologizing for her swift departure, telling him she had to go back to work.

His reply was one of surprise and regret, and he expressed the hope that he could come to London for the coronation in May. He finished the letter with words that stuck in her mind:

Marion, I do think of you every day. Please think of me occasionally. I couldn't bear for you to forget me. I will never forget you.

Until we meet again,
George

Marion did think of him, almost constantly – on the train down to London, as she started packing up Piccadilly, as the real work of the move to Buckingham Palace began. She did her best to throw herself into her duties, focusing on the enormous upheaval coming to the Princesses' lives, but George still lingered at the back of her mind.

Buckingham Palace, January 1937

Tommy, newly promoted to King George VI's private secretary, waded through the coronation invitation list. He had spent hours and hours over many meetings with the Prime Minister, the cabinet, and many Empire and world ambassadors in order to make certain that all the right people were invited. The last thing he wanted was an international row if any head of state felt they were neglected.

P-T had likened it to the christening of the princess in the Sleeping Beauty fairy tale. 'We don't need anyone cursing the King because they feel snubbed, now, do we?'

The palace itself was very quiet. The royal family were still at Sandringham and he thanked God for it. The last thing he needed was interference. They had already sent their list of the private friends and family to be invited. And it was going to be quite a squeeze to get everyone into Westminster Abbey.

Tommy also had dozens of meetings to sit in on with military heads and the security services, all outlining minute by minute, yard by yard, the royal procession. How many horses? Which carriages? Each point of the journey was timed to the second and there had already been night time rehearsals through the empty streets.

Then there was the ancient service itself. The Archbishop of Canterbury had his work cut out for him. One wrong word could make the entire process invalid.

At the Tower of London, the crown jewels were cleaned, and the crown altered to fit the King's head precisely.

Tommy's meticulous notes grew day by day.

In the middle of it all, he finally managed to get a weekend clear to go home.

'Darling, I have missed you. You must be exhausted,' Joan said when she picked him up at the station. 'Are you hungry?'

He settled himself into the passenger seat and tried not to wince at Joan's erratic driving. She was a wonderful woman: tall, with a generous body and hair that was, he noted, beginning to grey – but she was a dreadful driver.

'A little. What's for dinner?'

'I have a beef rib in the oven and apple crumble.'

'Good. I brought some gin with me.'

'Oh darling, we still have some left from Christmas.'

'Well, I shall take it back with me then.'

'I have some brandy for you.'

'Excellent. How are the children?'

'Some good reports from school. You'll be pleased.'

'Good reports?' He sighed. 'Where have we gone wrong?'

Joan laughed. 'They are all in for dinner and promise not to chatter.'

'Good.'

Tommy had met Joan in India back in 1920, just a year after he became aide-de-camp to the governor of Bombay. She was the daughter of the then Viceroy of India, Lord Chelmsford, and their meeting had been at a round-up of elephants in Mysore.

Joan was a sensible girl and well brought up. Tommy had liked her immediately but it was some time before he plucked up the courage to ask her to marry him. At the time he had not been considered much of a catch. He was from an aristocratic family, had powerful intellect and biting wit – but he had no real or permanent work or income. However, he did have the

Military Cross, won for gallantry in France during the Great War, and the wounds to prove it. It was enough for his father-in-law to think him a good fit for Joan.

Joan had fallen in love with him quite easily. He was undemanding, fun to be with, and independent – just as she was. If she were to marry and have children, she did not need a husband who would be under her feet all the time.

A year after their marriage, their first son, John, was born. Tommy, having come from a family who thoroughly enjoyed nicknames, immediately gave the poor boy the nomenclature Wool.

The year after that Lavinia – always known as Charles – arrived, and five years after her came Caroline, usually called Mrs Mooch.

The children were waiting at the door when he arrived home.

'Hello, sir.' Wool shook his father's hand. 'Good to see you.'

Charles gave her father a kiss on the cheek. 'Hello, Pa.'

'Daddy, I have missed you.' Mrs Mooch threw her arms around him. 'Have you been to any concerts?'

'One or two. Jolly good one at the Albert Hall. Schubert. Now do get off me – I need a drink.'

The rib of beef was perfect and the entire family ate in silence as usual. This was a custom that Tommy had insisted on long ago, when the children were small. 'I don't like chatter at the table,' he'd always said. 'I cannot hear myself think while I eat if there is chatter.' Joan had always agreed. She thought it was good for the children to learn some self-discipline and it certainly made for faster dinners.

Another rule that Tommy had instilled in them was that no one was to get up and walk about the room during mealtimes, Tommy being the exception. He often got up between courses to look out of the window and jingle the coins in his pocket. Whether he was puzzling over affairs of state or planning how to develop the herbaceous border, no one disturbed him. He was the head of the household and he could do what he jolly well wanted.

After dinner that evening, they settled down as a family to play whist. Joan watched Tommy gradually relax, laughing and conversing with the children while winning hand after hand. She had been worried about him. It had been a terrible year of strain for both of them, but at least she had the fresh air of Sussex, good friends and the garden. Dear Tommy had precious little peace in London.

'What has it really been like in London, Father?' Wool asked.

'Very, very, dull,' Tommy deadpanned. 'In fact, if I had my time again, I would never have been a courtier.'

'I don't believe that,' Joan said.

'Nor I,' said Charles.

'What would you have been then?' asked Mrs Mooch.

Not taking his eyes off his cards, he replied, 'I would breed horses. They are kind and gentle and truthful. Any kind of horse – racehorses, cart horses, wild horses.' He looked up at them all. 'Anything but a courtier.'

Chapter Thirty-Three

Dear Mother and Dad,

My first letter to you on Buckingham Palace notepaper!

I am still sleeping at 145, but I thought you'd like to see it.

I am so glad I came back early. There has been so much to do. I have the schoolroom at BP established now, which was no mean feat!

The new schoolroom is larger than the old one, but what it makes up for in size it loses in comfort. Everything is on a monumental scale here and the heating system can't have been changed since Queen Victoria's time. The radiators rattle and groan alarmingly. We have the fires lit, but when the winds moan, the draughty chimneys seem to suck all the warmth up to the clouds. I am very glad to have Scottish blood in my veins, and woollen socks on my feet!

Most of the furniture from 145 Piccadilly has been moved over to the Palace now and the staff are working all day to clean and refresh the royal apartments. It is beginning to look a bit more homely now, if I can call it a home. It is more an edifice, an office of international business.

The corridors are long and seemingly endless. When my lunch is brought to me it is usually cold, the walk from the kitchens to the schoolroom taking almost fifteen minutes.

My bedroom is rather a walk from the nursery. And, you might laugh, when I was opening the curtains to let in some daylight, the pelmet and curtains clattered to the floor and scattered a nest of mice living behind them.

There are so many mice here – and, I am told, rats too. Thankfully I haven't seen any . . . yet!

The family arrive in three days. Alah and Bobo have got the nursery and the Princesses' bedrooms looking very nice. It is so important for them to settle in with familiar possessions around them. Lilibet has her own sitting room now. Alah and Bobo have their own rooms, too, and there are two bathrooms, one for them and one for the Princesses. Very antiquated and with giant bath tubs that they could swim in!

Talking of which, there is a swimming pool here – indoor, so I shall make it my job to get the girls swimming well.

I hope you are both well?

Your

Marion

PS Have you seen George? Please tell him I was asking after him.

In her hurry to the Palace post room, she tripped on a short flight of carpeted, marble steps and landed hard on her right wrist. Disoriented and in pain, Marion remained on the floor for a few moments to recover herself.

A door opened to the left of her and a woman's voice said, 'Are you all right? Have you broken anything?'

Crawfie gingerly placed her good hand around her sore wrist. 'I think I have sprained my wrist.'

'Let's help you up.'

A pair of slender ankles shod in brown lace-up shoes came into Crawfie's eyeline. 'Come on. I've got you. These stairs are an absolute menace.'

Crawfie found herself standing upright and slightly breathless, but in one piece. She looked up to recognize Sir Alan's secretary. 'Thank you, Miss P-T. I was hurrying to catch the post.'

'Just P-T, darling. I'll get one of the girls to post that for you. You look as if you need a cup of tea.' She smiled. 'Good job I was working a bit late tonight, Miss Crawford, or we wouldn't have found you until the morning.' P-T looked her up and down. 'Now let's get the kettle on and I might find a biscuit or two. That's the best I can do.'

Another door opened behind them. 'What the hell is all the noise?'

P-T replied, 'May I borrow some of your ice, sir? This poor girl has a swollen wrist.'

Tommy raised his dark eyebrows in recognition. 'Goodness. We meet again, Miss Crawford. Come on into my office and sit down.'

'I was going to make a tea?' P-T said.

'Bugger tea. The woman needs a Scotch.'

Settled in Tommy's office with a tea towel full of ice on her wrist, Crawfie watched as Tommy poured three glasses of whisky and handed them out.

'Chin-chin.' He raised his glass, drank and sat at his desk. 'Still the dedicated governess, what?'

'Yes, sir. I never thanked you for tea.'

'It was Fortnum's, wasn't it?'

'Yes, sir.'

'How is it going?'

Crawfie looked at her wrist. 'Feeling better, thank you, sir.'

'I mean your work. Still keeping the Princesses' noses to the grindstone?'

'They are good students.'

'They need to be now.'

'Yes, sir.'

'And how is the move going?'

'Almost done.'

'Good. Finding your feet in this monolith of a building?'

'It is certainly a lot bigger than 145 Piccadilly.'

'And colder.' He nodded at her glass. 'Drink up. Very good for shock.'

P-T asked, 'Is anyone hungry? It seems ages since lunch. I can ring down for some sandwiches.'

'Good idea,' Tommy agreed. 'But haven't you two young women got young men waiting for you somewhere? It is Valentine's night, you know.'

P-T grinned. 'And how could I get a young man when I spend all the hours God sends working for you?' With a chuckle, she left to order the sandwiches.

'Point taken.' He looked over at Crawfie. 'What about you? No Bonnie Prince Charlie keening for you?'

'No, sir.'

He looked amazed. 'What the hell are the young men of today up to? I despair.' He picked up his glass. 'A toast, to young hearts everywhere and to the abdicated King and his Mrs Simpson. To foolish love.'

The whisky scorched down Crawfie's throat where a lump had suddenly appeared. She thought of George and wherever he was at that moment.

'Do you know,' Tommy began, 'he seemed the most admirable man I had ever met when I started working for him. I had a deep admiration for him and was convinced that the future of England would be safe in his hands. But it transpired that he is just a person like any other. After nine years working for him when he was Prince of Wales, my admiration changed to despair. His lack of sense of duty and his self-absorption made him unfit for his destiny. I wasn't wrong, was I? You must have met him. What did you make of him?'

Crawfie was shocked that he could speak so candidly and – in her opinion, disrespectfully – about the man who had been King. 'I met him only a couple of times,' she replied primly, 'and I thought he seemed very nice.'

'You were blinded by his looks, no doubt.'

The whisky was working its way into her system, provoking some bravado. 'He is as handsome as a King of England should be – a man whose only crime was to fall in love.' She felt the heat rising in her cheeks. 'And because of that simple, human emotion, he had his crown taken from him.'

'Taken from him?' Tommy frowned. 'My dear, he gave it away.'

'I respect the Crown, sir.'

'You think I'm disrespectful?'

'I do.'

Tommy's expression became serious. 'Good for you, Miss Crawford. But something I have learned in this life of service is to never give respect to those who don't earn it, or indeed want it. He wanted to love and be loved. Bugger his duty.'

P-T arrived, banging the door open with her hip and carrying a tray full of sandwiches. 'Here we are, sir. Chicken, ham or cheese?'

'Chicken, ham, cheese.' He laughed. 'The Crown or Mrs Simpson. Life is full of decisions. P-T, our glasses are empty.'

P-T dutifully topped up the glasses, even though Crawfie said no, and she began to tell an off-colour story about a footman, a chambermaid and a bicycle.

Gradually Crawfie relaxed into the comfortable atmosphere that alcohol and food very often induces. She listened as Tommy talked about his children, and P-T regaled them with tales of her flatmate who was working in the cabinet office.

'There's an awful lot of anxiety about Germany and Herr Hitler,' she said. 'Mr Baldwin is being talked into retirement. Making way for a younger Prime Minister, you know – one with the courage to stand up to foreign aggression.'

'Poor old Baldwin.' Tommy reached for a cheese sandwich. 'The abdication ballyhoo took it out of him. My money is on Winston Churchill for next PM. Mark my words.'

Crawfie read the newspapers every day, fascinated by the accounts of the people and events that she lived with. She had seen Mr Baldwin many times at 145 in the run-up to the abdication and saw how burdened he had seemed.

'My parents would prefer a Labour government to replace him,' she said.

Tommy turned his amused eyes on her. 'Off with their heads.'

P-T pretended shock. 'I never had you down as a revolutionary, Miss Crawford!'

Crawfie knew she was a little tipsy because her laugh came out more as a giggle. 'I said my parents, not me. Maybe I used to be a little revolutionary, but not now. Now I see how hard it is for all people in all walks of life.'

'Very hard indeed,' Tommy intoned. 'So many jewels and houses to deal with. The interesting people queueing up to fawn over one. Dreadful life.'

'I mean it,' Crawfie said, trying not to laugh. 'Their lives are not normal. I am privileged to be charged with the education of Princess Elizabeth and Princess Margaret, particularly now. If the Duke and Duchess are not blessed with a son, Lilibet will be Queen one day. My duty is to show her the real world before the doors close around her.'

P-T and Tommy looked at each other and raised their eyebrows. 'P-T, call the guards. We have a red under the bed.'

'I am not a red – and neither am I a blue!' Crawfie said crossly.

'I tell you what you are.' Tommy uncrossed his elegant legs and stood up. 'I'm still hungry. Come along – I am taking you two to dinner.'

They had a brisk ten-minute walk over to the Ritz, where Tommy effortlessly breezed in and was greeted by a welcoming waiter with, 'Your usual table, sir?'

Crawfie had never been inside the Ritz before, and pulled herself up to her full height as she allowed her coat to be taken and her chair pulled out. Dining with the elegant Sir Alan and P-T meant she could observe how the privileged spent their time. It was quite different in style to that of the over-formal behaviour at the Palace. Here, around each table, were monied people gossiping and keeping their eyes open for faces they knew. This was fun, expensive and fascinating to Crawfie – a world between the simplicity of Dunfermline and the stuffiness of the royal household. And she realized, suddenly, how oddly comfortable she felt within it.

Over fillets of sole Veronique, Crawfie let slip about George, leaving out the disaster of New Year's Eve. 'And he says he might come down for the coronation,' she finished.

'Might he indeed.' Tommy picked up his wine glass. 'And do you want to see him?'

P-T replied, 'Of course she does. He sounds *very* charming.'

Tommy hummed through a mouthful of rather good white burgundy. 'Hmmm. I shall give him the once-over when I meet him. It will be good practice for those callow Lochinvars who will beat their way to my own front door in pursuit of my daughters.'

Chapter Thirty-Four

It was the last day at 145 Piccadilly, and Crawfie felt a fresh wave of relief break over the household. At last, the hinterland of the abdication, followed by the Christmas break, was bridged. Tomorrow the family and household would move to Buckingham Palace.

The press were once again focused on the outside of 145 Piccadilly and Lilibet was enjoying peeking through the windows at them.

'There are so many, Crawfie.'

'Come away, please,' Crawfie said. 'We don't need a picture of you looking at them, thank you.'

Margaret was hopping about excitedly. She was wearing a new dress, a Christmas gift from her maternal grandmother, who was coming for tea shortly. She was swishing about in it. 'I would like them to take my photograph.'

'There will be plenty of time for that, but not today.'

Today there were no lessons. Crawfie was keeping the girls occupied while Alah and Bobo were at Buckingham Palace, putting the last of the laundry and bedlinen into ancient airing cupboards. The Duchess – no, Crawfie checked herself for the umpteenth time that day, the *Queen* – had invited her mother, and her friend Lady Cynthia Asquith, to tea, and Crawfie was getting the girls dressed in their prettiest dresses, ready to meet her.

'Let me brush your hair please, Lilibet.'

Lilibet was so easy to look after. She was almost eleven now and stood patiently, barely frowning as the hairbrush pulled a knot.

'Now, let me look at you!'

Lilibet did a twirl.

'Very nice indeed,' Crawfie told her. 'Now Margaret, please.'

Margaret frowned. 'I don't *want* my hair brushed. It hurts.'

'You want to look nice for your granny and for your mummy's friend, don't you?'

Margaret was six, with a mind of her own. She dragged herself towards Crawfie as if she were on her last legs. 'But I *hate* having my hair brushed . . . Ow!'

'I haven't even touched you yet. Stand still.'

Crawfie finally led the girls downstairs to their mother, then quickly ran back up to the nursery. Bobo and Alah had just returned from the Palace and were at the window overlooking the front door.

Bobo's face was pushed against the glass. 'Here she comes.'

Alah pushed her to one side. 'Is it Lady Asquith or the Countess?'

Bobo pushed through to see. 'Lady Asquith, I think.'

Alah sighed with pleasure. 'She is wonderful. A woman who understands what it means to be a wife. Unlike Mrs Simpson.'

'Alah!' Crawfie was surprised. 'What do you mean? She couldn't help falling in love.'

'Love?' Alah snorted. 'The only thing she loves is being the centre of attention. A woman who imagines her needs must come first. I believe the newspapers call it *bourgeois feminism*. What a load of rot.'

Below them, the ghastly Fleet Street mob immediately began to crowd the pavement, while two policemen tried to hold them back without success. The photographers snapped frantically as the distinguished wife of the former Prime Minister arrived. She posed politely and briefly for the cameras before entering the house.

Bobo was thinking. 'I think it is important to be feminine,' she said.

'Feminism does not mean feminine,' Crawfie told her. 'Quite the opposite, some say.'

'And it is,' said Alah. 'We are not the equal of men and never shall be, despite what these female radicals shout about.'

Another black car drew up beneath the window, and again the photographers surged forwards as the Queen's mother, the Countess of Strathmore, arrived. She did not stop or pause, but told the photographers in a clear and aristocratic voice, 'I shouldn't waste a photograph on me,' before disappearing through the glossed black door of 145.

Alah moved away from the window. 'Bobo, put the kettle on, would you?'

'Yes, ma'am.'

Alah settled in the chair by the fire, and Crawfie joined her.

'Female radicals?' Crawfie asked.

'They are a disgrace!' Alah sniffed. 'We have the vote and we can divorce on certain grounds, but the rest of it would be the ruination of society.'

'Would it? Do you not think that a woman could be as successful as a man if she wanted to?'

'Why would she want to? A woman's place is in the home. How would the King be able to do all he has to do, if the Queen decided to run for parliament or go out to work? And how is the Queen able to be the Queen without us caring for the Princesses? It is the balance of nature that we hold the fort.'

'I didn't realize you had such strong feelings about it, Alah.'

'Well, I do. I am so grateful that you show no sign of silly girlishness, running after young men and such like. You are single and you are not distracted from your work – just like me. Long may that be the case.'

'Supposing I did meet someone and wished to be married. What then?'

'What do you think? You would be dismissed.'

Downstairs the Queen was enjoying the final afternoon tea she was to hold in the sitting room of 145.

'You will miss this little home, won't you, darling?' Countess Strathmore asked her daughter.

'Bertie and I have some wonderful memories here,' replied the Queen. 'It does seem sad to leave. It is not what we were expecting, at all.'

'Quite a lot to take in, I expect.' Lady Asquith smiled. 'I have always hated moving house. Such a bother for everyone.'

The Queen smiled. 'It is, rather, but it's poor Bertie who is having the hardest time.'

'Packing the boxes as we speak, is he?' Lady Asquith was known for her wit, and everyone laughed.

'Would you like to see me dance?' Margaret piped up. 'Come on, Lilibet, let's dance.'

And the two girls, like any other little girls, got up and danced for their mother, grandmother and family friend.

Tea was drunk, sandwiches were eaten and gossip was whispered above the Princesses' heads. When the pretty French clock on the mantelpiece struck four, the ladies moved to collect their spectacles and gloves and the party broke up.

Lilibet escorted her grandmother and Lady Asquith to the door. On the hall table was a letter addressed to Her Majesty the Queen, and Lilibet pointed to it. 'That's Mummy now,' she explained.

As the door opened, a fresh blast of camera bulbs went off – but not at the two women who were leaving. The new King had just arrived and was getting out of his official car.

'Afternoon, Your Majesty,' the photographers called, jostling each other, desperate to get a picture of him looking towards them.

'Over here, sir, *Daily Telegraph*.'

'Give us a smile for the *Daily Express*, sir.'

He politely smiled and waved before entering his home for the last time.

Crawfie had been summoned to come downstairs and collect the girls. She stood in the shadow of the stairs, amused by the slightly chaotic crossover of leavers and arrivals.

Finally, the Countess and Lady Asquith were safely in their cars and the King stepped into the hall. The large black door was closed behind him, shutting out the doorstep clamour.

Crawfie hung back, allowing the girls to welcome their father. They were whispering to each other.

'Don't hold on to me,' Lilibet ordered Margaret. 'Do it like we used to for Granny and Grandpa when they were King and Queen.'

The King kissed his wife, then the Princesses took a step forward and swept to the floor in graceful curtseys. 'Welcome home, Your Majesty, Papa.'

As they smiled up into their father's weary face, Crawfie witnessed something she'd never forget. The King was taken aback. It was as though the reality of his position had swamped him again. His eyes glistened with tears as he stooped and took both girls into his arms. Time stood still for them.

Crawfie turned her gaze from the intimacy and melted back into the shadows.

Chapter Thirty-Five

Buckingham Palace, 17th February 1937

'Margaret, would you please stop cycling up and down this corridor!' Alah was rubbing her shin.

'Why?'

'Because you have run into me twice. And it hurts.'

Lilibet was grooming one of her toy horses. 'Come and help me, Margaret. We have to get all our horses to feel happy in their new home.'

'But it's so *boring.*'

Crawfie arrived. 'Alah, it's the oddest thing. I don't have a light switch in my bedroom. I looked everywhere and it's outside in the corridor, at least six feet from my door. Ouch!'

'Sorry!'

Alah lifted Margaret off her tricycle. 'That's it. I'm putting this away. Go and help Lilibet, please.'

Margaret immediately burst into tears and ran into her room, shouting, 'I don't like living here! I want to see Mummy!'

'Difficult morning?' Crawfie asked.

Alah sighed. 'You could say that, yes.'

The day continued in similar vein. The entire palace was overrun with removal men, painters and cleaners.

The Queen was busy with her maid, making her bedroom cosy and homely. The King had rejected the old King's bedroom and chosen his father's smaller dressing room. It held happy memories of watching his father dressing for dinner when he was a boy.

Life here was certainly very different. The Palace was the opposite of the homely warmth of 145 Piccadilly. It was enormous: endlessly long corridors, draughty rooms, vast and important works of art at every turn. Liveried staff and footmen with powdered wigs scurried through the unseen rat runs behind secret doors. All was pomp and ceremony.

The Palace steward headed up a staff of four hundred servants, including equerries, ladies of the bedchamber and ladies-in-waiting. Dining tables were laid with golden candelabra and bowls of red tulips.

The Queen's diary was heavy with appointments: dress-makers, ambassadors, letters to answer and portraits to sit for. Crawfie had twice seen her walking the corridors in full evening dress and a tiara at half past nine in the morning!

The King spent most of his days in his office, dealing with matters of state and practising his new signature: George R VI.

There were no more afternoon naps, and very few bath-time romps for the Princesses.

Crawfie, Alah and Bobo took a while to find their way around the miles of corridors and antiquated plumbing. The building was full of history, rusty pipes – and mice. When Alah found a mouse climbing her stocking, she shrieked, but the Princesses laughed. 'It's only a little mousie,' said Margaret. 'Lilibet and I feed him crumbs when he comes into our bedroom at night.'

Eventually, they all settled down in their new home, and after a visit from the Palace rodent catcher, no mouse was seen in the nursery again.

There had been so much going on that Crawfie didn't have time to stop and contemplate her new home, to absorb the fact that she, Miss Marion Crawford, was now living in a royal palace, with a King and Queen who employed her to care for two royal

Princesses. The reality of that was going to take some time to sink in.

And it wasn't only the Palace that was busy. In the Royal Mews, the Crown equerry oversaw the grooms and coachmen who tended the seventy-five horses and state carriages. The Princesses adored going to visit, their pockets full of apples and carrots.

Her Majesty Queen Mary, now the Dowager Queen, had stayed at Buckingham Palace since the death of her husband and abdication of her son, and appeared reluctant to move out. But go she had to, and after some negotiation, Crawfie heard she had agreed to move to Marlborough House, another mansion and only a stone's throw away, on the Mall.

On the eve of her departure, she invited the family and the more important members of the household, including Crawfie, Bobo and Alah, to the white drawing room, where they found two long tables with dozens of trinkets that the Dowager Queen had no use for.

'May I take this opportunity to thank you all for your loyal service to me and my late husband,' she said. 'I have many memories to take across the road to my new nest, Marlborough House. But before I go, I should like you to choose something from these tables around you as a keepsake from me.'

The Dowager Queen graciously accepted the warm rumble of thanks and applause, and insisted on staying to talk and oversee who wanted what.

Lilibet and Margaret were very excited and couldn't wait see what treasures she was leaving behind. They walked up and down with Crawfie, under the watchful eye of their grandmother, scrutinizing everything. Finally, Lilibet decided, 'Granny, please may I have the little china bowl of flowers?'

'You may. A very good choice. Now you, Margaret?'

'I would like the china dog please, the Labrador.'

'Then it is yours.' She looked to Crawfie. 'Miss Crawford, what would you like?'

Crawfie was taken by surprise. 'Thank you. I wonder, may I have the little glass jug? I have a sprig of lucky heather that would sit perfectly in it.'

The Dowager Queen bent her head in assent. 'The perfect thing.'

'You are very kind, ma'am. I shall treasure it.'

Bobo chose a box of lace handkerchiefs and Alah a pocket-sized prayer book. The Dowager Queen was delighted with their choices.

'Now remember,' she said, 'I am only moving across the road. You must come and have tea with me very often. And Miss Crawford, I am always keen to hear about Lilibet and Margaret's educational progress. If there is ever anything I can do to help, do let me know.'

Buckingham Palace, 20ᵗʰ February 1937

Dear Mother and Dad,

Well, here we are all finally moved in to Buckingham Palace. The last few days have been exhausting for everyone, including the King and Queen. I do worry for them – I never worry that they cannot do their duty, of course, but I am concerned about how widespread their duties are. Life is going to be very different, and I feel so privileged to be here, serving my country in a way I never expected.

The Princesses are adapting well. Margaret is very jealous of Lilibet's own little sitting room, which is her pride and joy. Margaret thinks it very unfair and keeps asking me why Lilibet gets her own room, when she has to stay in the nursery.

'Because she's eleven now,' I told her. 'And she is allowed to have a room of her own where she can do her homework and read in peace.'

'But why can't I share it with her?'

Being six is not all fun, and it took her all afternoon for her to leave behind her grumpiness.

Lilibet loves her room. She has placed all her books alphabetically on the shelves and there are two beautiful photographs of her parents on her mantelpiece. She has a little desk for homework and letter writing, a fire, a gate-legged drop-leaf table on which to dine, a small chintz sofa and an armchair with a little footstool.

I have been trying to think of ways to cheer Margaret up, so this afternoon I suggested that Lilibet send a written invitation to Margaret, asking her to come for afternoon tea.

At four o'clock the footman arrived with cucumber sandwiches, bread and butter and fruitcake – exactly as the Queen herself likes it. Alah and I kept an eye on them through the open door. Their conversation was so funny.

'And have you had a good day, Margaret?' Lilibet asked.

'Oh yes, thank you. We have moved into a new house.'

'And is it nice?'

'Yes. It's a palace. My father is King of England.'

'Gosh. How interesting.'

'Yes. And my sister will be Queen of England one day and I shall be the Queen's sister.' Margaret giggled, and a piece of bread and butter slipped off her plate and onto the rug. Lilibet couldn't tell her off because she was laughing too much as well.

Dookie (you remember the Corgi I banned from the schoolroom?) couldn't believe his luck. I honestly have no fondness for him.

I shall sign off now as I am very sleepy. Tomorrow I am being given a tour of the palace gardens by Sir Alan Lascelles, no less. He is the King's private secretary and known as Tommy. I was rather frightened of him at first, but he is actually very kind. I will tell you more next time.

With love,

Marion xx

'And what did you choose from Queen Mary's bric-a-brac table?' Tommy asked Crawfie as they stepped out onto the steps leading to the palace gardens, both of them keeping an eye on the Princesses who were running ahead.

'Hardly bric-a-brac.' Crawfie glanced over her shoulder. 'Someone may hear you.'

Tommy strode on, grinning. 'You must learn not to be so deferential, Miss Crawford. It's not good for you and it's not good for them. So, what did you choose?'

'A small jug which I shall treasure.'

'How very ungreedy of you. I picked a paperweight. Very heavy. Caithness glass. An excellent murder weapon.'

The Princesses had reached the palace lake and were standing perilously close to the edge. 'Wait, girls, please!' Crawfie called.

The girls waved back at her in acknowledgement.

'Admirable obedience,' Tommy noted. 'Do you think the Princess Elizabeth has the character to make a good Queen if and when the time comes?'

Crawfie was certain. 'She has a very fine character. Thoughtful and kind, never short of a question. And what's more, she listens to the answer.'

'A good head on young shoulders, you think?' Tommy asked.

'Aye.'

'Her grandmother, the Dowager Queen, sets an excellent example. I admire her very much. Did you know that her first engagement was to George V's older brother? Some sort of arrangement was made with Queen Victoria. Anyway, the poor blighter died and the younger George was pushed gently in her direction. Or perhaps it was the other way around, but it became an excellent match and a successful reign. She'll be happy in Marlborough House, eventually.'

Crawfie privately wished the Dowager Queen might have been allowed to remain at Buckingham Palace. To have lost her husband last year, and now to lose her home and her job seemed so very awful. But she kept her thought to herself.

A burst of sunshine suddenly lit up the bare trees and the reeds at the edge of the pond where it bounced off the water. A coot swam out of the shadows and picked its way through a patch of weed.

'Crawfie, look!' shouted Margaret. 'Duck!'

Tommy was an excellent naturalist, pointing out the crocuses poking through the grass and the buds on the trees. He played a bird-spotting game with the girls to see how many they could name.

Eventually, as the sky grew yellow above them, Crawfie shivered. 'I think we ought to be going in now. It's cold enough for snow.'

'Just one more thing to show you,' insisted Tommy. 'Follow me.'

Dutifully the Princesses and their governess trooped behind him as he led them to the very end of the garden, where a grassy incline took them to the top of the Palace's high perimeter wall. 'The best view in London,' he said. 'Come and see.'

'Look at all the people!' said Margaret, peering over the top on tiptoes.

Lilibet was at her side. 'I can see Hyde Park. Look at that boy on his bike.'

'Look at that girl there.' Margaret pointed. 'I should like a red coat like hers.'

'We are like spies up here.' Lilibet smiled. 'Let's see if we can hear what the people are talking about.'

Lilibet and Margaret giggled at how naughty this seemed, and Crawfie and Tommy found themselves listening too. The snippets they heard, while not earth-shattering, seemed strangely fascinating.

'I said to him' – a young lady was talking to her friend – 'you come home late again and it'll be curtains.'

An older lady was talking to her son about supper: 'Daddy doesn't like liver so we'll have sausages tonight.'

And a cabbie dropping a fare was saying, 'Cheers, mate.'

The air grew chilly, and Tommy put the collar of his coat up to protect his ears. 'I think we should head back now,' he told Crawfie.

Crawfie was watching the girls, who were still intent on listening to the park below. 'Thank you for showing us all this,' she said softly to Tommy. 'This garden will be such a secure haven for them.'

Tommy said quietly, 'You care very much for them, don't you?'

'I have become very fond of them, yes.'

'Wait until you have your own brood. How many children do you want?'

Crawfie was taken aback, and glanced around to check that the Princesses hadn't heard. 'Well, I hadn't really thought.' Keen to dismiss the conversation, she signalled to the girls that they ought to go, and to walk down the grassy slope.

'Come, come,' said Tommy, following her, 'don't all young girls dream about marriage, a home, a family? Or are you the exception to the rule – married to the job?'

Crawfie stopped and gave Tommy a hard look. 'Of course I would like those things. In time. But now, my attention is needed here.'

The first flakes of snow descended. 'Look, girls!' Crawfie caught a snowflake on her hand. 'It's snowing.'

Margaret jumped up and down with excitement. 'Can we build a snowman? *Pleeese?*'

'You'll be a snowman yourself if you don't hurry up and get inside. Come on!'

Chapter Thirty-Six

Darling Joan,

It was so difficult waving goodbye to you last night. Thank you for dropping me at the station. The train was cold and the buffet car closed, which did not improve my low spirits.

Impressions of the new King: good! His Majesty took me for a long walk this afternoon. He talks to me and I to him, most naturally. I really like him awfully. After a hesitant start, he is adjusting well to his new duties.

The new Queen is a delightful woman, although underneath I detect a necessary strength to protect the family from any more scandal, particularly where the new Duke of Windsor is concerned. After the abdication, they remained close for a time but it has been weeks now since they spoke. This is mostly because the Duke kept telephoning the King, asking for more and more. The latest request was for Mrs Simpson to have some money, respect, dignity and position. I ask you! Apparently she loathes wandering around Europe, joining the other countless titles roaming the continent meaning nothing. She wants the extra chic of HRH.

It is simply not going to happen.

I bumped into Cecil Beaton this morning, here taking charming photographs of the Queen. He said that the last time he saw the Duke of Windsor, he noticed his 'tragic eyes' and the 'weather-beaten hands of a little mechanic'.

I really do hope that the public cease to take him seriously and realize the truth – that his mental and moral development stopped dead when he was about fifteen, and that though he is a sad figure, he is no longer a particularly interesting one.

The sooner the coronation takes place, the better.

I do miss you, old thing.

Tommy

Buckingham Palace, 13th May 1937

Dear Mother and Dad,

How are you both? I am glad to hear Dad's tulips came up even after all the snow you had.

I have so much to tell you about the coronation yesterday.

The blossom in Hyde Park came out at the perfect time but was spoiled by last week's damp weather, and we've had quite a lot of rain. I do pity those loyal people who slept in the parks and on the pavements the night before in order to catch a glimpse of the new King and Queen – they must have been soaked to the skin!

The Princesses were on best behaviour for the entire ceremony. I was so proud of them. By the time this letter reaches you, you have probably already seen the photographs in the newspapers. Weren't their dresses pretty? Their first LONG dresses as Margaret proudly told me – and what about their ermine-edged cloaks and little coronets?

When they eventually got back to the Palace, it was onto the balcony to wave at the cheering crowds. When that bit was done, Alah provided sandwiches for the girls before the official photographs were to be taken. They were so tired that I thought another hour of standing and smiling might finish them off! I thought the King and Queen must be hungry too, but when I quietly suggested they might also like a sandwich, I was told that a light buffet had been set up in their 'dressing rooms' at the Abbey.

The Queen made me laugh. She whispered to me, 'We are not meant to be human, Crawfie.'

And so, our lives have changed forever. And by that I mean the entire Commonwealth, not just we who serve in the household. I really feel that we are heading into a bright future with a modern monarchy, a proper family. May God bless them.

I have a little piece of personal news too. George surprised me last week with a letter telling me he was coming to London for work. He arrived three days ago although I have not managed to see him yet, what with all the ballyhoo going on, but he is taking me out for an early dinner tomorrow. It has to be early because I need to be with the girls in Windsor for the weekend. There is to be a garden party this Sunday, although after this week, I think they would all prefer some ordinary family time.

My love to you both.

Marion xx

Chapter Thirty-Seven

Royal Lodge, 16th May 1937

Tommy stood on the platform at Windsor station, waiting for Joan's train to arrive. The King and Queen were having a Garden Party at Royal Lodge to thank those who had had so much input into the smooth running of the coronation, and wives were included.

Joan stepped off the train and Tommy took his hat off to kiss her. 'Darling, thank you for coming.'

'It's rather an honour to be invited,' she said, smoothing down her skirt. 'Do I look all right?' She was wearing a neatly-fitted powder-blue suit, belted at the waist, with a fox fur thrown around her shoulders.

'You look perfect. And I love the hat.'

'Is it all right? I was worried it might be too much. Do you think the Queen will approve?

'Most definitely.' He picked up her small valise and put his arm around her waist. 'I have a taxi waiting.'

The garden of Royal Lodge was already busy by the time Tommy and Joan arrived. Crawfie spotted them straight away, weaving amongst the many beautifully dressed people there. What a handsome couple they made: Tommy tall and distinguished, his wife effortlessly chic and wearing the smartest little hat. They seemed so right together that it made Crawfie's heart jump a little. She was still dizzy from the unexpected turn of events with George earlier that week.

Two nights ago, he had taken her for supper in a small French café in Victoria. George had been attentive and kind, showing more interest in her work than usual. He had asked so many questions about the behind-the-scenes stories of the coronation, wanting to know every detail.

'Now you must tell me about you,' she had asked. 'How is the bank?'

She noticed that he puffed out his chest a little as he sat back in his chair. 'It is going very well. Its reputation speaks for itself. Landowners, aristocrats, members of the world's royalty – they have heard how rock solid it is.' He leant forward to pick up his glass of wine. 'But if you wanted an account with them, I can swing it.'

Crawfie's eyebrows shot up. 'Goodness. I don't really have enough to warrant that kind of banking.'

'You never know. You are young and hardworking. You deserve to do well.'

'I am happy with everything I have.'

'You're only what, twenty-seven?'

She pulled a face. 'Twenty-eight next month.'

'And are you saving for your future?' He looked serious.

'I save a little.'

'That's good.' George stretched his hand across the table to take hers. His fingers were warm and strong. 'I do admire you, Marion. A working woman, independent, strong and loving.'

With those few words, Marion forgot all about their disastrous New Year's Eve, and the scant communication they had had from then until now. She looked at her watch to hide her flushed cheeks. 'My train to Windsor is in an hour.'

'Let me take you,' he had said.

He called a waiter over and paid the bill. Once they were outside, he hailed a taxi.

'Save your money.' Marion tried to stop him. 'We can take the bus.'

George picked up her bag and took her arm. 'A bus? You deserve a cab.'

The initial weekend rush for the country had thinned out by the time they got to Paddington. George led the way down the platform, looking for a quiet compartment.

'Here.' He stopped. 'This one's empty.'

Marion hesitated before stepping up into the train. 'Thank you, George. It's been lovely to see you.'

He was standing very still, looking at her intently. Crawfie held her hand out to take his, but his hands remained in his pockets.

'Marion, I never did tell you what I wanted to say to you on New Year's Eve.'

Marion didn't move, hearing the blood thunder in her ears. Was this it?

He shuffled his feet, coughed and spoke again. 'I realize I am well over ten years older than you, but, well, my respect for you is enormous. I have missed you very much and I . . .'

She tried to say something, but he stopped her.

'Please let me say what I should have said a long time ago. I have done a lot of thinking since New Year's Eve, and I realize I don't want you to slip through my fingers and into somebody else's arms.'

'George—'

'Marion, would you make me the happiest of men and become my wife?'

'George—' Tears swam in her eyes and her voice shook as she answered. 'Yes. Yes please.'

They embraced as last-minute commuters stepped around them to board the train, and Marion felt her heart swell. Releasing her, George helped her up the step and onto the train.

'The next time I see you, I will have an engagement ring,' he promised.

'When *will* I see you again?' she asked.

'I shall be back in London next month. I shall take you out for your birthday and we can celebrate our engagement.'

A guard walked past and slammed the door between them shut.

Marion pulled the window down. 'George, I can't take it all in, but you have made so happy. Thank you.'

'No, Marion, thank *you*.'

The train pulled away with a jolt, separating the two lovers for four long weeks.

'Hello, Crawfie. May I introduce you to Joan, my wife.' Tommy indicated the clearly well-bred woman by his side.

Joan smiled. 'My husband tells me you are working wonders with the Princesses.'

'She is,' said Tommy, 'Even though their mother doesn't see the value in educating them. After all, she had little or no education herself. A young Scottish girl from a good family only needed to know how to be gay and beautiful.'

Crawfie shook her head. 'You are being very unfair. The Queen is a wonderful mother.'

'I don't doubt it,' Tommy said, 'but is it not Queen Mary, their grandmother, who takes the most interest in your teaching?'

'Well, yes,' Crawfie conceded, 'but only because she has the time so to do.'

Tommy tapped her wrist with his elegant fingers. 'Now you are making excuses for her.' With a smile, he turned his attention to the garden. 'Everything looks very much better than when I was last here. Not quite so much of the feel of a municipal garden about it, all those serried rows of stiff plants, red, white and blue.'

Joan laughed. 'Forgive my husband, he is a garden snob.'

'Yesterday we were all hands to the pump.' Crawfie smiled. 'The King and Queen, the Princesses, even I, were commissioned to help dig, weed and plant. I am glad that you have noticed.'

'I suppose it must have helped them let off a little steam after such a momentous week?' Joan asked.

'Indeed.'

'Well, I suppose we ought to mingle.' Tommy took his wife's elbow. 'I can see a couple of dullards who really need to be kept on side. Come along, Joan.'

Crawfie didn't mind being left on her own. She found a seat in a shaded spot and sat with a plate of tiny sandwiches and a fruit juice, watching as the Prime Minister, the Home Secretary, the King's younger brothers and the Princess Royal greeted people and conversed with ease. All accompanied by their spouses. Crawfie's mind wandered to the day when she would be accompanied by George. Mr and Mrs Buthlay. How proud she would be of him.

'He is manager of the Aberdeen branch of Drummonds bank,' she would tell them. 'Yes, I am very proud of him. What do I do? I work with the royal family as governess to Princess Elizabeth and Princess Margaret Rose. Very rewarding indeed, yes. One day George and I hope to have a family of our own, of course.'

The vision was as clear as crystal. She hoped they would be married as soon as possible. The wedding would be wonderful. Perhaps the Princesses could be bridesmaids . . . She would have to tell the Queen about her engagement very soon.

But what if . . . ? A sensation of icy cold fingers ran down her spine. What if the Queen would not allow her to marry? Or what if she dismissed her? The law prevented women from remaining in the teaching profession when they married. When she and George were married, he would not be expected to leave his job in Scotland to live with her in London. A man could work, be married and have children, and expect a wife's plans to fall in line with his. She clenched her hands in frustration. If only she was a man – men's lives were so simple.

She checked her thoughts. Was she expressing the thoughts of a radical woman, the type Alah disapproved of? Oh Lord, she needed to stop that immediately. It would all work out. Of course it would. After all, her position was surely unique. The family needed her, trusted her – they relied on her entirely. She had been with them for five years now, and she dearly hoped they would see her as irreplaceable. True, she might no longer be able to live at the Palace if she were to live with George, but surely there would be a way . . .

'Hello, Crawfie.' Margaret was at her side. 'I am bored.'

'And how am I to help you?'

'Can we play Happy Families? I've got the cards in my pocket.'

'I couldn't think of a better game to play today.'

Buckingham Palace, 17th May 1937

Crawfie stood outside the Queen's sitting room, waiting to be called in. She had asked to see Her Majesty urgently, and had been granted five minutes between a meeting with her dressmaker and the American Ambassador's wife.

Eventually, the dressmaker left, a sheaf of designs in her hands and a pincushion on her wrist. Crawfie was ushered in.

The Queen was at her desk, looking at some swatches of silk. 'Ah, Crawfie dear. Which do you think the King would like? The peach?' She held it to her cheek. 'The blue? Or the lilac?'

'You suit all of them, but I think the blue really complements your eyes.'

'I think I agree. Dear Bertie does love blue.' She put the swatches down and indicated a chair nearest to her.

'Thank you for seeing me at such short notice, ma'am.'

'I have the American Ambassador's wife arriving shortly, but I was told you wished to see me as a matter of urgency. Are you ill?'

'No, ma'am. I am very well and very happy. In fact, I have good news.'

'I like good news.' The Queen smiled. 'Tell me.'

'I am going to be married.'

The Duchess's smile froze. 'Oh dear. When would this be?'

'We have not made a date yet, but neither of us wish to delay.'

'What a surprise and, may I say, a shock. My dear, what about your work here? What would the Princesses do without you? They are so fond of you. And with the move from 145, the stress of the coronation and Lilibet's dawning realization that she will one day be Queen, you leaving us would be a catastrophe. You must see that.'

'I was hoping that I might be allowed to continue my work after I am married. The Princesses' education and happiness is my first priority.'

'And yet you wish to seek your own happiness?'

'Well, yes – but I can do both.'

'Where would you live? I can't see how you can be married and still live here. It would be impossible for your husband to join you.'

'He works in Scotland and occasionally London, so we would be living apart a lot of the time.'

'And he would permit that?'

Crawfie hadn't discussed any of this with George. She hoped she could persuade him later. 'Oh yes. He knows how much my work here means to me.'

'And what if he wants you back in Scotland? What if you were to have children of your own? My husband and I and our daughters need someone we can totally rely on. It would never do to have a governess whose domestic arrangements might take her away at any moment.'

Crawfie tried to sound reassuring. 'I would see him during the holidays and he would come to London when he can.'

The Queen paused. 'And how long have you known this man?'

'Seventeen months, ma'am.'

The Queen looked at her governess, unblinking. Her pretty blue eyes that almost always twinkled were now shrewd and clouded with thought. She shook her head. 'I don't think it possible. It is simply not convenient for you to leave us. You must realize that this is the most difficult time for my husband and me. We need someone we trust, to care for the girls and give them stability. *We need* you, Crawfie, dear. You must see that?'

'I do, ma'am, but apart from perhaps being away for a few days to marry in Scotland, my life here will remain exactly the same. I would make sure of it.'

'In which case, there is little need for you to marry immediately. You must postpone your arrangements until the time is right. Please explain this to your fiancé. I am sure he will understand.'

The Queen folded her hands in her lap. The conversation was finished.

Crawfie had been stopped. She knew there was nothing she could do. She found she could hardly speak. 'Of course,' she made herself say. Her voice sounded quiet and hoarse. 'We shall wait until our timing is better suited.'

The white and gilded doors opened again, revealing a footman and a smartly dressed woman in a scarlet hat. 'Mrs Robert Bingham, ma'am.'

Crawfie curtseyed and left the room, determined not to cry.

In her room she wrote to George.

Darling George,

I don't know quite how to write this letter, so forgive my just diving in.

I am most awfully sorry but I find we must postpone our wedding – just for a little while. The Queen, while delighted by our news, apologizes profusely; what with the coronation just gone and all the new pressures on her and the King, she rightly feels that any disturbance of routine for the girls at this time would be disastrous for their happiness and education. The last year has certainly been a whirlwind for them all, what with a new home and new jobs, in a way. I am feeling the effects myself.

I am so disappointed because more than anything I wish to be your wife. Nothing will change my feelings for you. Please, please understand.

I do feel the short delay might be helpful for us. It might give us time to organize an unrushed and heavenly wedding, and a chance to work out where and how we live after our marriage.

I have been thinking, perhaps the bank would offer you a permanent job here in London. Wouldn't that be marvellous? We could look for a little home of our own here. That way, perhaps I could continue to work and bring in a second wage, which I think you would agree would be most useful. Of course, I don't expect to stay in London forever. I can picture us in a little Scottish house, nappies on the washing line, your pipe and slippers by the fire, and being terribly happy. I will buy you a pipe for Christmas so that you can start practising!

Please write to let me know you understand. It will not be a long wait.

How is Scotland? The scent of the heather you brought for me that time in Windsor still lingers, but how I wish I were out on the moors, walking next to you.

It would at least get me away from all the talk here of Germany and Mr Hitler. Apparently he is all for lifting the Germans out of the depression and poverty of the last war, by making jobs and building roads. The Prime Minister and the King talk about him rather a lot, I am told. The Prime Minister is worried about the fascist movement in Italy and thinks it could spread through Europe. I had to look up the meaning of fascist and if it means having an organized country, I can't see how that would be all bad. I am sure it will resolve itself without anyone coming to blows.

I have just read that bit back and I think I am just trying not to think too much about the delay for our wedding.

Please write soon. I hope you can see that a short delay is a positive thing. I can't wait too long to be Mrs Buthlay!

I do love you.

Marion xx

Dear Marion,

I have just received your letter. I am very disappointed that the Queen should persuade you to delay our happiness but perhaps we do need some time to gather the plans for our future. When I waved you goodbye at the station, I promised you that the next time we met I would have an engagement ring to place on your finger. You deserve fine diamonds and sapphires, but at the moment I could not afford it. Therefore, reluctantly, I accept that we must wait. It will give us the time we need to save some money so that you can have the ring and the home you deserve. I know how you worry, lassie, but don't fret. We have the rest of our lives ahead of us.

If I could, I would be on the next train down just to see you, but alas, I also have news. The bank needs me to stay put in Aberdeen for a while, and so I cannot be with you for your birthday. I will speak to them about the possibility of a transfer to London in the future.

I am not sure when I will see you again. I hope it may be soon, but know that I miss you as much as you miss me.

My love,

George x

PART THREE

Two years later

Chapter Thirty-Eight

Downing Street, January 1939

Tommy sat slightly apart from the conversation, making notes. The room was warm and cigar smoke hovered around the ceiling and over their heads, like an ominous thunder cloud.

The Prime Minister, Neville Chamberlain, was talking. 'And what if Germany continues to be the aggressor? God knows I will do anything to avoid war, even if it means appeasing Germany. We *have* to find the path of peace. And if we can't, then Great Britain's strength can only be enhanced by the strength of our Allies.'

The foreign secretary replied, 'Certainly those who border Germany will be looking to us to help – and to France, too. And then there are the Americans.'

Winston Churchill, an MP with a voice people listened to, blew out a stream of cigar smoke. He leant his elbows on the Prime Minister's desk and looked into the faces of those assembled. 'Mr Roosevelt is not keen to get involved in a war in Europe – too expensive, too far from home, and too damn dangerous. As you know, my mother was an American. I therefore have many American cousins. They tell me what they think. I listen. And the Americans are not too fond of us right now.'

The foreign secretary discredited this with a smile. 'I can't think why not.'

The PM's response was more measured. 'Why do you think that is, Winston?'

Churchill's answer was swift and brief. 'Because of the way we treated one of their own. Mrs Simpson.'

The foreign secretary raised his hands in disbelief. 'Poppycock.'

'Believe what you wish, sir.' Churchill lifted his elbows from the PM's desk and sat back in his chair. 'How would you like *your* wife to be humiliated by the whole world, just because she had fallen in love with *you*?'

Tommy wrote this insult down most carefully, hiding a smile.

The PM sat back and crossed his arms over his chest. 'How would you suggest we sweeten our friendship with America?'

Winston chuckled. 'Let's woo them with the one thing they lack, and long for. No member of our monarchy has set foot in the United States for one hundred and fifty years! Not since we were defeated in the American War of Independence. I think it's time we did. We send in our biggest guns: King George VI and Queen Elizabeth.'

Every man in the room fell silent.

Buckingham Palace, January 1939

His Majesty was dumbfounded. 'We will not do it!'

Winston Churchill nodded. 'I do understand your feeling, sir. However, I believe the time is right for the Empire to know what we stand for. The only person to deliver that message is you, sir, and the first to hear it must be the United States.'

A few hours had passed, and Churchill and Tommy were standing in the King's office at Buckingham Palace.

'America is no longer part of our Empire,' said the King.

'Which is why it is paramount that the USA is our starting point – an acknowledgement of their independence from us, and a show of no hard feelings.'

The King stubbed out a cigarette, immediately lit another, got up and began to pace the room. 'Have the Americans requested a visit?'

'No, sir.'

'Then we are assuredly not going. It would weaken us if we were seen to be pleading for friendship.'

Churchill's eyes gleamed for a moment. Tommy watched him as his great brain worked quickly. 'In that case,' said Churchill, 'let us not speak of it again.'

'Good.'

In the silence that followed, the King turned to Tommy. 'What do you think?'

Tommy stooped to place a folder of letters onto the King's desk. 'These are for signature, sir.'

'Damn the letters, Tommy,' the King stuttered. 'Do you think the Queen and I should present ourselves, cap in hand, to the Americans?'

'Sir, it is not for me to say, but one would hope that any conflict could be avoided with delicate and experienced diplomacy.'

Mr Churchill lit one of his famous cigars, the pungent smoke settling around him. 'Quite right. Jaw-jaw before war-war. But first of all, Mr Hitler must want to jaw with us.' He turned his gimlet eyes back to the King. 'I discovered something quite extraordinary the other day, sir.'

'Oh yes?'

'Your grandfather was the last member of the royal family to visit Canada. That must be well over forty years ago now.'

'Which is why, as their King and Queen, we are visiting Canada in the spring, as you very well know.' The King picked up his pen and made a start on signing his letters.

Mr Churchill continued. 'So I have heard. Such a beautiful part of the British Commonwealth, almost a home from home. I first visited in 1900 myself. It is the lynchpin of the English-speaking peoples.' Churchill gave the King a sly look. 'Everyone must see Niagara Falls at least once. I stood there with the thundering water filling my ears, and my eyes looked over the border and into America. An extraordinary sight, one I shall never forget. I have promised many times to take Mrs Churchill to see it for herself.'

The King continued signing papers. 'Yes, the Queen is very much looking forward to seeing Niagara Falls.' He stopped mid-signature and paused. 'What are you saying?'

'I am merely mentioning that a tour of Canada, followed by a little hop over to America while you are there, may be rather pleasant.'

Tommy allowed himself a small smile.

Chapter Thirty-Nine

Buckingham Palace, May 1939

Dear Mother and Dad,

I met Mr Norman Hartnell today! He is designing all the gowns for the royal tour of Canada and America. He is a young and slim man, maybe a little too intense. I heard someone call him a pansy and people laughed. I don't know what's so funny about a pansy. I liked him very much. He made me laugh and he does make very beautiful clothes.

The Queen's ladies-in-waiting are making preparations now for all the packing. Dozens of day clothes, work wear, relaxing wear, evening gowns, hats, gloves, bags, shoes, jewellery . . . the list goes on.

The Princesses will not be travelling with them but are very excited anyway. We have promised the Queen that we shall write often and if they can manage a telephone call to us we shall hold Dookie up to the mouthpiece so that the Queen can hear his panting. Margaret suggested pinching him to make him bark.

The Dowager Queen Mary has been very kind to me. When the King and Queen are away she has lined up several outings for the girls when they are not in the schoolroom with me. She will take them to museums, art galleries and even the Bank of England to see all the gold bars in the vault. How wonderful to have a grandmother who can open such doors to them.

I know you were asking about George in your last letter. I had a letter from him just yesterday and he is quite well. The bank keeps him busy in Aberdeen but I hope to see him in London soon. It seems strange to think our engagement has gone on for nearly two years now. My, how the time has flown! Mother, I know you wish to know when the wedding will be, but as I said in my last letter, we will have to wait a while longer. I cannot let the Princesses or their parents down. I would feel like a soldier who has deserted his post. With the royal tour approaching and all this talk of trouble in Europe, I simply cannot abandon them now. George completely understands, and if he is content to wait for me, could not you try to be content too?

But I don't mean to grumble at you, Mother. Anyway, you must look out for any photographs and articles about the royal trip to Canada and America. I shall be making a scrapbook with the Princesses to give to their parents on their return. And I am thinking of starting a Girl Guides group for the girls and the daughters of Palace employees.

With love,

Marion x

Quebec, May 1939

Dear Joan,

What an appalling crossing we have had the misfortune to encounter. The Atlantic was bleak and grey, shrouded in thick fog, and the horn was blowing incessantly. The melancholy blasts were echoed back like a twang on a piece of wire. We very nearly struck an iceberg. The poor captain was hassled by passengers telling him it was at the exact spot where the Titanic went down. As if they knew!

Landing in Quebec, we were met by an enormous crowd, all wanting to catch a glimpse of the King and Queen. I am told that the fashion papers applaud Mr Hartnell's designs and are holding the Queen up as a fashion plate. She is very gratified indeed.

We are now on the most vulgar train – a silver, blue and gold 'streamliner', I am told. It has a lounge car, offices, two royal bedrooms and many ordinary bedrooms or bunks for the rest of us. Thank God I have a bed, no matter how narrow.

With my highest esteem,

Tommy

Buckingham Palace, June 1939

Dear Mother and Dad,

The royal tour of Canada and America is going very well. Do you see the photos in the Scottish papers? I get every paper each day, for the Princesses are looking for articles to cut out and stick in their scrapbooks.

Lilibet is very interested in the reported speeches that her parents make, and the commentaries of the British journalists accompanying them.

Margaret loves the photographs of her parents looking so elegant or doing something funny.

Did you see the photograph of them at Niagara Falls? Spectacular! And now they are in America. I hear from Ainslie that the venture is going better than he could have imagined.

They are meeting with President Franklin D. Roosevelt and the First Lady Mrs Eleanor Roosevelt today or tomorrow. I can't work out the time differences. I have read that Mrs Roosevelt is very popular and very unaffected in her manners. She's described as 'Rather Homespun. Not concerned with balls or grand cuisine. She likes scrambled eggs and something called square dancing.' Doesn't that sound fun?

They have been away for nearly three weeks and we are all missing them.

I am missing George terribly, too. Thank you so much for looking after him for me. He is such a dear and praises your dinners so that I worry my cooking won't be up to your standards.

I can't wait to be back home for the summer. Christmas with you all seems a long time ago. I'll let you know my dates as soon as I have confirmation of when the family will be at Balmoral. We might go to the Braemar games again?

My love to you and Dad and please give George a hug from me when you see him next.

Marion xx

Buckingham Palace, 22ⁿᵈ June 1939

'Your Majesty, welcome home.' Crawfie dropped into her now-expert deep curtsey.

'Mummy!' Lilibet and Margaret jumped up from behind their desks and smothered their mother in hugs and kisses as she stood in the schoolroom door.

Margaret was beside herself. 'We were very good. We didn't wake you up even though we knew you and Daddy were home!'

'Where is Daddy?' asked Lilibet. 'I have missed you both so much.'

'And we have missed you very much. Daddy is working, but you will see him tonight.'

'Was the boat ride home nice?'

'Yes, Margaret, it was better than the first crossing. Very foggy with the foghorn booming all night and all day. Daddy slept through it all because he's used to being on boats, but it took me a while to get used to it.'

Lilibet left her mother's side and ran to the bookshelf. 'Look what we have made for you.' She carefully carried two large scrapbooks to her mother's lap.

'Ooh. And what is this?' the Queen asked. 'Crawfie, may I sit with you all to look through this? I would like to tell them some stories of the trip.'

'Of course, ma'am.'

The girls got settled next to the Queen, nuzzling against her as she turned the pages.

'Look, there's Mrs Roosevelt,' Margaret said.

'So it is. Do you know she writes her own newspaper column called "My Day"?' asked the Queen.

'What does she write about?' asked Lilibet.

'Oh, she talks about what she does with the President at work and at home.' She laughed. 'She tried to persuade me to do something similar, but what on earth would I have to say in a newspaper column?'

'You could talk about the people you meet,' Margaret offered, 'and our gardening and the games we play.'

'Darling, you will learn that we do not speak to the newspapers. I am certainly not going to write anything about *our* family life.'

'But why not?' asked Lilibet.

'Because people do not want to know that we are just like them. They'd be bored by us in a moment.'

'Oh.' Margaret turned another page. 'I stuck that one in. It's the President, isn't it?'

'Clever girl. Yes, that is Mr Roosevelt. He is our friend and he has promised to help us if we ever get into trouble with another country.'

Lilibet nodded. 'That's good. I like him.'

'So do Daddy and I,' the Queen said. 'And, on our last night Mr and Mrs Roosevelt organized a picnic at their own home, or rather their "backyard", as they call the garden. Daddy drank beer straight from the bottle and we ate hot dogs.'

'Hot dogs, euggh,' said Margaret. 'I don't like the sound of them.'

'You didn't eat a dog, did you, Mummy?' Lilibet asked anxiously.

'They are not real dogs. They are sausages in a large bridge roll, taken straight off the barbecue grill and served on paper plates. I asked the President how I should eat one, and he told me to push it into my mouth and keep pushing until it was gone! Daddy ate two like that, but I really didn't have the heart to follow suit. After some gentle enquiries, a knife and fork were found for me. It was delicious. I was delighted.'

Margaret and Lilibet looked at each other and then back at their mother. 'Can we have hot dogs for dinner?' they asked.

Chapter Forty

Marion was lying in bed in her old bedroom. It appeared to get smaller year by year, but the fading wallpaper of pink roses still made her smile. Her stepfather had put it up as a surprise for her homecoming, after a nasty bout of scarlet fever had hospitalized her. She remembered how weak she had been when her parents had collected her. Her stepfather had carried her up the stairs, and when she saw how he had transformed her room, she had cried, and clung to him.

Now she yawned and stretched.

It was day one of her summer holidays and she would see George in a couple of hours. She was glad to be out of London and away from the concern growing over Hitler's Germany. She knew now that fascism was not about simply organizing a country well, and was ashamed that she had been so naïve to have thought so. It was about dictatorship and prejudice and violence. In Germany it was called National Socialism, or Nazism, and they were attacking Jewish people. The previous November Nazi soldiers, shamefully helped by German civilians, had smashed and burned synagogues and Jewish homes all over Germany. The streets had been filled with broken glass and so it had been called Kristallnacht. Marion couldn't bear that they had given a murderous night such a pretty name.

She rubbed her eyes. She knew more than she should, because Mr Chamberlain, the Prime Minister and his colleague, Mr

Churchill, were at the Palace almost every day. What they had to say often filtered down to the servants' hall via footmen. She hadn't seen Tommy for a while, but he must be in the thick of it. She and Alah and Bobo had recently started a nighttime ritual of gathered prayer – just the three of them, praying that peace would hold and God's grace be with the world.

She had got home last night, tired but happy to catch up with all her parents' news, especially that of George. She longed to see him.

In return, she had told her mother about a day out on the royal yacht. She had accompanied the girls with the King and Queen on a short voyage to Dartmouth Naval College, and there they had met a delightful boy, who showed off to the Princesses by leaping over tennis court nets. He was a Greek prince called Philip. The Princesses, especially Lilibet, who was now thirteen, had seemed rather taken by him.

Someone knocked lightly on Marion's door. 'Come in, Dad.'

He poked his head round. 'How did you know it was me?'

'Because Mother would have made more noise.'

They both laughed.

'I've brought you tea,' he said, putting the cup and saucer on the table by her alarm clock, then sitting on the edge of her bed. 'She's on the phone to someone from church.'

'Oh no!' Marion sat up. 'I hope she's not organizing one of her tea parties. I hate it when they all come round and ask me questions.'

They kept still, straining their ears to hear Maggie's side of the conversation in the hall.

'And the royal yacht *Victoria and Albert* is wonderful,' Maggie was saying. 'It's like a palace inside – very Victorian, everything served on Crown Derby china. Of course, Marion is very used to that sort of thing now, but I would love to see it for myself.'

Marion was horrified. She leapt out of bed, bouncing her dad's tea into his saucer, and ran out on to the landing. 'Mother! *Mother*, would you stop gossiping!' she hissed.

'It's only Jeanie from church.' Maggie flapped a hand at her daughter and smiled. 'She'll not tell anyone. Sorry, Jeanie, Marion is upset about me talking to you . . . Aye, I've told her that . . .'

Marion clattered down the stairs and stood in front of her mother. 'Put the phone down,' she mouthed.

'I have to go now, Jeanie. I'm awful sorry . . . No no, I'm fine. I'll tell Marion. Bye, now.'

Marion was steaming. 'I am never telling you anything about my work again! How many times do I have to tell you, Mother? I could lose my job because of your tattling.'

'Och, away with you. I only mentioned your trip to Dartmouth and that young man who escorted Lilibet and Margaret all day.'

'*Mother!* She is the Princess Elizabeth to you.'

'Oh, here we go. Can I not be happy that *Lilibet* attracted a nice boy who rowed after the departing royal yacht until he had to turn back?' She turned and walked to the kitchen. 'Are we not allowed a little romance in these dark times?'

Marion was glowering at her. 'Mother, she is only thirteen!'

'Exactly. So, she's hardly going to meet him again, is she? It's all innocent enough.'

'That's not the point.'

The doorbell rang and startled Marion. 'That will be George, and I'm not dressed!'

Later, George drove Marion quietly away, saying nothing while she railed against her mother's loose tongue and general inability to be discreet. Finally, she ran out of anger and sighed. 'Thank you for taking me out of there.' She put her hand on his thigh and squeezed. 'How do you put up with me?'

'It's best you get it off your chest.'

She smiled. 'Where are you taking me?'

'Up to Loch Leven for some fresh air. I think you need some space.'

'Dear George. What a wonderful thought. If you had told me, I would have packed a rug and maybe a picnic.'

'Why would I spoil a surprise? And anyway, that's all taken care of.'

George's smile melted her heart. He was so good to her. He had his odd little angry moments every now and then, but that was just him. She understood why he had been so upset when she had postponed the wedding but neither of them expected it to be for over two years. Since then, they had both started saving hard and, although their long-distance love affair had survived, they were yet to set a date.

In the two years they had been engaged, she had fallen in love with him over and over again. It was true they weren't able to see each other nearly as often she'd like. George was usually working in Aberdeen, and was only able to come to London once every month or so; even when he was there, Marion found it hard to escape the Palace in order to see him. But when they were together, it felt safe and right. This summer, George had managed to get some time off work and had come to Dunfermline, ready to spend as much time with her as possible. Marion hoped this summer would be perfect.

They parked by the little ferry which would take them over to the island where Loch Leven Castle stood. George seemed to know the place, and once they were off the ferry he took Marion straight to a hidden grassy spot at the foot of the ruined castle walls, overlooking the water. Here they were sheltered from the breeze, and from prying eyes.

'You spread this out and sit down,' he said, throwing her a tartan blanket. 'I'll set up our lunch.'

She lay back on the rug, feeling the warmth of the Scottish sun on her. 'Is this where you picked my lucky heather?'

He looked puzzled.

She laughed. 'You remember, the heather you gave me when we met in Windsor Park? You said that every time I looked at it, you would be thinking of me.'

He smiled quickly. 'Absolutely, I picked it here. Have you still got it?'

'Of course, I have. It is really very special to me. As are you.'

He beamed, then handed her a sandwich wrapped in grease-proof paper. 'Smoked salmon.'

'Thank you.' She unwrapped it and took a bite. 'Delicious.'

George lay down next to her and propped himself up by one elbow. 'Am I really special to you?'

'Yes.' She understood he needed reassurance. 'You are.'

'Enough to set our wedding date?'

She hesitated.

'Marion, I don't think I can wait much longer. It's been two years. Working at Drummonds is as important to me as your work is to you but I need you to be *with* me. I am the manager of an important bank, and it's only right that I have a wife. And I miss you so much.'

'Oh George, I know.' She began to placate him, nervous that his mood might change and the day be spoiled. 'But we have lots of time.'

'You say that because you are young.' He turned his gaze to the water. 'Marion, I'm sixteen years older than you.'

She smiled. 'That doesn't matter. I like that you're older. I like the way you feel like my protector. I feel secure with you. Nothing will hurt me if I'm with you. I feel safe.'

'Marion, if we are fortunate enough to have children, I want to be young enough to enjoy them.'

She stopped eating. 'You really want children?'

'Yes. As long as you want them?'

'Yes.' She felt her heart warm, and said again more firmly, 'Yes!'

'Well, we had better get a move on.' He took her hand. 'After all, you are thirty now.'

'Only just! I may be an old spinster but there's plenty of life in me yet!'

'I am not joking, Marion. If a war does happen, I shall volunteer immediately, as I did in the Great War.'

Marion frowned. 'Surely not? Your age would be against you.'

'I have the rank of major still, and the active service experience. Unfortunately they will call the experienced servicemen first. I want to marry you before I die, to know you have a child to remind you of me. If God sees fit, I want a son to bear my name.'

Balmoral, 7ᵗʰ August 1939

Darling Joan,

Fourteen hours from King's Cross to Ballater – the royal train does not allow speed to interfere with comfort. I still get the child-like excitement of sleeping on a train and very comfortable my quarters were too. Rather good grub in the lavish dining car also.

The royal cars came on the train. Can you believe it? Driven very skilfully onto the enormous freight wagons.

The horses and dogs, poor creatures, have the misfortune to travel by road.

I have unpacked and was relieved to find I had remembered my slippers, as all royal houses are rather chilly – this one is particularly so.

Tomorrow there is fishing. Rain is forecast but that won't deter the King. He and the Queen are excellent fly fishers and will be standing waist-deep in the chill river no doubt. I may leave them to it and go riding with the Princesses. They are utterly fearless and I imagine we shall have some fun.

The Glorious Twelfth is almost upon us and I am told that the grouse are plentiful and simply begging to be shot. I shall offer my services as beater and picnic helper. The King likes to unpack the luncheon hampers while sitting in the heather and warding off the dogs.

Now it is off to dinner and charades. Last year my impersonation of a St Bernard's dog strained my vocal cords so severely

I could hardly speak the next day, and I recall that the Queen's newest corgi, Crackers, was abysmally sick on the carpet. Let us hope for better things from this evening.

It feels good to be away from the worries of London. Do try not to read the newspapers too much – they will only make you solemn. We must trust that the situation abroad will improve.

All love to you and the children,

Tommy xx

Chapter Forty-One

Dunfermline, 2ⁿᵈ September 1939

Marion was already packing. At 11.15 that morning she had received a telegram from Buckingham Palace, ordering her back to Balmoral. The Prime Minister was expected to give a radio broadcast the following day, announcing that Great Britain would be at war with Germany. Until then, the news was top secret.

Marion had scanned the telegram, folded it twice and hidden it in her pocket.

Her mother had watched her. 'Who was it from?'

Marion smiled quickly. 'I have been called to Balmoral. The King and Queen are returning to London at once. I am needed to go and see to the girls. I shall deliver them back to London in a few days.'

Maggie was white. 'It's war, then? I don't want you going back to live in London. It could be dangerous.'

'I can only tell you what was in the telegram,' Marion had said. 'The Princesses are still at Balmoral and the King and Queen will never put them in danger.' She snapped her case shut.

'Marion.' Her stepfather, panting slightly, was now coming up the stairs. 'George is downstairs.' He saw her suitcase. 'Here, let me take that. Are you leaving now?'

'The next train I can get to Ballater.' Marion's heart was racing but her mind was calm and focused. She hurried down the stairs.

In the hall, George was waiting anxiously.

'Darling!' Marion had never been so glad to see him. 'Would you give me a lift to the station?'

'Robert just told me you had to go. I understand.'

She reached the bottom stair. 'You don't mind? I am so sorry about our lunch. I was so looking forward to it.'

'Me too.' He took her hand and squeezed it. 'We'll do it as soon as we know what's happening.'

She hugged him quickly. 'Thank you, George.'

Maggie was wretched. 'We are going to war, aren't we?'

George and Robert swapped quick glances. 'I hope not,' said Robert, with a laugh

Maggie began to cry. 'I don't want you to be in London, Marion. Please stay at Balmoral. Please.'

Marion was brisk. 'Mother, dear, all is well. Mr Chamberlain is a good prime minister and I am sure he is doing everything he can to keep us safe.'

She hugged her parents, biting her lip to stem her own tears. 'I will let you know what the plan is as soon as I can. I love you both.'

George put her case in the car and came back to shake Robert's hand and kiss Maggie's cheek. 'Don't worry – I'll make sure she gets the right train.'

Maggie and Robert waved their daughter and her fiancé off in a blur of tears and anxiety, watching as Marion waved from the car window, promising to let them know any change in plans.

At the station, George held the suitcase with one hand and Marion with the other as they marched to the ticket office. 'Single to Ballater, please,' he commanded of the woman behind the glass.

'You've just missed one,' the woman said.

'When is the next one?'

'Well, it's Sunday, so there aren't that many.'

George snapped, 'Just tell me when the next bloody train is.'

She bridled. 'No need to speak to me like that. I can refuse to serve you, you know.'

Marion stepped in. 'George, let me.' He glared at the woman behind the glass, before giving her a muttered apology and stepping back.

Marion bought the ticket, then joined George on a wooden bench. 'Next one is in a couple of hours,' she said calmly.

'Two hours?' George's ire was still bubbling. 'I could drive you there in that time.'

'That's a lovely thought, but I will be fine.'

Sitting as they were, side by side, he took her hand and held it hard. 'I can't believe we're at war again.'

'I know.' She squeezed his hand. 'With luck this will all be over soon.'

'I want to marry you, Marion.'

'And I want to marry you, George. It will all be all right.'

He was silent for a time, and then he said, 'I'm going to join up.'

Marion felt her heart clench. She had known this was coming, of course, but . . .'What?'

'The army will need men like me and there's no way I am not going to do my bit.'

A bolt of fear shot through her and she gripped his arm. 'Please don't. You don't have to. What about your work?'

'What about *your* work? You won't leave them now, will you.' It was statement not a question.

'I . . . no,' she said, at last, 'but . . .'

'They mean more to you than I do.' He said it quietly, not angrily, and it sent a pang through Marion.

'Please don't say that. You must see I can't leave those girls now. They need me.'

'They need you, and the war effort needs me.' He stood up. 'It's your decision.'

'Where are you going?' she asked anxiously. 'Please, George, don't go.'

'You have a lot of thinking to do, Marion. And so do I.' He bent to kiss her. 'Let me know that you arrived safely. Goodbye, Marion.'

'George, please don't leave like this!'

He said nothing more, and she watched solemnly as he walked to his car and drove away.

A car had been sent to Ballater station to pick her up.

'Miss Crawford.' Jackson the chauffeur was waiting for her. 'Welcome to Ballater.'

'It's good to see you, Jackson. How is everyone?'

'Shocked by it all, I'd say.' He looked at her. 'If you don't mind my saying, you look shaken yourself.'

She supposed she did. Another war was a terrible thing. She had still been a young child when the first one ended, but she remembered the scars it left behind. Besides, her conversation with George had confused her. She felt weighed down by guilt, though what she was guilty of she had no idea.

'I think the news has shaken everyone,' she answered. 'How are the Princesses?'

'They can't wait to see you. As excited as kittens when they knew you were coming.'

'I'm excited to see them too.' As he helped her to the car, Crawfie said, 'We will get through this, won't we, Jackson?'

'No doubt about it, miss. No doubt at all.'

'Crawfie, Crawfie!' The Princesses were waiting for her and ran to hug her.

'Don't squeeze me so tightly,' she gasped, thrilled by their affection. 'Let me look at you both.'

They let go and stood back for her review. It surprised her, sometimes, how grown up they were getting. Lilibet was thirteen now, and Margaret had turned nine last month. She had been with them for so many years now; they had become such a huge part of her life. 'I see you have grown, Margaret. And Lilibet, your hair is a little longer.'

The girls beamed.

'We have missed you,' they said.

'And I have missed you.' Marion crouched down and took them both in her arms. These precious girls who she had known for more than seven wonderful years were now in her care.

The faith their mother and father had in her both gave her confidence and made her question whether she could do it. She would lay down her life for the Princesses, she knew that. Their warm bodies were so trusting. She slowly let them go and as they stood before her, she stroked their curls from their foreheads. 'What fun we shall have.'

The girls giggled before Lilibet added quietly, 'Why are Mummy and Papa going back to London? Do you think the Germans might come and catch them?'

Crawfie smiled, fighting down a lump in her throat. 'No chance.'

Balmoral, 3rd September 1939

> *Darling Joan,*
>
> *So, the balloon has gone up. I sat with the King and Queen, drinking tea – so very British – to listen to Mr Chamberlain's wireless announcement. The Queen was in silent tears.*
>
> *Afterwards she said, 'My last cup of tea in peace. My last bath at leisure.'*
>
> *They are going to London tomorrow, and I will go with them.*
>
> *The King has ordered that Queen Mary must be immediately evacuated to Badminton House for the duration, for fear she may be kidnapped.*
>
> *Balmoral Castle will be closed down and the Princesses and their necessary staff are to be moved to Birkhall, a smaller, very*

cosy house on the estate, where they will be less likely to attract attention. The plan is to make things as familiar as possible for them. The stalwart nursery staff, Alah and Bobo, are with them, and Miss Crawford has just arrived this afternoon. They make a formidable trio – exactly what is needed for the girls at this time. You met Miss Crawford in Windsor once. Tall for a woman, rather shapeless and with a generous nose? But she possesses a quick mind and a true heart. Alah is getting on a bit now – in her seventies, at my guess – a strict but loving martinet in the old Victorian way. Bobo is something of a child although in her mid-thirties: kind, caring and utterly loyal.

I want you to come to London just as much as you do, but I can't yet see the perfect solution. I think it is safer for you to stay in the country than to join me in the city.

You are so good and kind and efficient and it is a comfort to hear your voice on the telephone, and to know that you are seeing this thing in the right perspective. We are far luckier than so many thousands of others: I, in a job that will probably give me better chances of seeing you than if I were on active service, and you and the children, to my mind, in about the best place possible in England.

My immediate movements here are rather vague. I am unable to tell you too much, but I shall be sleeping at BP and I believe the King and Queen are too.

Speak soon, my darling,
Tommy

PART FOUR

Chapter Forty-Two

I have decided to start a diary. I am not allowed to let George or my parents know my exact whereabouts, and I miss writing, so I thought I might jot down my memories in a small note-book — not to show anyone in particular, but more as something I may look back on in the years I hope are to come.

Bobo, Alah and I left Birkhall on the Balmoral estate back in May. We'd had the whole place virtually to ourselves for an entire eight months. The war seemed a long way away and we were safe to walk the heathered hills, bird watching, picnicking and, in the warmer months, even paddling in the chuckling burns. We've kept as much of the war news away from the girls as possible, but Lilibet is always very keen to know more. Nonetheless we've edited the worst bits.

The King and Queen telephoned almost every evening when we were in Balmoral and the Princesses regaled them with stories of their adventures — the biggest one being the arrival of children from the Glasgow tenements, evacuated to the Balmoral estate farms around us: skinny little things with scuffed knees and worn shoes. I organized a picnic for some of them last weekend, thinking that sandwiches, little sausages and glasses of milk might be thoroughly enjoyed. The Princesses helped in the kitchen to put it all together and we carried it out onto the lawn. There were around twenty little people with very round eyes watching as we set it up on the trestles. But the funny thing was they were too shy to come forward immediately. Dear Margaret went straight to them, introduced herself and her sister and started offering round the plates of food as if she were at a cocktail party. There was barely a crumb left after that! Once they had eaten and drunk their fill, a game of chase was organized, followed by grandmother's footsteps for the girls and football for the boys.

They had never been to the countryside and they found almost everything strange, but the thing that frightened them most was the noise of the trees in the wind!

How different my life would have been if I had become the child psychologist I had planned to be all those years ago. What would I have been doing now? How many of those young lives could I have changed?

There is little point in regret. God had another path for me and what a path it is.

In February I received a telephone call from the Queen in London. 'Crawfie, I think you should bring the girls at once to Royal Lodge.' She and the King were clearly missing them.

It took a lot of packing up, but a few days later we were back in Windsor.

The Queen looked radiant when we all arrived. She never made a show of any of her concerns and in that way it kept up the spirits of those around her. After a couple of days of reacquainting themselves with their long lost toys, books and of course the dogs and horses, the girls settled down happily.

One evening after they had gone to bed, the Queen called me in to the sitting room.

'Crawfie,' she began, 'do you think me selfish in bringing our daughters back to Windsor, rather than keeping them safe in Scotland?'

I didn't know how to answer this question. It was not for me to decide, so I asked her, 'What is your heart telling you?'

She cast her eyes down and thought for a moment. Then she said, 'Some government ministers wish me to send them away, and I have noticed some of the newspapers have been asking the same thing. Of course they don't know where the Princesses have been these last months and they never will know. But I am sure that here in Windsor they shall be safe.'

'At Royal Lodge?' I asked.

'Windsor Castle,' she replied. 'It's a fortress that has survived almost a thousand years. I don't think even Mr Hitler could knock it down.' She smiled at me. 'And anyway, the children would not go anywhere without me, and I cannot possibly leave the King, and the King will never leave.'

'And what is selfish about that?' I concluded.

We stayed at Royal Lodge until just a few days ago, when we moved into Windsor Castle, and I fear we may be here for some time. London has been deemed too dangerous for the girls, but Balmoral too far away. The King and Queen want to be with their daughters, but they cannot be too far from the capital. So here we are.

Alah believes we will all be back in Buckingham Palace soon, and has brought only a few clothes for herself and the Princesses. I packed everything. I feel that we may be here for a long time.

This ancient castle is not a home. There are few comforts here, and all the treasures, pictures, furniture and chandeliers have had to be taken down. At night I can hear air raid wardens and others flitting about, their shoes ringing on the stone floors of the passageways.

My bedroom and sitting room are in the Victoria Tower, and I have to climb a stone circular staircase to reach it. My bathroom is up in the roof – chilly, and a terrific target for the German bombers.

We live in an underworld, even above ground. There are few electric lights and many power cuts. At night it can be difficult to find your way around or see what you are eating.

We had an air raid yesterday. I was helping at the castle's Red Cross post, responsible for medicines and dressings, when I heard the alarm. I locked up and ran to the shelter in the dungeons, expecting to find the girls there. But they weren't.

Against procedure, I ran back up the winding stairs to the nursery in Lancaster Tower, knowing I had to get Alah to safety. In recent months I have noticed her hearing is not as it was, so in my best impersonation of the Queen's voice, which I sometimes used to entertain Bobo, I shouted, 'Alah! Are you up here?'

'Yes, Your Majesty!' she called back, flustered.

'Alah, it's me, Crawfie.'

'Is the Queen here too?'

'No, but we are all waiting in the shelter. You must come down now!'

'We are dressing. We must dress. I am in my nightdress!'

'For goodness' sake, put a coat over it. And where are the Princesses?'

I heard Margaret's voice from her bedroom, and when I ran up I found her on her knees in front of her chest of drawers. 'What are you doing?' I said. 'Come on.'

'I am looking for the knickers that match my skirt.'

I had to smile.

Windsor Castle, September 1940

Dear Joan,

So, we have had our first air raid. Rather noisy. Young Miss Crawford was very sparky – sent out like a dove to find the Princesses and their nanny, who were deciding on the dress code.

The Good Servant

The Queen has had a rather splendid gown made by Norman Hartnell especially for the raids, and Crawfie, as she is fondly known, has had a boiler suit made, just like our new Prime Minister's, Mr Churchill. He calls his a 'Siren Suit' because it's the perfect thing to be wearing when the warning sirens go off. He has them in many colours and fabrics – I hear he even has one in green velvet to be worn at formal dinners. Crawfie looks very natty in hers. The Princesses are most envious. I am certain it won't be long before they have their own.

This place is never warm and the wind whistles through the tall windows. I often find the King wrapped in a travelling rug in his room to keep his feet warm.

I heard today that Hitler thinks the Queen is 'the most dangerous woman in Europe'. It has cheered her no end.

Yours, fondly,

Tommy

Windsor Castle, January 1941

Our nights in the dungeons have become more comfortable, even though my thoughts often turn to those who had been chained there centuries before. The girls are remarkably unafraid. Margaret snoozes on my knee and Lilibet reads her books by the dim light.

We have taken down beds and blankets, toys and books, and even a kettle and cups and saucers for tea. The shelter is becoming almost cosy.

Every night at 7.00 pm, the Princesses troop off with their little cases, wearing their new siren suits, as if they are off to catch a train. Then, when the all-clear sounds, Lilibet is told, with a bow from a courtier, 'You may now go to bed, ma'am.'

It is remarkable how one can make the ordinary out of the extraordinary. Lessons continue. Christmas has been and gone. Time passes, and the war rumbles on.

The King and Queen are often away, touring the country in the royal train and keeping up morale.

The Queen writes to me when they are away, asking after the girls and their wellbeing, and I had a very funny letter from her the other day after she had visited the Sandringham Women's Institute. I shall copy it here, for it made me smile. They treated her to patriotic tableaux.

'It was a hoot. Mrs Way, dressed as Neptune(!) glaring through a tangle of grey hair and seaweed. The verger's daughter, Miss Burroughs, as Britannia, was HEAVEN. The script was spoken by Mrs Fuller's cook, draped in a Union Jack. Crawfie, dear, you would have loved it. Give my love to the girls and thank Alah for her card. Tinkety tonk, Old Fruit, and down with Hitler!' I can't agree more. When will the blasted man give up?

Buckingham Palace, December 1941

Darling Joan,

Ever since Buckingham Palace was bombed, the King and Queen have been determined to increase their visits to fresh bomb sites. They stand and watch the tireless efforts of rescuers digging the trapped or killed from the rubble, or those who drowned in the burst water mains. The Queen hates these visits but never cries. I commended her the other day on her steadfastness and she said, 'I am a beastly coward. It breaks my heart. The destruction is so awful and the people so wonderful. They deserve a better world.' It is all so piteous. I pray every night for our John and try as far as possible to check on the whereabouts of his regiment. You know I can't tell you all I know, but I do know at this moment he is safe.

Meanwhile, the Princesses, with the help of Miss Crawford, are putting on a nativity play. Princess Elizabeth played a wise man and Princess Margaret played the child who gave the gift *of herself, and sang to the baby Jesus in his crib. The King told me 'I wept through most of it. It is a wonderful story.'*

Princess Elizabeth is preparing to give her first radio broadcast. She will speak to the children of England, those at home and those evacuated. She worries so much about their fear – their fathers fighting, their mothers alone. She is busy writing a lot of it herself, to be shaped by others later. I am certain it will bring tears to many eyes and a new post bag of cheer.

I will come down on Christmas Eve to be with you all but will have to return on Boxing Day. I think I know where I can get hold of some half decent wine. Ask no questions and I will tell no lies!

Your Tommy

Windsor Castle, spring 1942

Today I walked through Windsor Great Park by myself. The sun had more heat than I had expected and I had to take my coat off. I walked up to the Copper Horse and laid my coat on the grass, thinking of George. I sat and thought of the day we met up there and the heather he brought me from Scotland. It is now almost dust but I cannot let it go. I sat there for some time imagining him walking towards me through the daffodils which are such a hope of better things to come. I pray for him each and every night. He has been sent abroad – he can't tell me exactly where. It must be awfully difficult to get his letters out because I receive none for four or six weeks and then several come at once. When this awful business is over we will at last be married and I shall be the most loving of wives.

My parents are the same – stalwart and safe, although my stepfather is getting older and his hip is worse. My mother is knitting madly for the troops – socks and mufflers mostly. Princess Margaret was fascinated when I told her and insisted I taught her to knit. So far, her swift and nimble little fingers have produced five scarves and two pairs of rather ugly socks. Queen Mary is very proud of her but I noted she turned down Margaret's offer of fingerless mittens! 'That's so kind of you, Margaret; however, we must keep the wool for the soldiers.'

The Princesses have such fortitude and resilience. Lilibet is almost sixteen and Margaret twelve. Where does the time go? The war has made them mature beyond their years. They are such good companions, which, considering they have only the grenadier guards and the household around them, is a great thing!

Buckingham Palace, November 1942

My darling,

America's First Lady has arrived to visit the American troops newly stationed in the United Kingdom, and for us it is a chance to hopefully send the message that we Brits are most grateful and should be liked a little better.

Back in the States, I hear the voters are none too happy with the cost and danger to their men and country. Of course, if it wasn't for the Japanese attacking Pearl Harbor last year, Roosevelt would never have joined. But he had no choice.

Therefore 'Operation Sweeten the Americans', disguised as a Thanksgiving tea party, was launched at BP. Two hundred American officers arrived and were charmed by British hospitality and as many young ladies as we could muster, to cheer the whole thing up.

A certain Mrs Gould managed to gatecrash the event and make a nuisance of herself. She is co-owner of an American periodical called the Ladies' Home Journal. *Some time ago she persuaded Mrs Roosevelt to contribute to the magazine, writing a column called 'If You Ask Me . . . Essential advice from the First Lady.'*

Dangerous rot, I daresay.

The Good Servant

But now Mrs Gould has successfully wormed her way into the Foreign Office and the Ministry of Information, seducing them with the idea that the Queen should write something similar for them. 'It would ease tensions between us and America,' she bleated, or so I was told.

I told the FO that a queen can no more write an article for a magazine, than serve a pint in a pub. I drafted a letter turning Mrs Gould down firmly. I hoped to God she takes the hint and disappears.

No such luck.

Alas, she has come back with a letter via the Foreign Office which includes a highly fictitious account of a conversation she supposedly had with the Queen, wishing permission to publish!

As you well know, any request to me from anyone – and I include our own offspring here – I put to the test by asking: 'Will it do more harm than good?' In this instance the answer is blindingly clear: Yes!

The Queen summoned me to go round to the Ritz hotel, where Mr and Mrs Gould nest while in London.

'Tommy, dear,' HM said, 'would you go to the Ritz and tell Mrs Gould that the Queen has warm feelings for the Americans, but cannot agree to her request.'

My mission went well, I thought, and Mrs Gould appeared to accept that any business with the Queen would not be entertained.

Next thing I know, it is President Roosevelt himself who becomes a bother. This time to the King. He has been asked by the Duke of Windsor to ask Winston Churchill to ask me to pave the way for the Duchess of Windsor to be made HRH.

This is clearly another attempt to make the Americans like us more. It is rather doing the opposite for me.

Thank you for the handsome new pipe. It smokes very well and is wearing in nicely. You are a duck.

Fondly,
Tommy xxx

Windsor Castle, January 1943

I find myself in a bit of a low trough. I am trying very hard to pull myself together but last night I could not stop the tears. The truth is that I miss my parents and Scotland and George. I have never been besieged by so much emotion. It is almost a tangible entity – a black mist that sits over me and drains any energy or joy in life. I long to sleep, to have this war over. I cannot think of a future.

I hide this from the Princesses, who remain so gay and stalwart, but this evening, Alah took my hand and asked me how I was. Her words of kindness and understanding as I tried to put words to my misery opened a floodgate of embarrassing sobbing.

When the storm finally subsided, she made me a cup of Ovaltine and helped me to bed. I felt like a small child being protected, made to feel secure as she kissed my forehead and said good night. She told me that she will get me through this.

Tomorrow is another day, and I shall not allow this awful ennui to continue. There are people who have it far worse than me.

Chapter Forty-Three

'Come in, come in.' Tommy opened his office door to Crawfie. 'Sit down. I am having to make the tea myself this afternoon. P-T is doing her fire watch duty.'

'I did mine two nights ago. Jolly cold up on the roof. I hope P-T has a good coat.'

'She's a woman of good country stock,' Tommy answered, filling the small electric kettle from a large water jug. 'If I know her, she'll be as warm as toast.' He plugged the kettle in. 'Sugar? Milk?'

'No, thank you. Just black. Before this war, I used to have three teaspoons of sugar, but rationing has killed my sweet tooth.'

'I wish it had mine.' Tommy set up a tray with two saucers, two cups and a teapot into which he deployed a good amount of loose tea. 'I couldn't cook before the war – now look at me. Rustling up a cuppa at the drop of a hat.'

Marion smiled. During these war years, Tommy and she had become friends – not too close, but with an understanding of each other.

It had started in the dungeons on the long dark nights of air raids; Tommy noticed that she never showed any nerves or fear, always comforting the Princesses, and the first to make a hot drink for anyone who couldn't sleep. When the Princesses fell asleep, cosy in their blankets, Crawfie would bring a book out of her bag and read.

During one particularly close bombing raid, when the ancient foundations of the castle seemed to shake beneath them, Crawfie had showed no concern. She checked that the noise hadn't disturbed the girls, or Alah and Bobo, then serenely returned to her book. Her fortitude impressed Tommy, and in the next raid, he found himself sitting opposite her in one of the wider stone tunnels.

She was reading P.G. Wodehouse's *The Code of the Woosters* and it was clearly amusing her.

'That looks like the perfect antidote to an air raid,' he said softly, so as not to awaken those around him.

'Wodehouse?' replied Crawfie. 'He really is a good writer. It was the girls who started me on him. The Queen orders the books. Have you read any?'

'Oh, rather. *Carry On, Jeeves* kept me company when I was in India. Have you read Forster's *A Passage to India?*'

'No.'

'Well, you should.'

And so their shared interest had begun.

Now she spotted her copy of Osbert Sitwell's *A Place of One's Own* on Tommy's desk.

'How are you getting on with it?' she asked.

'Not bad but rather too fanciful for me. Would an elderly couple choose to buy a wreck of a house rumoured to be haunted?'

'I rather enjoy being scared.' Crawfie smiled. 'I began reading it aloud to Bobo and Alah around the nursery fire on evenings we aren't parcelled into the dungeons, but Alah had to tell me to stop because it was scaring Bobo too much.' Crawfie laughed. 'Yet she is never frightened of the real haunted dungeons we sleep in.'

'Which just goes to prove that fiction is more frightening than fact,' said Tommy. The kettle had boiled and he was pouring the steaming water into the teapot, giving it a good stir. 'Another culinary success.' He carried the tray to his desk and sat down. 'How did you get on with Forster's *A Passage to India?*'

'I thought it was thrilling. It made me want to go to India.'

'It's a wonderful place. Joan and I were married there. And wonderful people – they have nothing but would give you anything. In India, it is hard to live, but easy to exist; here in England it is easy to live but harder to exist – a Maharajah told me that as he sat in his many-roomed palace, and he wasn't wrong.' He poured the tea and passed her cup over. 'What news on your parents? How is your stepfather's hip?'

Family and friends had become another topic of conversation in the dungeons.

'It's a little better, I think. At least, that is what he told the doctor, or else he wouldn't have been able to join the Home Guard for Fife.' She said the last bit with comic pride.

'A Fife Home Guard – how about that! Your mother must be very proud.'

'Oh, she is. He has been part of a team manning the road blocks that Polish soldiers have organized.'

'Goodness.' Tommy stirred sugar into his cup. 'Quite right too. I hear that Fife is the chosen destination for Herr Hitler's invasion of our sceptred isle.'

Crawfie laughed. 'Once I would have thought you were awful, telling jokes like that. Now that kind of humour is the only thing that gets us through.'

Tommy dropped his gaze to his cup and asked carefully, 'And George? How is he?'

'Oh, he's all right,' she was saying now. 'His work at the relief agency is going well. I told you about that, didn't I? He coordinates the supply of food, medicines, fuel and shelter to victims of war. Isn't that marvellous? You can imagine how relieved I was when the army turned him down for re-entry. Eyesight too poor. I told him it was because he'd strained them looking at all those lines of tiny numbers on the bank's sheets.' She gave a small laugh then frowned. 'I think he's glad to be away from the bank for a time. He's a funny old stick.'

'Hmm,' Tommy answered. 'Jolly good.'

'And how about you? How are Joan and the children?'

'They are all in fine fettle. My dear wife will be coming to live with me in London when it's safer and the children are off her hands a bit. The trouble is, she might find me to have become a bit of a bachelor – used to coming and going as I please with very little of anything in the larder.' He looked off into the middle distance. 'It is my son, John, she worries about.'

'Oh. Which service?'

'British army. Grenadier guards.'

'You must be very proud.'

'Indeed.' He managed a smile. 'He's a good chap.'

Crawfie wanted to lean over and take his hand, but he was not the sort of man one could do that to. 'It must be very hard on her,' she said.

'I am more worried that Joan will have adored her single life and is dreading the thought of living with me and the children again.' He finished the last of his tea and looked at his watch. 'Well now, somewhere in the world it is after six o'clock, so how would you like a small whisky?'

The 'small one' was not very small and was followed by several larger ones.

Tommy was not the sort of man to reveal secrets when in his cups, but something had been bothering him all day, irritating him, so that he felt the need to share it.

'May I run something past you? Something a little delicate. I would value your opinion.'

'Of course, but please don't tell me any state secrets.' She grinned. 'I do not wish to carry that sort of burden.'

'Nothing like that. No, no, it's a little problem I have with two American journalists who are unable to take no for an answer.'

'American? What do they want?'

'In short, they want the Queen to spill her heart all over the pages of their ghastly magazine, telling tales of life with the King and their daughters – in short, of life as a monarch.'

Crawfie scoffed. 'But she would never do that.'

'Quite so, but try telling that to Mr and Mrs Gould. Today I received a message from them, opining that King George VI and Queen Elizabeth need a professional public relations team. Can you imagine? My whole life with the royal family has been devoting to keeping their private life private – and here I am being told to do the exact opposite.'

'Don't worry,' Crawfie told him. 'Our royal family would never stoop so low.'

'No, they won't, but certain people around them – house-maids, footmen, stable lads – may not have our scruples. In 1924 I was in Long Island with the then Prince of Wales – now Duke of Windsor – when a rodent of a journalist offered me a brand-new Lincoln motor car in return for "anonymously written articles about HRH's private life".'

Crawfie was shocked. 'What did you tell them?

'I laughed in their faces.'

'Good. I cannot understand how anyone could betray the royal family. I never would, even if they *did* offer me a big car.'

'Not even if it meant you and George could finally get married?'

Marion was taken aback by this unusually personal remark; Tommy usually circumvented anything emotional.

'Honestly, a wedding seems a long way off at the moment,' she said solemnly. 'We can't do anything until this war is over and the Princesses' education finished.'

'The Queen has told you that?'

'Not in so many words. In truth, I think I would like to post-pone our marriage until the girls are independent.'

'And George is amenable to that?'

She hesitated. 'He gets frustrated that we are so far apart. And I do miss him. I wish he would come down south more often. Last year we only saw each other three times. But we write and speak on the telephone.'

'Why can't he come down more often?'

'Clearly it's too dangerous, and besides, he may be sent to Italy soon. They need supplies of medicines and foods.'

There was a pause. 'Do you trust him?' Tommy asked.

'Of course.' Crawfie dropped her gaze. 'But – well, the other day I mentioned, as a joke more than anything, that the postmistress in the village told my mother that she had seen him out with a girl on his arm. I am sure she did it out of malice. Anyway, I chose the wrong time. George had had a drink and flew off the handle. It's his work. It is too stressful and I shouldn't have asked. He told me that I have too much time on my hands and need to do something for the war effort myself.'

Tommy was not impressed. 'What does he think you are doing here, for goodness' sake? Going to tea dances and galleries?'

She sighed. 'No, but – and you'll laugh at this – I thought he might have a point, so I went to the Women's Royal Navy Service recruiting office to see if they would take me.'

Tommy's eyebrows had shot up into his scalp. 'What on earth for?'

'To do my bit – and I like the uniform.' She laughed. 'Very shallow of me, I know, but I think I have been turned down anyway. In the box asking who my employer is, I wrote Her Majesty the Queen. That was a couple of weeks ago, and still no papers.'

Tommy threw back his head and laughed aloud. 'They will refuse you entry on grounds of insanity!'

'I know!'

Wiping his eyes, Tommy nodded to Crawfie's glass. 'But you will get married?'

'Yes. I want to be Mrs Buthlay very much but . . .'

'You want to stick with the job until it's finished.'

Marion nodded.

Tommy stood up. 'One more for the road?'

'Not for me. I told Alah I would be back in the nursery for tea. The Princesses are out tonight at a dinner dance at Eton College, so it's just the three of us.'

'They are growing up fast.' Tommy shook his head. 'Margaret is what – thirteen now?'

'Almost. And Lilibet eighteen.'

'Goodness. I saw her the other day in her ATS uniform, looking like a real duck.'

Marion smiled. 'Doesn't she? Every morning, Jackson brings the car round to chauffeur her to Camberley Barracks. Do you know, she is being taught how to strip a lorry's engine and put it back together again? Margaret is very jealous. She desperately wants to join up and have her own uniform. When she saw Lilibet in hers, she said it was the ugliest thing she had ever seen, out of spite.'

'Oh dear.'

'I told her off of course and she did apologize.'

'Well, I think it very dashing.' Tommy smiled. He twisted his glass, watching as the golden liquid moved within, small waves lapping the edges. 'You know that the Nazis are killing thousands of Jewish people, don't you?'

Crawfie had not expected the conversation to take such a turn. 'I know that they have imprisoned some. I read about it in the newspapers. But that was a while ago. Two years or so,' she said slowly.

'The newspapers were asked not to report on it after that. Bad for the morale of those at home already facing hardship and loss. What is actually happening in these camps is too much to bear for humankind. They are death camps. Jewish, Roma, Poles, Russians, Jehovah's Witnesses – anyone who Hitler declares are impure.'

Marion was chilled. 'What does that mean?'

'It means that Hitler wishes to create a pure Aryan race. Not tainted by the culture, religion or thought of anyone else. They are herded like animals onto railway trucks and taken to camps where they are held, starved, tortured, gassed or hanged – men, women and children. Clearing the way for the next delivery of poor souls.'

She stared at him. 'How do you know? How can this be kept out of the papers?'

'Because it is horrific. But it is true.' He rubbed his eyes. 'I am so damn tired of this war. Soviet soldiers liberated five hundred people yesterday from a camp called Majdanek in Poland. Reports tell us that the prisoners were like walking skeletons, and that there were literally hundreds more dead and heaped into piles.'

Crawfie was shaken. 'But we need to know about this.'

'Everyone will when the war is over. All those who did these things will be held to account. I was in a meeting with the Prime Minister and the King yesterday, and I can tell you, it is felt that the public would not be able to take in the immense horror. They really are anxious enough, waiting for their homes to be bombed, receiving a telegram to let them know their husband, father, brother has been killed. We can't tell them this.'

'But five hundred people saved is a good story. We have stopped the enemy.'

'No.' Tommy rubbed his temples. 'We haven't. Intelligence suggests that there are thousands of such camps across Germany. Hitler is hastening his Final Solution.'

'What?'

'His Final Solution – to murder all those who don't fit his criteria of a supreme human being. Premeditated mass murder. Genocide.'

'Dear God,' Crawfie murmured. 'Why have you told me this?'

'Because you have the strength of mind to bear it. And you will keep it to yourself. Forgive me, but I needed to tell someone.'

Now she reached over the desk and squeezed his hand. 'I won't tell a soul. You look all done in.' She stood up and placed her whisky glass on the tea tray. 'Go to bed, Tommy. You must sleep.'

'Thank you for allowing me to unburden myself for a moment. I shouldn't have.'

'That's what friends are for.' Marion walked to the door where she turned to look at him. His face gaunt and grey. 'Where would we be without men like you? Goodnight.'

Chapter Forty-Four

Crawfie watched as the two horses were led out of their stables, their hooves crunching on the frozen gravel, their foggy breath streaming from their nostrils. It was a cold start to the month. Today was Lilibet's day off from her ATS training, so she and Margaret were going riding in the park.

Both horses came to Crawfie and nuzzled her pockets. She always had something for them – this morning it was a carrot each.

The Princesses mounted gracefully. They were beautiful young women now. Lilibet just nineteen. Margaret almost fifteen.

'See you later, Crawfie,' they said and trotted off towards the park, followed by their detectives, also on horseback.

'Goodbye.' Crawfie waved. The days of the schoolroom were more or less done now; Margaret was quick and clever but easily bored, and wanted nothing more than to telephone her friends and organize small parties.

'I like her to enjoy herself,' the Queen had told Crawfie only recently. 'We don't need to bother with too much schoolroom now, surely?'

'As you wish, ma'am. The days are coming when you will need me no longer.'

'Goodness, no. Dear Crawfie, the girls need you more than ever but in different ways. A companion. A friend.'

Crawfie knew she should have asked then: when could she be spared to marry George? But the moment slipped through her fingers.

She was thirty-six. She would marry George as soon as the war was over. She had promised him that.

She tied her scarf a little tighter under her chin, in the same style as the Queen wore it, and, pulling on her gloves, she set off for a walk. The sun was throwing warmth onto the Long Walk, making the frost twinkle brightly. She shielded her eyes in time to watch the Princesses canter up to the Copper Horse, black silhouettes against the pale sky.

'Crawfie.'

She heard her name and turned. It was Tommy.

'Good morning.' She smiled. 'You've come for a spot of fresh air too?'

'Do you mind if I join you?'

'Not at all.'

Since Tommy had told Crawfie about the concentration camps – and she, good to her word, had not told a soul – she had become his trusted reticule of difficult secrets.

He looked around them now as they walked, trying to work out if any of the people around them were spies. The mother with the little boy chasing a puppy? The man on the bench with a newspaper? The old woman plying her basket of lucky heather? He waited until he and Crawfie were both well clear of anyone else, then said, 'I believe the war is coming to an end.'

Crawfie stopped dead and swivelled her face to him. 'What?' she exclaimed in delight, grinning.

'Shh.' His eyes darted around them once more. 'Keep walking and look bored, please.'

They set off again.

'Tell me then,' she whispered.

'The King has received a copy of an MI6 cipher sent to the Prime Minister. U-boats are being told to stop hostilities and return to base.'

'Really?'

He nodded. 'And in the last week the British and Allied troops have liberated the Bergen-Belsen concentration camp – sixty thousand emaciated prisoners, starving and suffering from typhus were found barely alive, and the dead numbered many, many more.'

'Dear God.'

'Herr Hitler is dead. Suicide. He knew the end was coming and shot himself.'

'Dead?' Crawfie's eyes sparked with hostility and abhorrence. 'Good!'

'The German armies are surrendering. On the western front eight hundred thousand of them are now captured.'

'So – we've won?'

'Looks like it. Stop smiling.'

Crawfie could feel the hope blooming within her. 'I can't help it.'

Windsor Castle, 2nd May 1945

Crawfie woke early. She dressed and left the castle quietly, heading to the nearest newsstand. Early commuters near Windsor station were collecting their morning newspapers. The air was raw with cold and the queue was stamping its feet and blowing on cold fingers.

'*The Times*, please.' She handed over the money to the vendor, an elderly woman well-wrapped for the morning cold, who passed her the paper.

''Ere you are, love. You need gloves. Minus nine it was, last night – does me arthritis no good.'

Crawfie nodded. Leaving the paper folded and under her arm, she walked quickly back to the castle.

In the nursery, no one was yet up. She lit the fire, made a cup of tea and unfolded the newspaper. The headlines were thrilling:

HITLER IS DEAD
PEACE BY WEEK'S END HINTED BY CHURCHILL

She wanted to wake Alah immediately and tell her the good news, but Alah had not been well recently and needed her sleep. So Crawfie hugged the news to herself, got down on her knees and gave a prayer of thanks.

It wasn't over yet, but it couldn't be too long now. If only she was with George right now . . .

Windsor Castle, 3rd May 1945

The weather was awful; sleet had turned to snow across the south of England, but the excitement in the Castle and across the country was building. Crawfie and Alah and the Princesses gathered around the nursery wireless for every radio broadcast, while poor Bobo was sent to fetch tea, make sandwiches and do the chores.

Each evening the King and Queen, who were in London, telephoned their daughters. Yesterday they had suggested that they should start packing to return to London at a moment's notice. They were to be ready when the call came.

Windsor Castle, 8th May 1945

Crawfie woke with a start. She had a strong feeling that today would be the day they all longed for, and she had a burning hunger to hear the news.

She had to get out and walk to use this inner energy. She needed to tire herself to settle her anxious nerves.

On the Long Walk, the horse chestnuts had forgotten the snow of two days ago. A warm wind was blowing through them, teasing their candles of pink and white flowers into bloom.

Crawfie's impatience was tangible and, walk as hard as she could, it only got stronger.

Finally, she turned and headed back to the castle kitchens. She would ask Ainslie to put a breakfast tray together for Alah and Bobo.

As soon as she entered she knew.

Shouting, clapping and laughter was coming from the servants' hall and, running towards it, she could hear Ainslie's voice. 'His Majesty has a message for us all.'

Crawfie was now in the doorway, and listened as Ainslie produced a letter and read:

Today we are at peace. The long years of war are ended. The Queen and I offer you our sincere thanks for all you have done to keep our ship afloat. Your care, hard work and loyalty mean so much to us and our family. These have been times of hardship, danger and sorrow. We shall remember those of our household who lost their lives on the field of battle, brave men and women who will shine in our memories. God bless you all.

Your servant,
George VI

Many of the female staff were wiping tears and Crawfie found herself being hugged and happily hugging in return.

Then Ainslie's voice cut through it all once again. '*God save the King!*' he roared, and his family of staff roared it right back at him.

That very afternoon, the Princesses' packed bags were loaded into a large van, and the Princesses themselves – Lilibet proudly wearing her ATS uniform – were chauffeured back to Buckingham Palace, the home they hadn't seen for almost six years.

Crawfie, Alah and Bobo stood in the silence of the old room in Windsor Castle – the nursery, as it was still called – with its books and jigsaw, Ludo and cards. The Princesses' rooms were cleared of clothes and ornaments.

'Feels a bit odd, doesn't it?' Bobo said.

'Unreal,' said Alah, slowly sitting down into her favourite chair.

Crawfie wrapped a blanket over Alah's legs. 'You must be tired.'

'Nonsense. Why would I be tired?'

'It's been a big day.' Crawfie smiled. 'Let me get you a cup of tea.'

'That would be nice.'

In the little kitchen, Bobo helped set the tea tray. 'You can get married now, Crawfie.'

'Oh yes.' Crawfie smiled. 'Yes, I think I can.'

'But you will still work here, won't you? Alah and I would miss you if you left. You will stay, won't you?'

Crawfie thought for a moment. 'I would like to, yes.'

Buckingham Palace, 9th August 1945

My darling Joan,

Three months since the end of war in Europe and at last the Americans have ended the war in Japan by dropping two H-bombs. Reports are ghastly. I hope to God we never use weapons like this ever again.

I fear this will also bring up, once more, the problem of Anglo-American relations.

The Duke of Windsor has reappeared after his stint as Governor of the Bahamas (or Bahammers as he now pronounces it, having adopted an American twang). He announced, quite seriously, that he would be the man to improve the USA and UK's friendship. Naturally, he is harping on again about getting his wife the dignity of an HRH. It is simply not going to happen.

In other, happier news, Princess Elizabeth has revealed a beau – Prince Philip of Greece. He has been seeing action, rather a lot of it I hear, with the Royal Navy, and by all accounts is a hero. His ship is due home any day.

This is the same young man who rowed out of Dartmouth to follow the royal yacht all those years ago. I know this because I had tea with Miss Crawford, who told me that letters have been exchanged frequently over the war years, and that Elizabeth had a photo of him with her constantly. I understand the King has decreed they should slow their courtship down. He feels Elizabeth is too young – she is only nineteen, after all – and Prince Philip is too much of an unknown quantity.

With the war behind us, the King is planning to take the whole family away to South Africa for an extensive, lengthy and important tour of the Commonwealth. We are in the planning stages now and they are expected to be away for several months. I shall have to accompany them, but I hope that will be my last big tour. I am too old to be away from you for such long periods of time.

You have been so patient and understanding. Our next holiday will be to any destination you wish. Get my old atlas out and start planning.

My love,
Tommy

PART FIVE

Two years later

Chapter Forty-Five

Buckingham Palace, 9th July 1947

Crawfie was in her own sitting room, reading a letter from George that had arrived that morning. It had upset her because he was lonely. And when he was lonely, he tended to write peevishly.

Dear Marion,

I write this, sitting alone in my home, thinking of you. I am glad you are happy in London with all it can offer – so much more than Dunfermline ever could.

The war has taken its toll on me – my work in Italy, supplying the many who had so little with everyday items like food and medicine, while all the time going out of my mind with worry over your safety.

The bank has offered me redundancy. So many young men, now demobbed, need to have work, and so an old war horse like me is the first to be put out to pasture. My small war pension will be a struggle to live on until we are married. I shall look for work as soon as possible.

My dear, our wedding plans were dashed so long ago – not your fault, of course, but, if you still want me, I am waiting. I have waited faithfully for nigh on eleven years, thinking of you working tirelessly behind the scenes, caring for the Princesses and their parents. I sometimes think the royal family mean more to you than I do, but my chest fills with pride that I have known you at all.

In your last letter, you invited me to London as soon as possible. Do you mean that? Or are you just being kind to a silly old man? I will come, if you want me. Could you help me with the fare? I hate to ask but I am a little short of money right now.

If I come to London, we must discuss our future. I proposed so long ago to you. Do you still want me?

My fondest love,

George

Marion sighed. No matter how much she reassured him, she knew he couldn't shake himself out of a mood until he was ready.

She went to her small desk and took out notepaper and pen, working out how she would apologize and tell him how much he meant to her. She knew they had been waiting a long time to marry. Had it really been ten years since they first became engaged? The war had felt like such an unreal time that it seemed impossible it had been so long. They loved each other – they both knew that – but circumstances were so against them.

There was a knock at the door.

'Come in.'

'Crawfie, do you have a moment?' Lilibet closed the door behind her and grinned. She was twenty-one now, the picture of a proper young woman. 'I have something to tell you.'

Crawfie gave her full attention. 'Come on then.'

'It's a secret.'

Crawfie grinned. 'Out with it.'

Lilibet held out her left hand, wiggling the fourth finger. 'Philip and I are engaged to be married.'

'Oh my goodness!' Crawfie stood up and hugged her. 'How wonderful. Congratulations!'

'Thank you. The public announcement is tomorrow.'

'Tomorrow! Let me see that ring.'

'Philip designed it. The stones are a gift from his mother, Princess Alice.'

'It's beautiful.' Crawfie squeezed Lilibet's hand with love. 'I'm so happy for you.'

Lilibet took a seat. 'Now that I'm twenty-one, Papa has finally given his consent.'

'Of course he has. You and Philip will be very happy together.' Crawfie smiled. She looked thoughtfully at Lilibet. The Princess had been just a little girl when Marion and George first met, but she was so grown up these days. Now that she was getting married, now that Margaret was nearing seventeen, perhaps it was finally time for Crawfie to make a change within her own life. 'Actually, I have a secret too,' she said.

Lilibet looked at her curiously. 'Well, do tell me.'

'I am engaged to be married too!'

Lilibet clapped her hands. 'How exciting! But you are not wearing a ring?'

'No.'

'I didn't know you had a beau? Who is he?'

'Major George Buthlay.'

'A soldier! Tell me about him.'

'He is a little older than me and he is a bank manager with Drummonds Bank.'

'A catch! When is the big day?'

'Well . . .' Marion hesitated. 'It has been a long engagement, but I think perhaps the wedding will be soon. I must ask the Queen first.'

'Oh, Mummy will be as pleased for you, I know, as I am! We will all want to come to the wedding. After all, you are our Crawfie.'

The two women chatted for several minutes, both delighted for each other, until they heard a scream from the nursery.

They exchanged worried looks and, in unison, jumped to their feet and ran towards the noise.

Bobo was standing by Alah's chair, shaking and crying pitifully.
'What on earth has happened, Bobo?' asked Crawfie.

Bobo pointed to Alah's chair. 'I can't wake her up,' she sobbed.

Crawfie's heart began pumping hard. 'Alah!' She shook her friend's arm. 'Alah, it's me, Crawfie. Can you hear me?'

Alah's arm flopped over the chair arm. 'Alah!' Crawfie's voice was rising. 'Bobo, call the doctor.'

Bobo was rooted to the spot.

'Bobo! Get the doctor!'

When she had gone, Crawfie and Lilibet knelt before Alah. Crawfie took her pulse as she had been taught in a wartime first aid course.

'Is she alive?' Lilibet asked, her voice a little shaky.

'Just. Very slow heartbeat. Let's get her on the floor and into the recovery position.'

They got her onto the floor and placed a small cushion under her head. 'Get a blanket, please, Lilibet.'

The two of them sat by the dear servant, talking to her and stroking her forehead. 'The doctor is on his way,' Lilibet told her. 'Don't worry. Help is coming and we'll get you as right as rain.'

Marion sat on her heels. 'She's had a chesty cough for a while now,' she said to Lilibet, in a low voice. 'She refused to see the doctor. Where is he?'

When he came, Dr Mackay felt for Alah's pulse, took her temperature and listened to her lungs. 'Pneumonia. We need to get her to hospital.'

'I will go with her,' Lilibet said.

'No, no, I will go,' Crawfie insisted. She felt almost sick with worry.

Dr Mackay agreed. 'Your Royal Highness, you must stay here. Please let Her Majesty know.'

'I will, of course.'

'Thank you, ma'am.'

*

Sitting in the ambulance and stroking Alah's hand, Crawfie spoke to her old friend as calmly as she could manage. 'Now, Alah, dear, I knew there was something wrong – didn't I say you should see the doctor? Thank goodness Dr Mackay was at the Palace today. Imagine, the King's own physician tending to you! You are so precious to us all. When you get better, I am going to make sure you have every afternoon off to rest. I shall personally tie you to your bed if you don't behave. And anyway, I want you at my wedding. You have to be there. Why didn't you admit to feeling so rough? Hang on tight. We are nearly at the hospital.'

Dr Mackay and the medical team swept Alah off into a treatment room while Crawfie sat in the long corridor outside. After a while, she needed the lavatory and a passing nurse directed her. 'The teashop is just near it if you need some refreshment.'

It was while Crawfie was buttering a toasted teacake that Dr Mackay found her. 'I am so sorry,' he said.

Crawfie dropped her knife. 'No? You don't mean—? No! She can't be gone?'

'We did all we could, but the pneumonia was too far advanced.'

Crawfie stared at him in horror. She almost fell back into her chair, barely able to stand, as she felt tears well in her eyes.

The nursery, when she returned to the Palace, was peaceful and quiet. Bobo was waiting for her and when Crawfie had delivered the terrible news, they clung to each other, their tears flowing freely.

Later, Crawfie washed Bobo's face and hands and put her to bed. 'You must get some sleep, Bobo. Grief is tiring. See you in the morning.'

Bobo closed her eyes obediently. It didn't take her long to fall asleep, and when she had, Crawfie tiptoed out of the room and closed the door silently.

Back in the nursery, she plumped up the cushions on Alah's chair and opened the big window to let her spirit free.

Outside, London rumbled past. From Green Park the scent of plane trees, mown grass and the song of a blackbird assaulted Crawfie's senses, as she sent a prayer to Alah, giving thanks for all the times they had shared, the laughs, tears and tiffs. She would miss her so dearly.

On her way to her bedroom, she hesitated outside the closed door of Alah's room but couldn't bear to go in. That would be for tomorrow. Now she had to write a reply to George.

My dearest George,

Thank you for your letter. Please never doubt my love for you. I hate it when we have misunderstandings. You have waited so patiently for me, I know, but I really am determined that we will be married soon. I just hope I am worth the wait.

I want so much to build a little home together. We may not be rich, but we will be happy.

I have made up my mind to talk to Queen Mary before I speak to the Queen. I hope she might discuss it with the Queen so that it won't be such a shock when I announce our plans. I know that sounds rather feeble of me, but I hate to upset them. In many ways, yes, they are my family and leaving them will be difficult. I shall explain that I won't be leaving them entirely after we are married – not just yet. I have to see it out until the end. I know you will understand. I will let you know the moment I have the royal assent.

With all my love, darling,
Marion xx

P.S. Dear Alah died today. I haven't the wherewithal to write more about that at the moment. I am too tired and too sad.

Chapter Forty-Six

Buckingham Palace, 11ᵗʰ July 1947

'Come in.' Tommy was sitting at his desk.

P-T, his loyal secretary, popped her head round his door. 'Miss Crawford to see you, sir.'

'Excellent. Show her in, and perhaps we could have some tea?'

P-T nodded, before leaving the room. A moment later Crawfie entered, looking a little anxious.

'Come along in and sit down.' Tommy offered her a seat.

'Thank you for seeing me.'

'Always a pleasure. How can I help you?'

Crawfie took a deep breath and let her words spill out. 'George and I want to finally get married.'

Tommy peered at her. 'I see.'

'I told Queen Mary this morning because she has always been such a support over the last fifteen years and I felt I could discuss it with her. But when I told her, she said that I couldn't leave the family now because they wouldn't manage without me. I'm sorry.' Crawfie pulled a handkerchief from her pocket and wiped her eyes. 'As you know, George and I have waited so long, I had rather hoped that this time . . .' She wiped her eyes again.

Tommy sat back in his chair. 'And you thought, by telling Queen Mary first, she might pave the way to the Queen's consent?'

'I suppose I did.'

P-T came in with two cups of tea. P-T glanced quietly at Crawfie's tearstained face, but Tommy gave a warning look she recognized as an order to say nothing and leave quietly.

When they were alone, Tommy poured the tea. 'Now you drink this, and tell me all about your fiancé.'

Through a few more tears and a little nose blowing, Crawfie told him. 'A major, eh? Jolly good. Gordon Highlanders, too. And he saw action, you said?'

'He fought in the Great War – he is a little older than me, you know – and was made Major then. As you know, he worked with a relief agency, organizing essential supplies to those made homeless or sick. Unfortunately he was invalided out with malaria.'

'Malaria? Remind me, where was he stationed?'

'Italy.'

He picked up his pen and jotted down these details, then asked, 'And how do you think I could help you?'

'I would like to make an appointment to see the Queen on an urgent, important and most personal matter.'

Buckingham Palace, 12th July 1947

The Queen listened as Crawfie put her case.

'So you see, ma'am, we have waited all these years to be married because I never wanted to leave you or the Princesses. It has been my duty and my honour to serve Your Majesties, and to have left would be very unfair on the Princesses when they most needed me.'

The Queen put her head to one side, in thought. 'I suppose you would be thinking of leaving us when you marry? You must see that this would be most inconvenient. A change at this late stage for Margaret would be undesirable.'

'I assure you I do not wish to upset your plans. For the time being, I would be happy to live and work at the Palace, even after my marriage. But my presence here will soon no longer be required. Princess Elizabeth will be married and Princess Margaret is almost seventeen.'

'Hmm.'

'I have a likeness of George, Major Buthlay, to show you, if you would care to see?'

Crawfie handed over the small photograph that she had treasured ever since he had given it to her. It was an old one of him in uniform, looking young and very smart.

There was a long silence as the Queen surveyed it. 'Why, Crawfie, that was a great sacrifice you made. I shall talk with the King.'

Buckingham Palace, 13th July 1947

Tommy had become very fond of Miss Crawford. Over the years she had shown herself to be utterly loyal, discreet and courageous. But he had never much liked the sound of this George Buthlay, and if it looked as though Miss Crawford was now really going to marry him, he had to made some enquiries.

And he found some disturbing news. With friends in high places, it had been easy for Tommy to get someone in the War Office to pull out Buthlay's records. They were now sitting on his desk in front of him and told a sorry story.

George had indeed fought in France during the First World War but had come out as a captain, not major. In the last war he was not declined for poor eyesight; he had not attempted to enlist in the first place. It was true he had worked for a relief agency, but he had not been invalided out with malaria – he had been cashiered because an inordinate quantity of essential supplies that he was in charge of (including food, medicine and fuel) had gone missing, presumed stolen and sold on the black market.

In short, the man was a liar and a cheat.

How on earth was he to tell Miss Crawford?

Chapter Forty-Seven

Buckingham Palace, 24ᵗʰ July 1947

Princess Elizabeth and Princess Margaret insisted on meeting George.

'He can come here,' Margaret decreed. Nearly seventeen now, she was always determined to get her own way.

'To Buckingham Palace?' Crawfie hadn't thought of where they were to meet. Imagining George actually in her place of work made her feel uneasy.

'Yes. He will be my and Lilibet's guest,' Margaret said airily. 'Any guest of ours is always welcome.'

Ten days later, George was on his way down from Aberdeen. Crawfie met him at the station.

Several heads turned as the tall young woman with a large nose embraced the much older, shorter, moustached gentlemen.

A couple of busybodies passed them and muttered, 'Every pot has a lid, I suppose.'

Crawfie heard none of it. She was too excited. At last she was able to show off her wonderful fiancé to the people she cared most about. If only Alah was still alive. She would have adored him, surely.

Arriving by taxi at Buckingham Palace, Marion swept George inside. Tommy was just on his way out and they ran into each other.

'Good afternoon, Miss Crawford,' he said, eyeing the small, dapper man next to her.

'This is my fiancé, Major George Buthlay,' Marion told him with pride.

'Ah. Major Buthlay.' Tommy held out his hand. 'Good to meet you.' So, this was the little pipsqueak who had wormed his way into Miss Crawford's life.

'Sir.' George was beaming. The cat who'd got the cream. Tommy made a note to have a word with him before he left.

George's eyes goggled and gleamed as Marion took him up impressive staircases and treasure-lined corridors.

'Might I bump into the King?' he asked. 'Or the Queen?'

'Shh. Keep your voice down,' Marion told him. 'And no, because they are not here today.'

'Shame. I think the King and I have a lot in common. Both servicemen. Where do they bank? Drummonds would be happy to look after them.'

Marion said nothing, but stopped outside the cream and gold door. 'Here we are.' She smoothed her dress and checked George's regimental tie before knocking twice. The door flew open.

'You are here at last.' Lilibet and Margaret stood before them, two beautiful young women in pretty summer dresses.

George almost saluted them.

'Major Buthlay, welcome,' said Princess Elizabeth. 'Do come in.'

'We have ordered tea,' said Princess Margaret.

For a moment Marion felt reality tilt. Her two worlds colliding almost made her dizzy. She had kept them separate for so long.

George was looking around the room, and Marion tried to imagine it through his eyes. It was certainly not ostentatious: two old-fashioned armchairs with a matching sofa, a desk from the time of Queen Victoria and a polished table covered in photographs of dogs and relatives. A large vase of summer flowers stood in the fireplace, and an ormolu clock struck the half hour on the mantelpiece.

'Isn't this a beautiful room, George?' Marion asked, with obvious pride.

'The Queen's sense of style,' Princess Elizabeth said with self-deprecation. 'She is very clever at these things. I wouldn't have a clue.'

'Look out of the window, Major Buthlay,' said Princess Margaret. 'You can see all the way down to the lake.'

He walked over and looked, but said nothing.

'Isn't it lovely?' Marion went to stand next to him, anxiously wanting him to show some appreciation of his surroundings.

'Aye. It's very nice. But not a patch on the Highlands.'

'George!' Marion said, with a small glare that only he could see.

Margaret laughed. 'I quite agree. Balmoral is spectacular and we love being there – but don't you think London is more exciting?'

Before he could answer, a footman and a maid came in with the tea tray.

'Oh, strawberries,' Princess Elizabeth said with delight. 'You must try those, Major Buthlay. We grow them here. All down to Crawfie. She had us planting a little fruit and veg patch years ago. Now, do come and sit down.'

Cups of tea were poured and delicate scones, still warm from the oven, were handed around with clotted cream and the fresh strawberries.

When they were settled, Princess Margaret asked teasingly, 'I hope you are going to keep Crawfie in order when you are married. She has been bullying us for the last sixteen years.'

'Oh, don't worry.' He laughed. 'I will.'

Marion smiled. 'We have had a long engagement,' she said. 'George has been most patient.'

'Some things are worth waiting for.' His smile was charming and the Princesses, Marion could tell, had taken to him.

For almost an hour the four of them chatted about things they enjoyed and pets they loved. Marion was pleased to see that George was at his most charming, full of little jokes and shows of interest.

'You three,' he said. 'You are so alike. Almost like sisters, all of you. You talk and laugh alike, and look at your mannerisms, the way you use your hands. It is uncanny.'

Marion blushed. 'George!'

'Crawfie is almost family,' agreed Princess Elizabeth. 'She has been a wonderful governess and friend since we were so little. When Crawfie first came here, she wasn't very much older than I am now.'

'Although we thought you were very grown up when we first knew you,' added Princess Margaret. 'Isn't that extraordinary!'

'You were tiny wee girls when I first arrived,' Marion said. 'And now look at you: two fine young women – and one of you almost married.'

Princess Elizabeth turned to George. 'Are you free in November, Major Buthlay? Our wedding is on the 20th, at Westminster Abbey.'

George beamed. 'I would be honoured to come.'

'Excellent. And have you and Crawfie fixed a date yet?'

George took Marion's hand in his. 'I haven't discussed this with you yet' – Marion's eyes widened – 'but I have spoken to the minister at Dunfermline Abbey, and the 16th September is available. It's a Tuesday.'

Marion gasped, her eyes gleaming. 'Have you really?'

'I wouldn't joke about something so important. Would midday be all right?'

'Yes. Yes, please.' Marion gripped his hand. 'Oh George, you are so good.'

He gave a modest shrug. 'I have wanted to tell you for the last week, and now to be able to tell you in front of your friends seems the right moment.'

Princess Margaret jumped up to call for a footman. 'We need champagne!' she declared.

Chapter Forty-Eight

Buckingham Palace, August 1947

'It is very kind of you to share your car with me, sir.' Crawfie relaxed into her seat and put her gloves on her lap.

'My pleasure,' Tommy said. 'Thank you, Jackson.'

The chauffeur shut the door on his two passengers and stepped smartly into the driving seat. The engine purred and the large heavy car moved through the Palace courtyard and out towards the gates. They were on their way to Windsor.

'It is such a treat not to have to carry my bags.' Marion waved at the policeman on duty before they turned right up Constitution Hill, heading for Park Lane and the west.

Tommy hoped that he looked outwardly calm, because inside he was in knots. He had engineered this journey for them both in order to tell Miss Crawford the unpalatable truth about her fiancé.

He slipped a finger between his collar and neck and eased the restriction in his throat. He had already asked Jackson to make sure the glass partition between the front and back of the car was in place, in order that the difficult conversation would not be overheard.

He coughed, fiddled with his pocket watch, straightened his trouser creases and dived in.

'My dear . . .'

'Yes?'

'I wonder if I might speak about a matter of some delicacy?'

Marion was worried immediately. 'Oh, have I done something wrong?'

'No, no. But it is about something that might be wrong.'

Marion frowned. 'Go on.'

'It's Mr Buthlay.'

She smiled. '*Major* Buthlay, you mean.'

'Ah, yes. Perhaps we could start with that.'

The following five minutes were most uncomfortable. Crawfie was in turns disbelieving, defensive and angry. When Tommy finished his demolishment of George's character – which included a suspected fondness for alcohol and women – Marion erupted.

'How dare you say such things about Major Buthlay? Have you ever actually spoken to him? Got to know him? Because I have. I have known him for many years. He is the man I love! Why are you making up such lies? I can't understand it.' She stopped for a moment, realization dawning. 'Oh, I see what you are up to. The Queen has spoken to you, I suppose – told you to say anything at all to stop me from marrying, from leaving? We can't possibly have the royal family inconvenienced by such a small thing as a good servant getting married! Is that what this is about?'

Tommy was appalled. 'Absolutely not! Everything I have said is entirely true. You know that the family have given you their blessing to marry.'

'I know how you do their dirty work for them.' Marion's voice cracked. 'Smoothing the way, ironing the awkward problems, always loyal. But the truth is, you are just like the rest of us. Just another servant. You might eat at smart gentlemen's clubs, enjoy the opera and keep your family in the country, but beneath it all, Tommy, you are just another hired hand. And for all your pomposity, you have not a shred of respect for the royal family. They are just pawns that you shunt around the board of diplomacy. They do not love you as they love me. And I love them! You are envious that I am part of the family while you are not.'

Tommy sighed. 'You may not believe this, Miss Crawford, but I care for you and I worry about your future happiness. I am trying to help you.'

'By trying to blacken my fiancé's name? By making me miserable?'

Tommy had made a hash of this. And he knew it. 'I am sorry to have caused such distress. I have explained my very real concerns, and it is up to you whether you wish to believe, or act on them. I cannot let you walk into a marriage without knowing the real facts.'

Marion was completely thrown. Her breathing was rapid and she was hot. Unwinding the car window, she drank in the cool air, her mind whirling.

How dare Sir Tommy Lascelles say that Major George Buthlay was a liar.

A fraud.

She turned back to Tommy. 'I shall be telling George exactly what you have said about him. He will be appalled that you should say such things to me. You'll be lucky if he doesn't have you for slander. He is a better man than you could ever be.'

Tommy looked her straight in the eye. 'I understand that you are upset and I applaud your defence. Loyalty like yours should be rewarded but, Miss Crawford, in this instance, I fear you will find only disappointment. I tell you this with the best and kindest of intentions.'

'*Pah*.' Crawfie's fury was white hot. Her voice low and not without threat. 'You will assure me that you will never peddle these false accusations to anyone. If you do, I shall make sure that the King and your colleagues and your family know that you are the liar.'

She turned away to the open window again. Her hands in knots on her lap. Her face pinched.

'As you wish,' he answered tersely.

Chapter Forty-Nine

Dunfermline, September 1947

A week after Tommy's sickening attempt to put Marion off marrying George, she had returned home for the happiest of reasons. She had told no one about the conversation. The only possible rationale for Tommy's behaviour was that he was jealous of her close ties to the family. She was needed by them, while he was just a cipher in a suit, there to do their bidding, to quell any storms brewing that might breach the royal walls. He was sick.

Here, sitting in the kitchen of her family home, she could put all her worries to one side. She would soon be Mrs George Buthlay and would be blissfully and supremely happy. The best revenge was a dish best served cold. Sir Tommy Lascelles would have to eat his words.

'You really had champagne with the Princesses? George told me all about it.' Maggie was frantic with joy.

Marion smiled. 'Yes. It was so special, and they loved George straight away.'

'Who wouldn't! You have done so well. Your first boyfriend, and he's been so patiently waiting all this time. You're lucky he did wait. I thought you'd never find anyone!'

Marion winced and tried to ignore her mother. She always managed to hurt her, somehow or other. Did she do it on purpose or was it simply thoughtlessness? She got up. 'Shall I make a start on the tea?'

'Yes, please, dear. I am awful tired. It's the hours your wedding dress has taken me. Your dad says I do too much.'

In the kitchen, Marion turned on the small radio on the windowsill and tried to quell her irritation. George and her father would be home soon. She hoped they had had a good day on the golf course.

She had decided against telling George about the horrible conversation with Tommy. It would be too upsetting and would spoil the happiness of the approaching wedding day. She didn't want anything to ruin this perfect time. Besides, George hadn't liked Tommy much when they had met briefly at Buckingham Palace. George was a very good judge of character.

Marion washed the potatoes and began peeling them, before putting the mince in the frying pan for the shepherd's pie.

She closed her eyes and imagined herself this time next week, cooking for George as Mrs Buthlay. The wedding was going to be small but perfect – only extended family, old friends and neighbours.

She would never again be referred to as 'Maggie's spinster daughter'.

Now her mother had a different refrain: 'You have left it very late to make me a grandmother.'

Marion wanted to slap her. But she didn't. With a smile she answered, 'Mother, I am only thirty-eight and there is nothing you can say to suffocate my happiness.'

'I am only just saying it for your own good. I don't want you to be disappointed when it doesn't happen.'

'*Mother!* For goodness' sake – I am a grown women who has lived in London these past fifteen years. I have lived through the war and kept the Princesses safe from the bombings that tore London apart.'

'You are not the only person to have seen the bombs, you know. We had two nights of it. Your father and I saw the bombers coming in – we heard them drop fifty miles away on Clydebank.

The sky was scarlet. Don't think we don't know about the horrors of war.'

'Mother, that's not what I am saying – you know that.'

Maggie went into one of her sulks, bottom lip sticking out.

Marion ignored it. She shut her eyes. Soon she'd be snug in her own little home.

She got up. 'Shall I make you a tea?'

The King and Queen had offered her a grace-and-favour house, a red-brick cottage in the grounds of Kensington Palace called Nottingham Cottage. She had been to look at it on her own and reported back to George. It was such a dear little place – and designed by Sir Christopher Wren! It needed some attention, but it had a small garden, with a little white fence and roses round the door. Inside there was a tiny but dear little kitchen, a dining room and sitting room and two bedrooms. Marion had agreed to sleep Monday to Thursday nights at the Palace until Lilibet was married, and to spend her weekends with George. His bank had finally agreed to transfer him to the London branch.

She couldn't wait to have her own front door.

She could have a cat if she wanted. Or a little dog. Pets are good for young children.

A baby of her own.

She longed for a baby.

Or two.

A boy first, followed by a baby girl.

Her thoughts were interrupted by the arrival of the men, back from their day of golf. George came straight to the kitchen to kiss her. 'Mmm. Something smells good.'

'Shepherd's pie.' Marion smiled.

'I mean you. You smell good.'

Marion's heart melted. 'Don't be so silly.'

'I can't wait to be married.' He slipped his hand from her hip to her bottom.

'George, don't. Mother and Dad might come in.'

'I can't wait for our wedding night,' he murmured, squeezing her buttock a little harder.

She wriggled away from him, and began mashing the boiled potatoes for the shepherd's pie topping. Marion was completely unversed in the physical side of love and had never had a close enough female friend to share the essential information. The only thing her mother had ever told her was, 'Men can get over-excited. You have to be careful.' Well George had been very excited on several occasions but she had never seen him naked and she had always, very definitely, kept all her clothes on. Her only preparation for her wedding night was to buy a pretty cotton nightdress with small buttons down the back which the saleslady had told her would be 'tantalizing'. Marion's word for it was 'terrifying'.

She looked at George, smiling at her across the kitchen and found the fear ebbing away.

Yes, her wedding day was going to be very exciting.

The only upset was that the royal family would not be attending. Engagements at Balmoral prevented them but the Queen had penned a lovely note and so had the Princesses.

Crawfie had popped the letters into a large biscuit tin, a souvenir for the upcoming royal wedding that she couldn't resist. As soon as it was empty, she had begun filling it with all the small notes and childhood paintings that she hadn't wanted to part with over the years – mementos from her life with the Princesses.

Chapter Fifty

Buckingham Palace, 19ᵗʰ September 1947

'Good morning, sir.' P-T, juggling an overflowing letter tray and a cup of tea, welcomed her boss as he arrived for work. 'Good weekend?'

'Very good, thank you.' He hung his jacket on the hat stand. 'Those for me?'

'Yes, sir, plus a letter from Crawfie to all the girls in the office. I thought you might like to read it.'

He took his cup from her and sat at his desk. 'Why would I wish to read a letter that wasn't mine to read?'

P-T put the letter tray down and stared at him. 'She's got married.'

Tommy ignored P-T and the letter, and riffled through the post beneath.

P-T stood her ground. 'You aren't happy for her?'

'Women get married every day. Do you expect me to do a cartwheel?'

P-T took the chair opposite his desk and sat down. 'What happened?'

'What on earth can you mean?' He sipped his tea. 'Stone cold.'

'I have only just made it.'

'Well, make me another.'

'Someone got out of the wrong side of the bed this morning, sir.' P-T remained where she was. 'I thought you and Miss Crawford were friends.'

Tommy sighed in exasperation. 'She's a colleague. That's all.'

'No, she is more than that. You have been good friends.'

He lifted his eyebrows and stared. 'What are you insinuating?'

'Nothing like that, sir, obviously not – but you have helped to guide her through and around royal tripwires, and she sees you as her . . . mentor, I suppose.'

He pushed his cup away. 'Poppycock.'

P-T reached for the cup and said, 'The master has fallen out with his pupil and it will do neither of you any good.'

'I could have you sacked for insubordination.'

P-T smiled. 'You can't sack your own goddaughter. Daddy would never speak to you again.'

Tommy watched her go. She really was getting a little chippy. Perhaps P-T needed to get married herself; a husband would sort the chippiness out of her.

Tommy drummed his fingers on his desk and slid Crawfie's letter from the top of his mail pile to the bottom. For the next two hours he worked his way through the rest, taking telephone calls or dictating notes to and from a decidedly cool P-T.

Finally, his desk was cleared and Crawfie's letter sitting starkly in front of him. There was nothing to do but read it.

Dear all,

George and I are finally married. It was a wonderful day. Even the Dunfermline sun shone on us. The minister's ceremony was beautiful and, you may think this nonsense, but I felt my heart fly to the roof of the Abbey. Silly, really. George was very handsome in his full highland dress and my parents looked so happy. I think they thought I would never marry, but they adore George as much as I do. George's oldest friend, Christopher, was best man and he made a most amusing speech.

We are now on our honeymoon! George booked a week in a little guest house near Loch Lomond. A whole week of getting used to being Mr and Mrs Buthlay.

> *By the time you read this, I hope George and I shall be back in London. We have the long weekend, a glorious few days to settle ourselves into Nottingham Cottage before my lessons with Margaret resume. I am so looking forward to George and me building our home together. Mother has given me some beautiful linen that she got when she first married, and George has bought me a sewing machine to make curtains! I have never made curtains before, but I am determined to try my best!*
>
> *I do hope you will all come and visit us.*
>
> *See you very soon,*
>
> *Mrs George Buthlay* AKA *Crawfie x*

Tommy folded the letter and pushed it back into its envelope. Mrs George Buthlay, eh? Good luck to her. Typical woman – impulsive, and strong-willed. Wouldn't listen, and now she's got herself married to a spiv. She'd regret it, that was for sure. If she were Tommy's daughter, he would have thrown Buthlay out by his lying ears.

Still, she had her job to rely on. The royal family might be built on self-preservation and duty, but they knew a good servant when they had one. Even now she was married she was to continue to teach Margaret and, if she played her cards right, she could continue her role to the next generation of royal children, exactly as Alah had.

Alah would have had something to say about all this. Funny how one could only see how important a person was when they died. Alah was the smooth hand on the tiller throughout the Queen's childhood and then the Queen's children's childhood. That was the proper way of things. Miss Crawford might still have a chance to emulate her.

Comforted by the thought, Tommy left his desk and went for an early lunch at his club. A pleasant hour of sensible, like-minded male company was exactly what he needed.

Nottingham Cottage, 19ᵗʰ September 1947

Marion carried her case into her new sitting room. 'Oh, George! Do come and look. The sun coming in through the window is so beautiful.'

George entered, carrying a large box which he put down on a carpet that had seen better days. 'This room is a bit on the small side,' he said slowly.

'It's big enough for us. We are lucky to have it, and furnished too.'

George looked at the ancient chintz sofa and armchair. 'If you can call it furniture.'

'In time we shall afford our own.' Nothing was going to burst Marion's happiness today. Putting her case down, she went to the window which faced the cottage garden. 'Our own little paradise. I am going to fill those flower beds with snapdragons and scented carnations.' She turned to her new husband. 'George, I am so happy.'

He smiled at her, a beam of love that made her heart glow. 'I'm glad.' He hooked his hand into hers and pulled her to him. 'I only want you to be happy.'

'And I want to make you happy.'

'What's it like upstairs?' He grinned a wolfish grin and pinched her bottom.

Marion flushed, more with apprehension than passion. She was finding the physical side of marriage rather awkward and uncomfortable. George was keen to teach her the ways in which both of them could enjoy it but he was definitely finding it more pleasant than she was. She pulled herself away from him gently.

'I will have to find the sheets first.'

He pulled her back to him. 'We don't need sheets. It's a warm day and I want to make love to my wife. That's OK, isn't it?'

'Well yes, of course, my love. But – and I know this sounds silly – I want everything to be perfect first. I want to unpack. Where are the other boxes?'

They had brought three large boxes down from Dunfermline on the train. Maggie and the neighbours had turned out their cupboards to gift the newlyweds their unwanted blankets, sheets and table linen, a toast rack, four egg cups, a pink tea set with a saucer missing, several ancient saucepans, a mismatched selection of bone-handled cutlery, two sharp knives and a fish slice. Marion hadn't wanted any of it, but her mother had told her, 'Beggars can't be choosers, Marion. When your father and I married we had nothing. These things may be old but there's years of life left in them yet.'

The boxes were now resting on the kitchen table.

George, annoyed, said, 'I'm hungry. What have we got?'

Marion laughed. 'Nothing. Why don't you go and do some shopping for me while I make things a bit more homely?' She went to her handbag and took out her ration book, giving it to George. 'See if you can get some butter and sugar and maybe some bacon? Eggs? Oh, and some bread, milk and tea.'

'I don't know my way around like you do. Come with me.'

'Oh, George. Kensington High Street is only at the end of the drive. It's full of shops.' She pressed two one-pound notes into his hand. 'It won't take you long. By the time you get back, I'll have everything straight.'

He took the money and the ration book, kissed his wife and made for the front door.

'Don't be too long,' she said.

'I won't.'

Marion was in her element. With sleeves rolled up and one of her mother's old pinafores tied around her waist, she started organizing the kitchen, then the drawing room and small dining room, then bustled upstairs to make up the waiting brass bed. The bed may have been second- or maybe third-hand, but the mattress was brand new and rather stiff. Plundering the gifts from Dunfermline, she added sheets and blankets, pillows and pillowcases until the whole thing was most inviting. She couldn't resist lying down on top of the quilt and stretching out.

The day had been long, saying goodbye to Mother and Dad, starting out on the earliest train and now throwing herself into all these jobs. She was tired. Turning on her side, she gazed out at the view from her window. She could see a corner of Kensington Palace, the tall trees of the park beyond and the comforting drone of traffic on the High Street.

She noticed that the curtains at her window, while not of her choice, were of good quality. They would do until she had time to get out her new sewing machine and run something better up.

If only Alah was still alive. She would have shown her how to do that.

The bed really was rather comfortable. George would be back soon, hopefully with a quarter pound of tea and some milk. She could do with a cup of tea.

Marion closed her eyes and thought of all the changes she might make to her new home. Soon she drifted off to sleep.

George had had a wonderful few hours, exploring the pubs of Kensington. He'd met some jolly good fellows too. After several rounds of whisky and, at some point, a decent plate of ham, eggs and chips, he was ready to go home to his wife and claim his conjugal rights. He couldn't deny he was fond of Marion. She was a good woman, would do anything for him – and he now had a swanky address, even though the cottage was rather shabby. His future looked comfortable, very comfortable indeed.

Approaching the gates of Kensington Palace, he was stopped by the on-duty policeman. 'Excuse me, sir, are you expected?'

'Expected? I damn well live here!'

The policeman caught the aroma of whisky. 'May I have your name, sir?'

George drew himself up and pushed out his chest. 'I am Major George Buthlay.'

The policeman checked his list of names that were permitted through the gates. 'And who are you visiting, sir?'

'My wife. *Mrs* George Buthlay.'

'I am sorry, sir, but I cannot find you on my list.'

'Oh for . . .' George mumbled some swear words. 'We moved in today. Nottingham Cottage.'

The policeman checked his list once more and nodded. 'Ah yes. Miss Marion Crawford. I met her when she first came to look over Nott Cott, as we call it. A very nice lady. She told me she was marrying.'

'Yes. *Me*.' George tapped his chest.

'Congratulations, Major Buthlay, and may you be very happy here.'

George grunted and walked up the long drive towards his new home.

Marion was roused by the sound of gravel being thrown at her window.

'George?' She tidied her sleep-flattened hair and shouted from the window, 'Is that you?'

'Who do you think it is? Mahatma Gandhi?' He sounded cross.

'I'm coming.' She was anxious. How long had she been asleep? She hoped George hadn't been waiting too long.

'Sorry, George. I must have dropped off. Come in.' She noticed he had no shopping with him. 'Oh dear, were the shops shut?' She closed the door on the setting sun and took his coat. 'What time is it? You must be hungry.'

George yawned. 'I had a bite to eat in a pub.' He leant in to kiss her. 'How about a nightcap before bed, eh?'

She smelt the whisky on his breath as her stomach rumbled. 'We don't have any, dear.'

'Well, bed it is then.' He headed for the stairs. 'Come along, old girl.'

She hesitated. 'I'll be up in a minute.'

In the kitchen she poured herself a glass of water and sat at the little table. She began to a write a shopping list.

In two days she would be back at work, and she wanted George to be as comfortable as possible while she was away from him.

When she had finished, she refreshed her glass of water, turned out the light and climbed the stairs.

George was already asleep.

Chapter Fifty-One

Tommy's walk to work that morning had been an utter delight. The September sky was newly washed and cloud-less. A drift of swifts were chattering on telephone wires, readying themselves for the long flight south, and the trees were turning from summer green to autumn gold. Refreshed and at ease with the world, he strolled to his office with a cheery hello for P-T and the other girls, and installed himself behind his familiar desk.

P-T brought him his morning cuppa and the post.

'Good weekend, sir?'

'Splendid, thank you. Anything interesting today?' He gestured to the letters in her hand.

'One from Mr Morrah, at *The Times*.'

'Morrah, eh? I wonder what he wants. Decent chap. Played chess with him on the South African Tour.' Tommy leant back into his chair, thinking back. 'He wrote Princess Elizabeth's 21st birthday speech.' He cleared his throat. '"I declare before you all that my whole life, whether it be long or short, shall be devoted to your service" . . . Brings a tear even now.'

'So young to make such a promise,' P-T said. 'God bless her.' She went to the door. 'Tea at eleven, sir?'

'Thank you, yes.'

He opened the letter and began to read.

My dear Lascelles,

I have something of interest to run past you. The Foreign Office have been approached by the editors of the Ladies' Home Journal, *a very successful American women's magazine with a huge circulation. They are well-known for attracting influential women columnists to write about their lives, ambitions and thoughts on key issues of the day – the most notable, you may remember, being the First Lady, Mrs Roosevelt.*

I believe you have met Mrs Beatrice Gould, joint editor with her husband, Mr Bruce Gould?

The magazine was very interested in getting Her Majesty the Queen to author a column, but, unfortunately, the offer was dismissed by the Palace. I am sure you remember that!

As you know, relations between the UK and USA have been strained since the war. America feels that its service to the United Kingdom and Europe between 1941 and 1945, and the many lives of their servicemen lost during that time, has not been properly acknowledged.

As it was explained to me, 'They need to feel a little love from across the pond.'

Perhaps we could discuss this further over dinner at the club. Are you free next Thursday?

D.M.

Buckingham Palace, 27th September 1947

'Bobo!' Crawfie tucked her head around the door and grinned at her old friend.

Bobo looked up from her ironing and squealed in delight. 'You're back! How are you? Tell me, tell me, tell me everything.'

'Finish your ironing and I will make us tea.'

'I haven't got much left to do – just these last two blouses for the Princesses. You'd have thought there wouldn't be so much to do now they are grown up. I thought I was busy when they were little, but there's no end to looking after two beautiful young women. The stockings they go through that need mending – and you know Margaret! Likes to change several times a day and can never wear anything twice without it needing washing.'

Crawfie smiled. 'I don't know what they'd do without you.'

With the tea brewing and the iron and board put away, the two women settled in front of the fire.

'I have a photograph to show you.' Crawfie pulled a large envelope from her bag. 'Here.'

Bobo stared at it, her fingers running gently over it. 'Oh, you look so beautiful. What colour was your dress? It looks like cream satin?'

'Yes. Mother thought the white was too bright for older skin and I think the cream is a warmer shade anyway.'

'Older skin!' Bobo scoffed. 'You are pure peaches and cream – Alah used to say so. And you went for calf-length?'

'Yes. I wondered about full-length but Mother said the shorter length was more suitable.' What she'd actually said was that Marion would look like mutton. 'But Dad chose my veil and the little crystal tiara. I've brought them back with me to show you.'

Bobo clutched her hands to her small bosom. 'I should love to see them.'

'Nothing like the ones Lilibet will wear at her wedding.'

'It's the love that they carry, not the cost,' Bobo said. 'Is that a bunch of heather you're carrying?'

'Yes. White heather. The first flower George ever gave me.'

'That little bunch, all dried up in the vase from Queen Mary?'

'Yes.'

'And look at the Major in full highland dress. Very handsome.'

'Bobo, when I saw him waiting for me at the altar . . . I felt exactly like a princess.'

'But without all the television cameras trained on you.' Bobo shook her head in incomprehension. 'How our Lilibet is going to cope with the whole world watching, I don't know.'

'I do.' Crawfie smiled. 'She will see Philip waiting for her and he will be all she needs. That's how I felt.'

'Well, I am happy for you.' Bobo raised her cup. 'To happiness! If Alah were here, she'd open up the sherry.'

Later, Crawfie found her old Palace bedroom totally unchanged. She'd been away such a short time and yet her whole life had changed since she'd last been here.

She put her small bag, packed with minimal essentials, on to the dressing table and sat down. She missed George already. She had grown used to being apart from him during all the long years of their engagement, but now that they were man and wife, it felt wrong not to be together.

She had filled the larder of Nottingham Cottage with everything she could get hold of, using up most of his rations and all of hers to do so. At least she knew he would not starve until she got back on Friday evening. Apart from that first night when he had come home in a difficult mood – she blamed the whisky – he had been so attentive and kind since their wedding day.

He didn't mind that she would be away from Nottingham Cottage during the week – indeed, he had encouraged her. He himself would be busy at the Drummonds branch in London, working as a manager, now that a suitable position had finally come up.

'While we both work,' George had said, 'we can save for a little car, perhaps? Now you are married, you should ask for a pay rise. And how much is your pension worth?'

'Gosh,' she said, 'I have no idea. I haven't thought of retiring just yet.'

'Marion, these are serious things you ought to be thinking about. You need to ask someone.'

She didn't quite know who to ask about that. Before his extraordinary outburst in the car to Windsor, she would have asked Tommy, but that option was now closed to her. She tried to avoid him around the Palace wherever possible. Her anger would not allow her to put herself in a position where he thought she needed him. Absolutely not.

She caught her reflection in the dressing-table mirror. With Lilibet and Margaret no longer tied to the schoolroom, what exactly was her position? Margaret was still having some lessons, but they were becoming fewer and further between. Still, she would be helpful in the run-up to Lilibet's wedding, and there was plenty to help Bobo with, and she could assist with any of the Princesses' personal arrangements without getting in the way of the new ladies-in-waiting.

She realized that she had had vague, imagined thoughts of carrying on as governess to Lilibet and Margaret's children – the reliable, loyal, trusted and much loved retainer.

She shivered suddenly.

Maybe the future would not be quite like that.

And anyway, this time next year, she might have a child of her own.

She couldn't continue to work if she became a mother, could she? No, George wouldn't want her to work. He was a proud man who would want to look after his family. At least she – *they* – had Nottingham Cottage. The Queen had made it quite clear that the grace-and-favour home would be hers for the rest of her life. But what if something happened and George outlived her? Would he be allowed to stay? She was definitely going to have to ask someone.

Dermot Morrah's Club, 29ᵗʰ September 1947

'Dermot, old man.' Tommy loped into the club smoking room. 'I was told you'd be lurking in here. How the devil are you?' The two men shook hands and clapped each other on the shoulders.

'I'm fine. All the better for seeing you. How is Joan?'

'Marvellous. An absolute brick, as always. And your family?'

'Good, thank you. Brandy?'

'Rather.'

The steward was summoned and two large brandies ordered.

'So, what's all this about, Morrah?' Tommy asked.

Morrah looked Tommy straight in the eye. 'You have a problem and I can help to fix it.'

Tommy raised his eyebrows. 'I have a problem?'

'I will be blunt. The special relationship we have with America is at risk unless your employers—'

Tommy coughed delicately. 'The British Monarchy.'

'Don't split hairs, old boy. This is a serious matter. The King and Queen need to help build the decidedly rickety bridge between us and them – the United States of America.'

Tommy sipped his drink, smiling. 'They do not, and will never, cooperate by selling chummy interviews to ladies' magazines.'

'That is exactly what I expected you to say.' Morrah delivered his *coup de grâce*. 'But can we find someone who has inside knowledge? Someone who can paint a very positive picture of life in the Palace and how much the King and Queen value everything the USA did for us during the war?'

Tommy gave a hollow laugh. 'I am not for sale.'

'Not you, Tommy, although you would be excellent. Listen, with the royal wedding coming up, and interest in Princess Elizabeth and her handsome Prince growing by the minute, there must be someone in the palace, someone with daily contact, someone the royal family can trust to tell a few innocent, heart-warming stories?'

Tommy uncrossed his elegant, long slender legs and leant in to Morrah. He said, firmly, 'No.'

Chapter Fifty-Two

Buckingham Palace, early November 1947

'More wedding presents!' Bobo came in clutching two parcels, followed by a footman pushing a loaded post trolley.

The large Palace reception room had long trestle tables lined up around it, ready to accept the many thousands of wedding presents for Princess Elizabeth and Prince Philip.

Bobo and Crawfie were part of a team who had been drafted in to help unpack and list every gift that arrived and from whom it came.

Lilibet and Margaret had joined them.

'Good God! What on earth is this?' Margaret had pulled a woven piece of cloth from its wrapping.

'Who is it from?' asked Lilibet.

'Hang on, I'll read the label.' Margaret peered at it. 'It says: *I have woven this tray cloth with my own hands, in the hope that it will be useful and bring you pleasant memories of your wedding day. With sincere best wishes, Mahatma Gandhi.*'

'Goodness!' Lilibet said. 'What an extraordinary gift. How thoughtful.'

Margaret held the cloth up to the light. 'It's very fine work.'

'Hello, you two.' Prince Philip strode into the chaos. 'What's that?'

Margaret explained.

'Well, if anyone asks, I shall tell them it's Mr Gandhi's loin-cloth,' Philip said.

Margaret rolled with laughter, while her sister tutted. 'Don't you dare!'

Lilibet was alive with happiness and was the still centre of a storm that whirled around her. Philip knelt amongst the discarded wrapping paper to help. 'Now, these are useful.' He held up three pairs of nylons.

Margaret made a grab for them. 'Can I have a pair?'

Lilibet got there first. 'Excuse me.' She turned the packets over in her hands. 'These are lovely. Aren't people kind, spending their rations on me? I have so much. I do feel very guilty.'

Margaret scoffed. 'Darling, give them to me if it will make you feel better.'

'I think they should go to someone more deserving.' Lilibet held them out in front of her. 'Crawfie?'

Marion was carefully folding some brown paper. 'Yes?'

'Please have a pair of these stockings, to wear at the wedding. And there is a pair for Bobo too.'

Crawfie couldn't believe it. 'That is so kind. I haven't had new stockings for a long time.'

Bobo, almost crying with joy, took them and held them to her heart. 'Oh ma'am. They are much too good for me.'

Lilibet flashed her a happy smile. 'They certainly are not. Enjoy them. Oh, and Crawfie, I would like you to make a list of things you might like for your little cottage?'

'You have already given me a beautiful coffee set as our wedding present, and Margaret, the bedside lamps you gave us look perfect.'

'What about a complete dinner service?' asked Margaret, pointing to seven such things placed on a table. 'Lilibet can't need all those.'

'Thank you, but Queen Mary generously sent me a most attractive dining service.'

'Did she?' Lilibet asked. 'Well, that was jolly nice of her. But honestly, we have so much here. Make a list of anything that could be useful.'

Before Crawfie could object, Mr Norman Hartnell arrived, sweeping into the room as grandly as any Duchess.

'Your Royal Highnesses.' He delivered a theatrical bow.

'Good morning, Mr Hartnell,' Lilibet said, beaming. 'Another fitting?"

'Indeed, ma'am.'

He and his young assistants were endlessly appearing, carrying heavy boxes spilling with tissue paper, raining pins, scissors and tape measures.

Bobo never stopped providing them with refreshments, while trying to get a good view of *the* dress – without much luck.

'I can't wait to see it,' she told Crawfie one evening over cocoa. 'I know it has lots of embroidery and pearls and a beautiful veil. One of the seamstresses told me that much.'

'Well, don't you pass that on to anyone else. The walls have ears, you know,' Crawfie told her, while not admitting that Lilibet had shown her some sketches of the dress.

'I'm not silly.' Bobo huffed. 'I *have* been here longer than you have. I know the rules. And, by the way, as soon as she is married, I am to be her personal dresser.'

Crawfie was pleased. 'Is that so? Congratulations. Alah would be so proud of you.'

'Do you think she would?'

Crawfie smiled. 'Absolutely.'

'Do you know, I was as nervous as a kitten when I started. I had no idea what I was to do or how I was to do it. Alah had to teach me everything and I was so homesick.' She bit her lip. 'The first year was very hard for me.'

Crawfie nodded in agreement. 'To tell the truth, Alah taught me, too. I had no idea how a governess was to operate in a family like this one. I was terrified of the Duke and Duchess, the Princesses, even Ainslie! But Alah was the scariest.'

Bobo began to giggle. 'You were frightened of her? But she was frightened of you! She would often tell me how assured and confident you seemed, how you had the Princesses and their timetable totally organized. She had ruled supreme until you arrived. You put her on the back foot.'

'Never! Did I?'

'Oh yes.'

'Goodness.' The two women sat with their memories in the quiet.

'She would have loved all this, wouldn't she?' Bobo said quietly. 'Seeing her Lilibet so happy and preparing to marry.'

'She really would.' Crawfie picked up her cocoa mug and raised it. 'To Alah.'

Bobo joined her. 'To Alah.'

Buckingham Palace, 18ᵗʰ November 1947

Crawfie and Bobo were at the nursery window, looking out at the gravel courtyard below as Lilibet and Philip said their last goodbyes before they met tomorrow at Westminster Abbey.

'Look at her,' Bobo breathed. 'See how she's touching his collar and straightening his tie?'

'It's a true romance,' Crawfie said. 'I know a little of how she feels. The night before I married George I was bursting with excitement and nerves. My mother and I sat together in the kitchen with a sherry each.'

Bobo smiled. 'Her little girl becoming a married woman.'

Crawfie looked into her drink, recalling the horror of her mother's birds and bees speech. She never wanted to think about it again.

'Something like that.'

'And look!' Bobo's breath was misting the pane. 'They're kissing.'

They watched as Philip reluctantly parted from his Princess and jumped into his little car. He made a turn towards the Palace gates, spraying gravel as he did so. Lilibet waved at him madly until, with a last toot, he disappeared.

Bobo and Crawfie were busily getting their wedding outfits steamed and sorted for the next day when there was a knock at the door and Lilibet popped her head round. 'Hello.'

'Lilibet! What are you doing up here? Shouldn't you be having an early night?'

'I think I am going to find it hard to sleep tonight. Philip has left to stay at Kensington Palace with his mother and grandmother. But before that he is having a party at the Dorchester for his friends. Gentlemen only, I am assured.' She gave a little laugh. 'I might have to have some aspirin hidden in my flowers for him tomorrow.'

'I am sure he'll be all right. He is a sensible man,' Crawfie said. 'He is devoted to you. You know that.'

'Yes, I suppose I do.' Lilibet sat down in Alah's old chair. 'May I have a cup of tea with you both, just to calm my nerves?'

'How about a spot of sherry instead?' Bobo asked. 'I found one of Alah's bottles of Bristol Cream a few months ago.'

'Alah liked sherry?' Lilibet asked.

'Oh yes.' Crawfie laughed. 'A small drop would often find its way, accidentally of course, into her bedtime cocoa.'

'All right then.' Lilibet ran a hand over her engagement ring. 'Then we will make a toast to Alah – the finest nanny ever.'

'Hear hear,' Bobo said

Over the flickering of the fire and their sherry-laced cocoas, the three women talked about old times in the schoolroom.

'Do you remember when I tipped that bottle of ink over my head, Crawfie?' Lilibet asked.

'I do indeed.'

'You weren't cross, though.'

Crawfie smiled at the memory. 'It was good to see you behaving like a normal child.'

'Are you cross that you had to wait so long to marry Major Buthlay, though?' Lilibet said.

Crawfie took a deep breath, thinking. 'I am married now and that is all that matters.'

'But did you feel that we had stopped you?' Lilibet looked thoughtful. 'That you had put your life second to ours?'

'No, ma'am. To serve you and your family will always come first. It has been – and is – my pleasure.'

Lilibet yawned. 'Golly, I think I had better go to bed. Bobo, will you wake me in the morning?'

'Of course I will.'

Buckingham Palace, 20th November 1947, 7.30 a.m.

Bobo carried the pretty silver tea tray to Lilibet's bedroom and knocked gently before entering.

'Good morning, ma'am. I have your tea.'

Lilibet stirred and opened her eyes. 'What time is it?'

'Seven thirty.' Bobo put the tray down and crossed the room to draw the curtains. 'There's a beautiful sunrise.'

'I hope all those people who have camped outside aren't too cold or wet.' Lilibet sat up to drink her tea. 'It's so good of them to come.'

Outside on the terrace, a lone piper began playing.

'Oh Bobo, he's playing "Mairi's Wedding". Isn't that fun?'

'Now you just concentrate on your tea,' Bobo fussed. 'Mr Hartnell will be here to dress you at nine and you need to be ready. Shall I draw a bath for you?'

The Good Servant

'Do I look all right?'

Lilibet was standing in her dress, before the Queen, Mr Norman Hartnell, Bobo and Crawfie.

All three women had tears in their eyes. 'Darling, you look wonderful,' her mother told her with a handkerchief to her eyes.

'It has taken an hour to get me into it all,' said Lilibet.

Mr Hartnell stood back, surveying his creation. 'One can't hurry perfection, ma'am.'

Bobo clasped her hands to her breast in rapture. 'You look beautiful.'

Crawfie beamed. Lilibet really did look stunning. She could not quite believe the little girl she had met so many years before had become this beautiful, grown-up woman.

The Queen moved forward to kiss the bride on both cheeks. 'You look so happy and Papa and I are so proud of you.' She held her daughter at arm's length for a moment, checking every feature. 'Don't forget to put your pearls on.'

Lilibet gasped. 'Oh gosh. Would someone fetch them for me please?'

'I'll go. Where are they?' asked Crawfie.

'They were at the jewellers. The clasp needed fixing. Who went to collect them?' asked Lilibet, always calm, looking at herself in the long mirror and checking each angle. This wedding would be the first royal wedding to be broadcast on television, so she had to be just right.

'I will ask Ainslie,' said Crawfie, dashing out of the room.

Mr Hartnell looked about him. 'Where are your flowers? It would be good for you to rehearse carrying them. They will be heavy, and with the long train and your veil, you must feel utterly comfortable and balanced.'

A cursory rummage followed by a more thorough search through the entire room revealed that the flowers were not to be seen.

Bobo leapt at the chance to help. 'I'll go and find them. Ainslie will know.'

Buckingham Palace, 20ᵗʰ November 1947, 10.45 a.m.

Crawfie and Bobo bumped into each other in the corridor outside Lilibet's dressing room.

'I had to run to St James's Palace,' panted Crawfie. 'But I have them!' she waved a leather jewel box. 'The pavements were crowded with well-wishers. It took me an age to get through them.'

Bobo was holding a huge white box. 'And I have the flowers. It's taken me half an hour to find them. They'd been put in a cold cupboard but nobody could think *which* cold cupboard.'

Crawfie took a deep breath and blew it out to calm her breathing. 'We have saved the day, Bobo.'

'Excuse me.' A young man was running towards them. 'Can you tell me where the bride's changing room is, please?'

'Who needs to know?' Crawfie asked with suspicion.

'I'm from Garrard, the royal jeweller. I have come to mend the bride's tiara. It has snapped.'

'Follow us!'

At 11.15, spot on time, the King and Lilibet set off in the Irish state coach for Westminster Abbey. Palace staff lined up to wave them off and watch as the carriage went through the gates, disappearing into the swell and noise of the cheering crowds.

Bobo and Crawfie dashed to a waiting car which got them to the Abbey well before the Princess and the King arrived.

Chapter Fifty-Three

Dear Mother and Dad,

Wasn't it wonderful! I am so glad that you managed to share Mrs Clark's television to see it. You had a better view than I did, I expect. Not that I am complaining – George and I were seated in Poets' Corner and watched as my little Lilibet and the Duke of Edinburgh (what a lovely new title – a surprise from the King) knelt on those two satin boxes. You will never guess what they were made of . . . orange boxes! Really. Rationing and austerity applies to royalty too.

From where we were sitting, I could see the light bounce off the beautiful crystals on Lilibet's dress. The Duke of Edinburgh, as we must now call him, is a very lucky man.

Outside the Abbey, the bells pealed and the crowd cheered as Bobo and I waited for our car to Buckingham Palace and the wedding breakfast.

I had to say goodbye to George because he did not have an invitation to the breakfast, only to the service. He was put out about it, but I tried to cheer him with news that there was a homemade chicken pie waiting for him at Nott Cott.

It was a wonderful lunch, gay and merry. The happiness of everybody there was tangible. Lilibet was radiant, the light of the chandeliers and candles catching every crystal on her dress. I knew then that she would be very happy with Philip and that he knew he was a lucky man.

The King came to find me later and said, 'Well done, Crawfie. I think she's happy, don't you?'

I told him that I had no doubt. Then the Queen kissed me and said what a wonderful day it had been. And I told her, yes, but that I too felt as if I had lost a daughter. And she said, 'I am sure you do, Crawfie, but we must make the best of it.' So gracious.

When I eventually got home, there was no sign of George. I didn't worry too much because he has made friends with a crowd in the little pub at the bottom of the Kensington Palace drive.

After all the great build-up, the Palace – indeed all London – is quiet.

George and I are moving to a small hotel in Kensington tomorrow, because Nott Cott is having some repairs made to it. I had to pack up the few things I had put out in the kitchen and around the house, so I am back to square one – living out of a suitcase with darling George. I have not even had the chance to fully unpack. Queen Mary's dinner service is still carefully wrapped, as are the table lamps from Princess Margaret. The coffee set from Lilibet had to be rewrapped and put away.

I have to agree with George about our little house. The plumbing is awfully old and the whole thing needs rewiring and decorating – none of which I have time for, as I am at the Palace during the week taking care of Princess Margaret, who misses her sister very much. She and I will be on our own a lot because the King and Queen are travelling so much these days.

At least we still have the old guard here at the Palace. Dear Bobo, Ainslie and even Jackson the chauffeur. You remember him? He is married now with children of his own. How time flies. Bobo has become the Princesses' personal dresser and is delighted, of course.

George is getting used to living in London and is enjoying meeting up with his old chums in old haunts. I know he misses me during the week, and we have talked at length about how long I shall continue working, but for now I am to remain. We are able to save money – and besides, the family still need me.

I hoped we could come up to Dunfermline for Christmas but you can see how we are fixed. As soon as the cottage is ready, I want you both to come down and stay. I can take you to Oxford Street for shopping and the theatre too. That will be my Christmas present to you.

All my love,

Marion

Crawfie folded her letter, and put it into an envelope ready for the post.

She was desperate to have some time to herself and eager to be a proper housewife to George.

Margaret was longing to visit the cottage. She had been asking for days. 'When can I come and see your lovely new home?' she would say. 'I could help you choose colours and curtains. *Please?*'

Today, Crawfie finally gave in. 'We could go this afternoon, I suppose. I would like to see how the workmen are doing. George is keeping an eye on things and he says they are coming on wonderfully well.'

A few hours later, Jackson drove them the short distance from Buckingham Palace to Kensington Palace, then asked if he could come and see the little house too.

'The more the merrier,' laughed Margaret.

Glowing with expectation and pride, Crawfie led them to her home. 'Look at our sign.' She waved at the small plaque bearing the words NOTTINGHAM COTTAGE on the gate.

'Adorable,' said Margaret, as she went through the gate and straight to the open front door. 'Hellooo,' she called.

The sound of banging coming from the upstairs stopped, and footsteps overhead made their way to the top of the stairs.

'Who's there?' A man appeared, wearing a flat cap and workman's overalls. He stared down at them. 'Can I help you, miss?' he asked.

'Yes.' Princess Margaret grinned. 'I should like to come in and see what you are up to.'

Crawfie tried to intervene, but Margaret mischievously stopped her, whispering, 'Let's have some fun.'

The man frowned. 'I can't let you in here. This is crown property – private. You'd better hop off quick.'

'But it belongs to my family.' She smiled, stepping into the hall.

'This belongs to the King, love. Now, if you don't mind, I . . .' He looked again at the beautiful young woman and recognition dawned in his eyes. He almost fell down the stairs in his hurry to reach her. 'Oh, my gawd, Your Majesty, I didn't know . . . I mean . . . blinkin' 'eck!' He stood before her and whipped his cap off, bowing as best he could. 'I had no idea, Your Majesty.'

'That's quite all right. And only my parents are Their Majesties – I am Her Royal Highness Princess Margaret. This is Mrs Buthlay, my governess, and the lady who will be living here as soon as the work is done, and that's Jackson, my chauffeur. Do you have a cigarette on you?'

He patted a pocket and pulled out a Senior Service box. 'Would one of these do?'

'You smoke the same brand as the King. Therefore one would certainly do. Thank you.'

More footsteps were heard upstairs, and a man's voice called, 'Put the kettle on while you're down there, Pete.'

'We got visitors, Cyril.'

'Tell 'em we're busy.'

'Cyril?' Princess Margaret called up. 'Do come down. We are dying to meet you.'

They heard Cyril grumbling to himself and then his footsteps on the stairs. At the bottom, he noted a youngish man in a driver's uniform, a tall, skinny woman with a prominent nose, and finally one of the most recognizable faces in the world. He stood speechless, his mouth hanging loosely.

'Hello, Cyril,' Princess Margaret said laughingly. 'Are you and Pete going to make the tea, or should I?'

'Oh Mummy, it was so funny.' They were having tea back at the Palace and Margaret was telling the story. 'The men were terribly sweet and gave us the least cracked of the cups. Jackson had a good look round and told them they'd better get a move on because Mr and Mrs Buthlay needed their home sooner rather than later.'

'And are you pleased with how they are doing, Crawfie, dear?' asked the Queen.

'Yes, ma'am. Thank you. It's a beautiful wee place.'

'But Mummy, Crawfie will need all sorts to put into it: floor coverings, curtains, pictures.'

Crawfie stopped her. 'We can make do until we can afford those things.'

'I don't think you should.' Margaret smiled. 'I think I shall have a word with Granny. She has an awful lot of stuff she doesn't need.'

Buckingham Palace, early December 1947

It was around ten o'clock at night and Crawfie was in her Palace bedroom, getting ready for bed. The King and Queen and Margaret were away for two nights in Somerset for a shooting weekend. She was spending the time making a list of plants she would have in her cottage garden, using one of the King's gardening books.

'Crawfie?' a familiar voice called from the corridor. 'Are you awake?'

It was Lilibet, fresh off the train from her honeymoon in Hampshire at Broadlands, the home of the Duke's uncle, Earl Mountbatten of Burma.

'Lilibet.' Crawfie embraced her. 'You look so well. How was Broadlands?'

'Glorious, thank you. Lots of space, fresh air and fun. Philip has made it all so wonderful.'

'And are you happy?'

'Well, I was very happy until I discovered that my horrid sister seems to have lost all the dog leads. Puppy Susan is adorable, but she needs a lead before we go to Balmoral for the rest of the honeymoon. We are on the night train, so I only have twenty minutes before Philip will be shouting for me. Are there any up here?'

The search proved fruitless until a footman found a rather chewed lead with a ragged collar at the back of a cupboard.

'Oh, that's marvellous. Thank you.'

Lilibet gave Crawfie a quick hug, and then she gaily jogged down the long corridor to find her husband. Happiness poured from her. She was so young and she and Philip had so much to look forward to – their new home, Clarence House, was ready to move into and was already creaking with the mountain of wedding presents which they had no idea what to do with.

Getting into her single bed, Crawfie compared her life with that of her ex-pupil. Living apart from her husband, who she knew was not happy staying in the hotel alone, with a home she could never furnish the way she wished. And no word on her retirement or what she might expect as a pension.

All in all, this was not how she had expected things to be.

She reached up to her bedside lamp and turned it off. *Come on, Marion,* she told herself, *this is just a bad patch. It won't be long before George and I will be back together. The garden will bloom in the spring, and maybe we will be blessed with a baby, too. Nice curtains and carpets are not important. Count your blessings and go to sleep.*

She rolled over on to her left side, closed her eyes and drifted off.

Chapter Fifty-Four

Buckingham Palace, December 1947

P-T, in her outer office, rang through to the intercom on Tommy's desk.

'Mr Dermot Morrah from *The Times* on the line, sir.'

'Put him through.'

Tommy sighed. What did Morrah want this time?

'Tommy?' the cultured voice asked.

'Yes indeed. Good morning. How can I help?'

'Don't get on the defensive.' Morrah chuckled. 'I am writing a piece about Princess Elizabeth and her new home – or should I say homes? My editor requires a colourful domestic picture of the newlyweds.'

'You know that is something I would never advise.'

'Oh, come on, old man. They are doing awfully well. Clarence House for town, Windlesham for the country and I hear Malta for the Commonwealth?'

Tommy rubbed his index finger over his clipped moustache. 'What are you getting at?'

'Let's start with Malta.'

'I shall send you a press release when we are ready,' Tommy drawled.

Morrah continued to press him. 'Can you confirm that Prince Philip is to be stationed at HMS *Magpie*? And that the Princess and he will live there for two years? You can't deny those facts.'

'An official briefing will appear in due course.'

'Oh, come on old man. Give me a little something.'

'Ha.' Tommy almost laughed. 'Absolutely not.'

'Oh, and by the way, Lady Astor is bringing Mrs Gould to tea at BP next week. Guests of the Queen.'

Tommy laughed. 'You can't catch me out that easily, old man.'

'Never said a truer word. I will book a table at the club on Thursday. By then you will want to talk to me, I assure you.'

Putting the phone down, Tommy frowned. How did Morrah know that Lady Astor and Mrs Gould were coming to BP to see the Queen?

He summoned P-T.

'Yes, sir?'

'Has Her Majesty any female visitors coming for tea next week?'

'Let me check, sir.'

Moments later, she was back. 'Wednesday, 3.30 p.m., tea with Lady Astor and a Mrs Gould.'

'Thank you, P-T.'

Then, 'Damn the woman,' Tommy said to the empty room.

Buckingham Palace, December 1947

'And how is Nottingham Cottage coming along, Crawfie? Have the builders finished now?' Lilibet asked, pouring them both a cup of tea.

'Yes, they have. It's very comfortable, thank you.' She didn't mention that the plumbing still had a mind of its own. 'George is bringing a Christmas tree home tonight. I am so looking forward to decorating it.'

'Mummy and Granny love that bit too. They are off to Sandringham tomorrow to do ours. Philip and I will travel down next week.' Lilibet smiled. 'Are your family coming for Christmas?'

'No. George and I wanted to spend our first one together. Mother and Dad will come in the spring, perhaps.'

George had been most adamant that Maggie and Robert stayed in Scotland, and Marion had reluctantly agreed.

'Oh, that will be nice,' Lilibet said. 'Granny told me she has been over to visit.'

'Oh yes. So kind of her. The workmen didn't know what to do with themselves. Lots of bowing.'

Lilibet laughed. 'Was she being stern Queen Mary?'

'No, she was lovely to them – chatting about the war and their part in it. They were eating out of her hand by the time she left.'

'I heard she sent over some of her furniture?'

'Yes. Beautiful paintings, a cabinet, a bookcase and a George III chest of drawers.'

'And do you like them? Or did you feel your hand was forced to accept them? Granny can be very insistent.'

'Not at all. Everything looks perfect,' Crawfie lied.

'Philip and I will come and visit before we go to Sandringham.'

Crawfie sipped her tea. 'George and I shall look forward to that.'

Dermot Morrah's Club, December 1947

The clatter and chatter of the club's dining room would have been comforting to Tommy – if only he had not been here to find out more about Morrah's mission to target the Queen and Princesses as fodder for the American press.

The maître d' glided over to him as he waited to be seated.

'Sir Alan, do follow me. Mr Morrah sends his apologies. He is delayed at the office and will be a little late.'

Tommy's irritation went up another couple of notches.

They reached a well-appointed table for two. 'Mr Morrah's preferred table,' the waiter told him, as he pulled out a chair. 'May I get a drink for you, sir?'

'Scotch and soda, please.'

Tommy looked around him. Of course this would be Morrah's preferred table: no one near enough to overhear but perfectly positioned to see and be seen by everybody.

Since Lady Astor had brought Mrs Gould to tea with the Queen, Tommy's brain had been working overtime. He hadn't seen Mrs Gould for several years, and in that time had had to brush her off twice. By God, the woman must have skin as thick as a hippo. Tommy found that people like Mrs Beatrice Gould were completely beyond his understanding of women.

The woman was ruthless. She was determined to get a series of syrupy columns about the British royal family in the periodical she owned with her husband, Mr Bruce Gould. The *Ladies' Home Journal* was America's most widely read magazine for women. Mrs Gould was selling the idea as a way of 'enhancing the friendship between America and Great Britain'. She'd said, 'Our people love the British and they want to see that the British love them too. Especially when so many American servicemen lost their lives in helping out with World War II. In a way, you owe us.'

Tommy shuddered. He knew exactly what Mrs Gould wanted: she wanted to sell magazines.

He had made sure he intercepted Lady Astor and Mrs Gould on the day of tea party, just as they were about to leave the Palace.

'Goodness! Lady Astor. How lovely to see you. I didn't know you were here.' His performance had been charming.

'Tommy, dear,' answered Lady Astor, offering her powdered cheek. 'We have had the most delightful tea with Her Majesty. May I introduce you to Mrs Gould?'

Mrs Gould reached out a gloved hand. 'We met once at the Ritz.'

'Oh goodness, so we did.' Tommy smiled. 'Would you care to join me in my office? I can offer tea, or something a little stronger?'

'We must get on,' Lady Astor demurred.

'No, honey, wait.' Mrs Gould had placed a hand on Lady Astor's arm. 'I would love a drink.'

'Sorry, old man,' Dermot Morrah said now, arriving fifteen minutes late. 'What're you having? Scotch and soda?' He turned to the hovering waiter. 'I will have the same.'

They exchanged pleasantries and enquiries about wives and children as they read the menu, Dermot eventually plumping for the steak and kidney pie while Tommy went for the pork.

Once the waiter had left, Dermot cut to the chase. 'So, Mrs Gould tells me that you cleverly got her and Lady Astor to yourself?'

Tommy inclined his head. 'That is true. They both enjoyed a small Dubonnet.'

'Yes. She told me that too. I am surprised she accepted. But then, a gentleman would never attempt to loosen a lady's tongue, would he?'

'She didn't need to be encouraged. I know what she wants, and I have communicated to her, once again, that it is impossible.'

Dermot gave a wry smile. 'Tommy! This is the twentieth century. We are moving in a free world, in a time of movie stars and rich men. People like to be given a glimpse of how their idols live. You must see that allowing a peek into a small corner of our royal family's lives will pay enormous dividends in the bank of popularity.'

'The role of the royal family is not to be popular.' Tommy moved his napkin to his lap as the waiter placed their plates.

Dermot shook his head. 'Not to be popular? How ludicrous you sound. Antiquated opinions like that cannot exist today. Listen, I am talking to the Foreign Office who are talking to Bruce Gould, the husband, and all they want are some innocuous stories. In America they adore Princess Elizabeth and the Duke of Edinburgh. It's perfect. A young and handsome couple, she destined to be the Queen of England. What was she like growing up? What hobbies did she have? What is she reading? Who is her favourite film star, Clarke Gable or Cary Grant? What music does she listen to? It's that simple.'

'I cannot recommend any of it,' Tommy said firmly. 'Can you actually see the Queen sitting down and writing that sort of guff, when she has spent her entire life being a mystery? Or the Princess? We cannot lose the importance of the family's otherness. It is because of their enigma that they *are* so popular.'

Dermot shook his head. 'Tommy, when I wrote that speech for the Princess's twenty-first birthday – you remember, *whether my life be short or long* – you wrote me the most wonderful letter, thanking me for hitting the right note. I am telling you now that we can hit another right note and open the oyster just a crack, shine a little inside and then put it back in the water. No harm done. The Foreign Office is for it. The Prime Minister is for it. And the Queen, once she has spoken to the King, will be for it, too. You will lose the battle.' Dermot smiled and sipped his drink. 'You are on your own, Tommy.'

Chapter Fifty-Five

Westminster Hospital, December 1947

George was unwell. He was in hospital, having tests for possible kidney stones, and Crawfie couldn't help but feel anxious. She had spent the day at his bedside while he had drifted in and out of sleep. The medication to kill the excruciating pain made him very drowsy But the nurses and doctor were reassuring.

'The stones may be small and will hopefully pass themselves, which could be rather painful,' the doctor told her. 'We are giving him lots of fluid intravenously and have added a little something to help break the stone or stones up. I reckon, in a couple of days, he should be home as right as rain.'

'Thank you, doctor.' Crawfie looked at George's pale face against the sheets and stroked his cold hand. 'The pain came on so suddenly.'

'Tell me, does he drink a lot of sugary drinks?'

'He has sugar in his tea.'

'What is his alcohol intake?'

Marion bit her lip. George was spending a lot of time in the pub, and more often than not came home a little drunk. He had even shoved her last week when he had come home to find his dinner dried up in the bottom of the oven – but he had apologized so profusely the next day. 'No, not really. But he's a Scot, so he has the odd whisky.' She smiled.

'I recommend that he leave that alone for a while. There's a lot of sugar in alcohol, and we know that too much sugar can cause these stones.'

'I see. Of course.'

'I should get off home if I were you. He'll sleep most of the night now and you need your own rest.'

'Thank you, but I will stay just a little while longer. I believe dinner is on its way and I will see if I can tempt him with a little.'

'As you wish, but you must take care of yourself too.'

Marion stayed another two hours.

Dinner was beef stew. When George woke up, Marion offered him some, but he pushed her hand away.

'It's almost as bad as your cooking,' he muttered.

One of the nurses on the ward noticed and turned to Marion. 'Don't worry, Mrs Buthlay. It's the drugs. Makes people do and say strange things.'

Marion made her way home on the bus, feeling low. London was dark but the sparkling of the Christmas lights in the shop windows cheered her. This would be her first Christmas as Mrs Buthlay but her first without her parents. She hoped George was well enough to be home in time. Perhaps he would be in a better mood when the pain was gone.

Nottingham Cottage was dark and cold when she got in.

She lit the fire, put the kettle to boil on the new gas cooker, and went upstairs to run a bath. As soon as she opened the tap, the old and antiquated boiler clanked into life. The plumbers had not been able to fix it properly and she hoped a new, more modern boiler might be supplied soon. In the meantime, she played a form of Russian roulette, never knowing if the water would run icy or scalding.

She pulled back quickly. This evening it was red hot.

Twiddling both taps, she finally found something that was temperate. As the water pressure was low, she knew it would take at least ten minutes to fill – time enough to make her tea and stoke the fire.

In the end, the bath was tepid, but reasonable enough to wash her hair.

She dried herself, put on her nightie and dressing gown and wrapped her hair with a towel.

The bare Christmas tree that George had brought home two nights ago was sitting forlornly in its pot by the window. A box of baubles and a string of coloured lights lay next to it. She should dress it before George came home. The empty branches felt so dull and solemn.

Unwrapping her hair and brushing it by the firelight, she wondered what she would have for her dinner. She always tried to make an effort for George, but she wasn't very hungry tonight, and she was on her own. Maybe a bowl of soup and some toast would do.

Then the doorbell rang, making her jump. She went quickly to the door.

'Who is it?' she called anxiously.

'It's me. Lilibet. Philip and I have come to pay our official call.'

Marion glanced at the clock. It was not late, only six o'clock, but she had not been expecting anyone and had planned for an early night. She straightened her dressing gown and ran her fingers through her damp hair. She could not let them wait on the doorstep, even if she was hardly dressed for the occasion.

'Come in. Forgive my attire.'

'Oh! Are we disturbing you?' Lilibet strode in with Philip after her, lowering his head so as not to bang it on the door jamb.

'Not at all. I have been out all day and was going to have an early night. George is . . . away.' She felt somehow a little embarrassed to mention that he was in hospital. 'Actually, I was thinking about dressing the tree for his return. Would you like a drink?'

'Tea would be nice.'

'Do take a seat.' Marion indicated the two chairs either side of the fire.

'I would rather have a look round, if I may. Do you remember Margaret and I showing you around our Little House at Royal Lodge, all those years ago? Your cottage almost reminds me of it.'

'One of the first adventures you took me on,' Marion said, with a smile at the thought. 'Shall we start upstairs?'

Princess Elizabeth enjoyed her tour. She insisted on opening every cupboard upstairs and down.

Prince Philip was intrigued by the boiler. 'Has this come out of the ark?' he said, tapping it with his knuckles.

'It *is* rather eccentric.' Marion laughed. 'I never know quite what temperature it will produce.'

'You girls go and make the tea, and let me have a tinker. I know my way around a ship's engine room. It can't be much different.'

Marion made a large pot of tea and brought it into the sitting room, where she found Lilibet looking through the Christmas baubles.

'Shall we do this together?' she asked.

'No, have your tea, I can do that later,' Marion protested – but Lilibet had already started on it.

'Papa always says the lights should go on before the baubles,' she was saying to herself. 'So that is where we shall start.'

Marion was amused. 'It wasn't so long ago that I was the one putting the tree up in the nursery, you and Margaret arguing over who put what where.'

'And now you and I are both married and Margaret is living her own life.' Lilibet threaded a length of cotton through the loop of a red bauble. 'Do you ever think about what you are going to do next, Crawfie?'

'What do you mean?'

'Now you are married?'

'Oh, I am happy as I am. Perhaps when Margaret comes of age, there may be a change. At twenty-one, she really won't need me.'

'Do you not want a family of your own?'

'If it were to happen for George and me, then yes, that would be marvellous. But one cannot assume.'

'I suppose not.'

'But you, Lilibet, are young and healthy, and I am certain you have a wonderful family to look forward to.'

A smile lit Lilibet's features. 'Well, yes, Philip and I would both like that. He is to be stationed in Malta in the new year, and I shall go with him. Just us. Won't that be lovely? He is still a naval officer, you know, and has been offered second-in-command of HMS *Chequers*, which is the lead ship of the flotilla operating in the Mediterranean. I shall be a proper naval wife, looking after my husband and my home.'

Prince Philip appeared. 'I don't need any looking after,' he said, with a laugh. 'Crawfie, where is your husband's tool box? I need a spanner.'

When Lilibet and Philip finally said goodnight, the boiler was sounding a little less clanky and the tree looked perfect.

'Merry Christmas, Crawfie.' Lilibet hugged her old governess. 'And you, too.'

Philip shook her hand and as a joke, Crawfie saluted. 'Thank you for fixing my plumbing, sir.'

'Any time, Able Seaman Crawfie. Any time.'

Chapter Fifty-Six

Buckingham Palace, February 1948

'Good morning, sir.' P-T, as ever on time, brought Tommy's copies of the day's newspapers and his cup of tea. 'Did you have a good weekend?'

'Splendid, thank you. Joan and I took a long walk over the South Downs. Lunched in a delightful pub. Went home and had a decent snooze. Feel all the better for it.'

'Glad to hear it.' P-T turned to go but at the door said, 'The Foreign Office have asked to see you at eleven. There is nothing else in the diary, so I said I would confirm with you?'

'That's fine. I wonder what they want. Do I go there or are they coming here?'

'Here, sir. They have a meeting with the Queen first.'

'Oh. Well, I shall be waiting for them.'

P-T knocked at Tommy's door at two minutes past eleven. 'Sir, Mr Edwin Jones and Mr Julius Rosenstein from the Foreign Office are here to see you.'

Tommy stood up and came around the front of his desk to welcome his visitors.

Once the niceties were over and they were all sitting down, Tommy raised one quizzical eyebrow and asked, 'And how may I help you?'

Mr Rosenstein, the older and presumably more senior of the two, spoke first. 'I am sure you are aware of enquiries as to the possibility of a little lifting of the public profile of the royal family both here and in America and, indeed, globally?'

'Ah.' Tommy sat back in his chair and surveyed the two men. He had thought Morrah and these ghastly Goulds had gone away for good. It was madness. The royal family were on an even keel now – as popular as ever, if not more so, after the interest and excitement of the marriage of Princess Elizabeth and the Duke of Edinburgh. They had no need to sell themselves to a couple of American hacks. 'If you mean Mr and Mrs Gould of the *Ladies' Home Journal*,' Tommy said, 'I am indeed aware and dead against it.'

Mr Rosenstein frowned, but continued. 'And it follows that you also know we have come to you directly from an audience with Her Majesty.'

'I do.'

Mr Jones – young, callow and barely of shaving age – coughed and opened the briefcase by his side to take out a closely typed page. He held it out to Tommy. 'We have drawn up some proposals. The Queen has looked at them and has tentatively agreed to some careful press access to Princess Elizabeth.'

Tommy left the page dangling in Mr Jones's fingers. 'Has she?'

'She understands the very real value of public relations with our American cousins, the Commonwealth and the world beyond.' Mr Rosenstein smiled.

Tommy did not move a muscle. 'Does she?'

'She asked us to talk to you.' Mr Rosenstein produced another, silkier smile.

'About what exactly?' Tommy folded his hands.

'Mr and Mrs Gould are excellent journalists,' Mr Jones said, 'who have been trusted by many significant people, in publishing uplifting and informative articles about their lives, including Mrs Roosevelt when she was the First Lady.'

'Yes.' Tommy sniffed. 'I am aware.'

Mr Jones perked up. 'Their wish is to commission Princess Elizabeth to write a series of informal articles about her life married to a naval officer. Her hobbies, charity work, favourite recipe. You know the sort of thing.'

Tommy shuddered. 'Her hobbies? Favourite recipe? Ha!' Tommy's laugh was mirthless. 'They really want that sort of bumf, do they? Good Lord. That's the marvel of being an American, isn't it? Anyone can be president and anyone can get anyone else to do anything. And the answer, chaps, is *no*. We Brits do things differently. Our constitution and the people within it are not for sale.'

Mr Rosenstein crossed his legs, pinching the fabric of his trousers a little and then smoothing it back again. 'Lady Astor was in this morning's meeting with Her Majesty. She suggested that rather than Princess Elizabeth writing the articles herself, they could be written by a third party – someone close to both sisters, who would share a few charming and harmless tales.'

Tommy had a terrible feeling that he might know who they meant. 'And?'

'The Princesses' governess? Miss . . .' Mr Rosenstein looked over to Mr Jones who supplied the surname.

'Miss Crawford.'

Tommy clenched his hands. 'No.'

'But Her Majesty thought Miss Crawford might be perfect?' Mr Rosenstein pressed. 'Providing that the articles were anonymous and that Miss Crawford's name and position were never mentioned. It would be a marvellous opportunity for the royal family to boost their followers in the States – Princess Elizabeth, the Duke, Princess Margaret, and of course the King and Queen, all of them charming. It would be a delightful and positive venture. You must see that?'

'I see it all too clearly.' Pulling out every fibre of the courtier within, Tommy concluded the meeting. 'Mr and Mrs Gould's motive is to feed our royal family to the masses, like an advertisement for a soap powder. And their only desire is to line their fat pockets. Good day, gentlemen. Do send my regards to the foreign secretary.'

Nottingham Cottage, May 1948

'Post for you!' George shouted up the stairs.

'I'll be down in a moment!'

Marion was getting ready to go to work. She fastened her string of pearls and looked at her reflection in the long mirror. Her tweed skirt was fitted nicely around her hips and her powder-blue twinset was neat and sensible. The pearls gave the whole outfit a feel of the regal. How she had changed since 1932, when her mother had sent her off with a case full of homemade clothes. Now she looked every inch the smart wife and royal servant.

George shouted again. 'Your porridge is getting cold.'

She checked her makeup, picked up her bag and jacket and went down.

'Very nice,' George said appreciatively. 'Your letter is by your porridge. Sit down and eat up.'

'Thank you, dear.' She noticed the empty whisky bottle by the sink but said nothing as she opened her letter. She had grown used to saying nothing about George's increasingly regular nights of drink. 'It's from Lilibet.' She turned the envelope to George, 'A Maltese stamp.'

'Oh quick, let me get my stamp album.' He sat down opposite her. He was looking dreadful.

'Are you feeling any better today, dear?' she asked. 'Any more pain? Only the doctor did say . . .'

'That I shouldn't have too much sugar. I know. And I don't.'

She blinked nervously, a small habit she'd recently caught herself doing more and more. 'You were late to bed last night.'

'Well done, Holmes.' He caught her steal a glance towards the empty bottle. 'And yes, as a matter of fact, I did finish the bottle. There was only a drop left. So don't worry. Read your letter.'

She started to read.

'Out loud!' he told her. 'I want to hear what the lovely Lilibet has to say about married life.'

'Yes, of course.' She cleared her throat and began.

Dear Crawfie,

Malta is wonderful. A home from home. I can go out and about as I like and no one bothers me. The other naval wives have been very sweet and helpful. I know the best places for fish, vegetables and fresh bread. Twice a week I go to the market where I can get huge bunches of fresh flowers for next to nothing. They brighten the house.

My driver is a sweet woman, Petty Officer Blake WRNS. She's very smart. I remember you wanting to wear the Women's Royal Naval uniform and you were right – it is far nicer than the ATS one that I had.

I have a cook and a housekeeper, and two policemen of course, but I am learning how to iron Philip's shirts almost as well as Bobo.

Philip is very happy and when he is happy, so am I.

I have some news for you.

Crawfie stopped reading. Her eyes had run ahead of her lips to news that was utterly confidential.

George urged her on. 'What is the news?'

Crawfie skipped over the next two lines and continued:

We are going on a picnic at the weekend, on a pleasure boat. Philip wants to show off his water-skiing abilities. But obviously I will not be joining him.

'Why not?' George said, with a laugh. 'Doesn't want to get her bloody hair wet?'

'George! Language.'

'Oh dear. Sorry, I forget. You not only dress like an off-duty queen – you sound like one too. Queen Marion.'

Crawfie quickly folded the letter and popped it in her bag, trying to ignore the pang of hurt his comment gave her. 'I had better get off. See you later.'

'You haven't touched your porridge.'

'It's lovely, darling, but I must go.' She kissed his head and closed the door.

Outside, she took a big breath of fresh air. It was a fine May morning and the walk to Buckingham Palace would be a pleasurable one, especially now that she had such a secret to think about.

Lilibet was expecting a baby. Due in November. She would come home to have the baby and then share her time between here and Valletta.

Crawfie hugged the news to herself. If only Alah could know.

Maybe Crawfie could be governess to the new arrival? But it would be years away before the child would be ready for the schoolroom, and George was already pestering her to stop working.

After his illness at Christmas, he had left the bank. He was still not back to his usual self. They had been very generous with a lump sum redundancy payment and a decent enough pension.

Her own work at the Palace was slowing down. She no longer needed to stay overnight, which George was very happy about. He liked knowing she was at home, even if he was out.

Crawfie knew that the end of her career was approaching. Princess Margaret had totally outgrown the need for the schoolroom or a chaperone. She now ran with a fast set of wealthy and fashionable friends. Crawfie was not sure she approved; they liked to party until the early hours and stay in bed until noon; they were always playing silly pranks, like daring to knock off a policeman's helmet.

Crawfie was beginning to feel unwanted on voyage. Her time was coming to an end.

But she had her little cottage, a husband, her health. There was no sign of the longed-for baby yet but she still had time. She tried not to feel a little sad at the thought of Lilibet's coming child.

The plane trees of Hyde Park were in fresh leaf, their smooth bark bright in the sun. She slowed her pace. She had no need to hurry. On the Serpentine, toddlers with their nannies threw bread to the ducks, while dogs tumbled and chased each other happily.

The rumble of Constitution Hill reached her ears as she went through Green Park – and bumped straight into Tommy.

'I'm so sorry,' they both said at once, before realizing who they were each speaking to.

'Oh, Miss Crawford.'

'Tommy.'

'On your way to the Palace as well?'

'Yes.'

'We may as well walk together.'

They walked in silence for some moments. Tommy was remembering how he had tried to warn her against marrying the Buthlay chap. Crawfie, meanwhile, was thinking of the anger she still felt, and the unsettling worry nagging at her that maybe she should have listened.

She tried to push the thought away. Yes, perhaps George drank a little too much, and his illness made him restless and irritable, but surely they were just going through a difficult patch. She loved George, and he loved her.

'I trust married life is working well for you,' Tommy said.

'Yes, thank you,' she returned with feigned joie de vivre. 'And how is Lady Lascelles?'

'Very well.'

'Good.'

On the edge of the park, they crossed the road to the Palace and its gates.

The policeman nodded. 'Morning sir, ma'am.'

'Good morning, constable.'

'Lovely day.'

'Indeed, sir, ma'am.'

They continued walking. As they reached the doors, Tommy turned to her suddenly. 'Miss Crawford, I regret the things I said at our last meeting. Please accept my apology. It was wrong of me and none of my business. And I am happy to see that I was wrong.'

Crawfie was startled. She looked at her shoes, then at the sky and finally at Tommy. 'It was terrible of you. Hurtful and horrid. But I accept your apology.'

'Thank you.' He smiled with pained relief. 'Perhaps I could take you to lunch to make it up to you?'

'When?'

'Today?'

She hesitated, then smiled. 'Thank you. I should like that very much.'

As it was such a beautiful day, Tommy suggested that they eat at the small café by the Serpentine.

'We can watch the ducks,' he said, 'and I do so like to hear the birds singing.'

A table came free just as they arrived, with a good view of the boating lake while having the benefit of a little shade. They sat down opposite one another.

'I love eating outside,' Crawfie told him. 'I always feel as if I am on holiday.'

'I know what you mean.'

The waitress brought them the menu: soup, omelettes, sandwiches or Cheddar ploughman's.

'What will you have, Crawfie?'

'I would like the ploughman's.'

Tommy turned to the waitress. 'Two ploughman's and I think a small jug of beer for us to share?' He raised his eyebrows at Crawfie for her confirmation.

'Perfect,' she replied.

Crawfie had been a little apprehensive about their lunch together, but the conversation was easy and light between them. The awkwardness and upset of the last few months had dissipated. It was very good to see him again. They were unlikely friends but true friends, platonic in every sense.

'Bring the bread you didn't eat,' Tommy told her, as he settled the bill. 'We'll walk around the lake and feed the ducks.'

Arriving back at the Palace later, they saw a large car, driver in full livery, on its way out. Tommy took Crawfie's elbow and guided her out of the way, but the car stopped and Lady Astor peered out of the car's back window.

'Tommy!' she called. 'And Miss Crawford, too. This is a very fortunate meeting. Do wait a moment.' She leant forwards to stop her driver. 'Turn around, would you? I shall stay a little longer.'

Tommy sighed. 'Oh Lord.'

Lady Astor corralled both Tommy and Crawfie into an empty side room.

'Miss Crawford,' she began.

'Yes?' said Crawfie, wondering what this was all about.

'We think you would be the person to share a few harmless anecdotes about the royal family in an article for a magazine.'

Tommy intercepted. 'And who would *we* be?'

Lady Astor was pleased with her reply. 'The Queen and the Foreign Office.'

Tommy shook his head. 'Lady Astor, nothing will happen without it first coming across my desk, and my current position is an emphatic *refusal*.'

'Excuse me,' Crawfie said, looking between the two of them. 'What on earth is this about?'

*

'I can see the benefits to them, but what about you?' George said that evening. They were sitting at the dinner table, and he had been listening to Marion's news. 'Will they pay you?'

'Oh George, I don't want paying, I am happy to help. My name won't be on any of the stories and they will only be short recollections for a little article in a magazine that no one in Britain will ever read.'

'Don't be so sure. Has this sort of thing been done before?'

'I don't think so.'

'In that case, your wee stories will be worth a lot of money.'

'I don't want any . . .'

'You say that now, my dear, but I can smell hocus pocus here.' He scratched his chin. 'Someone will be making a lot of money or they wouldn't be interested in it.'

Marion shrugged her shoulders. 'Mr and Mrs Gould want to meet me. They have asked if I could do the day after tomorrow.'

'Then I shall come with you, to make sure no one is taking advantage of your goodwill.' George emptied the glass by his side. 'Have we any more whisky?'

'I don't think so. Sorry, I should have bought some for you.'

'In that case' – George rocked himself out of his chair – 'I'm off to the pub. Don't wait up.'

Chapter Fifty-Seven

The Ritz Hotel Piccadilly, May 1948

Bruce Gould, journalist and proprietor of the bestselling American magazine, the *Ladies' Home Journal*, was checking himself in the cheval mirror of his hotel suite.

'Honey?' he called.

'Yes, sweetie?' His wife, Beatrice, came out of the bedroom. 'Oh my, you look very handsome.' She went to him and smoothed the shoulders of his well-tailored suit. 'When did you get so adorable?'

He smiled at her reflection. 'You can still say that, after all these years?'

'Sure I can. Now, would you do up my zipper?'

'I love this dress,' he said. 'Now turn around.' He zipped her up.

Together they stood side by side, looking at themselves in the mirror. They were both in their early fifties. Beatrice, with her slender figure, her well-preserved face, her hair dyed jet black and rolled into tight curls, was the perfect image of a successful New York woman, who balanced work with her wifely duties effortlessly. Bruce was still athletic-looking, tall, balding, but with an honest, open face that had stolen the trust of many. He was good at making money and was not ashamed to admit it. He also made it for those he exploited, so who was complaining?

He watched as Beatrice painted on her coral lipstick.

'You've still got it, honey.'

'Right back at you, handsome.'

There was a knock at the door.

'That'll be room service. I asked them to bring some coffee and cookies and stock up the cocktail bar.'

Marion and George had walked to the Ritz and were climbing the front steps. A uniformed doorman opened the door for them and Marion, who had been there before, walked straight to reception, quickly followed by George.

'May I help you?' the young woman on duty enquired.

George answered. 'Mr and Mrs Gould are expecting us, I believe. Major and Mrs Buthlay.'

'Oh yes, sir. Take the lift to the top floor. Their suite is the first door on the left.'

'Do I look all right?' Marion asked nervously, as they got into the lift.

George, without looking, said, 'Top floor, please.'

The lift boy answered for him. 'You look very nice, madam.'

George gave the boy a dangerous look. 'And you look like a pansy.'

'George, please!' Marion was mortified.

She hadn't wanted George to come with her at all. 'It's just a meeting to see if we like each other,' she'd said, earlier that day. 'I will be fine on my own.'

'I'm not good enough for you? Is that it?' George had said, pushing his florid face in to hers so that she could smell last night's alcohol.

'No, dear, but I think you need to rest. You still don't look very well, and . . .'

'You are worried I will embarrass you in front of your posh friends?'

'No, dear, not at all.'

'Then get out of my way.' He had shoved her so hard that she almost fell. 'Where the hell is my good suit?'

The lift boy, now crimson, pressed the button to the top floor. He kept his eyes fixed on the door.

'Top floor.'

George stepped out. Behind him Marion mouthed 'sorry' to the poor boy.

The first door on the left had a sign that read THE PICCADILLY SUITE. George pushed Marion forward. 'Well, knock on it then.'

The room they walked into was grander than any of the rooms in the royal homes Crawfie had seen. It dripped with fresh paint, gold embellishments and the very last word in stylish furniture. It was all *new*. She almost lost her footing on the deeply tufted carpet.

'Miss Crawford, how very nice to meet you.' Beatrice's welcome was warm.

'Mrs Gould, thank you for seeing me.'

'Beatrice, please. And may I call you Marion or even . . .' She laughed a little, clutching her pearls. 'Crawfie?'

'Either is fine. May I introduce my husband, Major George Buthlay?'

'Lovely to meet you, George, and this is my husband, Bruce.'

'How do you do, George?' The men shook hands. 'Can I fix you a coffee or maybe something stronger?' Bruce asked.

George's eyes gleamed. 'Scotch and ice, please.'

'On the rocks? Nice. I'll join you.'

Marion accepted a coffee before each couple arranged themselves on the two sofas. A coffee table stood between them.

'So, Marion.' Beatrice set the ball rolling. 'Do you know just what the Queen thinks of you? She adores you.'

Marion felt herself relax. 'She is a wonderful person.'

'She is! And Lady Astor too. She was the one who recommended you for this little enterprise.'

George finished his drink and Bruce quickly refilled it. 'Thank you, Bruno,' he said.

Bruce raised an eyebrow. 'It's Bruce.'

George nodded. 'Bruce, of course. Now, what my wife needs to know is, what exactly is this little enterprise?'

Beatrice sat back. 'Oh, it is going to be just wonderful. I will let Bruce explain.'

Bruce looked at Marion with admiration. 'Crawfie – and this is so important – you hold in your hands the love of the royal Princesses and the King and Queen of Britain. In America we are so darn jealous of your British history. We really want to get a little bit of it. We adore your royal family, and when Princess Elizabeth got married to her Duke – well, we couldn't get enough of it.'

Beatrice put her hand on her husband's knee. 'We got up so early to watch it on television. I mean, it was still dark outside. And it was so beautiful. We would have loved to have been there, wouldn't we, Bruce?'

'We *were* there,' George told them.

'Oh my God! You were there? You saw everything?' Beatrice's eyes were wide with the thrill.

'Yes,' Marion said. 'It was wonderful.'

'My wife went to the wedding breakfast,' George boasted. 'Unfortunately I had to work.'

'*No!*' Beatrice looked as if she were in heaven.

'Oh yes,' said Marion. 'In fact, the night before, she came up to the nursery and had a long chat with me and Bobo. Bobo is her personal dresser but used to be the nurserymaid. She's a dear. In fact, it was Bobo who took her tea tray in the next morning. She was the first person to see the Princess on her wedding day.'

'This is *wonderful*,' Beatrice said breathily. 'Bruce, don't you think this is wonderful?'

'It's – it's incredible.' Bruce grinned at his wife. 'Quite incredible. And did you speak to the Princess on the morning of her wedding, Crawfie?'

'Yes, it was quite funny really. She had mislaid the pearl necklace she wanted to wear and no one could find it, but then we realized it might be at St James's Palace because it had been sent there to have its clasp fixed. So, I ran out of the Palace, down the Mall, through all the crowds, found it and brought it back.'

Bruce and Beatrice locked eyes with each other and nodded. 'Miss Crawford, these are the stories that the American public would cherish. You know we love you all in the States, right? But this kind of stuff will make America worship your royal family and the whole of Great Britain.'

Crawfie suddenly worried she might have said too much. 'I would need the Queen's approval before I say anything,' she said carefully.

'Of course, that's no problem. We wouldn't want you to get into trouble, would we?' Beatrice gave a tinkling laugh, which went some way to allaying Crawfie's unease.

George had finished his second glass of whisky, but Bruce did not get him another, which irritated him. He did his best deals after a few whiskies – always had done, especially at the bank. A decent lunch with a new customer always managed to fatten the bank's coffers.

Unfortunately, one such client, a wealthy widow, had complained to his bosses after he had clumsily felt her thigh under the table, and under her skirt. He was almost sacked on the spot, until he explained that to sack the husband of the royal family's governess, when the royal family held prodigious accounts at the bank, was not a good idea. He got away with a decent pension and a lump sum of 'redundancy pay'. If anybody asked, he said he had left on account of his health.

Now, sitting in this swanky hotel suite, with two wealthy business people who wanted his Marion, he smelt the dollars. He had sat and listened long enough. It was time for him to take control.

'Would you be paying my wife for her stories?'

Beatrice momentarily dropped her smile, but quickly picked it up again. 'Certainly. I understand that you have not been married long. A sum to help you with your new life together would of course be paid.'

George was pleased. He had set his marker down and these two swindlers would recognize it. He wasn't a man to be messed with. 'I look forward to opening our negotiations.' He stood up. 'Thank you for your hospitality.'

'It has been our pleasure.' Bruce shook George's hand. 'We shall be in touch. It's good to know, in principle, that Mrs Buthlay is on board.'

'As long as I have the explicit permission of the Queen,' Marion repeated.

Beatrice smiled, and came to hug Marion. 'My dear, we can't wait to get started. Bruce and I are returning to the States tomorrow and we will get the ball rolling. It may take a few months before we can come back to England. We have a lot to organize!'

Outside on the pavement, George looped his arm through Marion's. 'You were fantastic in there – you way you hooked them in. They can't wait to get their greedy little hands all over you. And they will pay. You, my dear, are an unmined asset.'

Marion was nervous. 'I don't want to make trouble, George.'

He smiled at her. 'Trouble? This could be the end of all our troubles.'

Chapter Fifty-Eight

Nottingham Cottage, 5ᵗʰ June 1948

In the kitchen, Crawfie was making her morning cup of tea. George was sleeping off a late night and she was grateful to have some peace before he woke up – grumpy, more often than not.

She opened the back door onto the garden. The sun was warming up and the early birds were chattering around her bird table.

Wrapping her dressing gown securely around her, Marion picked up her tea, stepped out of her slippers and walked barefoot across her lovingly tended lawn, to say good morning to her flowers.

The purple lavender, pink peony, sweetly scented heliotrope and tall white lupins had become her babies. 'Good morning, everyone.' She smiled at them. 'What a lovely morning.' She studied them for greenfly and droop, then settled herself on the small bench under a cherry tree. She closed her eyes and focused on what she could hear, smell, feel. This had become part of her daily routine. The garden was sheltered and hard for anyone to see her. She ran her toes over the grass. Her skin on the cool earth felt good. She opened her eyes and studied her hands. Short clean nails, tendons showing clearly, freckled.

'Happy birthday,' she said to them.

She heard the telephone ringing inside and knew it would be her mother. She wondered whether George might pick it up or let it ring. She wasn't in the mood to hear her mother's opinion on being forty. Marion stood up. If she didn't answer it, no one would.

'I was about to hang up. Where were you?'

'Good morning, Mother. I was making tea for George and me.'

'How is he?'

'He's fine, Mother.'

'I hope you are looking after him?'

Marion rubbed her forehead in despair. 'Why do you always ask me that?'

'Because you work too much and a man needs to know he's cherished and needed.'

Marion wanted to scream down the telephone that wives need to feel cherished and needed too, but all she said was, 'Nice of you to ring to me up.'

'Well, thirty-nine years since I gave birth to you is a big day. One I shall never forget. Sick every day carrying you, I was – even on the delivery table. And you never slept. I remember making your father promise me that we wouldn't have any more children.'

'You tell me that every birthday, Mother.'

'And now you are nearly forty, and there's little chance of children of your own.'

Marion lifted her gaze, looking out through her kitchen window. She could see the sun on the lawn and a blackbird hopping in the grass, looking for worms – like her mother constantly pecking at her, sucking the life out of her.

'How's Dad?'

'In the garden, of course, picking over his tomato plants. He is even thinking of digging a *pond!* I said to him, what do we need a pond for? And he said it would be something peaceful to look at. Peaceful, I said? With rats running in and out of it?'

Marion felt drained. 'Do you have rats?'

'No, but we will. You mark my words.'

She sighed. 'Mother, why are you phoning me?'

'To see that you got my presents.'

'They came yesterday. I have them here. Delightful.' She looked over at the three lace doilies on the kitchen table. 'Very pretty.'

'I wish you had rung up yesterday to let me know they'd been delivered.'

'Mother, I have to go. Thank you so much for the doilies and for telephoning. Send my love to Dad. Goodbye.' She put the phone down, slumped into a kitchen chair and laid her head on the cool of the table.

She would have stayed like that all day if she could, but she heard George's footsteps above and the flush of the lavatory, so she pulled herself together and began to make breakfast.

George was never his best in the morning, and today was no exception, but she knew what irritated him and what didn't. Appeasement was becoming her middle name.

'Good morning, dear.' She smiled brightly. 'Sit down and I'll bring you your breakfast. Full Scottish?'

By lunchtime, fed and watered, George was in a much better state, and insisted that he take her to the pub for a birthday lunch.

She agreed as if it were the very best of ideas.

She was expecting to be taken to his local on Kensington High Street. She heard a lot about the friends he had made there, and she didn't think she liked the sound of any of them. But he surprised her, pleasantly, by suggesting a small pub on the Thames.

'We can sit outside in the beer garden and watch the pleasure boats go by. Let's walk.'

'How thoughtful.' She smiled. 'Thank you.'

He took her hand as they walked and was more like the old George. Marion began to relax. 'Mother called this morning.'

'Did she?'

'She wanted to know if I was looking after you.'

He chuckled. 'Bless your mother.'

'Mm. She said that now I am a year away from forty, there would be no hope of having children.'

He winked. 'We'll prove her wrong.'

'George, would you really like a child?'

He squeezed her hand. 'I'd like to talk to you about that. I think the reason why it hasn't happened yet is because of the long hours you work. You are always so tired. You have given everything to that family but the time has come for you to leave them.'

Marion started, taken aback. 'What?'

'My dear, perhaps it's time that you retire.'

'I don't think I can—'

'Oh yes you can. You have worked with them for eighteen years and never put yourself first.'

'There was the abdication and the war and—'

'Ssh.' He stopped walking and put an index finger to her lips. 'No more. It's time for you and me to put us, and our future family, first. I had an overseas call from Bruce Gould in the week.'

'You didn't say.'

'You were at work.' He shrugged. 'But the point is, I have been discussing your contract.'

'Oh, George. Do we have to have contracts? It's just a few little anecdotes.'

'Be that as it may, those few anecdotes will be read by thousands of people who will buy thousands of copies of his magazine. The magazine will make a lot of money. And you deserve a share of that. In fact, Bruce gave me the impression that it will be a nice little nest egg, which, with our pensions, will take us nicely into old age.'

Marion looked at her husband. He was tricky, difficult, sometimes cruel, but on days like this he was the man she had fallen in love with all those years ago. He had stood by her for over a decade, faithful and long-suffering.

He put his arm around her waist and hugged her to him. 'What do you say? This is for your own good. I like having you at home with me. I miss you when you're at work. We could spend days out like this whenever we wanted.'

'Oh George, you really have been thinking about this, haven't you?'

'I don't like seeing you tired and running around after them. We need more time for each other.'

'Let me think about it.' She kissed him, his little moustache tickling, which made her smile.

'You haven't kissed me like that for a long time,' he said tenderly. 'Maybe we will get the baby we want sooner than we thought.'

'Oh, George.' She lightly smacked his hand.

'But first, we are going to walk up to Westminster Pier and catch a cruise along the Thames. I might even buy you an ice cream.' He tucked his arm through hers. 'Happy Birthday, Mrs Buthlay.'

Chapter Fifty-Nine

Buckingham Palace, September 1948

'Her Majesty will see you now.'

The liveried footman opened the door to the Queen's drawing room. The Queen was in a lilac tea dress, sitting at her desk and looking at a set of photographs. She looked up.

'Crawfie, do come in. Mr Cecil Beaton has taken some new pictures of the King and me. I think they are very good but it is so hard to choose.'

'You photograph very well, ma'am.'

'You would say that because you are a dear.' She shuffled the photographs neatly, then stood up and walked to the two sofas either side of the empty fireplace. 'Do sit down.' She sighed. 'I have received and read your letter of resignation and I quite understand your reasons. Princess Margaret is utterly done with education and is . . . spreading her wings, shall we say?'

'She is certainly a vibrant young woman. Naturally she wants to have some fun.'

'She misses Lilibet terribly, but is very excited about becoming an aunt.'

'She will be a wonderful aunt. And how is Lilibet?'

'She is doing very well. Married life in Malta suits her, but of course she will come home soon for the birth.'

'She will need you.'

'Possibly, although perhaps I may be more of a hindrance than a help.' She smiled, cocking her head like a bird. 'Queen

Mary is jubilant to think she will be a great-grandmother.' She clasped her hands to her knees, her diamond rings sparkling. 'Crawfie, you have been marvellous here, and we shall be very sorry to see you go.'

'I shall be sorry to leave. It has been my privilege to serve you and to share some wonderful times.'

The Queen nodded in agreement, then added warily, 'I hear you have met Mr and Mrs Gould – the American publishers?'

'Yes.'

'And that you are to share with them some light stories of your time with us?'

'Well, yes – if you are happy for me to do so.'

'I can trust you not to discuss anything too personal, I am sure.'

'You can, ma'am.'

'And you understand that you are to be entirely anonymous? Your name must not appear anywhere.'

'I do understand that, yes.'

'It might not seem as if you are doing anything of great service to the King, but my dear, it will help him a lot. My husband and I wish to share our gratitude with the American people for all they did for us in the war. Our two countries have a special relationship, both personally and politically, and I am persuaded that Mr and Mrs Gould's popular magazine will demonstrate our feelings.'

'I see.' Marion was both flattered and worried. 'You will be reading everything that I offer them before publication, won't you?'

'Lady Astor will make sure of it.'

Marion smiled. 'That makes me feel so much better.'

'Just one more thing before you go.' The Queen hesitated. 'The King knows nothing about this yet.'

The Good Servant

Buckingham Palace, October 1949

'Come in, my dear, come in.' Tommy beamed as Crawfie came into his office. 'Sit down and tell me how you are.'

Crawfie took the seat he had offered. 'I must say, now that the decision has been taken and accepted, I am rather looking forward to retirement. George was the catalyst.'

'Was he? Gentle persuasion rather than an arm up the back, I hope?' Tommy chuckled at the thought.

'No. Of course not.' Crawfie was immediately on the defensive. 'What makes you think that?'

Tommy was surprised at her reaction. 'Just a silly figure of speech.'

'George is thinking only of me.'

'Good. Good.' He smiled. 'I expect you are wondering why I have called you in?'

'A little.'

'It would not normally be something I would deal with but I wanted to make sure that your retirement settlement was done properly. Therefore, I have made it my business to oversee the paperwork.' He picked up a sheet of paper from his desk and passed it to her. 'This is your pension.'

Crawfie looked at the figures carefully. 'This is more than I expected.'

'Don't worry, you haven't been given special treatment. You have earned it. As a long-serving member of the household, that is your rightful due.'

'Thank you.' Marion smiled, thinking how pleased George would be.

Tommy was passing her a second piece of paper. 'And this states that Nottingham Cottage is granted to you in the grace and favour of Their Majesties and is yours until you shuffle off this mortal coil.'

Crawfie frowned slightly. 'And if I were to die before my husband, would he be able to stay until his death?'

Tommy spread his hands. 'Ah, that is always a tricky one. But I think, in your circumstances and providing you don't fall under a bus, Major Buthlay, being your senior, may pop off before you do.'

'You can't guarantee he could stay?'

'In short, no. Same for us all.'

She looked down at the paper solemnly. 'I see.'

'I can tell you are discomfited by that, but, moving on, and this is strictly hush-hush, the Queen has in mind a token of her appreciation for you. I can say no more, but do monitor your post box for the next couple of weeks.' He folded his hands. 'Now, how about a catch-up over a cup of tea?'

Nottingham Cottage, the same day

'George?' Marion shut the front door and took her coat off. 'George? I'm home!'

She walked through to the kitchen, where the back door was open onto the garden. 'George?'

George was sitting on the bench under the tree, a bottle of Scotch on the grass and a full tumbler in his hand. He was trying to focus on her. 'Where the hell have you been?'

'At work.' She went to him. 'Are you all right?'

'You're late.'

Crawfie recognized stormy waters ahead. 'Yes, I met up with Tommy. He was giving me all the details of my pension and the tenure of our little home.'

'You are a bloody hour late. Having it off with him, are you?'

'No! You know I would never be unfaithful to you.'

'Oh, that's what they all say but I know. I can see it in your eyes.' George lurched towards her and sniffed her collar.

She pushed him away. 'What are you doing?'

'I can smell him on you.'

Her pulse began to race in fear. 'Please, George. Don't go getting yourself in one of your states. You need a cup of tea and a sleep. It's been a hot day and you have had just a little too much to drink.' She took his arm and tried to lift him onto his feet.

'Let go of me, you!'

'Shh. People can hear you.'

'They need to know what you are really like.'

'Darling, please.' She tried again to lift him, but he swung his left fist at her and punched her in the ribs.

Marion fell painfully on her side. She didn't think her ribs were broken; she knew what broken ribs felt like. 'Please stop, George,' she said, her voice shaking.

'Not the bloody waterworks. Get up, you silly cow.'

She rose slowly to her feet. 'I have a pork chop for your supper. I am going in to cook it now. I will call you when it's ready.'

The next morning, Marion woke early. She winced when she turned over to check the alarm clock – 6.30. It was a beautiful day by the look of the light creeping around the edges of her curtains. George was next to her, out cold.

If she had any tears left, she would cry.

But what good would that do?

She was married to a man who liked a drink and when he was drunk, and sometimes sober, he liked to lash out. She shouldn't have stayed the extra hour with Tommy. It was her fault. Poor George had a jealous streak.

Her body felt sore. With the aid of the bedside table, she stumbled to her feet and silently got herself ready for work.

She made sure she got home early that night.

George was waiting for her, sober and sheepish, with a bunch of roses in one hand and a letter in the other.

She tested the water. 'Hello, dear. How are you?'

'Ashamed.'

She shook herself out of her coat. 'No need.'

'These are for you.' He offered her the flowers, looking as anxious and sweet as a seven-year-old boy.

Her heart softened, as it always did. 'Thank you.'

'I am so sorry. I don't remember anything that happened yesterday. Marion, listen to me – I am not well. I have been very sick today. I think it's my kidneys. I have an infection.'

Marion knew he was looking for sympathy, while batting away the obvious. 'Well, we had better go back to the doctor, hadn't we?'

'And this came for you.' He handed her the envelope – it was thick and cream, with the royal cipher stamped in red. 'It's from the Queen.'

'I can see that.'

'Will you read it to me?'

He groaned as he sat down, and she rubbed the small of his back. Her ribs were still sore from yesterday, but she said nothing. She opened the envelope and slid out the single sheet of paper.

My dear Crawfie,

The King and I wish to show our great appreciation for the service you have given us over so many years.

It is in our special gift to recommend that you be made Commander of the Victorian Order to show you the gratitude you deserve and the esteem in which we hold you.

You will be invested on 15th March next year in the Ballroom of Buckingham Palace. Three guests may be invited.

King George VI Elizabeth R

Chapter Sixty

Nottingham Cottage, 8th March 1949

'I have nothing to wear!' Maggie bleated down the telephone. 'Mother, why don't you come down a couple of days early and we can go shopping?'

'There's nothing in London that can't be bought here in Dunfermline. Hats are expensive everywhere. I have seen a very nice green suit. What do you think? Will a suit be too warm? What will you be wearing?'

'I have a cream dress with a navy jacket and navy hat.'

'Oh no. If you are wearing blue, I can't wear green, can I!'

Marion was not going to allow her mother to spoil her joy at being given the CVO, so she just laughed. 'Mother, you will look gorgeous. Now, stop fretting and get yourselves down here. The spare room at Nott Cott is waiting for you.'

'Is George wearing a kilt, because if he is I will get your stepfather to hire one?'

'He might, but honestly, Dad can come in his gardening trousers for all I care. Now shush and I will see you next week. Bye, Mother.'

Buckingham Palace, 15th March 1949

Marion waited nervously in the corridor outside the ballroom with a line of equally quaking honourees. Her mother had almost driven her mad that morning, taking over the bathroom and the kitchen, then the only long mirror Marion had.

George and her stepfather were in full highland dress. Marion almost cried when she saw them. 'You would both do this for me?' Her voice had wobbled.

Robert grinned. 'Enjoy it while you can. I'll not be doing it again.'

And later, when Marion was ready and walking down the stairs, it was he who shed a tear. 'You look beautiful, Marion, love.'

Now, standing in the line, she thought of her parents and George seated in the ballroom and it reminded her of the school concerts they had come to when she was a girl, to watch her play the recorder or take part in a display of Scottish country dancing. And now, here she was, about to receive one of the highest awards a monarch could give to a member of his household.

'Marion?' Someone touched her elbow.

'Oh Tommy, I was miles away. What are you doing here?'

'I came just to wish you luck. You look awfully nice.'

'Thank you. Are you going to watch?'

'Sadly not. Lunch date with Joan.' He took her hand. 'Congratulations, Mrs Buthlay, CVO. Don't be a stranger.'

He pushed his way back through the line and disappeared.

And then it was her turn. The door in front of her was opened and the packed ballroom – the biggest room in the entire Palace – was before her. People were craning their heads to see who was coming in next.

She kept her eyes straight ahead as she walked the red carpet towards the dais and its two thrones, where the King was waiting for her.

The equerry by his side called out, 'Mrs Marion Buthlay, awarded Commander of the Victorian Order for service to the sovereign.'

Marion was sure she heard her mother say something but she kept her concentration on what was happening. This was a day she must not forget.

She curtsied to the King who, in a low voice, called her forward. 'Crawfie, thank you for devoting so much of your life to the Queen and me and the Princesses. We shall never forget you. Lilibet and Margaret send their congratulations.'

He pinned the beautiful insignia to her jacket as she beamed with pleasure.

Another shake of the hands, a curtsey, and then she was back out into a different corridor, catching her breath.

Outside the Palace, her parents and George were waiting for her.

Her mother hugged her tight. 'Oh Marion, to think I was in the same room as the King! I could see you were nervous though – your first curtsey was not as good as the second one.'

Marion laughed. 'Thank you, Mother.'

Her stepfather was waving his Brownie camera. 'Maggie, Marion, let's have a picture.' He clicked away before pushing George in. 'Now, one of the three of you. Smile!'

'I want one of all of us,' Maggie said and she grabbed a man going by. 'Would you mind taking a picture of us all, please?'

Marion cringed. 'Mother!'

'I don't mind,' said the stranger.

The celebration lunch was in a little Italian restaurant on Buckingham Gate. The table was small but welcoming. Maggie sat down with a sigh. 'I'm exhausted.'

Marion exchanged an amused glance with her dad, while the waiter appeared with a bottle of champagne. 'Congratulations, Mrs Buthlay. Your husband thought you might like this.'

Marion was moved. 'Did you?' she asked George.

'Aye. Nothing is too good for my wife today.'

She kissed him. 'Thank you.'

'I can't drink champagne,' Maggie told the waiter. 'It gives me a headache.'

'More for us!' Marion laughed.

Maggie rallied. 'I might have a drop. Just to keep you company.'

After four days, Maggie and Robert were put on the train back to Dunfermline, and as Marion waved the chugging train off, George tugged her sleeve. 'Thank God they're gone.'

'I'm sorry. Mother can be very tiring.'

'It makes me glad my parents are dead.'

'Oh George, don't say that!'

'You wouldn't disagree with me if you'd met them.' He sighed. 'Let's go home.'

Chapter Sixty-One

Nottingham Cottage, May 1949

'Look at your medal. It is *adorable*!' Beatrice Gould was standing in the drawing room of Nott Cott, staring at Marion's CVO on the mantelpiece. 'I love the red leather case it comes in. May I touch it?'

'Yes, do.' Marion liked it to be admired. 'The enamelling is exquisite, isn't it?'

'It is. Can I try it on? Hey, Bruce, come and look at this.'

'That's swell, honey. Congratulations,' Bruce said, coming in with a glass of whisky. 'George here has been telling me all about the ceremony. He is very proud of you, Marion.'

'I am!' George raised his glass of whisky. 'To you, Marion.'

Marion was dismayed to see George drinking. It was only four thirty in the afternoon. The doctor had advised that George didn't drink at all for six months because his liver was showing signs of inflammation. He had been very good since the last time, but now here he was, glass in hand and already slightly glassy-eyed. She would have to tread very carefully tonight.

'I must say your house is wonderful,' Bruce was saying. 'So old and quaint.'

'Darling, it was designed by Sir Christopher Wren!' Beatrice told him.

George went to his armchair and settled in. Marion saw an opened bottle of Scotch at his side. 'Well, he was a bloody awful

435

plumber. You never know if the water is going to be freezing or bloody boiling.' He glanced at Marion. 'Have you shown Bruce the letter you had?'

'Not yet.'

'Well, get it.'

Marion went to the small desk, one of the pieces Queen Mary had given her, and took an envelope from one of the small drawers.

'Read it out,' George ordered.

'It's a letter from the Queen,' she told them, and hesitated before reading it aloud:

My dear Crawfie,

We look upon you now and always as a true and trustworthy friend. I can never tell you how grateful I am for all your devotion and love for Lilibet and Margaret. It was such a relief to me during the war to know that they were by your side through sirens, bombs and pantomimes, keeping everything cool and balanced and good-humoured. Thank you with all my heart.

Now you will be able to devote more time to the hub of your universe, your husband and your home.

She folded the letter and saw Bruce and Beatrice staring, their mouths open.

'Oh my God, that's so wonderful and insightful.' Beatrice gasped. 'What do you say, Bruce, honey?'

'Incredible. That is the Queen of England giving you permission to share some of your stories, because she trusts you.'

Crawfie shook her head. 'No, it is not that.'

'But you have spoken to her about your work with us?' Beatrice asked.

'Yes, I have and she was most definite when she asked me not to have my name associated in any way with the articles. They must remain anonymous.'

'Exactly as we agreed with Lady Astor, who has spoken to the Queen as well.' Bruce was at his most avuncular. 'So you see, we have double confirmation now.'

Marion looked over at George for support. 'What do you think?'

George winked one of his red eyes at her. 'I think we have a deal.'

Immediately the Goulds snapped into business mode. 'That's terrific. We will get a copy of a contract over to you to take a look at as soon as we get back to the States.'

Bruce shook George's hand, and Beatrice put her arm around Marion's shoulder.

'In the meantime,' she said, 'I am going to bring back with me one of my dearest friends. She will type every story you tell her so that you don't have to. You just talk naturally, telling her the stories, as you would to a friend, and she takes it all down. Simple.' She let go of Marion and reached for her handbag. 'OK, you guys. We'll leave you in peace and see you very soon. We'll let ourselves out.'

Marion followed them to the door and waved them off.

She couldn't shake off the doubts she had. She trusted the Goulds and the Queen trusted her, and Lady Astor wouldn't involve herself in anything that was wrong but . . . it didn't feel right. She walked back into the drawing room.

'George, do you think this is going to be all right?'

George had given up any pretence of being sober and was now draped in his chair, emptying the remains of the whisky bottle into his glass. 'All right? It'll be better than that. That stuck-up bitch you call boss is going to get what's coming to her.'

'George! Don't speak about the Queen like that. She has been so wonderful to us.'

'Ha!' He jerked his hand to punctuate a point, slopping his drink down his shirt. 'What has she ever done for me? Eh? Kept me away from you for over eleven years, that's what. And left me to spend my last years with you in a house that should be condemned. What's so bloody wonderful about that?'

'George, you don't mean that.' She tried to appease him. 'We have so much to be thankful for. A roof over our heads, an income and my CVO.'

George carefully stood up and swayed over to the mantelpiece, where her medal was shining in its box. 'This,' he slurred, holding it up in front of her face, 'this is a piece of shit. Fairground tat. You are worth so much more than this and I am going to make sure you get it.'

Nottingham Cottage, July 1949

Marion had mistakenly thought retirement would mean a slower pace of life. How wrong she was.

At least three days a week, she received a telegram from the Goulds in New York:

MORE DETAIL ON MRS WALLIS SIMPSON STOP

HAS HIS MAJESTY MET UP WITH HIS BRO DUKE OF WINDSOR? STOP

WHAT WAS REACTION IN UK WHEN US TROOPS JOINED WAR? STOP

She was scared stiff each time the knocker went.
And on top of that, George was unwell.

'Major Buthlay, how much do you drink every day?' the doctor asked.
Marion glanced anxiously at George.
'Just a wee dram before bed. Helps me to sleep.'
Marion held her tongue but couldn't help her worried expression. The doctor saw it.
'Would you agree with that, Mrs Buthlay?'
Marion sidestepped the question. 'He has trouble sleeping sometimes.'

The doctor pursed his lips in doubt and continued to examine George. 'Look at the colour of your eyes. They should be white, not yellow. Have you noticed that?'

'I had malaria serving overseas in the last war. It flares up.'

'Hmmm.' The doctor reached for his stethoscope. 'Take your shirt off please, and lie down on the couch.'

Marion stood by George and took his hand, which he immediately snatched away. 'I am not a child! There is nothing wrong with me.'

Marion made room for the doctor, who pressed George's abdomen.

'Ow!'

'Does that hurt?'

'No.'

'How about this?' He pressed again.

George gasped.

'You have lost some weight since I last saw you and yet your abdomen is rather swollen.'

Marion spoke. 'He has lost his appetite recently.'

'Hmm.' The doctor inspected George's feet, ankles and calves. 'Oedema in lower leg. Do you take much exercise?'

'Oh yes. Marion and I walk every day.'

The doctor glanced at Marion for confirmation.

'We haven't walked so much for a couple of weeks. He gets tired very quickly.'

'Aye,' George said, 'because I don't sleep well at night. I have told you that.'

'Indeed.' The doctor returned to his desk. 'You can get dressed now, but I am sending you for a blood test. Come back next week for the results and in the meantime, no alcohol.'

George got dressed, and he and Marion left with a blood test form and directions to the phlebotomy unit.

They walked in silence until Marion spotted an arrow pointing to PHLEBOTOMY.

'We go left here, George.'

'I am not having a damn blood test. We're going home.'

'But George!' The anxiety that lived permanently in Marion's stomach rose up. 'You have to. Please.'

'I am going home. I need a drink.'

There was a furious row over George's determination not to return to the hospital or give up drinking. Marion felt helpless. She wanted to help him, but his anger, resulting in her getting a black eye one Sunday evening, meant that she decided to ignore the problem.

It was a heavy secret to hold. It ate her up each day and night. The only thing that calmed him was talk of the Goulds and their money.

They had wired to say they were on their way and would be at Nottingham Cottage in three days. Beatrice's friend, the stenographer who would type every word Marion said, was coming with them.

Chapter Sixty-Two

Buckingham Palace, August 1949

Tommy bowed as he entered. 'How may I help you, ma'am?'

'Tommy, I fear that I may have been misunderstood on something.' The Queen dabbed her nose nervously with an exquisite lace handkerchief.

'How may I help?'

'I think Miss Crawford, in whom I had the utmost trust, could be selling stories about the children to an American magazine.'

'Ah.'

'It was suggested to me by Lady Astor. She mentioned that the Foreign Office were keen to improve our popularity in the United States. I talked to the King last night about it and, well, let us say we had words. I explained that I had done nothing other than to listen to Lady Astor and meet with Miss Crawford, but there was no talk of *selling* stories. I need you to explain to Miss Crawford yourself that it is simply out of the question.'

Tommy knew that the Queen was being a little economical with the truth and could only imagine the King's fury. He himself had been on the other end of one of the monarch's tirades and he knew how unpleasant they were.

After a moment's thinking, he said, 'Supposing I draft a letter explaining the mix up?'

'Oh yes, that would be most helpful.' The Queen looked reassured – and relieved.

'However' – Tommy coughed – 'the letter must be signed by you.'

'Me?'

'Yes, it will send a much clearer view of things than if I were to sign it.'

The Queen thought for a moment. 'I suppose it might.'

'It would, most definitely. I can draft something today.' He smiled. 'Nip it in the bud.'

'Dear Tommy. That is most kind and I would be grateful if you didn't mention it to the King until it is posted. Then I shall tell him myself.'

'Of course, ma'am.'

Buckingham Palace, the next day

The postman, a very inquisitive man, handed Marion the letter. 'Still keep in touch, I see. That's nice.'

Marion smiled, said 'Thank you,' and closed the door on him. Really, people were so nosy.

She opened the letter in happy anticipation.

My dear Crawfie,

After some conversation with my private secretary, Sir Alan Lascelles, I do feel most definitely that you should not write or sign any articles about the children. People in positions of confidence with us must be utterly oyster. You have been so wonderfully discreet for all the years you have been with us, and you would lose all your friends. I do hope you put all the American temptations aside, very firmly, and say no, no, no to any offers of dollars for something as private and precious as our family.

I know you will do the right thing.

Elizabeth R

Marion's heart almost leapt out of her chest. The Queen had discussed her situation with Tommy? She read the letter again and felt she could detect the parts written in Tommy's voice and the parts the Queen had added.

What was she going to do?

The Goulds were arriving tomorrow.

She would have to stop them.

George was in the kitchen making tea for them both, probably adding whisky to his. She had to show him the letter. He had had a little breakfast and this was the golden hour between his hangover and the next bout of drinking.

He read it and scowled. 'Insurance – that's all. She's covering her tracks. Don't worry about it. She wants the articles written or she wouldn't have asked you. Forget it.'

'It frightens me. I don't want to be in any trouble. Can we not just say no to the Goulds? It's not too late, is it?'

'Marion, it *is* too late. They will be here tomorrow, sitting in our wee drawing room, and you will give them all the stories that you have. You are not letting state secrets out. They can't drag you off to the Tower. It's 1949!'

She sat at the kitchen table, clasping her cup of tea. 'I feel awful. What does she mean, I won't have any friends?'

'As if Bobo and Sir Snooty wouldn't still be your pals! They will all still be there, just sorry they didn't have the chance to make a few quid themselves.'

'I hope that's true.'

George sat down next to her and took her hand. 'Darling, I have been meaning to say some things about that family, which I think you should hear.'

'What things?'

He took a deep breath. 'They have treated you appallingly from the start. They dictated your life. You and I could have been married years ago. We could have a wee family by now. Not only have they deprived you of your own children – they have deprived me of mine! And look at this house. It's totally unsuitable – it's a wreck. Even your mother told me it was.'

Marion stared at him. 'Not this again, George. I love it here and am so grateful. Mother said she liked it too.'

'She didn't want to burst your balloon. No, she doesn't like it. She feels sorry for you. Knows you deserve more. She says it needs pulling down and I have to agree with her. Look around you, Marion. The plumbing, the damp patch by the chimney, and the furniture foisted on you by the old lady!'

'Queen Mary was very generous.'

'No, she wasn't. She wanted to get rid of it and she couldn't very well take it down to a jumble sale, could she?'

'Don't say that. I like having her things.'

'Well, I don't. And what about the wedding presents? A coffee set we will never use, a dinner service which would be grand if we could fit more than four people round this table, or had a dining room, and a couple of table lamps? All of it is an insult considering how you have subjugated your life for them.'

Marion started to cry. 'That's not true. Please, George, don't say such things. I have been so happy. It was my job. They love me.'

'Do you think so?' He paused and reached into his trouser pocket for his handkerchief. 'Here. Wipe your eyes. You gave them your whole heart but they saw you coming.' He feigned a clipped English accent. '*Give her a hovel to live in, pay her a pauper's pension and, what fun, the final insult, give her a CVO.*'

'Don't say that! The CVO means so much to me. It is a very special honour to show their respect for my work.' She was finding it hard to get the words out through her tears.

'No, no, my love. You should have had a DCVO. Dame Commander of the Victorian Order. Not just Commander. They cheated you, gave you second best, as they always have. And that is why we are going to work with Bruce and Beatrice.'

Chapter Sixty-Three

Nottingham Cottage, September 1949

The little drawing room of Nott Cott was bulging with the five of them.

Dorothy Black, Beatrice's typist friend, had set her typewriter up on the Victorian gate-legged table, handed down to Crawfie by Queen Mary. Bruce was explaining how the articles would be written.

'Dorothy will be immensely helpful in crafting your memories. The Queen will love how our readers take to her.'

Beatrice pulled out a sheaf of news cuttings from her bag. 'If you are in any doubt, take a look at what the papers in the States are saying about her and the King. They do not make pretty reading.'

Marion scanned them. The headlines were unkind and anti-British as well as anti-royalist. She frowned. 'Is this what they really think?'

'I am afraid so. But they are ill-informed and unnecessarily hostile, don't you think?'

'I do.' Marion was shaken by them.

'Only you can write the truth and help your royal friends.'

'You have too much faith in me.'

'Don't you trust our journalistic experience?'

'I do, but . . .'

'Uh-uh, no buts. This your chance to tell the world what you know, and bring both our great nations together again. You know what?'

'What?'

'I have it on pretty high authority that the Queen herself will write a preface to these articles in her own handwriting.'

This made Crawfie brighten. 'Really?'

'Oh yes, honey.' Beatrice turned to Dorothy. 'OK, Bruce and I will leave you two together now. We have meetings in London and then Paris before we head back to New York. We'll be back in four weeks to pick up the manuscript.'

Bruce kissed Marion, then shook George's hand. 'We will have the contract ready to sign, with your amendments included. You drive a hard bargain, sir.'

'Have you not heard about the canniness of the Scots?' George slapped Bruce's shoulder. 'See you soon.'

Every day for the next four weeks, Dorothy coaxed reminiscence after reminiscence out of Marion, constantly asking her for more 'colour', as she put it.

'Describe the Queen's bedroom.'

'What perfume does she wear?'

'How handsome is the Duke of Windsor?'

'What was Mrs Simpson wearing? Describe her jewellery.'

'What presents were exchanged at Christmas?'

'What colour was your bedroom?'

'Tell me about the scent of the flowers in summer?'

'Chronicle the war years.'

'Recount tales of life in the nursery and the schoolroom.'

In her mind, Marion had to believe that what she was telling Dorothy was good for the family. She trod as carefully as she could around the most personal questions ('What lingerie does the Queen favour? Do she and the King still share a bed?'), telling the truth but drawing a line where she felt it should be drawn.

Dorothy encouraged and provoked, and at the end of each day congratulated her on her recall and charming stories.

George was completely supportive, always praising her. 'Darling, you are doing the right thing. This will earn you the DCVO that you deserve.'

He was still drinking, but not as much. He stayed sober enough to make the endless cups of tea and coffee for Marion and Dorothy throughout the long days, and then produce simple suppers for Marion in the evenings.

Eventually, Dorothy pulled the last sheet of paper from the type-writer and announced, 'We are done! What you have here is a love letter to Great Britain and its royal family. It has been my privilege to commit your words to paper.'

'Thank you. May I read it now?'

'Oh, no. I told you at the beginning, no peeking. Wait until you see it tidied up. Beatrice and Bruce are terrific editors. I promise that when you see the final work, you will be so proud.'

Marion tried to smile. 'I hope so.'

'I know so.' Dorothy began to pack up her small office. The many pages she typed each day were put into a black box file that she took away with her each evening. 'Bruce and Beatrice will come over from New York very soon to pick this up. I will call them tonight from the hotel.'

'How soon is soon?' Marion asked.

'I'd say forty-eight hours. They will want to see this as soon as possible.' She tucked the box file under her arm and picked up her coat. 'I'll send for the typewriter later.'

The two women exchanged kisses, and then Dorothy Black was gone.

Marion was mentally and physically exhausted. She sat down heavily in an armchair, as George poured more praise on her and a large whisky for himself.

'You have done it, Mrs Buthlay,' he said with a smile. 'Congratulations.'

*

Marion didn't sleep well that night. She rarely slept well now-adays. Her most regular dream involved being handcuffed and thrown into the dungeons she had known so well during the war. George's assessment of how badly she had been treated, by the Queen in particular, had a ring of truth, but it was so difficult to match with the reality she had experienced. She knew that she loved the royal family, and that they, in their way, had loved her.

She had to have faith that the articles being written, without her name attached, would be seen as positive.

She had so much to be grateful for, so much to trust.

Nottingham Cottage, November 1949

'We bring champagne!' Beatrice Gould, standing on the doorstep of Nottingham Cottage, held up a bottle of Pol Roger.

Bruce stood next to her, his arms opened wide. 'Marion – my favourite author! You have a great big success on your hands!'

'Really? I have been so worried.' She stepped back to let them in.

'Worried? What is there to worry about!' Bruce hugged her. 'Where's George?'

'In the sitting room.'

Bruce walked past her. 'Hey George, you son of a gun, you have one hell of a wife!'

'I know.'

George was not looking well, and Bruce was immediately concerned. 'How are you?'

'A bout of malaria. I'm fine.'

'Poor you. Beatrice, hear this – George has malaria.'

Beatrice came in and put her bag and the bottle of champagne down, then embraced George. 'You poor man! Have you seen a doctor?'

'No,' Marion said. 'He hasn't.'

George flapped his hand. 'I am fine.'

'You need a holiday.' Beatrice smiled at Bruce. 'Do you want to tell him, sweetie?'

'Sure, OK. This is the big one.' Bruce stretched his arms wide. 'You can go on holiday to wherever you want, whenever you want, as soon as you have signed this.' He dipped his hand into the inside pocket of his jacket and pulled out a folded piece of paper.

George's yellow-tinged eyes gleamed. 'The contract?'

'That's it!' Beatrice was bouncing with glee. 'Marion, get some glasses. You are going to sign this and then we will pop that cork.'

Marion went to the kitchen and brought back four tumblers. 'I am so sorry, we don't have any champagne glasses.'

Beatrice laughed. 'Marion, you will have all the champagne glasses you want once you've signed this.'

George was reading through the two-page document. Bruce had his fountain pen ready.

George turned over the top page, leaving the second one to her. 'Sign here, Marion.'

She put the glasses down and took the proffered pen. 'Can I just read it all first?'

George pulled a face. 'Darling, it's a lot of legalese. Don't worry. I've checked it and it's all good.'

'All right.' She hesitated. 'Has the Queen given her approval?'

'Sure she has,' Beatrice said, with absolute sincerity.

'Good.' Marion took a deep breath and signed on the dotted line.

'Congratulations!' Bruce popped the Pol Roger. 'Your husband made you a great deal.'

'Did he?'

'He hasn't told you?'

'No. Not yet.'

Beatrice looked at George questioningly. 'Are we spoiling something here?'

'Not at all. I just wanted to surprise her.'

'Well, tell the poor girl now!' Beatrice put her hand on Marion's arm. 'You might want to sit down.'

'OK.' Marion took a seat, feeling suddenly anxious. 'Tell me.'

George told her, very slowly, 'You have just earned eighty-five thousand dollars.'

The shock was immense. Marion's head began to spin and she thought she might faint. She quickly put her head on her knees and began to take deep breaths.

Beatrice found a tea towel in the kitchen and put it under the cold tap. 'Here you are, put this on the back of your neck. Stay low and let the oxygen back into your brain.'

After a minute or so Marion managed to raise her head. 'How much was that again?'

They told her.

She shook her head. 'All that for a few articles?'

'We have news on that, too.' Bruce passed her a glass of champagne. 'You have given us enough material for a book, and so' – he paused for dramatic effect – 'we are going to publish it as a *book*!'

'A book? But you will not use my name, will you? I promised the Queen that no one would know that I had anything to do with it.'

Beatrice soothed her. 'Honey, let's get it looking like a book first and then the Queen will read it and she'll love it. That reminds me – we would like to put photographs in, as well. I'm sure you have lots of sweet personal ones?'

Bruce grinned. 'Sure she has. And let's keep this all to ourselves until we publish. We don't want to spoil the surprise.'

Chapter Sixty-Four

Westminster Hospital, Christmas 1949

'How are you today?' Marion sat by George's bed, her hand on his. 'I've brought you a newspaper and some grapes.'

He gripped her hand. 'Please get me out of here. I want to go home.'

'And I want you home. I put the tree up and we have had Christmas cards from Lilibet and Philip and baby Charles, and from Margaret and the Queen.'

George turned his puffy face to see her better. 'I want to go home.'

'I know. We shall ask the doctor when he comes. The nurse said he won't be long.'

Drowsily, George closed his eyes. He had been like this for two days now, sleeping on and off.

Marion always felt less upset when he slept. Awake, he often struggled against the pain and spoke in confused riddles.

She stayed with him, accepting a cup of tea from the kindly WRVS ladies who brought their trollies round each teatime. They always stopped for a chat. Today it was a mousy woman in her seventies, Marion judged, with her grey curls tucked under a hair net. She was Marion's favourite.

'He's looking better than he did on Tuesday.' She smiled, revealing her very neat dentures which amplified her mouselike appearance.

'He is, isn't he?' Marion said.

'You must be tired, me duck. All the hours you visit – and then I bet you don't sleep much when you are home.'

Marion was touched and felt the tears sting her throat. 'Oh, you know. I spent last night putting the decorations up for when he comes home.'

'Oh, that's lovely, but you have to look after yourself, you know. How about a bit of fruit cake with your tea?'

'Thank you. I am a bit peckish.'

'Not feeding yourself properly, I expect. I was the same when my old man came home from France. Lost his leg.' She bent down to pull something from the bottom of her trolley. 'Got the evening paper here – some bloke in X-ray left it in the waiting room. You have it. Do the crossword. It'll make the time pass.'

Marion wondered about the kindness of strangers and how perfectly timed the kindnesses came – unasked for, uninvited and yet given selflessly. She thought of the Bible lessons she taught to the Princesses and the one from Hebrews which Lilibet had often repeated: *Do not forget to show love to strangers, for they may be angels in disguise.* Marion smiled to herself. It would be just like God to make an angel out of a tea lady.

She drank the tea and ate the delicious cake before starting on the crossword.

After a peaceful hour, the doctor arrived. The nurse attending him drew the curtains around the bed, so they could speak in private.

'Sleeping, is he? When did he last have his meds, nurse?'

'About an hour and a half ago,' she replied.

'Ah. No wonder he is sleeping. And how are you, Mrs Buthlay?'

'I'm well thank you,' said Marion, 'but worried for George.'

'Naturally. Are you all ready for Christmas?'

'Just some wrapping to do.'

'Good, because Mr Buthlay can go home tomorrow. He has responded very well to treatment and not being able to get hold of any alcohol. He's been lucky. If he had carried on the way he has been, he would be very seriously ill indeed.'

Marion swallowed hard. 'How can I help him?'

'No alcohol in the house – none at all. Regular healthy meals, plenty of water and some exercise in the fresh air. I'll send him home with his medication. Make sure he takes it, and I hope I don't have to see him again.'

'Thank you, doctor.'

'Now you go home,' he replied. 'Collect him at ten o'clock tomorrow and have a jolly good Christmas.'

'We will – and you too. Thank you.'

She went home feeling much happier. After the shock of the contract and the arrival of the money in their joint account, George had begun his old routine: nights in the pub and days recovering or shouting at her – or both.

Walking back home from the bus stop, she wondered how she would manage to stop George drinking through Christmas. It was going to be hard. He wouldn't like it and he wouldn't like her for imposing it. She turned this over in her mind all the way to her front door.

As she slipped the key in the lock, she heard her telephone start to ring.

'Hello?' She slammed the door shut with her foot and disentangled herself from her bag.

'Marion? It's Tommy. Tommy Lascelles.'

Marion relaxed. 'Hello, Tommy, how are you?'

'Very well, thank you, but I am calling you on rather a delicate matter.'

Immediately Marion's anxiety flared. 'What would that be?'

She heard him clear his throat before answering. 'Have you signed a contract with Mr and Mrs Bruce Gould? The publishers from New York.'

'Yes.' Her voice was soft. 'Yes, I have.'

He slid his finger between his collar and throat. This was going to be difficult. 'Ah. I see. We have a snag this end. Lady Astor has received a proof copy of your stories and has shown it to the Queen.'

Marion felt her blood run cold. 'But why? My name isn't on it.'

'Unfortunately, it is. Maybe we could have got around that except for the content within . . .'

Crawfie began to shake. 'You have seen it?'

'Yes. I have read it – all of it – and there are certain events and conversations described that I know not to be true because I was there.'

'But I was most circumspect with what I said. There were no untruths.'

Tommy's heart went out to her, but he had to be tough. 'Listen, Crawfie, I believe the Goulds have taken you for a fool. It appears they have falsified the truth. I know you are a truthful person, one who would never lie. I am certain they have twisted your words and crafted them to their liking.' He paused.

'Oh my God.' Crawfie crumpled. 'But my name – they promised me it was not to be included. I only signed the contract because George had read it and told me . . .' She began to cry, her words coming out in gulps. 'He told me they were not using my name.'

'I am sorry to tell you he lied.'

'No! No! George would never do that. He is an unwell man. He is in hospital. I have just returned home. And why would he lie?'

Tommy never felt comfortable around tearful women but he had to plough on. 'I have the book in front of me. The cover says *The Little Princesses* by Marion Crawford.'

Marion cried noisily. Tommy waited a full two minutes, hoping it would subside.

Eventually Marion was able to speak again. 'What has the Queen said?'

'She . . .' Tommy did not want to describe the terrible scene in the Queen's drawing room. 'She is upset, naturally.'

'I must go and see her – to explain. This is not what I thought was going to happen at all.'

'I think it best you don't see her at the moment. You recall the letter she sent you, asking that you should not have anything to do with the Goulds or accept any money from them?'

Ice slipped inside Marion's chest. 'Yes.'

'Have you accepted money from them?'

Marion wanted to throw the phone down and run away. 'Yes.'

'A lot of money, I hope – because after this, life will be hard.'

'What will happen?' she asked fearfully.

'To you?'

'Yes.'

'There is little that can be done,' he replied softly. 'You have not broken the law. But you have broken a trust for which you will pay heavily. Not financially, but in the way people will view you.'

'I will lose my friends? That is what she wrote in that letter.'

'I know. I . . . helped her to write it. I tried to warn you.'

'Oh Tommy, please don't say that!'

'The Queen will not forgive you for this, I'm afraid.'

'Yes, she will. In time. When she sees how well loved she and the family are. The book will be a success here and in America.'

'Is that what they told you? The Goulds?'

'Yes,' she said, gathering her conviction. 'Yes, they did. You will see. I shall be thanked.'

Tommy took a long pause. 'You know how much I have valued our friendship, but I will not be contacting you again. That is the Queen's choice.' His voice was low, and she heard the emotion in it, the resignation. 'You understand? I do wish you well.'

'But the Princesses! Lilibet and Margaret, they will understand.' Marion was distraught. 'They have sent me Christmas cards.'

'I fear they will be your last.' Tommy pinched the top of his nose. 'Spend the money wisely, won't you?'

Her throat was tight with tears. 'I never wanted the money.'

She heard him sigh. 'I believe you didn't. I am very sorry for you. Look after yourself, Crawfie. Goodbye.'

He had called her Crawfie. The last person who would ever call her that.

She was finished.

She put the phone back on its cradle. This couldn't be happening. George would sort it all out when he came home. He would explain to them.

Distraught, she paced the small cottage, flinging her arms and raking her fingers through her hair. Finally she dropped onto the sofa and sobbed.

When it was over, she wiped her eyes and her nose. She had done nothing wrong – nothing at all. The Goulds were the ones at fault. They had misled her. Cheated her into signing the contract. George must have been cheated, too. He would never let her sign something that was wrong. The Queen would understand that it was not her fault. Her only stupidity was loving her employers too much and assuming they loved her. She had done what she had done for them.

But she had taken the money.' The twenty pieces of silver, to betray the people she loved.

George had been right to get some money for her. And what a lot of money it was. Better than a rundown cottage and a lifetime of service had brought her. It would not mend the hurt she felt, but it certainly helped.

She stood up shakily, and felt a weary anger rise in her. She was suddenly determined. From now on, she was going to concentrate on getting George better and enjoying life on her own terms.

Damn the lot of them.

Chapter Sixty-Five

Rubislaw Den South, Aberdeen, September 1950

'Isn't it lovely?' Marion walked through the large hall of her new home. 'So much space to stretch out in. What do you think, Mother?'

'I don't understand why you haven't bought somewhere closer to me.' Maggie was peeved. 'There's a hundred miles between here and Dunfermline.'

'But I am back in Scotland,' said Marion. 'I thought you'd be pleased.'

Maggie walked from the hall, with its impressive staircase, into one of the four reception rooms which overlooked the large front garden. Through the window she could see George walking Robert through 'the grounds', as he had started to call them.

Her mother ran a critical hand over the windowsill. 'Very dusty.'

'It's been empty for a while.'

'And too close to the road.' Maggie sniffed. 'Although we all know why you chose it – a stone's throw from Balmoral.'

Marion baulked. 'No, it has nothing to do with that. I just happen to like this area and so does George. The fresh air up here will do him good.'

'So you won't be waving at the bottom of the drive when the royal cars come through then?'

'Why on earth would I do that?' Marion swallowed the perennial irritation that came with any contact with her mother.

At that moment, a large removals van turned into the drive. 'Ah, here they are.'

Moving from the compact Nott Cott to this grand Victorian granite bungalow was a salve for her heart and dignity. Yes, she, Crawfie the governess, could afford to buy a splendid home of her own.

Leaving London behind her had been heart-wrenching, but necessary. Her old friends and colleagues had shunned her, just as Tommy had predicted. Her neighbours at Kensington Palace and friends from Buckingham Palace were afraid to speak to her in case they were accused by association. Even Bobo had not returned her telephone calls or replied to her letters. The stench of the traitor clung to her and George like ivy.

There was nothing else to do but leave London with as much dignity as she could and return to Scotland.

The Little Princesses had been published and become an overnight sensation in America. The Goulds added another half a million new subscribers to the *Ladies' Home Journal* magazine, which ran excerpts from the book to drive phenomenal sales. Fifteen million readers lapped it up in the US alone. Its success and the positive interest it created around the British royal family meant that there were no objections to publishing it in the UK.

The popularity of the King, Queen and Princesses had never been higher.

Mr and Mrs Gould were even invited to a Royal Garden Party in Buckingham Palace Gardens. When Marion had read that in the newspapers, with an accompanying photograph of the Goulds shaking hands with the royal family, she had run into the garden and thrown up.

The Goulds were forgiven for their impudence and treachery, while she had been cast out.

The new house gave her fortification and substance. A grand home for a great woman. She deserved it.

When the removal men arranged the furniture from Nottingham Cottage into the new rooms, they were lost, their size diminished. But she made certain that all the pieces from Queen Mary and gifts from the Princesses were placed where the few visitors couldn't help but see them. Her CVO was still in pride of place on the marble mantelpiece, but her joy in it was soured.

George and she were just rubbing along. The horror and pain of her shame had damaged the little pleasure they had had in their relationship, and they found that they had nothing much to say to each other. They had become a tiny, contemptible footnote in history. The adventure had come to an end.

George's alcohol consumption had escalated very quickly on his return to Scotland, with new pubs and new drinking pals. His health was unsteady, his fits of drunken anger more regular.

George had honed his insults so that each one pierced her to the core.

'You don't think I married you for your looks, do you?' he said one day. 'Face it, you're no oil painting. Imagine if we had had a child – what an ugly little brat that would be. I am glad you couldn't have children. Barren and frigid. You are a miserable old woman. A nasty, spiky old woman. You have no friends – and no wonder. Your arrogance and assumed airs and graces push them all away.'

On and on, every day, drunk or sober, she faced his barrage of verbal abuse.

Marion was ashamed of him. But no more ashamed of him than she was of herself. While shopping in Ballater, she'd had bread rolls thrown at her by two women. They'd called her a traitor and a money grabber. 'No better than a common tart,' one had shouted.

Marion had left the shop with her head down and disgrace following her.

She soon found she could ignore the things that were muttered around her, the stares and pointing fingers. She held her head up high. What did these people know of her life? She had been at the centre of the universe for seventeen years. Two little girls had loved her. She had made them the women they were. And she could bet that any one of the people who followed her, whispering snide remarks, would have loved to have seen the things she had seen, met the people she had met.

She had her biscuit tin still and another larger box, both full of the lovingly drawn cards, photos, notes and letters the Princesses had given to her: the photos of them on the royal train; the small reels of cine film with precious images of her, the Queen and the girls dancing the Lambeth Walk aboard the royal yacht; the coronation menu signed by Bobo and Alah; the small vase from Queen Mary in which she had kept the sprig of heather George had given her in Windsor until it became dust.

She could have been a child psychologist, invisible to history, no matter what good she had done.

She was Miss Marion Crawford CVO, governess to the Royal Princesses of the United Kingdom. Keeper of secrets. Her loyalty remained intact, no matter how they tried to rub her out.

She was a part of history, and nobody – not the King and Queen, not her parents, not the public, not even George – could ever take that from her.

EPILOGUE

It was a damp and rather chilly day, unlike other Augusts when she had had to wear a panama hat to protect her from the sun. Never mind – Crawfie always had the right clothes for the right occasion. She pulled out a warm dress and a cardigan. With her good shoes and her large umbrella, the pink one with roses on, she would look all right.

She rose slowly from her chair. It was harder work these days. She was seventy-five years old.

She was not quite sure where all the time had gone. George had been dead a year now – the drink had finally killed him – and her mother and stepfather were long gone, too. It was just her now.

She had made her will. Everything was to go towards the education of the underprivileged children of Scotland. Finally, after all this time, she would achieve her early ambition.

There was one other bequest. The large biscuit tin and card-board box that she had kept near her at all times was to go to Windsor Castle, to be kept in the royal archives. She wanted it to go back to the Castle, so that Lilibet and Margaret would know she had not betrayed them. If she were really a traitor, she would have sold the lot for a great deal of money long ago. But she never had, and she never would.

It was time.

She went to the window and looked out.

Maybe this year, Lilibet would spot her. She had already checked that the train from London had left on time and would be arriving in Ballater as scheduled. She knew exactly how long it would take for the royal cars to reach her house.

With fifteen minutes to spare, she left her front door and walked slowly down the short drive to the road to Balmoral at the bottom.

The rain had stopped, so she wouldn't be needing her umbrella. She shook it. Maybe she would put it up – they would definitely see her if she did.

She checked her watch, shifted her position. Seven more minutes. Seven minutes was 420 seconds. She began to count.

At 395 seconds, the police motorcycle outriders came by, blue lights flashing, and then there were the royal cars. Crawfie stood erect and proud. A Range Rover with detectives was leading, followed by Lilibet's Rolls-Royce. Crawfie lifted her right arm and waved as Lilibet, now Queen Elizabeth II, swept by without any sign of recognition.

The Queen Mother's car came next. Again Crawfie waved, more frantically this time, but again no recognition came. The last Range Rover with detectives was passing now. She waved for the sake of it and got a reaction from someone in the back seat – an elderly man with a small moustache.

Was it . . . yes . . . Tommy. The name escaped her lips as a shout.

'Tommy!'

He was level with her now and turned to see where the sound had come from.

'Tommy!' she shouted again.

She watched his face. He was trying to place her and then suddenly he knew and with slightly parted lips and a quickly raised hand, he was driven by.

She had stood at the bottom of her drive at the start of the royal family's Balmoral holiday many, many times before. This was the first year she had been acknowledged.

Tommy had seen her and he had waved.

Crawfie walked slowly back up the drive to her front door. She had not felt this alive for a long time. She had missed Tommy, more than she had admitted to herself. She had read the obituary for his wife, Joan, in *The Times* – it must have been seven or so years ago. They had had a good marriage, and after he had retired in 1953, Joan had finally moved up to London and into the grace-and-favour home Tommy had been given. She imagined how happy they must have been.

Happier than her and George.

Tommy had warned her, and she had ignored the proof he'd given her of George's lies, drinking and womanizing – all the things that had followed her into her marriage.

She had been a fool, so keen to prove everyone wrong about George, deluding herself that he was the love of her life, always and forever in her corner. What a joke.

He and the Goulds had coerced her into signing the damn contract for the book that changed her life in every way.

She had been labelled greedy, a fantasist, a liar. Her reputation and guts spilled and kicked into the dust and eaten by the vultures she had attracted.

And yet, did she regret the book?

No.

It was a good book, which opened the public's eyes to the reality of life behind the red velvet curtains of monarchy.

She had given them a priceless place in the world's heart.

She had that at least to be proud of.

Tommy and Alah had warned her that the royal family could ruthlessly dispense with anyone who spelt danger, but she hadn't believed them. She had truly believed that her special place in the monarchical fold meant she was safe.

She hadn't written to Tommy when Joan passed away, or when his beloved son, John, had died. She had been too bitter and too unforgiving to contact him.

It shamed her now that she had been so cruel. There were other reasons, of course. George had forbidden her to have any contact with the Palace and had arranged lucrative lecture tours around America, to feed the hunger for her revelations. She gladly took the money and was grateful.

What did that make her?

The Old Stables, Kensington Palace, September 1978

Tommy took the front door key out of its lock and stepped into his hallway. It was good to be home from Scotland. Balmoral never changed, its tartan-clad chill unbeatable no matter his old thermal long johns. It still had its grandeur. The Queen and the Duke of Edinburgh never failed to invite him for the Glorious Twelfth and its start of the massacre of red grouse and ptarmigan. He didn't shoot now. At the age of ninety-one, why would he? But the picnics in the heather and gentle fly fishing with Her Majesty the Queen Mother brought him enormous pleasure. She had always been kind and loyal to him and they had many shared stories to recall.

He had travelled home earlier today, sleeping on the train even as he tried to keep his eyes open to watch the scenery go by and imprint it firmly in his memory. This might be his last journey back from Scotland. He was getting old, and you never knew when the grim reaper might take you.

Setting his suitcase down, he closed his front door and wandered into his study.

His daily woman had placed a bowl of bright chrysanthemums in a vase on his desk. He tutted. He hated them. They seemed to him like streetwalkers or barmaids, too blowsy and garish. Joan never grew them and P-T – the dear girl was now married with twin sons and two daughters – would never have put them in his office.

He sighed and sat behind his desk, ready to tackle the neat pile of post that Mrs Wilmshaw had placed there.

He flicked through the circulars and bills, a postcard from a cousin and a note of fees from his club, until he came to an envelope in a hand that he recognized but was unable to think why. He opened it, intrigued.

My dear Tommy,

It is a long time since we have spoken. Seeing you, and your acknowledgement of me, brought back so many emotions.

Firstly, I want to apologize for my mistakes and for not listening to your advice all those years ago. Youth and naivety are my only defence.

You were right about George. He was all the things that you told me, but I loved him then and couldn't believe you. Can you understand that? Love is foolish and blind. I paid for my error, though – not financially, obviously; I have a house and money in the bank. I can live very well – if a life without friends is living well.

George died a few years ago. We had long forgotten to be kind to each other. In his will he specified that I was to be kept away from the scattering of his ashes. By then I didn't care. Is that very bad of me?

Life when you and I knew each other, with Lilibet, Margaret, Alah and Bobo seems almost unreal to me now: the disbelief of the abdication, our nights in the castle dungeons during the air raids, the books we shared and the whiskies in your office . . . I think of these things with gratitude and they lift my spirits, just as the sight of you today did.

I needed that.

Two weeks ago, I foolishly let all my woes get on top of me. I was weak, I admit. I took too many tablets, deliberately. I was found and taken to hospital where my stomach was pumped – unpleasant and not to be recommended. Why did I do it? I am lonely. I have no one who knows the real me, the Crawfie I was and the things I experienced. There is no one left who wants to hear about them.

I don't think you and I will ever meet again, but I want you to know how sorry I am to have let you down. You were my friend then and I hope you can forgive me and feel that friendship still, as I do.

I still have all the mementoes of my time with the Princesses. I shall send them to Windsor Castle to be placed in the royal archive. I hope you will get a chance to look at them and see that I loved Lilibet and Margaret, and that they loved me.

God bless you, Tommy.

Marion Crawford

AKA Crawfie

PS No reply necessary

Tommy slowly put the letter down and sat deep in thought. Should he reply? He was in two minds. Poor Crawfie . . . good-hearted and bright, amusing and loyal, a good servant who could still be in the royal service if she had played her cards right, as Bobo had – she was still revered by all.

Tommy made himself a small whisky and soda, and went to bed. He would sleep before he decided on a reply.

The Royal Archives, Windsor Castle, Kensington Palace, February 1979

Tommy had not replied to Marion. She had made her decisions even after his warnings, and he was too old to take on the past, but he was curious to hear from the office of the royal archives, some time later, that a parcel had arrived at Windsor

Castle for him to inspect. The archivist's name was Angela, and after greeting him and walking him down to a room surrounded by shelves of box files, she showed him to a middle table, where a biscuit tin and a cardboard box stood. An envelope addressed to him lay by their side.

'This is what came for you,' she told him. 'I have opened nothing, as instructed.'

Tommy was intrigued.

'I shall leave you to it, Sir Alan. Shout if you need me. My office is just next door.'

'Thank you,' Tommy said, his eyes not leaving the objects in front of him.

Alone, he put his glasses on and drew up a chair.

He opened the envelope. There were two sheets of paper within. The top sheet read:

Dear Tommy,
    As promised.
    Crawfie

The second page was more formal.

To whom it may concern,
    As solicitor for Mrs Marion Buthlay, and according to her wishes, I send one biscuit tin and one cardboard box containing mementos of her time in the employment of the royal household 1932–1950. Her greatest desire is that these are held in the royal archives of Windsor Castle for posterity and a testament to her loyalty.
    She wants it to be known that her life in service is remembered with deep honour.
    Yours faithfully,
    Peterkin, Smith and Thompson Solicitors

Sir Alan Lascelles had not cried when his son, John, or his wife, Joan, had died. He had kept his courtier's stiff upper lip always intact in public, while inside his heart was left with an irreparable schism.

But now, opening the tin and finding one woman's memories of a faded life and time, he bent his head and let his tears run free.

Buckingham Palace, 12ᵗʰ February 1988

'Have you read *The Times*, Mummy?' Queen Elizabeth II asked over the breakfast table.

'Not yet, darling,' replied the Queen Mother.

'Mind if I take a look?'

'Help yourself.'

Lilibet picked it up and began reading.

The Queen Mother, Queen Elizabeth II, and Princess Margaret sat in comfortable silence, munching toast and reading their chosen papers, until Lilibet dropped *The Times*.

'What is it, dear?' the Queen Mother asked.

'Marion Crawford has died.'

The Queen Mother continued with her *Daily Mail*. 'Who?'

'Crawfie – remember, our governess. She has died.'

'Oh dear.' The Queen Mother was enjoying the *Daily Mail*'s diarist and gossipmonger Nigel Dempster.

'Her obituary says that she died peacefully in an Aberdeen nursing home and that she had attempted suicide twice before,' Lilibet read solemnly.

'Why on earth would she do that?' the Queen Mother asked.

'Should we send flowers?' Lilibet asked.

'I don't think so,' her mother replied. 'Better not to make a fuss.'

READING GROUP QUESTIONS

1. Did you find any characters relatable despite the extraordinary setting?
2. What was your favourite moment in the book?
3. Letters and diary entries make up much of the story. What do you think this adds?
4. How does the book contrast Maggie and the Duchess as mothers? Do they have any similarities?
5. Do you agree that Marion was taken advantage of? Was she too naïve?
6. How does the book explore themes of love and loyalty?
7. What surprised you most about the book?
8. How does Marion compare to the women featured in Fern Britton's other books?
9. Did the story encourage you to find out more about the history that inspired it? Did it change your opinion on anything?
10. How did you feel after finishing the book? What would you say when recommending it to someone else?

AFTERWORD

This is a fictionalized account of a true story.

Marion Crawford, AKA Crawfie, governess to Her Majesty Queen Elizabeth II and her younger sister, Her Royal Highness Margaret, Countess of Snowdon, is known by many: the employee who felt her duty to the royal family very keenly, and yet in retirement sold the story of their lives in her infamous book, *The Little Princesses*.

Why did she do it?

Was she coerced?

Was it out of a desire to make money?

Or was it simple spite?

Whatever the reason, her story has fascinated me for a very long time. What makes a person do the unexpected? And how could the royal family banish her from their lives and break her heart in the process?

During my research for this book, I have read as many sides of the story as I could find and have kept to the essential facts as closely as I could. However, none of us will ever know the exact conversations that occurred during this time, the exact relationships formed, so I admit to creating many fictional conversations and events.

During my research, I read the diaries of Sir Alan 'Tommy' Lascelles, who was assistant private secretary to King George V, King Edward VIII, and private secretary to King George VI and Queen Elizabeth II. He was one of the courtiers who oiled the wheels of royal life and had a hand in controlling many royal scandals. He worked to keep the monarchy strong and safe. Reading his writings, some of which are very funny, I found a man who respected his work but also saw through the pomp of royalty. He saw the royal family as mere humans, making a mess of their lives, as we all do, and covering up their flaws.

I know that he met Marion Crawford at least once – they shared a car to Windsor – and I have put these two unlikely people together in a growing friendship of mutual affection and trust.

Marion, who would do anything for the monarchy – even postponing her marriage for over ten years – had her life and reputation destroyed with her book. Tommy had a healthy disrespect for the royal family, yet he survived unscathed.

Personally, I like both of them very much and would have loved to have met them. But it's up to you to decide whether Marion Crawford got what she deserved, or was grossly mistreated.

I believe she was grossly mistreated.

Marion Crawford attempted to take her life twice in her final years and eventually died in 1988 in an Aberdeen nursing home, disillusioned by her marriage and embittered by her experiences in life. Her funeral was lonely and there were no wreaths from the royal family. Her royal pension was paid until the day she died.

Tommy Lascelles retired from service in 1953 and settled into the Old Stables, a grace-and-favour property at Kensington Palace. He described it 'one of the nicest houses in London'.

He lived there until his death in August 1981 aged 94, having avidly followed and enjoyed the wedding of the Prince of Wales to Lady Diana Spencer the month before.

BIBLIOGRAPHY

The Little Princesses, by Marion Crawford, Seven Dials (2003, first published 1950)

King's Counsellor: Abdication and War: The Diaries of Sir Alan Lascelles, edited by Duff Hart-Davis, Weidenfeld & Nicolson (2006)

A King's Story: The Memoirs of HRH The Duke of Windsor KG, Prion Books Ltd (1998, first published 1947)

Princes at War: The British Royal Family's Private Battle in the Second World War, by Deborah Cadbury, Bloomsbury (2015)

Elizabeth: A Biography of Her Majesty the Queen, by Sarah Bradford, Penguin (2002)

George VI, by Sarah Bradford, Penguin (2011)

The Quest for Queen Mary, by James Pope-Hennessy, edited by Hugo Vickers, Hodder & Stoughton (2018)

Queen Elizabeth: The Queen Mother: The Official Biography, by William Shawcross, Macmillan (2009)

Elizabeth, The Queen Mother, by Hugo Vickers, Hutchinson (2005)

Read on for an extract from

Daughters of Cornwall

PROLOGUE

Caroline, Callyzion, Cornwall

Present day

It is said that the failings of a family bloodline repeat themselves through the generations until eventually someone, possibly centuries later, breaks the mould. Whether they break that mould with a newly acquired error of personality, or by bringing in a fresh bloodline with its own chaotic genetic make-up, it's hard to tell.

Whatever, I am certain your family will be no different to mine; a long line of women who have toughened themselves on the anvil of life. All with broken marriages, broken hearts and long-held secrets.

The story I am about to tell you is the one I have observed from my birth. Tales I have picked up, as any child does, sitting quietly and forgotten, eavesdropping as the adults reveal their shocking truths.

They dropped their pebbles in the pond and the ripples

spread outward through their lives and into my own, where they lap still.

Everything I have, I have worked hard for.

Everything.

I bear no grudge.

I am not a materialistic woman. I am a widow living within my means watching my beautiful daughter take the leap from adolescence to adulthood, carving her own path. She will find a suitable boy, settle down and be a wonderful wife and mother. As I was.

As my mother almost was.

As her mother, Clara, certainly wasn't.

Glamorous, strong and passionate, she lived her life by one rule. 'To be a liar, you have to have a very good memory.'

And she should know.

I didn't know any of this until very recently, and I must say it has rather disturbed my equilibrium. I like to think of myself as a woman who does not wear her emotions on her sleeve.

Losing my mother was dreadful, of course, as was my husband's illness and death. I was proud of my outward stoicism; my resilience in the spotlight of grief.

That was until I overheard one of the church ladies talking about me behind my back. I heard them in the choir stalls discussing my 'lack of emotion', my 'cold-bloodedness', and then something I would prefer not to think about, it being so crude and unpleasant. All I will say is that their unkind laughter followed me for days afterwards.

I miss my husband dreadfully. His kindness. His affection. His success. He climbed the ladder of the corporate world and gave me the secure world I craved. Darling Tom.

He knew how hard my fatherless upbringing was and how

hard I have striven to lead a normal life after the rackety one my mother brought me into.

All that has paled into insignificance now, for I have discovered another family skeleton. My mother was not the only one to have her secrets. To get pregnant out of wedlock.

Everything I thought I knew is a lie.

It arrived on my doorstep just a few days ago. A huge steamer trunk made in the days when people travelled the world by ship rather than hopped on an aircraft. The courier thrust his docket at me to sign. 'This has travelled a long way to find you,' he said, as if personally affronted. 'All the way from Malaysia, via Singapore and Kent, by the looks of things. And it's bloody heavy.'

'Are you sure you have the right address?'

'You are Caroline Bolitho?'

'Yes. Well I was, that's my maiden name.'

'Then yes this is the right address. I went to the Vicarage just up the road in Callyzion first. But the woman there said the only Bolitho she knew was you and she gave me this address.' He handed me a docket.

'Sign and print please, and I hope you don't find a body in there.' He laughed until I gave him 'The Look', the one my husband and daughter feared.

I signed the piece of paper and opened the door wider for him to carry it into the hall for me.

'Sorry, love. My job is to deliver to the door. That's as far as I'm allowed to go. Cheers. Oh, hang on.' He patted the top pocket of his shirt. 'Here. You'll need this. It's the key.' He handed me a small brown envelope and left me with the mysterious cargo.

By the time I had dragged the trunk into the lounge, I needed a cup of coffee to give me the energy to open the thing.

To be honest I was more than a little wary of the contents. What could they be? Why had it been sent to me? Who had sent it to me?

I finished the last of the two digestive biscuits that I had allowed myself and rinsed my coffee cup, putting it on the drainer.

'Come on, Caroline,' I told myself. 'The time has come.'

Back in the lounge, the trunk sat waiting. I circled it, reading the various labels. Most were aged and illegible but there was a name printed along the front edge. I went back to the kitchen and got a duster and an aerosol can of furniture polish.

The trunk was leather and, as I removed the grime, the natural hide began to shine. I made out the letters E.H.B. and an address for a rubber plantation on the island of Penang, Malaysia. I recognised the initials. Ernest Hugh Bolitho, my grandfather. My mother's father. All I knew about him was that he had died in Penang, back in the Seventies, having never returned to his English family.

I kept on polishing until the entire bag emerged, old but gleaming. I had been through so much of late that the idea of opening up the past was both comforting and terrifying. I had kept my family tucked out of sight for years and only Tom knew the circumstances of my birth.

I often wonder if keeping my secret to myself actually pushed people away from me.

Tom was my first boyfriend. I couldn't believe it when he spoke to me one Easter Sunday after Church. His parents were High Anglicans and kept the sort of decent, normal home that I had longed for as a child.

The trunk was almost clean now but I kept on polishing until there was nothing more to do.

The time had come to open it.